The Living Shards

Arianna Swain

DEDICATION

This book is dedicated to Ms. Annette Ross, the best English teacher an aspiring writer could ever dream to have. You allowed me to explore the world of my imagination without restrictions and I can never thank you enough for that. I promised you a long time ago standing in your classroom that I would dedicate my first book to you. I remembered and I sincerely hope that you enjoy it.

ACKNOWLEDGMENTS

I would also like to thank all of the wonderful, amazing, talented individuals without whom this book would not exist: my family for their continued love, support, and tolerance of the insanity that is my life, all of my friends who read, edited, and bled for this book just as much as I did, my editors and the various friends and family members who so graciously lent me a piece of themselves to make up pieces of the characters laid out before you. To name a few of you: mom, dad, all of my grandparents, Maggie, Marie, Hilde, Erica, Claire, and Enda. If I forgot a name please forgive me. To the person who has always been the best part of me, even before I knew you, there are no words to express how grateful and blessed I am to have you in my life. A very special thank you also goes out to the members of Incubus, Muse, Ryan Star, and the always amazing 30 Seconds to Mars who provided the soundtrack that I wrote this to.

What would you do to save your soul? What if it was literally half of your soul in someone else's body? You can fill your brain with platitudes and romantic notions but you never really know what you're willing to do for someone else, how far you'll go until you're there. When you're in that situation it's better if you don't have time to think, just act on pure instinct. Pure instinct got me as far as my car and through the first few states I had to cross. The last couple of hundred miles gave me far too much time to think. Now as I drive my insanely beautiful new 1971 steel gray Corvette Stingray down some long-forgotten road in the rain, crossing the last few miles to save another, the doubt and the fear began to set in. I turn the fear to anger and keep driving. The snowflakes swirling around me, caught in the glare of my headlights remind me that it's the middle of the night and I'm driving like a demon to God-knows where backwoods Ohio in the winter to once again save my soul mate's dumb ass which feeds the anger. Anger is safe so I let myself indulge a bit, spurring on my internal monologue. If I get into an accident or so much as nick the clear coat on my car, he's a dead man. I am not good without caffeine and there is not a diner, or a streetlight for that matter, anywhere to be found.

A little back story while I'm testing the engine on my car: Hi, my name is James Morgan and I am an alcoholic, caffeine addict, and I don't do mornings. To address all of your inevitable questions in order: 1) No, my parents were not expecting a boy. Do not call me Jamie. 2) In recovery and less pissed about that. 3) It's dawn, I've been up searching for Aaron for three days and there's no coffee. If I still drank I'd at least have one good Jack and Coke in me now. How did I get here? Well, let's just say there are lots of ways that I don't fit in with the Brady's.

For one, I'm known to shoot sparks out of my fingertips. Handy for lighting candles, not so much for making friends. I also have what's been referred to as "mood ring" eyes. No, Aaron did not name them that; he's not that poetic or creative. He just thought they were "far out". They started out as plain brown. When Aaron and I "met" they became dual colored, brown and green, black when I'm really beyond angry. Now they shift constantly between blue, green, brown, black, gray, violet, and any other halfway neutral color that you can come up with. I sometimes favor dark sunglasses.

Back to Aaron. My and Aaron's story is well, interesting for lack of a better or more descriptive word. While we are soul mates, quite literally perfect halves of one soul, the Fates kind of screwed us over in this lifetime. The issue seemed to arise just before we were born. We were destined to be brother and sister in this life, twins actually. We were already in the womb when something happened to change Aaron's destiny. The boy who beat Aaron out for one apparently more important destiny suffered an untimely demise causing the understudy to become the principle and we were separated. The woman who should have been our mother miscarried. Aaron was recreated first then I was born three years later: next door.

Now the problem is, while we're currently programmed to be lovers, some of the old brother and sister programming is still there. It's kind of like trying to record over an 8-track. The new song's there but there's always that blip of the old song at the beginning that kind of screws everything up. That's kind of how we are. All of the new stuff's there, there's just the tiny memory of what used to be and that's

2

the excuse that Aaron uses every time he wants to screw around with some trick in a shorter skirt than mine. And for some idiot reason I always take him back. Except this time. This time the trick's different. I don't know if her skirt was shorter or her shirt more transparent, but this time he decided he was in love. So Aaron went with her to the backwoods of freaking Ohio in the middle of winter. And of course, he fell for the succubus. The same succubus who is currently, literally sucking the life out of him. Which is not good. While I've threatened to kill him myself on several occasions and have honestly thought about it, the fact is, I like my life, the complication of him notwithstanding. We have this tiny problem, Aaron and I. If he stubs his toe, mine hurts. If I get sick, he gets sick. Therefore, it stands to reason, if he dies, I die. And I'm not too keen on dying at eighteen because he got horny. So I am braving all manners of inclimate weather to save his scrawny ass one more time. And then I'm turning him into a six year old girl. Damn the repercussions. At least I won't have to worry about him and his mood swings anymore. Unfortunately, I'm very quickly running out of time.

The weaker Aaron gets, the weaker I get, which is making it increasingly more difficult to drive like an insane person through what's turning into a blinding snowstorm. I have to get there. I can hear him scream, I feel him losing hope. It's like he's dying in the car beside me. I'm reasoning that if I can still drive my car, then there's still hope that we'll both make it out of this. There are lots of levels on which I will not live without Aaron. And I'm at about thirteen on a scale from one to ten right now. I can see the lights from the cabin and I know that she can see me through his eyes. I hope she feels the poison I'm going to pump into her veins for touching Aaron, for hurting us. I will not lose him. And that determination is probably the only thing keeping my car on the road as the lights from the cabin get brighter and my vision gets dimmer.

Just as I turned up the long dirt driveway a piercing pain struck my chest and Aaron's vision overtook mine for the briefest of moments.

The succubus suddenly loomed over me as her hand slid through my ribcage like it was butter and the rage I felt began to spill out of me along with my blood. I can feel that bitch ripping Aaron's heart out and it makes me want to scream. I want to scream at him for being so stupid, for putting us both in such a terrible situation. I want to scream because I know what's coming. I have to face the inevitable and there's no peace within myself for that now. I want to scream now for all of the things neither of us will never do, will never become, for the kids that I won't have as I'm suddenly reminded of the adorable little boy who lives across the street from us who told me my eyes looked like his mommy's mood ring. Pain sears through my chest and I look down, watching the blood gush out of my chest from a wound that wasn't inflicted on me. I cry as my car veers off the road, because I know I'm going to die in the snow a thousand miles away from the beach near the bayou where I was born and no one will find either of us until spring. And as my car stops in front of the cabin where my Aaron is bleeding through the pine floor, I stumble out into the snow, leaving a gruesome trail behind me to color the white with blood and things I'd rather not think about. My surety in our fate is confirmed as I watch the ice fall on my skin and realize that I can no longer feel the cold. I make it through the cabin door and see Aaron lying there, curled on his side, the red like a halo around his dark head, and I hear her laughing as she tries to pull what's left from his broken aura. The world went a little black, my focus sharpening for just an instant as I fell to the floor and grabbed his outstretched hand.

"I'm sorry, JJ." Blood started seeping from his eyes like tears.

"Be sorry later, fight with me now." I stared into Aaron's chocolate colored eyes for the last time as energy shot out of our joined bodies and we sent the succubus back to hell. I allowed a single tear to fall from my eyes as Aaron gripped my hand tighter with fear and we let go of our last breath.

Several hundred miles away, a little boy with Caribbean blue eyes was tucked tightly in his bed, sleeping, safe from the monsters that prowled the night. That little boy's remarkable eyes opened the instant he felt the woman with eyes like his mommy's mood ring leave the earth. His rapidly developing young mind registered that this was significant, but for what reason he did not know. The reason didn't matter. He knew she needed to live, he prayed to the God his mother taught him, and the one she didn't know about to be allowed to help find her. After that night he dreamed about the woman every night when he went to sleep. And on his tenth birthday he got the only present he had wished for in five years: he knew the exact moment when she was born again. As he drifted off to sleep that night, he vowed it would be the last time that he rested until he found her.

1

Have you ever noticed that there are no stars in Los Angeles? No, I'm not talking about the self-absorbed, self-destructing celebutants lining Sunset Boulevard from the Junction all the way to the ocean and back again about five thousand or so times. I mean the glowing balls of planetary mass and gases that dot the night sky. People don't look up here and we have one of the clearest, most beautiful skies in the world, minus the smog, at least in my opinion. I love the sky here but it makes me wonder how many lovers have made wishes on planes rather than falling stars. I've spent the last twenty minutes of my generally very short life lying in the street staring at the planes and few distant orbs that colored the night sky wondering what the hell I was doing. No, not why am I lying in the street, I know the answer to that. I mean, "What am I doing" in the larger sense of the phrase. I'm lying in the street because I enjoy pacing quiet residential streets in various parts of town at 3 a.m. when I have writer's block or am trying to figure something out. At 3 a.m. there are few cars and fewer pedestrians, even in the exclusive neighborhoods of the hills. So I randomly picked a neighborhood close to a Starbucks and started walking. My neck got tired of looking up and the coffee wore off so I lay down in a pool of light by the walled entrance of a stranger's home on the side of the street and stared up. I'm sure their not-so-state-of-the-art security system is catching some really not interesting footage.

I'm also equally positive that if this doesn't happen to be a morally descent person's home that the footage of me lying outside their gates on public property will be shown on TMZ tomorrow. Not that it matters. I'm a writer, which means that I'm allowed a certain measure of eccentricity. It's a little expected. Particularly when you factor in the idea that I am one of a handful of easily recognizable writers in this town, thanks in large part to my fiancé's high profile affairs and a few racy photo shoots of my own. Not racy for the nearly always nude models or actresses traipsing up the boulevard, but racy for a horror writer. Whatever, I don't care what those idiot motherfuckers think. I've got bigger problems.

As I stare up at the sky lying on the windswept, uneven pavement littered with dry leaves and potholes watching tiny balls of light move across the early morning sky I see flashes of my nightmares painted on the lens of my wide-open eyes and it drives me crazy.

I don't understand where it came from. Maybe nightmare is the wrong word. The dreams are more comforting and sometimes erotic but they always feel like home. That's what causes the nightmare correlation because I know where home is; I know who I'm meant to be with and he's not the stranger whose image floats across the backs of my eyelids at night. I accepted a long time ago that I am stuck with Zane. That's his name in this lifetime, Zane, electronic musical genius, magically neutered soul mate with little memory or concern of our previous lives. Oh, and he's also a philandering drug addict. Yeah, living the dream here. How does a girl get so lucky? 976 years and not a damn thing has changed except that our powers grow weaker with each passing year which makes me unreasonably nervous knowing that I'm the one who will have to protect us. Zane and I've made a lot of enemies over the years and I'm not the only one who remembers.

Stand up, dust self off, start walking, quit scaring the neighbors of people you don't know.

Yes, I remember the nearly thousand years of my time spent on earth. I can also see things I shouldn't see, feel things that I shouldn't feel, and know things I shouldn't know. Go figure. I'm not narcissistic enough to believe that we're special or the only ones with a few extra brain cells. I do know that out of all of the things floating through my brain that I shouldn't know one thing that I'm missing is the reason for all of this. I believe in reasons, I believe in a higher purpose, I don't for a second believe that we could have been through all of this, died so many horrible deaths for nothing. So weird that it's just this one long, potentially endless cycle. I keep waiting for something to change, something to be different. Here the difference is that I have a sister who got some of my powers and, of course, my mystery man. I worry about placing too much emphasis on the differences. There's always been something different, just nothing different worth noting. It's always ended the same way. Money, love, status, intent, choices, none of it changes anything. So much for the myth of free will.

Take long, deep breaths, keep walking. There's a more direct route back to my car but I don't really see the point in taking it. I'm not tired, I'm in no rush, and Zane sure as hell won't be home. Not unless he's not alone and I definitely do not want to deal with that again this week. I deal with that too often as it is. A quick flashback of memory shows me a time not so long ago when Zane and I were happy, stronger as a couple than we are as roommates pretending to be in one. At least I thought we were happy. Then I came home to find him in our bed with another woman. He was sad, apologetic, and repentant that first time. I forgave him, we continued on, and then me walking in on him with other women just became the norm. I hated it but I knew deep down he still loved me. Now I'm just apathetic to the whole situation. Beat something enough times and no matter what it's made out of eventually it will break. It hurt when that thing inside me that held hope for our relationship, for our happiness broke. Now we stay together because we can't leave each other. The icing on the cake of my romantic turmoil is that I have one guy driving me crazy in person and another causing me grief mentally. It annoys me more than

I like to admit to myself that I am no closer to identifying him than I was ten years ago. It's my own personal Rubik's cube. I pick it up when the visions are strongest and try to solve the puzzle, forgetting about it when reality distracts me. I mindlessly put one foot in front of the other, my brain flying through a millennia of memories, searching for something that would explain who this guy is and why he keeps invading my brain. Even my strongest shields don't keep him away for long. In the fifteen years that I've seen him in my head I've talked with him, I've felt him watching me through my own eyes, and I've never been afraid, never been worried, never held fear of who he is or what he may want from me. My lack of fear frightens me. Unless you're born into my life, I don't trust you. Sorry, I know there are good people out there but in my experience most of the ones that seek me out aren't the good people. They're the bad guys. And that means that I have to try and take them out before they take me or Zane out. Zane's the guy but he's positively useless in a fight. He always thinks that things will go his way because he's charming, he's special, he's him. Our death is usually what cures him of that until we're reborn and he takes the opportunity to have learned absolutely nothing of use. So we start again. Now we're nearly thirty and it's the first time we've been this old in any of our lifetimes. I'm in uncharted territory and I'm not sure that I know how to protect us. That scares me. I don't hope for real love, or marriage, or children. I don't get that and I wouldn't know what the hell to do with it if I did. I do hope to live though, to have a moderately peaceful life. This is the closest we've ever gotten. And I feel like I'm waiting for the other shoe to drop.

Pull the leaves out of my hair, take deep breaths of the cool night air, keep walking along the dark, winding mountain road. I have my MP3 player but I don't want to ruin the peacefulness of the evening with music played through a tin can. The best way to listen to any music other than electronic is on vinyl or in person. It's the only way that you get the feeling out of it. I feel like downloads rape something from music, especially good rock music. Though there is something to be said for being able to carry an entire library on something the size of a postage stamp. I'm watching the world die one gigabyte at a time without much inclination to try and save it. Mankind will always evolve. I don't. I make a living off remembering the worst parts of my cumulative life. I don't think that's really considered moving forward. I'll ask my life coach.

Not really surprisingly Zane was out when I got back. I checked the clock, noting that I had about an hour before his post-dawn walk of shame. Just to get a point across and keep him from waking me up I locked all of the bolts on the front door of the condo including the one that a key won't open. He could sleep on the doormat or call the fire department to break down the door. I don't care which option he goes with. Whatever he's doing now with whatever possibly underage celebrity wannabe bitch is going to embarrass me on the local entertainment news tomorrow. He deserves a little discomfort. What was really the cap on my already fabulous morning was walking into our bedroom and smelling the overwhelmingly disgusting scent of another woman's perfume. I've never understood why some women feel the need to layer scents like they work in a potpourri factory or why Zane can't manage to change the sheets. I don't remember the last time he and I had sex in that bed. Maybe I should buy a new bed. I opened the windows, the balcony doors, and stripped the linens before lying down to stare at the ceiling fan for the next two hours. Banging on the door ruined my contemplation of the sunrise. I smiled and plugged in my headphones to drown out the racket. Time to wake my sister up and go to work. I was already two weeks past my deadline on the latest installment in the book series exploiting my life. This is the last one before I have to start making shit up. My problem with reality isn't when it's real, it's when all that's there are the lies.

When I was finally ready to leave for the day, or at least for the morning, I climbed over Zane's sleeping body in the hallway on my way to meet my assistant/sister. I considered not waking him up, just leaving him there, but the protector part of me wouldn't allow it. I put down my coffee, laptop bag, and cell phone to drag Zane into the condo. I made it as far as our dining room with him before he woke up. I let my shields slip enough to feel the drunken, drugged-out haze that permeated his brain and groaned, snapping the mental shields back in place like a steel trap slamming before his chemically induced drowsiness could affect me. I can't really keep Zane out, he's like an extended part of me, but when he doesn't put any effort in to trying it's pretty easy to shut myself off. Unless he's dying, of course. Or injured, or sick, or just needy. Then whatever he's going through consumes me too. The knife cuts both ways but, unlike my own personal demon, I try to not cause us trouble. I just clean up the mess. Zane's bout with consciousness only lasted long enough for him to register that he was in our condo before he rolled over in the floor and passed out again. I collected my belongings from the doorway and walked down the hall. Elevator or stairs? I usually take the stairs just for the extra exercise but today I felt slack so I took the elevator up two floors to my twin's condo. There were two units available when we moved into this building. Karina and her husband Craig preferred the smaller condo with the better view. Zane and I each needed our own space so we took the much larger one on the third floor. Craig hates the close proximity. I'm actually pretty sure that he hates me. Karina's my twin sister, as well as my assistant, so he deals with me and my crazy for her. Outside of the two men who float through my head at will she's the only person who knows that the stories are true, that the media personality I've built up is nothing but a front and that the real person is a fairly fluid entity that gets suppressed at will. One day I'll find a better outlet for myself other than books. Right now the one I've got pays the bills.

When I reached the fifth floor I paused in front of Karina's door. On a normal day I'd just barge right on in. With a sigh I realized finally that today was destined to be anything but normal. Karina and Craig were fighting. Again. If I couldn't have felt her sadness and frustration radiating out of the apartment I could definitely hear the screaming match going on. By the volume I guessed that they were in the living room. An insane urge to break down the door and push my brother-in-law over the balcony for making my sister feel like shit caused my hand to tremble on the doorknob and I backed up before Karina noticed the noise. I closed my eyes and reached out with whatever sense it was that let me hear people's thoughts. Oh, not a good, we're-going-to-stop-yelling-and-have-make-up-sex-fight. The snatches of conversation that I could "hear" over the emotional tidal wave told me that once again Craig's annoyed by the time that Karina spends with me in what he calls our imaginary world. Karina's pissed that Craig still ignores a large part of her because he flat out doesn't want to understand. It goes against his very conservative, very strict Christian upbringing, which doesn't allow for things like telepathy, past lives, or other such "supernatural" nonsense. I waited for a break in the shouting, sipping my coffee in the hallway, silently taking in bits and pieces of the conversation, some through telepathy, some through just everyday normal human hearing. At least Zane and I don't fight like this anymore. The sad thing is that we don't care enough to fight with each other anymore. It's just a wasted effort. I reached the end of my cup, realized that we were now half an hour past the time when I usually show up and groaned because I know Karina must know that I'm standing out here now. Guess I'll knock and see what happens.

A very tired looking Craig answered the door and stepped aside for me to enter. I fought to control the smirk on my face as I entered, said "hello", and marched straight for the kitchen. I was definitely going to need more coffee if I was going to keep from hitting him. Maybe I'll take Karina out for coffee. I fought to not clench my fists or grind my teeth while I walked through the condo, Karina's utter despair radiating through the small space and breaking what was left of the organ previously known as my heart. I wanted to go to her but I knew I couldn't let Craig know what I'd heard and it would just further embarrass my sister. As a bonus, if Craig's home at this hour he's not going to work today. With him in Karina's apartment and Zane asleep in the entryway of ours, that leaves Starbucks for work without distractions. Maybe we should invest in an office space. Of course then neither one of us would ever make it to the office. No one likes to get up and move quickly on a schedule in the morning, least of all my sister and me. Maybe it's genetic. Bless my sister, even in the midst of World War III with Craig she managed to make an entire pot of coffee. I filled up my mug and continued into the living room where Karina was pacing the room in front of the large sliding doors that overlooked the Pacific. I heard Craig sigh heavily and walk into the bedroom that held his computer and desk, shutting the door firmly behind him. A moment later the opening strands of the theme song to a video game began to play. Zane's a moron but I still wouldn't deal with him spending the amount of time in front of a computer monitor that Craig does without anything productive coming from it. At least we manage to work while looking at the blinking dot of a cursor. Well sometimes. When I'm on a writing spree I find that I very rarely look down at what I'm writing, it just sort of comes out of my fingertips. It's times like that when the words start really floating out of my brain and down my hands that I'm happy I no longer shoot sparks out of my fingers. Excess electricity is hell on electronics.

Karina and I don't look exactly alike. We don't have the same build. I'm more of an hourglass shape while she's more like an ironing board with boobs. It works for her though. My eyes change color, dominant colors being green and brown; her eyes are uniformly gray green. She's my best friend and my sounding board. When the big, bad ugly rears its head from lifetimes past, I tell her about it and we deal with it. When I randomly freak out about something, usually Zane and my severe lack of a life outside of my past lives, she's there for me and talks me down off the proverbial ledge. No, I wouldn't jump. I already know what that feels like. Zane took a flying lesson off the side of a bridge a few lifetimes ago and I haven't forgotten the sensation of being crushed to death while lying in my bed yet. I have been tempted to numb my brain with alcohol and pills until my inevitable death arrives. We all know that I wouldn't do it though. The easy way out doesn't really entice me.

My sister opened the glass doors and stepped out onto the large balcony without looking back to see if I would follow. I left my laptop bag on the coffee table and took the coffee outside, gently closing the door behind me to prevent Craig from overhearing without getting close enough for one of us to sense his presence. Karina sat down at the small bistro table, her back to me. I stretched out on the all-weather chaise and contemplated the horizon. I knew she'd talk when she was ready and would clam up if I prodded, so I waited. In the meantime there was still a storyline to map out in my head and coffee to drink. Nice, hot coffee that smelled like vanilla and caramel with just a hint of chocolate. Trust Kari to purchase coffee that tastes like dessert without adding sugar or creamer. It took her about five full minutes to turn to me and speak.

"I know what you heard."

"Want to talk about it?"

Karina laughed bitterly and I could feel her heartbreak. "Not much left to say."

"You know that he loves you, right? You don't have to have my particular skill set to know that. If he didn't he wouldn't still be here. Try to be patient with him a little longer."

"Does he really love me or does he love the idea of me? Because the two things aren't the same. I'm not going to ever be the cute little southern preacher's wife he wants. If I don't have an outlet for all of this then it will just build up until it explodes out of me and does something fun like raise my own personal poltergeist." She sighed. "It'll be all right, he'll get over it, eventually. He always does. Want to work on the book or do you want to talk about my marriage?"

I swung my legs to the ground, turning to face her. "I want to talk about whatever you need to talk about."

15

"Well right now I need a distraction. Oh, I meant to tell you, I dreamed about you last night."

I laughed and allowed her to change the subject without objection. We'd talk about Craig when she was ready and if she needed a distraction her dreams were definitely a good one. Kari's dreams were often the stuff of very creative fantasies, further embellished in the retelling. "Dare I ask what this dream entailed?"

Karina rolled her eyes and stood up, opening the door to the cool interior of the apartment. "We were in a large closet but instead of clothes on the hangers there were men, well their skins anyway. I think we were picking out a new man for you. We picked the only one with a real body. He was kinda hot."

"What did this "kinda hot" guy look like? Please tell me it wasn't Zane." I closed the door behind me and sat down on the dark green plaid couch. My sister needed a decorator. She's the only person I can imagine in Malibu in a completely clean, modern high rise with a green plaid couch. Ugly as the thing was it's still pretty comfy.

Karina frowned at me like I was a naughty student asking a stupid question in the middle of a lecture. "Of course it's not Zane. How anti-climactic would that be? No, the guy in my dream, once we got him off of his hanger, was cute. Tall, thin like you like but with a few muscles, bright eyes. Couldn't really tell what color they were, they looked light. Great smile though. And dark hair. That would be a change for you after the bleach incident that claimed Zane's head." She laughed but the smile didn't really reach her eyes. I knew that but at the same time I didn't want to push her. If she preferred to hide what she was feeling, well there really isn't a lot that I can say about that. I'm the world's worst example of what a well-adjusted adult should look like. That and her description of the guy reminded me of my late night nap in the street. I should have given up on searching for that stranger's face in a crowd a long time ago. The clearest image I've ever gotten of him is currently about fifteen years out of date. And there's no reason for me to search him out. What would I say? "Hi, my name's Jane. I've been dreaming about you and talking to your spirit since I was a kid. Any chance that you remember me?" Yeah, that would go over well. To a patient in the psych ward.

Rather than tell Karina all of the thoughts that were running through my brain I laughed it off. "Yeah, I blame the bleach for Zane's consistent bad choices. Maybe if he hadn't dyed his hair white our relationship would stand a chance."

"It doesn't now? You're sure?"

I shook my head sadly even though there wasn't a lot of sadness in my response. I'd come to terms with the fact that I was hopelessly trapped in a loveless relationship with a moron. It's okay; there are worse ways to go. No chance of having my heart broken this way. I'd have to have one first. "Relationship died a long time ago. Now all that's holding us together is history and there's definitely a lot of that." I took a swallow of my rapidly cooling coffee in order to keep from showing any type of emotion. If Kari saw how this made me feel she might be a little afraid and I couldn't do that to her, watch my sister look at me like I'm the unfeeling bitch that I know I can be. That I'm trying to be right now toward Zane. Doesn't hurt as much if you don't feel it. I console myself with that anyway. Sadly just thinking it doesn't always make it true.

"You could venture out on your own, find someone who's a helluva lot better in bed," Karina smiled but behind that I could see that she was serious.

"We've had this conversation, Kari. I have to keep focus. I lose my focus and we get killed. I can't separate myself from Zane, we've tried and everything's failed. What's the point?" I gave up on the coffee and placed the mug on the table with a sigh. "I can have a meaningless relationship that lasts right up until he gets me killed, turns into some type of demon, or I have to explain Zane to him. That is if he doesn't figure out that I have a fiancé minute one from the giant ring on my finger." I held up my right hand in illustration.

"First, that ring goes on your left hand for it to mean something. Second, you know it does come off, right?" Karina pulled the diamond off my hand and dropped it onto the wooden coffee table beside my mug. "See? Took the ring off and the world didn't come to an end. It can happen. Give it a chance."

"No prospects."

"You turn them all away."

"Might be the whole media circus around my engagement thing."

"No offense, but it doesn't seem to be hurting Zane's prospects. Maybe you should leave Zane, the ring, and your inhibitions at home. Go somewhere that no one will know who you are and just give it a shot. Maybe you'll find a frog worth kissing. You could use some kissing. How long has it been?"

"Since I kissed someone? I don't know, awhile. Zane and I aren't exactly intimate anymore and it wasn't that good when we were. I would've thought sex with your soul mate would be a little more interesting."

"How long since someone gave you an orgasm?"

I laughed in earnest. I so was not going to have this conversation with anyone, little less my mostly happily married sister. "You won the husband lottery; let's just leave it at that. If only one of us gets a happily ever after I'm glad it's you. Now let's get to work. I need more coffee." I got up to walk into the kitchen.

"Your agent called again this morning."

That stopped me cold in my tracks. Two weeks past my due date for an entire manuscript with nothing to show the publisher was an uneasy place to be. The publisher could cancel my contract for that. Not that I was hurting for money or anything but a cancelled writing contract could end my career. And out of everyone I've met this lifetime my agent is probably the most tenaciously frightening. "What did she say?"

"She said she wants to know where the book she gave you a very large advance for was. I think she knows that it's just in your head right now."

"Can you distract her with our notes?"

"We tried that a month ago."

"How much time do we have?"

"Before she shows up here demanding pages or before she murders you in your sleep?"

"Both." I returned with my mug happily full of warm coffee and cracked open my laptop, the beginnings of both a storyline and a headache growing behind my eyes.

"I'd say you've got a week before she shows up, two days before she demands pages, and maybe a month before she kills you. You've gotta give them something, J." Karina glanced up from her computer to check my reaction.

"I will. It's just not coming out of my head yet."

"You're writing about your life. Did you forget how the story goes?"

"No, the story's still going. It resonates in my head. It makes me fearful of snow drifts and the random people that Zane sleeps with and getting close to anyone because I know that it hasn't been that long and that there is a whole race of people that would love to kill us both if they knew we were alive because we killed one of theirs thirty-odd years ago. I'm afraid of what happens if I let this story out."

"You can always change it. You don't have to die; you don't have to kill a succubus. James and Aaron can go on to live a perfectly normal life after escaping the cabin in the woods. It's fiction, Jane. Maybe this is your opportunity to rewrite the past."

"I don't want to draw unnecessary attention. I don't want to die."

"Maybe you won't. Who knows if this group even reads fantasy novels? The whole point is that it's supposed to be fiction."

"But it's not. It never has been."

"Well some of it is. You've managed to take the base story and spin something slightly more fantastic out of it. Otherwise you wouldn't have the readers you do and a franchise offer." Karina peeked at me over the computer screen, holding her breath while she felt out what I was thinking at the revelation.

"Frightening that my life has to be made into something slightly more fantastic. What did you say about a franchise?"

"Oh, nothing. I was just checking your messages this morning and there was one from some film studio wanting to option your books for a movie with the possibility of turning it into a franchise. I'm sure you're not interested."

"Are you kidding me? That's amazing! I can't do it but it's amazing."

"Why not?" Karina moaned in frustration. "If you don't start living your life I'm gonna do it for you just to show you how it's really done."

"You do that in all of your spare time from running your life. In the meantime give me a notebook. We're gonna try this old school before I sit here staring at a cursor on a blank page for the two hundred and sixty-ninth day in a row." Karina passed me a brand new blank notebook and my favorite pen. I sat down to write while she started the research that would make my knowledge of the subject matter credible. I willed the correct words to flow out of my brain and on to the page. Several hours and an IPod full of rock music later I had one two hundred page notebook full of newly written story, a cramp in my fingers, ringing in my ears and an ache in my stomach. I briefly considered calling out for delivery but as I looked across the table to where Karina sat staring out the windows at the darkening sky rather than typing the twenty new pages I had just handed her I decided it would be better if I left her and Craig to their own devices. We had a third of the first draft of the book almost finished, more than enough to quiet my agent and way more than most writers accomplish in the same amount of time. Once the story was given the okay from my brain it just fell out in this giant tidal wave, making my life a helluva lot easier by not slowly leaking out like the last two novels had. Maybe it was that this story hadn't happened all that long ago, it was easier to remember the details, the smells, the tastes. I'd write the end a bit slower. Right now we were just up to the part where I realized that Aaron didn't love me as James, that he had probably never loved me at all and had run off with a school teacher. That had hurt. It had been the first time he had actually abandoned me for another woman rather than just disappeared for a night. I remember that as the day that I fell out of love with him. The memories would hurt worse in the next couple of days when I had to break down and write the end, remembering in detail the way it felt when my heart was ripped out of my chest, how my blood soaked through my clothes and covered the dashboard of my Corvette. I loved that car. I couldn't remember now if I had wrecked it or not that night. I just remember that it had mercifully come to a stop before I stumbled out into the snow to die. *James*, I corrected myself. James stumbled out into the snow to die. I am still alive. I felt my stomach rumble and changed that opinion slightly. I was alive until my growling stomach decided to eat me for dinner. Then I might have a problem.

I nudged Karina with my toe to wake her from her reverie. "I'm gonna go."

"Think that 102 pages is enough work for one day?" She smirked but I could see the tired lines beside her eyes.

"Yeah, don't want to be too much of an overachiever. Might give my publisher the wrong idea, then they'll start expecting more than two books out of me a year. Return that studio call in the morning. If they're still interested I'll consider it."

"What changed your mind?"

"You. You're right. What's the point of life if I'm not living it?" I smiled and watched some of the worry fade out of her expression. Her constant concern was leading me to consider that maybe I needed to rethink some things, try something new. Change was scary when you haven't done it in a few hundred years. "Let's just make sure that this book is finished before I accidently kill myself." I packed up my notebooks and laptop, heading for the door. "Get some rest."

"Sure you don't want to stay for dinner?"

"It's already after eight. Maybe you should unearth Craig from his man cave." I nodded in the direction of the still closed bedroom door and slipped out the front door. When I reached the third floor Zane was in our apartment, awake, dressed, and working on a new track in his home studio. I left him to it and took a shower. I thought about trying Karina's idea out. I wasn't looking for romance but maybe I could find someone to play with for the evening, at least have a decent conversation. Zane did it all the time, why couldn't I experiment for a day with being myself? Rather than choosing my typical jeans and tight t-shirt I opted for a denim mini skirt with the highest heels I owned and a low cut tank top. Anywhere else in the country this would look like something a hooker would wear. In Los Angeles it was conservative. I looked at the clock and groaned. Nine in the evening and I was just now thinking strongly about dinner. Alone. On the way out the door I grabbed a book to take with me just in case whatever restaurant I ended up at provided boring company. While I'd like to spend the evening indulging in witty conversation with a handsome stranger there was the much more likely concept that I would spend the evening nursing a glass of wine over my Plato book. I wasn't alive during the time of the great Greek and Roman Empires in any of my lives. I had a lot of history to catch up on.

Zane wandered out of his studio holding a cold, congealed bowl of condensed soup just as I dropped my phone and book into one of those giant shoulder bags that are so popular with anemic size 00 starlets. Welcome to Hollywood, home of the hipster and the eating disorder. I was neither but I could put on a good show if the situation called for it. That and you could fit half my belongings in this bag. Perfect for disguising the book that would give away that I have an IQ over 20. I watched Zane shuffle to the kitchen and then wander back, his glazed over eyes finally acknowledging my existence. It was then that I felt his minor push on my mental shields and realized he was high. Again. I've never seen someone so continuously hell bent on self-destruction.

"Hi, Janey. Got a hot date?" he remarked snidely, one hand dropping down to readjust his crotch. I grimaced at the bile rising in my throat.

"I'm going out for sushi. Want me to bring you anything?"

"Nope. You know I don't eat that fish bait shit. I may be out when you get back."

"I don't doubt that. Just don't bring her back here this time, okay? I can't deal with another whore in my bed."

"I don't pay for it." He smiled and rubbed his blurred eyes. "You sound a little jealous. Reconsidering our arrangement?"

"Reconsidering sleeping with other women?"

He lost his smile and the cockiness in his voice. When Zane spoke again he just sounded resigned. "You love me, you know that."

"Despite all odds, Zane." I rolled my eyes and picked up my bag. "Enjoy your evening."

"When will you be back?"

"Are you going to miss me?" I paused with my hand on the doorknob, suddenly having a moment of insecurity about leaving him alone.

His smile returned as my thoughts slipped into his head, telling him of my momentary insanity. "I want to know where you are."

"Not in nearly as much trouble as you cause." I took off my engagement ring and left it on the entryway table. "Have a good night, Zane." I kissed him on the forehead and left before he could badger me with further commentary. I've got a nice new sports car, a '67 wine red Mustang that was a gift from Zane back when he still bribed me with gifts to cover up the cracks in our relationship. I picked out my own present that time, being a classic car girl and all. Zane overcompensates by driving a silver Porsche. As I slid into the leather driver's seat I smiled, feeling that the engine could use a little testing tonight. So much for local cuisine.

2

Forty-five minutes later found me parked in front of a random sushi restaurant in the Valley. San Fernando Valley has a sushi restaurant on almost every corner. The ones that don't have sushi have Starbucks. Some have both. Not a bad place to live. I parked a little down the street in an alley where I could watch the patrons coming and going. I wasn't looking for a menu rating based on the people who ate there; I was looking to see what my prospects would be if I decided to sit at a table alone rather than the bar. I haven't done this in a while but I'm assuming most people don't look at their possible selection of dinner partners like a clinical exam. Makes me feel a little bit like those gold-digging whores Zane likes to string along.

I'd decided to rev up my engine and get out of here, find a nice, quiet 24 hour diner where I could hide in the back, eat, and read my book in peace. It had been a nice thought to see if I could participate in a night out as a single person but apparently I couldn't. My heart just wasn't in it. And that's when I saw him. How cheesy does that sound? I'm leaving and then this hot guy crosses my path. The irony of it almost made me leave anyway. But then he stepped under a streetlight and I saw his face. My midnight musings about a man I'd never known rushed back into my head. He didn't glance up as he entered the restaurant alone, didn't completely show his face again before the door obscured it completely. What I had seen was enough to shake me, to ramp up my curiosity. At least that meant that I felt something, even if it wasn't a sexually related emotion. I slid out of the car, barely remembering to grab my shoulder bag. I had to get a closer look. It was probably nothing but my overworked imagination playing tricks but it could still be an adventure. And I desperately needed one of those.

Jared Stateton was not born to be a rock star, at least not in his opinion. He actually knew, for a fact, that he had been born to do other things, the tragedy being that he didn't give a shit so he spent his time making music in his own personal bubble that other people like to call Los Angeles. Rather than working in the family business that his father had always hoped he and his brother would inherit, Jared preferred to mingle in this giant melting pot of a few million people, ignore his father's threats, and play relatively normal human for a while. He wouldn't get to go on forever this way he knew that, so he reasoned that he might as well enjoy it while it lasted. Though he was never sure if it helped him or not when he was trying to blend in that he wasn't physically attractive in the current traditional sense. Rather than looking like a model for a franchise-clothing store, Jared's physique was taller, more like five hundred years ago--- classical--- in a Michelangelo carved him from marble the colors of a beach sunset kind of way. In deference to his current chosen profession, Jared conceded to wear black eyeliner and chipped black nail polish at shows. The nail polish sometimes survived the shows, the eyeliner didn't. He honestly couldn't stand having things like makeup on his face. Reminded him far too frequently of the mask he slipped on anytime his family was near. Despite the emo label that it put on his notoriously futuristic work, he did prefer to dress mostly in monochrome blacks, grays, and white, but regardless of what his legions of fans, mostly female, thought, it was just generally because they were easy colors and looked good with his black hair and bright blue eyes, successfully masking his lanky build. *Caribbean blue eyes…* He hadn't thought about that in what seemed like forever. It had been at least ten years since he'd given up

26

on looking for a girl with mood ring eyes, a dream from his youth. The resulting single-minded obsession had given his band one hell of a hit song though. He shook the dark memories off and crossed the street to his favorite sushi bar, just a bit off the beaten path so many take to the Hollywood Hills, grateful that while he had a recognizable face, he lived in a place where there were so many that he could blend in on a night like this, when he just wanted some avocado rolls and peace.

He slid into his favorite dingy back corner booth, a nook where he could see everyone in the tiny, overly crowded restaurant, but where he wasn't immediately noticeable, and pulled out his lyric notebook just as his server brought over a pot of hot tea. Jared ordered his veggie rolls and settled in to write, letting the emotions of the room flow over him like a carefully controlled tidal wave. Being an empath had made certain careers impossible, such as becoming a doctor, no matter how well he could control the outside emotions and thoughts that wormed their way into his brain. Hospitals are not a good place for someone who can feel every emotion from every person around them. It can morph into a rather incapacitating skill even when you know how to control it. Rather than attempting to completely shield against the things that go bump in the night in other people's heads, Jared taught himself to allow a small amount of it to flow through his consciousness and slide out through the various creative outlets he allowed himself. One of those was his writing. The writing morphed into lyrics which his brother turned into songs and here he was fifteen years later, the rock star sitting alone in the corner of a sushi dive, waiting on his avocado rolls and feeding off of everyone else's emotions. The tiny release of control that he allowed himself in a place like this permitted his abilities to feed, giving him an outlet, however small which kept the impulse to dive into the emotions of everyone he met at bay. Though empathy was his least favorite of his "special gifts" it did help to keep him human, let him feel connected to something other than his family. No matter how young he looked, after so many years it became difficult for Jared to hold on to even the most basic elements of human existence, such as emotions and a conscience. It didn't help his cause that the last human he had cared about had died viciously. The memory of that night flashed back through his mind, a thought that he quickly squashed and sent back into the void, refusing to return even for a moment to the dark place that had once consumed his soul.

Jared sat back in the corner of his booth, took a sip of his tea and closed his eyes, his shaggy black hair partially concealing his face, seeing the room through his mind rather than his human eyes. Casual observers who never gave him a second glance were suddenly sparring for dominance in his head, sending his ears ringing with their mundane discussions and internal monologues. In the midst of all of this new conversation it mildly entertained him that he was still very much aware of everything that was going on around him, the people talking aloud, the servers moving dishes through the crowded restaurant. The voices permeating his brain slowly fell into order and he began to make sense out of the words, his mind identifying the voices while his eyes readjusted to couple the words with the face. Like the man sitting with his wife, guilty over leaving work before eight. Or the teenage girl secretly lusting after him at the sushi bar with her friends. Without a glance in her direction, he gave the girl a small wave, just to be polite. No need to really encourage the jailbait. Which he quickly realized was the wrong move as her lust turned to confusion when she realized he hadn't looked at her and then wondered who he was waving at. He turned his head to smother a smile behind his hand, not wishing to frighten her any further. When he straightened, he noticed that her lust had returned and that she had begun to work her way over to him. Jared felt a moment of panic that was quickly overwhelmed by the reeking curiosity of another, newer presence in the room. He delved into her mind further and realized with a start that he was the subject of her silent query. And she knew precisely what he was doing. Jared looked up in time to watch the woman who matched the voice in his head slip in front of the approaching teenager to take the seat across from him. The woman smiled and helped herself to his rapidly cooling tea.

"You know, if you're going to play with people you really should be less obvious." Jared watched the pretty brunette sip from his teacup and grimace at the temperature. She touched three fingers to the outside of the cup, closed her eyes for the briefest of moments, and he sat stunned as steam began to rise from the cup. While he sat there contemplating her audacity at revealing her gift to him in such a public venue, she summoned the server over. "Will you please bring another cup? And I'll have whatever he's having." The server reappeared a moment later with the cup, which the woman promptly filled with tea, heated with her hand, and passed over to Jared. "Trust me; it's much better warm. And I thought you'd appreciate the fresh cup since I just drank from yours."

"Who the fuck are you?" Jared's forehead pinched as he tried to control the riot of thoughts bleeding from her head into his. It took him a minute to realize that the flood of random thoughts was intentional on her part. She was trying to drown his mental abilities so that he couldn't use them on her. He snapped his mental shields in place, effectively shutting her out until he could feel her drop the pretense.

"And why am I sitting at your table, right?" She laughed, though he could sense the nervousness in her voice. He got the idea that it wasn't commonplace for her to approach strangers without provocation. "Haven't you figured it out yet?" Without waiting for an answer, she held her right hand across the table, the same one she'd used to heat both cups. "Jane Jamison." She laughed nervously again when he hesitated to shake her hand. "Don't worry, empath, I won't hurt you. I only shoot real fire out of my hands when I'm really pissed. Or lighting candles." Jane sipped her tea, her bright hazel eyes dancing as she watched him from across the table. Jared felt her lightly prod at his shields without pushing hard enough to set off any alarms. "I'm kidding! Just heat, no real fire. It's an ability that I used to have once upon a time; this is just what's left over." She laughed again and it sounded like silk sliding across the table and up his spine. Jared shifted

29

uncomfortably at the feeling as odd sparks of forgotten memories flashed through his mind. "Do you have a name or should I make one up for you?" She set her cup down and moved to rise from the table. "On second thought, maybe I'll just go ask your friend over there…"

Alarm causing him to shake off the strange feelings, Jared leaned across the table, catching her by the arm and pulling her back down into the booth. Jane blessed him with a wicked smile borne of true confidence that he could see radiating off of her and slid her straight almost black hair back over her shoulder. Watching her, Jared felt his body hum in places he didn't want to think about at the moment and garnered that the sensation might be new for her too. "Jared Stateton. How did you know?"

"We're of a similar kind, Jared Stateton, and I hated to see you get caught when you so clearly thought you knew what you were doing." Jane's voice grew more confident, beginning to match her smile.

He laughed, a bit taken aback by her rash assumption. "You think I don't know what I'm doing?"

She raised an eyebrow in question. "Obviously you don't. And don't give me that disgusted, I'm-insulted look. I'd hate for your eyes to get stuck rolled up in your head. I've been reading you since you walked in the door, avocado boy, and you didn't even notice. By the way, I don't listen to your music, but what kind of name is Stateton for a rocker? Sounds more like a politician."

"Do you always talk this much to people you don't know?"

"I'm not entirely sure that I don't know you, though I'm positive we've never met before." Jane watched him as she leaned back, stretching her legs across her side of the booth and she sipped her tea, silently noting his reaction. Jared shook his head to rid himself of the thoughts her tanned legs conjured in his brain. He thought for the briefest of moments about what it would be like to take advantage of the situation she had presented him with, though the thought vanished

30

as quickly as it had come on the knowledge that she wasn't quite that simple to read. He felt too much fear sliding off of her despite her new-found optimism. Her smile broadened and he felt that twang of familiarity again, dismissing it in favor of encouraging her with a single erotic thought. "Naughty boy. I'm taken."

"Telepath." He didn't need her confirmation but he was curious to see where she was going with this game.

"Among other things, yes. Now I know your dirty little secret and you know mine. At least one of them, anyway." Her smile continued to widen. "Keep going with that thought. You're terribly creative in the most wicked ways. I'm enjoying it."

"Don't expect me to be embarrassed. I'm not. And you haven't seen my creativity yet. It comes across much better in reality than in theory." He grinned and felt her control slip a bit. He was surprised when she didn't immediately rush to recover it.

"Tease." Jane accused, smiling from behind her teacup, settling into the conversation.

"I'm not taken." Jared settled in to his side of the table, enjoying the interruption that Jane presented. A quiet wave of anticipation rolled across the table and Jared lapped it up before it was swallowed back up into her hesitation and the ever-present fear that held her wavering willpower in check. "To answer your question, Stateton is my birth name; I had no choice. But I agree with you, it's not a terribly intimidating name for a rock star." He laughed. "I suppose I could've been given some hippie name like Fire Moon or something. Would that have served my calling in life better?"

She tilted her head to one side, carefully regarding him while she considered the implications of her words. He felt the moment that she decided that she was more interested in his reaction than the possible repercussions of the moment. And that he knew was nothing that she considered to be a logical response to the situation. An irrational thought containing all the possibilities of what could happen that night slid through her brain and prodded her to honestly answer his question. "Angelo Caduto."

"Assuming the first is obvious, is there a specific translation or am I supposed to guess?" He leaned on the table, bracing his upper body on his elbows, intrigued by the pyro-telepath taking up residence across from him.

"It means 'fallen angel' in Italian. Some people are a living work of art, more exquisite because of their life than they ever would be were they simply carved likenesses of themselves." Her eyes came up to meet his and his breath caught in his throat for a moment. "You, Jared Stateton, have the potential to be one of those people. Too exquisite to be real which makes it a damn good thing that you're not exactly human in the traditional sense."

"Why do you think it would matter?"

Unbidden, Jane allowed her fingertips to slide across the delicate skin encasing his hand, her eyes following her hand. "Because good art shouldn't be so easily destroyed."

"Why are you here?" His elbows resting on the table, he leaned forward, moving as close as he could get with the table in between them.

She mimicked his actions, eyes sparkling with good humor. "In the restaurant or at this table?"

"Both." He caught her fingertips in his, short nails grazing the underside of her wrist. Hazel eyes met blue and he noticed for the first time that the color was artificial.

"I believe I already answered that, however if you'd like a slightly different explanation along the same vein, I like sushi and you looked lonely."

Jared's fingers slid across hers, and her breath caught. "Is that the only reason?" He could almost feel the thoughts twirling through her head behind the barriers that she'd made for herself. "I think you're lying to me."

"I was reminded of a promise I made to find an adventure. The search had to start somewhere." Her smile faded around the edges. "You're not exactly what you seem, are you, Jared?" She tilted her head to one side, regarding him quietly. "What I really can't decide is whether you need saving or you're searching for something to save." Jane watched a faint look of surprise followed by a sort of recognition that she didn't understand flit across his face.

Jared noticed her interest as she watched him and clamped down on his emotions before she saw something inside of him that he wasn't ready for her to see. His curiosity at the odd nature of the comment took only seconds to elicit a response. "What exactly am I supposed to be saving?"

Jane smiled and slid her hand back into her lap, taking her napkin with it. "Right now? Your fingers for your chopsticks. Dinner's here."

Jared laughed as the server set a large plate of sushi in the middle of the table along with smaller plates for their individual choices. "Very smooth. I wonder how you would've gotten out of that if the food hadn't come right then."

Jane added wasabi to her soy sauce, stirred the concoction with her chopsticks, and then began adding sushi rolls to her plate, taking her time in an attempt to regain lost space with him, fortifying her mental barriers. "Ah, but since it did, I guess you'll have to live with the mystery." She glanced over at him under the fringe of her eyelashes to gauge his reaction. He felt the dip in her chest when he unknowingly reacted, giving her exactly what she wanted.

"Is there a mystery that you'll allow me to solve?" Jared watched her as he added pickled ginger to his sauce dish, smiling as she fidgeted nervously under his gaze.

"Of course. Why is the sky blue?" The corner of her mouth rose in a half-smile as she started in on her sushi, her eyes glancing up from her plate to glance at his. She laughed at his enchanted face. "What? I'm not apologizing for not being one of those chicks that doesn't eat in front of a guy. I like food."

"No, it's nice to see a woman unafraid to be herself. To answer your question, the sky isn't actually blue; it just appears that way. What is it that you do out in the world under the seemingly blue sky?" He chewed on a piece of his avocado roll as he waited for her answer. He tried to monitor her emotions, blatantly ignoring the recurring electrical impulses he felt emanating off of her.

"This and that. If you mean my career, since I know yours, I'm a novelist. I search Valley sushi dives with peeling paint and smoke rimmed ceilings in search of hot, reclusive, slightly psychotic rock stars to chat up for character profiles." Jane smiled at his mental prodding and slid her barriers in to place, effectively slamming a steel door on his intrusion before he could find anything of use. He was attractive, charming, and not nearly as irresistible as she caught him thinking he was.

He coughed, nearly choking on his sushi as he interpreted her words and drew into himself, still reeling from the force of being propelled from her mind. "Is that code for paparazzi stalker?" He reached for his tea and Jane idly warmed it for him again as he brought the tiny china cup to his lips.

She laughed at the surprised reaction he tried so desperately to hide. "No, it quite literally means that I write books, fictional ones, science fiction horror novels to be exact."

"You don't strike me as the type to be able to do that kind of work." He didn't bother to hide his interest both intellectually and physically as she slid back into her seat, relieved that he hadn't misread her intentions.

"And what type would that be? Dark, depressed, morose, or more like a space cadet with a tinfoil helmet?"

Jared laughed at the image her words conjured. "Okay, maybe not! So you're Jane Jamison, famous fiction writer?"

"Not exactly. This is just the only career I've found where I can apply my life experiences without being involuntarily committed to the psych ward." Jane's expression was secretive. "Tell me about you. Maybe I'll use it in a book." She popped a bite of sushi in her mouth and smiled as she chewed.

Jared opted to blatantly ignore her query, pushing her to reveal more of herself to him first. "So what color are your eyes really?"

"Hazel."

"Liar. Those are contacts."

"They're different," she conceded. "I'd be impressed if you could tell me and get it right." She smiled a small, wistful smile to herself, and propped an elbow on the table as she concentrated overly hard on the chunks of melded rice and vegetables in front of her.

"Mood ring," he answered without looking up from his plate.

Jane jumped involuntarily at the phrase, nearly dropped her chopsticks. "What did you say?" She fought to control her face, willing her mind to be a total blank before Jared slipped past her defenses.

He laughed at her shocked expression trying to encourage her to override her protective instincts and let him in. "You really don't listen to my music, do you? I'd bet you my vintage handmade Stratocaster that you are the girl with mood ring eyes."

"Is she better than the girl with crimson nails?" Jane teased while silently berating herself for putting those pictures on the backs of her books and then reacting.

"U2. "Vertigo." A good, yet commercial song. You're infinitely more interesting."

"Now I am suitably impressed. Very few people understand that reference."

"Was I right?" His grin masked his curiosity as he refused to allow the change in subject.

Jane smiled sweetly. "I'll let you know."

Acknowledging momentary defeat but refusing to believe he was wrong, he decided to hold her attention with a compromise. "One week." Jared continued to eat, his gaze never leaving her face.

"Care to elaborate?" Jane sipped her green tea, ignoring the warm feeling stealing through her stomach at the opportunity to see him again.

"I'm asking you out on a date. One week from today, from the minute you sat down at my table, meet me here. I'll reserve this crap booth in this dump if I have to, but I want us to be right here seven days from now." He banged on the table with his open palm, emphasizing his point.

Jane giggled, giving him a mock salute with her chopsticks and continued to pick through the platter of sushi. "You picked the date and time, so I get to order the food. These cucumber rolls suck. They have no flavor. Doesn't this place have shitake rolls?"

Deep laughter rang out across the table. "I don't think I've had this much fun at one dinner. You're eating them wrong." He picked one up with his chopsticks, dunked it in his own sauce dish and held it out to her. "May I?" Jane leaned across the table and opened her mouth obediently. She slid the cucumber roll from between his chopsticks with her tongue and dropped back in her seat to chew thoughtfully. "You're right, it is better."

Jared shook his head trying to clear the seductive thoughts that were rapidly flooding his brain. "Would you mind just licking my chopsticks like that one more time?"

Jane rose from her seat and motioned for him to meet her halfway across the table. She leaned in close enough to whisper in his ear, her breath hot on his skin. "If you could only choose one place, one time, are you sure that's where you'd want my tongue?"

He turned his head so that his face was hidden in her neck, giving in to the sexual heat building between them, closing his eyes to help keep some semblance of control over the situation. She had slid under his skin as surely as a knife and she knew it. "God, no. Several others come to mind." Jared breathed in her scent and opened his bright blue eyes, forcing his vision to focus. "And if you don't like the idea of exploring each and every one of them in this booth, I suggest you damn well stop talking like that." Nothing but sheer force of will kept him even close to in his seat. His white-knuckled fingers gripped the tabletop so hard that he legitimately feared breaking it. The carefully checked desire that leaked from her body to his was nearly enough to cause him to not care who he was or where they were and the overwhelming reaction nearly knocked him to his knees.

She met his stare, closer than a prayer from her face and smiled her expression an inch away from devilish as she pushed to see how far he'd go just for the sheer pleasure of knowing he wanted her and he could feel everything she threw at him. Jane watched his thoughts turn from a PG-13 rating straight to NC17 without a stop in the middle.

She could visibly see the tension in his body and she still wanted to push him past that carefully held control just to see what he would do, how he would react. Jared Stateton was proving to be a worthy advisory and it had been far too long since Jane had someone to play with who could match her powers. "How about we just stop talking?" His eyes met hers and Jane felt a sharp shard of desire slide through her as his breath tickled her throat and it wasn't a forced reaction.

He licked his lips, the tip of his tongue sliding across the edges of his perfect teeth and he forced his hands to lie flat on the table to resist touching her. "You're not on my side of the table."

"And you're not on mine. Yet." Her disguised eyes dared him and he could've sworn he saw sparks of violet behind the hazel lenses.

Jared sat back in his seat dragging his muddled senses out of the metaphorical gutter they seemed to have fallen into, his cramped hands dropping dully in his lap. "No. Nuh-uh. I don't know if you're making this fiancé of yours up or not, but this is not happening. Not like this anyway." He smiled tightly, trying hard to relax. "But damn, if you're not good."

"Sweetheart, you wouldn't know." Jane sat back and offered him a halfway genuine smile, pulling her emotions back under control until she saw the curious blank his powers as an empath pulled from her reflected in his face. "You're a good man, Jared Stateton."

"Convince a tabloid of that. Eat your sushi."

Jane's smile turned more genuine as she continued to eat. "Yes, sir. So tell me more about Jared Stateton. What do you do when you're not giving the paparazzi big pay days or accusing random women of wanting to jump you in sushi bars?"

"I write and record music, do an insane amount of PR work, manage a band that's turned into a global brand, and for the record, I did not accuse you of anything. You offered." He pointed at her with his chopsticks before sending them diving to his plate for the last piece of sushi.

Jane laughed outright causing more than a few people to stare. "Bullshit! And for the record, I believe my offer only involved my tongue and it was really more of an inquiry than anything else. I was just curious," she shrugged, smiling innocently.

"You're wasting the innocent expression." Jared swallowed the last piece of his sushi and set his chopsticks aside.

"You didn't answer my question," she challenged.

He sighed dramatically then grinned. "Give me your hand." Jane set aside her chopsticks and placed her right hand in his left. He flipped it over and traced the lines on her palm with the index finger of his right hand. "What's this scar?"

"It shows a promise I made a long time ago. Nothing life-altering." She shrugged.

"It must be old. The line's very light." He traced the line then opened his own right hand. "I have a matching one. So does my brother. That's…odd." He rubbed it and continued studying her palm. "You're right handed. You trust me. I could break every bone in your dominant hand before you could pull it back and you gave it to me."

"I'm ambidextrous and if you even think about breaking my hand, I'll break your balls." She picked up her chopsticks with her left hand and propped one of her stilettoed feet between his legs in illustration. "I trust you because I have no reason not to. Are you going to give me one?" She wiggled her foot against his thigh suddenly bored by the serious turn of the conversation.

"I'd like to give you a reason to trust me more." Jared brought her hand to his mouth and kissed her open palm.

Jane sighed, annoyed by the triteness of his come-on tactics and the reaction that her body had come up with all on its own. It saddened her to watch him resort to teenage courtship tactics when she'd had so much hope for the creativity she'd seen displayed prominently in his mind since she'd sat down at his table yet she still felt a little blush creep into her cheeks. She rolled her eyes, attempting to pull her hand back with no success and enjoying his attention just a little more than she wanted to admit even to herself. "Please don't."

"Sometimes a kiss can just be a kiss. Or a touch just a touch…" he let his voice trail off as he licked the inside of her wrist, his free hand sliding down to caress the perfect leg resting between his thighs. "You taste better than dessert."

"I like flirting with you, you're fun to play with, but this table's not coming out from between us." She smiled cattily, toying with him as she struggled to keep him at a safe distance as his hand slid closer to her thigh. Jane stabbed her chopsticks across the wrist that he still had on the table, clamping it down in one place. "Remove your hand or I'll remove this one for you."

He laughed, his hands not budging an inch. "You won't hurt me."

All humor was lost from the gaze that met his. "What do you think my emotions tell you now, avocado boy?"

"You think I'm hot."

"You're not that cute," she countered, dropping her chopsticks in her almost empty plate and withdrawing her leg.

"You're sure about that?" His head bent back down toward her fingertips.

Jane snatched her hand back, saving herself from another advance that was not as unwelcome as part of her wished it was and stated the obvious. "You don't know me. Why would you want to?"

"Because you sought me out. You sat down at my table. You showed me a taste of who you are. Should I ask for forgiveness for being intrigued and wanting to know the rest, at least some of it?"

"There's a difference between knowing someone and touching them intimately like that. Apparently I shouldn't have…"

"Shouldn't have what?" Jared's eyes narrowed as she withdrew from him.

"Sat down at this table."

"Why not?"

"Because I like you more than I should," she said quietly, her eyes daring him to push her further or deny her claim.

Jared dropped some money on the table and held out his hand. "Come on. Outside."

Jane ignored his hand but followed him through the crowded restaurant and out onto the street. She turned and started down the sidewalk. When he didn't follow, she stopped and turned, her eyes searching him out in the deepening twilight. "Are you coming?"

"Where are you going?"

"Car's down here." She pointed to the alley beside the sushi bar.

"I'm across the street. Care to walk with me? We can finish our conversation. I'll drive you back," he offered gallantly.

"Dessert involved?" she teased, her previous good humor returning though her eyes and mind were still heavily shielded from him.

Jared eyed the tan legs visible underneath her denim miniskirt, his gaze travelling up to take in her tight shirt. "I think that could be arranged."

Jane laughed and took his arm. "I meant the edible kind."

He looked at her with mock shock. "What I was thinking of is edible."

"Sure. I believe you. Be my escort and hold me closer while we walk. This looks like I'm your sister."

"One brother, no sisters. And, in continuation, I'm not supposed to touch you, remember?" He slid his arm around her waist and pulled her closer in illustration of his commitment to not touch her, his fingertips moving ever so slightly underneath her shirt hem to caress her lower back. He smiled as she shivered beneath his touch and leaned into his hands.

"Big difference between you offering me your arm and me jumping you in a public place." Her body nestled into his side, surprised at how oddly comfortable she was touching this stranger and with how quickly she'd allowed the flirtation to progress. On a normal day Jane liked people she didn't know to keep their distance. On an abnormal day that became an "or else" situation. A perverse part of her looked forward to those days. Tonight she was grateful for her benevolent mood.

"Quit stalling and give me your explanation." He pulled her tighter against him.

"Explanation? You want the real, no holds barred one?" She waited for his affirmative nod and then continued as they walked down the street together, completely oblivious to the people surrounding them. "All right. My fiancé is a glutton for punishment who has a hobby of publicly running around on me. I'm his doormat for when he decides he wants to play house because his affairs with shallow whores didn't work out. And I ignore the affairs and keep him close because we're so closely attached that if he stubs his toe, mine breaks, so if something should happen and he dies then so do I and I don't want to go out that way again. You really should read my work. Makes the explanation much easier, less convoluted. And slightly less uncomfortable for me to talk about with people I don't know," Jane grimaced, sneaking a peek at his face.

"Again? Like past life again?" Ghosts from the past surfaced and swirled through Jared's head mingling with the fleeting memories that had been pestering him ever since she sat down at his table.

"Want to run in the other direction yet? Think I'm a total psycho, avocado roll boy?" She leaned back to watch the shadows play across his handsome face.

Jared hesitated for a moment before rushing headlong into the metaphorical fire. "I don't want to watch you die trying to save him again, James."

Jane stopped and turned to look at him under the fluorescent glow of a streetlight. "I think you have me confused with someone else." She felt the old panic start to rise in her chest as she stepped away from him.

"Why? Because you don't know what I'm talking about or because you don't want to answer the questions that might come with it?" The more he watched her the less he doubted himself.

"Haven't we already had enough deep talk for the night? Whatever this is that you've got going, just let it go, Jared. Besides, you've got the wrong person. Was your James even a girl?" She skipped ahead of him on the sidewalk.

"Yes, James was a woman. But you know that already, don't you?" He took a step toward her and she took one step back toward the street. "She's the girl with mood ring eyes."

"I don't know who you are other than the obvious, but you're creeping me out and I was enjoying walking. It's not attractive for a man to ask about another woman, you know." She sighed tiredly when his expression didn't change. "Please don't ask about that." The smile left her face completely and her whole body tensed as she stepped further away from him.

"I'd worry if I was asking about another woman."

"People don't often tell you that things are none of your business, do they?"

"How do you know what I'm going to ask?"

"You want me to trust you?" He nodded. "Then accept that I don't want to talk about it. The past isn't important. Besides, it might not be safe for you. Or for me," she mused, maintaining her distance.

"You're gonna have to give me something better than a safety hazard." His arms reached for her, not quite willing to let her slip away yet and more than a little confused by her reaction.

She turned on him angrily. "Fine, you want me to be honest? The truth is that I don't want to die, Jared. Zane and I are eight years past last time and you asking these questions just brings more attention to us that I don't need. So whatever's in your head, whatever story you've heard, just let it go." Jane stepped away from him and began walking back to her car. "There's nothing worth this; no one deserves this life, but it's the one I've got and I'd like to keep it, thank you very much."

"Holy mother…you really are her." He caught her and held her face in his hands so that he could see her eyes. "Show me," he demanded.

Jane stared up at him from behind her colored lens. "Nothing is worth dying for. Sometimes you can't change things no matter how hard you try, Jared." She stepped away from him.

"You don't remember me, do you?"

She stopped and gazed up at him. "Why should I?" When he remained silent, she stepped away. "Thank you for dinner. It was nice to meet you. Maybe I'll see you in a week. If I don't, do us both a favor and forget you ever met me, Jared Stateton."

Jared watched her walk away. "Sooner. I'm not waiting another week." He walked off to his own black SUV.

3

Everyone has a bit of insanity in their lives, in their minds. I'm starting to think that I might have more than most because I don't know what the fucking hell I was thinking. I'm just being honest.

I decide that I'm going to put myself "out there"; I'm going to search for an "adventure". This could not have been more of a clusterfuck. Not only did I find an attractive, smart guy who understands my random references in conversation, but he's also mentally stalking me. Which may be why he understands said random references. This was not the goal of the evening. Why can't just one thing in my life be uncomplicated? Rather than falling out of James's life I've managed to step further into the past. And my cute little should-have-been-a-one-night-stand boy remembers me as her. I have no idea how this happened. I should have walked away. No, I should have run in the other direction. Quickly. Now I'm stuck trying to figure out if this guy's a threat and if I should try to take out the random celebrity I met in a sushi bar or if Zane and I need to disappear. And damnit if I don't still want to kiss him.

I didn't wait until I got home. I sat in my car and Googled him just to see if he was telling me the truth. A ten second search pulled up so much stuff that I've got no idea how I missed him for this long. According to the press I glanced through we've been running in the same circles for a good decade or so. It gave me a whole new set of overanalyzed issues to deal with, starting with the idea that Jared Stateton might have been hunting us all this time. Truly frightening that this could have been going on under my nose, that this guy could have worked his way into my head through a spell and I didn't notice it, allowed myself to feel so safe that I ignored it. I would have kicked myself but dealing with the injury would just make me more irritated. I took a few deep breaths, trying to calm myself before I did something outrageous and stupid. I thought about following him and just finishing it, but there's still too much of me that's attracted to him rather than afraid or potentially infuriated with him. And that was truly dangerous. Though don't think that the thought that death at Jared Stateton's hands might not be so bad as long as there was an amazing orgasm in it for me hadn't crossed my mind. Don't judge, it's been awhile and Zane wasn't that good to begin with.

When I arrived back at my building I skipped over my condo and Zane's immense uselessness and went to Karina's unit. I stopped at the door, reconsidering waking her particularly in light of the way things were when I left. I paused with my hand just short of touching the door and felt out the apartment. Karina was awake. She slipped inside my mind and walked quickly to the outer door. Her backpack containing a travel herb kit was in her hand. Wordlessly we took the stairs down to the third floor where I retrieved two sweaters, one of my laptops, and a notebook before we stepped outside to the pool terrace and the beach below. The first thing that I did was to conduct a more thorough Internet search. More than I cared to admit to anyone, I needed to know if Jared was a demon, a threat, or just a random guy that I happened across. Karina sat beside me, silently taking notes and writing down ideas for other ways to get information. Google, not surprisingly, only turned up the standard press release line that he had given me over dinner, which was only helpful on a superficial level. I did find a surprising amount of heartbroken almost-starlets in his wake which really shouldn't have amused me half as much as it did. I couldn't imagine that one of those vapid wastes of oxygen could really hold her own next to a man who'd probably seen the rise and fall of the Roman Empire. I didn't need any type of confirmation to know that he's much older than I am, and I'm not a newborn. We left the computer on the vacant terrace and walked out on to the beach. More than anyone else Karina truly understood my insane need for caution. She opened the notebook and held it out to me so that I could take notes while she worked with her herbs.

"Are you sure you want to do this? I know that you like him."

"Doesn't matter if I like him. He knows too much, he knows me as James. No matter how cute he is there's no way he should know what he knows and be that young in this life. And that makes him dangerous no matter what flavor of talented he is."

"All right. Let's see what we can find out about Mr. Stateton. For your sake I hope this turns out to be nothing."

"Why?"

Karina looked up and grinned. "Because he's hot!"

I wrinkled my nose and tried to push back the immediate picture that popped into my head of Jared's face sliding intimately against my neck. My body shivered at the thought of things that couldn't happen and the fantasy of how much I'd wanted them to in that moment. I swallowed the emotional response down and repeatedly cleansed my aura until the thoughts weren't there anymore. "Doesn't matter. I have to protect us. That we all survive is all that matters."

My sister's face reflected the sadness that I felt coming from her and I shrugged it off like it was nothing because to let it in would show too much weakness and I needed to get through this right now. I could have my breakdown later. It could be better directed later anyway when I knew more about what I should be afraid of.

49

One long ass explanation and several hours later we'd found nothing. Actually we'd found less than nothing. This guy didn't seem to be on any radar, was immune to pretty much every type of spell we cast to gain information on him. While that did not make me feel any better it seemed to amuse my sister to no end. I should've known that she would see a pretty face and just assume he was inherently good. I don't have that much faith in people, magical or not.

"While I appreciate you waking me up to tell me you met a cute boy, you could have done this on your own. We've found nothing that he didn't already tell you himself." Karina lay back in the sand, staring up at the stars. "He is hot though. I'd do him."

"That is not the question I need answered." Rather than relax in the early morning light I decided to flip back through my notepad and reread my notes on Mr. Stateton. "I can't afford to be careless right now, Kari. I need to know what his agenda is."

"What if he has no agenda?" Karina opened one eye and turned her head to stare at me. I sighed knowing the answer she was looking for and not sure which one I was willing to give her. I opted for honesty since she'd read it out of my mind anyway.

"I don't know." I lay down next to her and stared unseeing at the slowly lightening sky. "I don't know what to do if he's just some random, normal guy who's interested in me. Actually, I take that back, he's not interested in me, he's interested in James and I'm trying really hard right now to separate myself from that life. I don't need someone dragging me back in. And it's too much of a coincidence to me that he would show up now, after all these years and suddenly be interested in my past."

My sister giggled at the sky. "Maybe he's a plant from your editor to get you to hurry up and finish this book."

"And my editor would know to send someone who looks scarily similar to a guy I've been dreaming about for the last decade and a half who has some of the same extra brain cells I do? That's a lot of coincidences for people who don't really believe in them."

"How do you know he's the same guy from your dreams? You said yourself that you don't really know what he would look like now, that the last clear vision you had of his face was over a decade ago. People can change a lot in a decade."

I shook my head, irritated but convinced that the man I met last night was the same one that had invaded my brain years earlier. I love how the things you stop looking for you can just randomly stumble across. That little bit of the universe annoys the shit out of me. I don't understand why it can't just be straightforward. You know what you know, I know what I know, now let's deal with it. I just didn't know how he didn't know it. Or maybe he did and he didn't want to tell me. Where was a vacant street to lie on and contemplate the ways Fate was screwing you over when you needed one? I am so unbelievably sick with being the one person that the gods continually screw with. No one I'd managed to kill in a past life had been that bad of a travesty to earn me an eternity of unending torment and questions. Finding Jared Stateton wasn't proving to be the relief I'd hoped for, he just added more questions to my already swirling mind. Kari didn't know what to say to make me feel better and I didn't know what to say to give either of us an answer I had faith in. Avoidance can sometimes be your friend, particularly when you think acknowledgement might land you in the middle of your own personal apocalypse.

"How's Craig? I'm sorry I didn't ask earlier."

"He's not good. He wants me to be someone I'm not and I can't do that for him anymore." Karina closed her eyes against the rising sun.

"I know you've tried talking to him but have you really tried to understand what it is that's bothering him? It can't be that he's just now figured out you're special. You told him years ago."

"Yes, but unlike you who has a very visible, active power, mine are all interior. It's really difficult to prove empathy and telekinesis to someone who is so visibly angry all of the time." I watched my sister's hands pound the sand in frustration and I just wanted to hurl a fireball at her husband for making her feel this way. I was seriously beginning to change my mind about Craig being one of the good guys. He was starting to resemble as much of a rat fink bastard as Zane exhibited on a daily basis. It wasn't fair that we both ended up with jerks.

"You know that he loves you. He's just got to realize that he loves all of you, not just the bits that he prefers. It's that whole "for better or for worse" thing."

Karina giggled and propped herself up on her elbows. "Speaking of wedding vows, are you and Zane decided on if that's really going to happen this time?"

"I'm thinking of asking him to move out. I think you're right, I want a life this time, at least for as long as I can live it. Complications of crazy people from my past resurfacing notwithstanding, of course." I grimaced and pulled myself up out of the sand. "Kari, I don't know if I can do this. I can't let Zane get too far away from me; I don't know what it's like to live my own life. What if I fail?"

"Then at least you tried. You can start with this guy though," she brandished a printout of one of Jared's photographs. "He's at least a distraction."

I ripped the printout from her hands and tore it to shreds that were shoved into the front of my notebook to keep them from blowing down the beach. "That man is not a distraction, he's suicide."

"Ah, but wouldn't he be a nice way to go?" Kari grinned, lying back down. "You know, I do think you've got a free pass lying around somewhere that entitles you to make Zane suffer a meaningless death at some point. Maybe you should live a little and see if you'd be forced to use it this go 'round."

"So you want me dead?"

"No, I want you happy and this is the most active I've seen you in years. Something about this guy gets under your skin. I think you owe it to yourself and possibly him to find out what that is. From what you said he sounds pretty determined." She turned on her side to look at me. "You know how boys in the schoolyard pull on girls' pigtails? This would be the grown up version. It's a good thing. Just go with it."

"He wants me to meet him at the sushi bar again on Friday." I grinned in spite of my best efforts to remain neutral. Damnit.

"Well that's one way to get your questions answered."

"Go get some sleep. I'm going to see what Zane knows, if anything if he's home, and then get some rest myself. I'm told humans should sleep every once in a while." I stretched and stood, gathering my belongings as I went.

"Craig will be up soon. Maybe he'll feel like a little make-up sex before he leaves for work. Meet you at your place in a bit?" Karina tossed her kit back together, burying the used herbs and saying a hasty prayer over the space. I nodded and watched her leave, preferring to watch the sunrise while I contemplated my dwindling options.

"Zane! I'm back!" I jumped almost high enough to smack my head on the ceiling as the front door slammed shut with the draft from the open patio doors. It had been a really long night. "We have got to get that fixed."

"J, not now." Zane cursed. I walked into his studio and watched as he changed a couple of dials on his soundboards and pushed his headphones down harder onto his ears, flattening his spiked white blonde hair. His dark eyes narrowed in his dark, thin face as he tweaked the recording. I wondered how I'd ever fallen in love with him.

53

Deciding it was far too late, or early depending how you looked at it, to deal with Zane's normal level of working bullshit, I sauntered into the home recording studio and slid between his chair and the soundboards, unplugging the headphones. "Take a break. I need to talk to you about something."

Zane gripped my waist in his tattooed hands, moving me away from his precious soundboards while I noticed the track marks on his arms. Thank God and Goddess I was shielding against him like a sonofabitch. He fell to one side, resting his head wearily on my torso, causing my otherwise flat stomach to twitch. "Sorry, baby, I can't. I've got to get this beat right."

"Five minutes? Something really weird happened tonight. I met someone who knows who James was, knows about our past. I need to know if you know anything about him. I can't figure out how he knows us."

"Anyone important?" Zane pushed away from me and even though I couldn't feel it, I could see that he was annoyed at the common theme of conversation. He was probably waiting for me to either drop it or devolve into a fight. I wasn't giving him either tonight. I watched him vainly attempt to ignore me for a few seconds while he worried with the plug on his headphones.

"Don't know yet. I really need to talk to you about this." I smacked the cord from his grasp. "I'm concerned, Zane. You know there's still people who'd like to see us dead again. Have you been doing anything different, met anyone new recently?"

He glared up at me, his brown eyes nearly black with his annoyance at the unasked question. Like I don't know he screws around. "Don't ask questions that you don't want the answer to. We're careful. Can we talk about this in the morning? I really need to finish this tonight." He rubbed his temples, trying to keep his irritation from showing and failing.

"It is morning, Zane."

"Fine. Will this get me killed, right now, today?"

"I don't know."

"Well neither do I because you damn well know that I don't remember as much as you. Let me know when we're at DEFCON one and I'll be concerned." Zane returned stubbornly to his recording.

All right. That was it; I'd had it. Fuck him and his dumb ass. Right now I wasn't much caring if he lived or died and we'd just see what happened to me. I somehow managed to just shake my head and stepped away from him. "You still don't get it. I don't care who you fuck. I care about staying alive which is a helluva lot easier if you'd work with me just a little bit on it. Drugs and whores don't exactly leave you in the best shape to deal with a threat. I know that we don't talk about it because it starts a fight, but damnit we should. I shouldn't have to come home to strange women in my bed or shield against you because I don't want to spend my life in a drug induced stupor. Read a paper, or turn on the television to something other than porn. I wish you'd just do something with your life. Grow up and help me deal with this for five seconds." I watched his glassy eyes stare stubbornly at his boards for a few moments before I finally just gave up. You can't save someone who doesn't want to be saved. Zane didn't want anything anymore. "I'm going to bed. Please don't bother me."

He was silent for a long moment before I got an answer that sounded more like it came from a lost child. And it broke a little of what was left of my heart because I knew then that he was well and truly lost. "It's not like that and you know it. And I can't watch porn anymore. You blocked the channels like I'm some eight year-old or something. Hey, did you get a take-out menu from the sushi place? You were gone a long time just for takeout. Do they deliver hibachi?"

I smiled sadly and kissed him on the cheek, knowing that the adult version of my soul mate was no longer running the controls on his body, not with the amount of narcotics he'd ingested. "Just trying to make sure you didn't get carpel tunnel in your hand. And no, we're not exactly in their delivery area." I squeezed his shoulder and walked to the door, taking what little I could find of his stash with me to flush down the toilet.

"You ate there alone?" His gaze didn't move an inch from the equipment directly in front of him.

"Don't worry about it. You don't like sushi; I do. I'm going to do some research and go to bed." Remembering my original reason for daring to enter his man cave, I stuck my head back around the doorframe. "Zane, what do you know about our past lives? I mean really know?"

He barely looked up from his keyboards but I knew the Zane I normally dealt with was back. "I know I need to get these beats laid before morning. I know nothing that you don't know about our past lives or why you're asking about them, other than the obvious nor do I care. This new research for a book, or are you still on your mystery person who dared ask a question that reminded you of something that you should know nothing about?"

"One day you're gonna wish you'd paid a little bit of attention to our conversations. Thanks for listening." I smacked the doorframe with my hand as I left, wincing at the smarting pain it caused to drip across my palm. "Good luck with the song." When the door slammed shut to the bedroom, I didn't flinch. I vainly hoped that Zane did though.

4

"You're doing it wrong." Truly green eyes inspected the outfit critically from a nearly mirror image of my face. I took a quick look at my sister's very safe jeans and polo shirt outfit and briefly considered just buying the shirt for her.

"Well, fix it!" I turned obediently and held the strappy, wayward black leather shirt in place while my sister followed me back into the dressing room and began to wind it correctly. I hate shopping unless I have something specific to look for. My sister loves it though and right now I'd go through about any self-imposed torture to make her happy.

"Why is it that I'm expected to fix everything that goes wrong in your life?" Karina worked to unsnarl the ends of the leather jacket, her concentration entirely focused on the task at hand.

"Because I fixed everything that went wrong in your life for the first twenty years. Um, can't breathe!" I glared at her in the mirror, a look that she summarily dismissed, my chest constricting painfully in the tight black leather as Karina cinched it like one of Scarlett O'Hara's corsets.

"This life or the last one? Breathe shallowly, it'll pass in a few minutes." She rolled her eyes, tied the last knot and stepped back to admire her handiwork. "There. Jared will lose his mind."

I turned to look my reflection over critically in the mirror and had to admit that even though my stomach now had a pulse it looked good. I would never be able to fight someone off in this. "It's not for him. I kinda like this." My sister grinned triumphantly; one of the few perks of her using me as a dress-up doll.

"You look hot and bull-fucking-shit. Zane never gave you the look you had on your face when you showed up at my house last night and you know it."

I sighed realizing there was absolutely no way to avoid the conversation. Inwardly groaning, I picked up my cell phone, checked the display and dropped it again. "I'm just glad the guy didn't turn out to be some kind of demon, though we still don't know what he is or how he knows about me. And who I fuck is irrelevant."

"Only if you were getting any," Karina snickered. "A good way to find out what he wants is to spend more time with him. Say on Friday night?"

I rolled my eyes. "I need to spend less time with him. We don't know anything about him and I like him too much in dangerous ways. Besides, even if I don't show on Friday I wonder how long it will take him to find me. The man's too persistent to give up that easily."

"Why does that always have to be a bad thing with you? The man's hot! I'd fuck his brains out and consider it worth it if he killed me afterward. Not like you've got Zane waiting for you at home. And may I point out, you started this. He didn't approach you."

"I did not start this mess. You know Zane still hasn't noticed that I'm gone. We sleep in the same bed for cripe's sake. Well, when he sleeps in our condo. I'm asking him today to move to the other bedroom. It's not like we use it for anything and honestly, I'm tired of his snoring. I don't see a reason to delay it any longer."

"I'm telling you that giant diamond was just to keep you quiet." Karina lifted my right hand to emphasize the large emerald cut white diamond resting there and let it drop as she continued hanging discarded clothing. "You and Zane are not in a relationship. The two of you pretend at one. And in the meantime he's banging Miss Sweet Sixteen and you're sneaking off to meet rock stars in weird restaurants in the Valley."

"I think you're over dramatizing the situation. The sixteen year old is a paparazzi rumor, and I met Jared last night, I didn't go there to meet him, there's a difference. And yes, Zane and I are going through a rough patch. All right, another rough patch," I conceded, shrinking in the face of my sister's knowing stare, "but you know how he gets when he's in these creative funks. He always comes out of it and things always go right back to the way they were. The point is that I'm not going to accept it this time as my only option, at least not until it is my only option." I picked at the knots in the leather, trying to choose my words carefully. "Seemingly nice guys like Jared Stateton don't need to get caught up in this mess." I paused, returning momentarily to my examination of my reflection in the dressing room mirror, trying to focus my attention anywhere else for the moment. "I don't think I'm going to get this. I can't get myself in it."

"Did you ever think that maybe you deserve better than Zane and his psychosis?"

"Talk to the Fates. Last time I checked I wasn't given many options other than my imminent demise."

"I will. We will find a loophole, Jane, I promise. In the meantime you're buying this jacket. I'll get you in it. You can think about who you want to get you out of it," Karina teased, forcing me to take one last look at myself in the mirror.

"Fine. But don't go there."

Karina smiled coyly and cocked an eyebrow. "Where would you like for me to go? How about how desperate you were to find out that Jared Stateton's not a demon or a black witch?"

"I was not desperate, I was concerned. I'm still concerned. There's a lot that doesn't make sense. He knows too much and that still creeps me out a little." Pent-up frustration led to me yanking on the leather bindings, untying the tight jacket and reaching for my t-shirt.

"You're sure James didn't know any Statetons? I mean, how else would he know?"

"We came up with nothing, Kari. Nothing. I don't even know how it's possible to come up with nothing with everything that's on the Internet. He's magical but he's not evil. And he's a celebrity. If he'd ever lived near Biloxi it would've been in there somewhere."

"Then how do you explain it?"

"I can't." I couldn't help the mild temper tantrum that followed that statement. I jerked my t-shirt over my head angrily and stomped out of the dressing room carrying the leather jacket. "Do you realize how much that irritates me?"

"Oh, that's pretty hard to miss. I think you kinda like him," Karina grinned as we made our way to the sales counter.

"I think you're full of it." I paid for the jacket that I still wasn't overly sure I wanted but knew I didn't want Kari to bully me into purchasing, and then stepped away from prying ears. "But damn if he's not hot. I shouldn't like him. Why do I like him?"

"The aforementioned "he's hot" and maybe the fact that it's been a long time since you let a real man into your life. He might be good for you in more ways than one," Karina teased, dancing a few steps

60

ahead of me. I wasn't sure if I wanted to laugh, toss the jacket at her, or do both just to mess with her.

"He might be the end of me if I let him get too close. And I mean that literally."

"He doesn't have to get that close for you to play with him, dear. Relax, have some fun. It's doesn't all have to be blood, death, and the four horsemen of the apocalypse. "

I felt my cheeks turn pink and I couldn't help just laughing in the face of the insane situation. "True. And he would be fun. You should see the evil things that flit through his mind."

"Ooh, do tell."

"Why don't you find out for yourself? I don't have to tell you everything."

"Right. Since when?"

I slung my free arm around my twin's shoulder and tried to gently guide her toward the front of the store. "Love you too. We read each other's minds. Look and see what ideas avocado boy came up with. In the meantime, let's go buy you something fun to show your soon-to-be adoring husband."

"You're beating that awfully hard for it to be a prized possession," Tyler noted watching his brother's agitation with his Blackberry. "Writer's block?"

"No, damn Internet's not moving fast enough." Jared checked the Blackberry's screen and popped it against his knee again as if it would make the connection sense his frustration. The one time he really needed the little bit of electronic connections to work and it was failing him miserably. Either that or it was just his patience that wasn't working properly. Jared checked the status bar on the screen and smacked the phone on his leg again. He couldn't believe that he'd allowed her to walk away from him again. She wasn't going to disappear again, not this time.

Tyler sat on the couch beside his brother, ignoring his impatience, and flipped open the screen of the laptop resting not four feet away on the coffee table. Two keystrokes later the Internet was up and waiting. "What are you searching for?"

Jared quickly discarded the Blackberry on the couch beside him and moved up so that he had a better view of the screen. "A fiction writer named Jane Jamison."

"Is this a group project or a personal one?" Tyler asked nonchalantly as he typed.

Jared glared. "I'll let you know in a minute."

"Personal. It's about time. And...here we go." He angled the computer so that Jared could follow as he read aloud. "'Jane Jamison, author, writes horror novels. Born October 26, 1981, has one sister, unknown. Lives in Los Angeles with electronic recording artist Zane Waters.' No picture except the one on the back of the books and...damn is that her?"

Jared leaned closer. The picture wasn't the run of the mill press shot that most authors put on the covers of their books. It was a black and white still of a woman sitting sideways in a wooden chair, her knees tucked under her chin, no clothing covering her trim body except a pair of dark panties and a long curtain of dark hair hiding her face and upper body from the camera's view. She was looking over her right shoulder and the only color in the photo, the only part of the face you could see clearly was her eyes. The irises were a molten ring of three colors, green, gold, and blue, like a glowing artist's pallet of paints that had just begun to melt into each other.

"Shit." Jared leaned closer to stare at the digitized picture, his fingertips idly tracing her outline, pausing over a tiny black tattoo on her shoulder.

Tyler groaned as he caught the look of fascination on his brother's face. He snapped the computer shut and sat back, running his fingers through his short caramel colored hair. "Jer, do not start this shit again. It's not her. It's never her. James is dead. This girl, whoever she is, is not going to help you recover some long lost love from your childhood."

"You haven't met her." His brother stared at him with haunted, unblinking eyes. "I sat across from her at a table all night last night, Ty. It's her. I'm right this time, I know it."

"This is not going to end well. You know that this is not going to end well."

"You know that I have to find out. She's alive, somewhere."

"You know I'm right. You know she's breathing, so why isn't that enough?"

"I don't know! You think if I knew I'd be doing this?"

"You've wasted your whole life trying to find her and you nearly went insane which is very difficult for someone in our family. What happens when you're wrong again? She's with someone else."

"And if I'm right, then he's the bastard who got her killed. Ty, I have to try. If you don't want to be a part of this then you can stay out of it."

"Everything we've ever done has been together. Why the fuck would I abandon you now?" Tyler opened his computer and began typing again.

"What are you doing?"

"Looking for an address and an agenda." He punched something into Jared's abandoned Blackberry and headed for the door, handing him the phone along the way. "Some days it pays to be the assistant to the biggest rock star on the planet." He picked up his keys. "You coming or not?"

"Where are we going?"

"Shopping. Where we're going you can't wear black jeans and eyeliner."

"Since when are you my assistant? I could've sworn you play bass next to me on stage every night."

"Well someone's gotta keep your ass in line. I'll look at hiring someone if it means that much to you." Tyler slammed the door behind them.

"So, do you want to go to this charity gala for me tonight? Zane's not going, as usual, I'm exhausted, and I don't care. You enjoy dressing up more anyway. I just want to hide." I gathered up our purchases, far more than I would have made on my own, and we left the boutique, turning down the street away from the glittering throngs admiring themselves in the late morning sun as they toured Robertson's offering of boutique shops.

"Aren't you supposed to be mistress of ceremonies or something fun like that?"

"Not necessarily. Jane Jamison is mistress of ceremonies. You and I look so much alike no one will know the difference."

"I love how you and Zane were supposed to be twins in this life, you got screwed over, so me, the only child, got you as my twin sister."

"Well, at least you're aware of it. Where is Coffee Bean?"

"Three blocks in the other direction." We turned around and walked back.

"You know we're not all as lucky as you who just woke up one day and said "I think I'll get married" and did a couple of months later. Some of us ended up with a more entertaining fate where we're tied to someone who doesn't know their head from a hole in the ground but we can't leave them because if something happens to said morally unbound idiot, we still die, whether we choose to be with them or not. And since Zane and I are bound at our souls by Fate, I really don't see a good way of getting out of it, do you?" I sighed my frustration as I finished my rant. I tried to keep my annoyance to a minimum as we slipped through the crowds unnoticed.

"My life isn't as pretty as the picture you just painted, but thank you for the vote of confidence. Do you love him?" Karina watched the bland reaction that I couldn't hide to the question carefully.

"Do I love who? Zane? I don't know, I guess a part of me will always love him. We've been together several times now so it's kind of improbable that I wouldn't care about him in some way. I am definitely not in love with him anymore, not that I'm sure it does me a damn bit of good either way. I've been on this earth for nearly a thousand years off and on with nothing to show for it but a broken heart and a ruined will. All these lifetimes of loving him, of fighting, and he still doesn't get it. He'd rather keep me as a safety net for when things go wrong and screw around. At least here there's espresso."

"You really don't love him." Karina said softly, grabbing me by the arm to keep my attention. I love my sister but she was acting like the thought had just occurred to her, like we hadn't already had this conversation. All I could do is shake my head negatively while she watched me sadly from the sidewalk beside me. I had no words left to explain how disaffected I was emotionally by Zane. I didn't bother to hide the way I was feeling from Karina and she didn't bother to try and hide her concern from me.

"Then why are you doing this?"

"Because I've tried everything to unattach myself and I can't. If I could, if I wasn't a threat to him, I would've kissed Jared Stateton last night, demon or not. Maybe more," I felt the intimate thoughts from Jared's head last night creeping into mine and I tried to think of something, anything different, hoping that the man in question wasn't close enough to pick up on them. "As it is, I'm afraid I'll get him killed."

"If he knows who you are maybe he can also protect himself. We're not the only people like us out there you know."

I held the door for Karina as we entered the coffee shop. "So, do you want to be me for a night?"

"What does it entail?"

We took our place in line and I verbally ran down the list of duties for the night in what I thought of as my most charismatic game show host voice. "You're auctioning off L.A.'s most eligible bachelors for charity in my new Dolce gown. Fourteen hot guys, all at your mercy. Anyone you don't like you can sell off to someone truly heinous. You may not use my bank account to buy one, I don't care how cute he is," I warned, my voice returning to its normal sarcastic lilt.

"I'm not that much like you, dear. Besides, I'm married and you're engaged so what would we do with him?" Karina bit her lip, batting her eyelashes coyly, causing me to giggle at the unvoiced thought.

"There are always whips and chains." I rolled my eyes and stepped up to the counter. "What do you want?"

"Don't tease." Karina shook her finger at me laughing while summarily ignoring the girl at the counter. "I'll have a hot chocolate with extra chocolate and no whipped cream."

"Weirdo." I acknowledged the overeager barista. "Can I get a hot chocolate with extra chocolate, no whipped cream, and a very large latte with five shots of espresso?"

"Planning on being awake til next week?" the teenager joked as she entered the order. I hate it when teenagers try to be cute with me. It makes me briefly grateful that I'll never have children so I won't have to worry about charges being filed when I lock them in a closet from the age of thirteen til they're twenty-one.

"I don't sleep, this just assists the process." I inwardly groaned, annoyed with the tiny blonde teenager's perkiness and her criticism of my coffee drink of choice.

"$11.17."

I smiled brightly, flashing enough teeth to frighten a saner person and swiped my debit card through the store's reader before stepping to the side. "Have a good day."

"You too! Pick up's at the end of the bar."

"Is it my imagination or do they get younger and perkier every time we come in here?" I muttered to Karina as we walked to the end of the coffee bar to pick up our waiting drinks. Hey, at least the place was fast.

"Oh, I think she just felt guilty about sleeping with your fiancé. Or am I wrong in believing there's no one in a tri-county radius that he's missed?"

"Why do you think he has to go on tour?"

A loud laugh escaped Karina before she clamped her hand over her mouth to smother her giggling. I couldn't help laughing out loud as we exited the coffee bar. After a certain point you just stop caring if other people look at you like you just escaped the mental ward. Sometimes they should just be happy that you're not obviously armed.

"Are you going to tell me now where I'm going?" Jared fought to stand perfectly still as the tailor measured and pinned his new suit on him.

Tyler stood equally still, his green gaze meeting his brother's blue one in the full length mirrors as another tailor worked just as industriously around him. "I donated us to charity."

Jared fought not to laugh. All these years and his brother could still surprise him. "You did what? We may need a tax write-off but I don't think we're that bad off yet."

"I'm serious."

"I got that. Is there an explanation or do I get to be surprised?"

"Your girl is hosting a charity bachelor auction tonight in Beverly Hills. You wanted in, they needed volunteers. Since I'm once again sacrificing myself for you, you can thank me later."

"Sacrificing yourself? You put us both up for auction!"

"Oh, shove it! You'll get some hot little fuck-me-now socialite and I'll get her mother. It's the way these things always work."

"I'll trade you and you can spend a night getting groped by some ill-mannered horny underage kid who can't pronounce your last name and has no idea that you can string more than two words together in a coherent sentence that doesn't include the words "like" and "Britney", or "Justin" and "hot"."

Tyler burst out laughing and was rewarded with a pin poke from the tailor. "Ow!" He sobered up immediately. "That was mean; you shouldn't make me laugh."

"You shouldn't give us off to charity either like you're selling our dead bodies to science."

"You're getting what you wanted; another shot at Ms. Jamison. And just to reiterate, I still think this is a waste of time. Either way, we do suits really well." Tyler grinned at his reflection.

Jared gave his younger brother a suggestive, thorough once-over before commenting in a mock teenage girl tone, "Yeah, you are so hot! I love the way your blonde hair makes your green eyes sparkle."

"Just what I always wanted to hear, and from my big brother." Tyler attempted in vain to flatten his short hair. "You scare me, you know that?"

Jared shrugged, regarding his own reflection. "Everyone's gotta have a hobby."

"Dad called us today." Tyler stared straight ahead, studying his reflection in the full-length mirrors.

Jared turned abruptly, earning another pin-poke from the tailor and not caring as momentary panic set in at the mention of their family. "What do you mean he "called us"?"

"He called. He used the phone. Some sort of cell phone I would guess. I don't think they have landlines where he lives, you know?"

"What did he want?" he batted the tailor away, distracted by his brother's words. The tailor finally took the hint and pulled his colleague to the side to allow the brothers a moment of perceived privacy.

"To talk to us--mainly to you. He still expects a decision this time." Tyler glanced up and over at Jared.

"Fuck his plan. His plan has gotten us nowhere so far."

"His will kept the woman you love alive for you. And you agreed, not me. You thought he wouldn't cash in on that? He has good reason this time. Just consider it, okay?"

"I'm working on it." He paused. "Consider her or consider what dad wants?"

"Aren't they both the same thing?"

"Not really," Jared grimaced, straightening his already straight shirt cuffs and wishing like hell his brother couldn't read his mind at will.

Tyler tried not to laugh and studiously stayed out of his brother's thoughts. "You want to enlighten me with your age old wisdom, wise man?"

Jared rolled his eyes. "Not really." He hesitated. "She's still engaged, remember?"

Tyler stared straight ahead at his own reflection as the tailor returned to finish his adjustments to the suit. "I didn't forget. I just thought you didn't care." He glanced over at his brother's troubled expression. "Maybe I'm wrong."

Jared caught him watching and straightened abruptly, plastering on his best, charismatic PR smile. "Don't stress yourself. I'm fine. Everything's great. Quit looking so worried."

"I'm not worried. Do I need to be worried?"

"Nope. Everything's fine."

"Great, now I'm worried." Tyler frowned at his brother's fake smile as the tailor finished his work.

Karina fidgeted with the top of the black silk and leather halter dress. "Can you make this a little looser?"

70

"Nope." I pulled the leather laces on the corset stomacher tighter trying vainly to force my sister's ramrod straight body into a slightly curvier figure. I laughed at the irony after this morning's shopping trip. "Breathe shallowly, it'll pass." I pushed the short silk train out of the way with my foot so that I could step closer to tie the laces tighter. "One of the curses of being me. There, you're perfect." I stared at our nearly identical reflections in the full-length mirror. It always caught me off guard how much the right clothes, cosmetics, and a little hair dye could make us look like the same person. It also scared me a little for Karina. I know she likes living vicariously through me sometimes but I don't like to leave her alone when she does even though I appreciate the gesture. Does get me out of being a performing monkey at some of these appearances though. Never have understood why she loves it so much. If you combined us we'd be the perfect woman. "Are you wearing the contacts tonight?"

Karina leaned closer to the mirror to examine her green eyes, glancing back at mine which were in the process of morphing from blue to steel gray. "The one way that no one would ever mistake me for you. Can't you just make yours green for the evening?"

"Doesn't really work that way. Do you know how hard it is to pick eye shadow when your eyes can cover the entire color spectrum in under five minutes? Besides, all the attention will be on you tonight and you don't have this particular problem. It's probably better if we don't match." I put in a pair of the hazel contacts that masked the bright colors of my natural eyes. My long dark hair got unceremoniously yanked up into a twist and I dug around in a drawer for a gold clip while watching my sister study herself in the mirror. I finally found the clip, slid it into my hair, straightened my short black cocktail dress and couldn't help wondering what a certain pseudo-celebrity would think if he saw it. Not good thoughts. "You know what I love? My eyes are almost never brown and I can't count the number of times some idiot's quoted "Brown Eyed Girl" to me. I hate that song."

"Does Zane even know that your eyes change?" Karina fingered the ends of the long dark wig covering her shorter, dyed auburn hair.

"Nah, they're almost always dark gray with anger when he sees them." I slipped on my bright red high-heeled shoes and dropped Karina's wedding rings in her evening bag before stepping up beside my sister. "You may not want to lose this."

"Thanks." Karina took the handbag, laughing at our reflections. "You look just like my assistant."

"Sometimes I think you enjoy this a little too much."

"Your idea."

"I didn't twist your arm."

"It was the dress. I love this dress. And after tonight you can't wear it again for five years til it comes back in style." Karina smoothed the skirt, admiring her reflection. It was well worth the price of the dress to see her that happy. I still wanted to go upstairs and bludgeon Craig with my stilettos. He hadn't spoken to her all day and though she tried to hide it I knew it hurt her, which made me want to hurt him. I settled for keeping her amused and distracted.

"Oh, I'll be safe as long as I wear it far from the shining lights of Hollywood."

"And when do you go there?"

"I go to New York for book releases," I retorted defensively as I grinned.

"Will you ever tell him your real name?"

I steadied my gaze and squared my shoulders as I picked up my handbag. "He'll give me a reason to. Not that it matters. He already knows."

72

"You sound sure about that." Karina's surprise was genuine. "You'll really tell him he's right? You don't know anything about him."

"You were just advocating for him!"

"As a play thing, not as a confidant. There's a giant difference."

I sighed, not knowing how to explain what I felt in my gut was right but hoping that she could read it from my thoughts in a coherent manner. "I know what he's not and that's all right for now."

"Be careful what you wish for."

I pulled my engagement ring off my right hand, barely registering it as I passed it to my sister. "If I got what I wished for the world would be a very different place. Or at least my world would be. I think it would be better but maybe it wouldn't be. I don't know. Maybe you're right and there is a better way out there."

"Maybe you should take your chances and walk away," Karina broached the old argument and I felt her heartache watching the anguish flit across my face.

"Kari, I can't. There are no choices for me. This is what destiny looks like and it sucks. If nothing else Jared Stateton is just a carrot being dangled in my face, tempting me with something that I can't have. As long as I just toy with said carrot and don't bite, Zane and I should be just fine and maybe I can have a little fun in the process."

"Destinies can change. Maybe yours has. My magic can protect you, at least for a little bit. And if it's only for a while, isn't it better to live your life than to be miserable?"

"Sweetheart, we don't know that I can live without Zane. So far he's managed to kill me half a dozen times, most of those without me there."

"For your sake I hope there's a reason to try."

I laughed, thinking of the one thing that would possibly change the course of the conversation. "You sound just like mom."

"Gee, thanks for the horror flashback." She paused. "You wouldn't really trade lives with me."

"No, I wouldn't wish this on you. You're the charmed sister and I'm cursed, at least in love. This time I'm alive, but I'm not free."

"It's never that simple, Jane."

I laughed again and this time it was a harsh, bitter sound. "Sadly it might be the only thing in my life that is simple."

"If you were free though…"

"If I was we wouldn't be having this conversation."

"Fine, be that way. I downloaded some new music to your IPod for our ride to Beverly Hills tonight. Think you might like it. You might be being given an option. And he's hot. Just think about it."

"Bitch."

"Slut."

"Working on it, dear." I stuck my tongue out at her and walked toward the bedroom door. "Come on, Ms. Jamison. You get to be famous tonight."

Karina obediently led the way out to the elevator, past Zane who was still absorbed in his project. "Bye, honey!"

"Bye, J. Have fun tonight. I may not be home when you get here," his voice was distracted and he did not even spare a glance as we passed.

I shot my sister a warning look. Karina winked and completely ignored me. I somehow had the feeling that this was going to come back to bite me in the ass. "Tell your other girlfriend I said hi. Make sure you double wrap." She laughed aloud as I shoved her none too gently out the door.

"Um-hmm," Zane responded. His head jerked up as the door snapped shut. "J! What?"

I really couldn't help the giggle that escaped as the elevator doors shut and we were whisked down to the bottom floor. "You really shouldn't have said that."

"Why not? You would have and for the next six hours I'm you. Besides, he agreed, so what's the problem? Let me tease him, just a little," she held her hands wide apart in demonstration.

"A little bit, huh?" I raised an eyebrow in question. "Think he's figured out what he agreed to yet?" We walked through the lobby to the outer doors and slipped into the backseat of the waiting limousine.

"Well, he's blonde this go-round, so probably not. You know, we really should quick picking on him."

"But why? He makes it so easy!" Karina pouted. "Oh, fine! Since you supposedly are bound to him and everything, I'll behave. Any last minute instructions?"

I stared out the window seeing the silver threads that tied me to Zane rather than the passing concrete scenery. "Yeah. Thanks for giving me the night off."

"You're still going. Why don't you just run off somewhere and relax? I can handle this."

"Maybe I will once things get started."

"Maybe you should buy a bachelor and have some fun for the evening?"

I playfully nudged my sister. "Yeah, I could see that making the front page once he figured out who I am. Besides, none of them are that interesting anyway. A model, an actor, a couple of guys that think they're awesome and aren't..."

"Just pick one that's so hot he can't walk and chew gum at the same time. Guarantee he won't know the difference between us."

I couldn't help laughing at the mental image her comment conjured in my brain. "Oh, that's a dream date. He'll look at himself in a spoon."

"Maybe we should find a certain rock star." Karina passed me the IPod and I groaned when I saw the selected artist, turning off the contraption before its contents could further corrupt my mental processes. I was going to find someone to amuse myself with tonight if it killed me just to rid my brain of the two men who suddenly seemed to occupy my every thought. None of this was productive and I didn't believe for a second that I had time to not be productive in this life. Taking things for granted makes you lazy.

I treated Karina to a wry stare and tossed the tiny music player back at her. "Shut up."

"Make me. You know you want to."

I sighed dramatically, bored of the conversation and annoyed with her persistence. There was nothing I could do about it so I saw no point in continuing to speculate. "This is what I get for admitting that I find someone attractive?"

"Maybe you should just admit that you like him." Karina turned sideways in the seat. "I'll make a deal with you. He shows up at

76

this gig tonight, you give him a shot. He doesn't, I won't bother you about it again."

I thought about it for a moment and did a cursory sweep of Karina's mind before nodding my head in agreement. "Okay, deal."

"Good because I signed him and his brother up as bachelors today and told his assistant that you would be there." Karina smiled like a Cheshire cat.

"You did what? Isn't that somehow cheating?"

Karina shrugged noncommittally. "You agreed to it."

78

5

"You really think this is going to work?" Jared pulled nervously on the sleeves of his new suit jacket, feeling inside for the cufflinks on his shirt that he already knew were there but checking anyway to have something to do with his hands and to make sure that nothing was suddenly disappearing on him. He glanced around them at the rapidly filling hotel ballroom, the evening's eligible bachelors calmly awaiting their turn on the catwalk to be auctioned off and wondered how they could possibly be standing so still. He silently willed one or more of them to move so that he wouldn't appear so nervous.

Tyler discreetly slapped at Jared's hands, earning his brother's undivided attention momentarily. "Yes, this will work. No, this does not validate your reasoning. I still think you're wrong."

"At least you're honest. I appreciate that."

"In the spirit of being honest, I think this is insane. And I thought the music video we shot on the mouth of the active volcano was genius. That being said, I hope this either works or you get this out of your system tonight because it's been great having my brother as himself for the last ten years and if this chick is what makes you all obsessive and crazy, I'll kill her myself. Whether you like it or not." Tyler smiled tightly at his brother's disbelieving face. "I don't care that you fought for her, I don't care that she's only alive because of your magic, will, or whatever. If she tries to hurt my family, I'll fucking kill her."

"Do I want to know who you're talking about or should I pretend that I didn't hear the end of that conversation?" Karina as Jane slid up behind the brothers, her notecards in hand. "You might want to sign in so that I get your information. We begin in a few moments and it would be my great joy to take certain liberties with the introductions." She tried to keep a straight, disinterested look on her face as she silently gave both men a once-over glance, ignoring the tension and surprise that she felt rolling off of Jared. Tyler wordlessly passed her their completed note cards. Karina smiled briefly at him before returning to her cards, taking note of their names and barely containing her amusement that they had both actually shown up. "Good luck, gentlemen. See you on stage." She turned and walked off toward the main ballroom and the waiting crowd of social elite.

Jared watched her walk away, his mouth hanging open in surprise. "What the hell? She didn't even look at me, acknowledge me, nothing." He moved to go after her.

Tyler put a hand on Jared's arm to hold him back. "Let her go." He waited until she was securely in the adjoining ballroom making her opening speech before pulling his brother into the back corner of the room, away from prying ears. "Tell me about this girl again. What exactly can she do?"

"Telepath, generates heat with her hands, I don't know, maybe something else. Probably something else. Why?"

"That's not her. I don't know who you had dinner with, but whoever was sitting across from you at that table is not that Jane Jamison."

His brother stopped fighting him. Bits of his conversation with Jane the night before came rushing back to greet him and the answer was so simple that it caught him off guard that they hadn't thought of it before. Jared heard his name called and walked to the back of the catwalk. "Then she's here and I have to find her. Though it gives me an idea of why the sister's listed as unknown." He stepped out on the stage and smiled as Karina began her introduction. Looking at her now he wanted to chastise himself for having fallen for the act. When you knew what you were looking for they didn't look a damn thing alike.

"Rocker Jared Stateton is pretty easy on the eyes, right ladies?" Polite laughter and clapping greeted him as he strutted down the runway. He made a turn at the end, winking at Karina. If she wanted to play who was he to stop her? "This bad boy enjoys ethnic food, late nights, and intelligent conversation. For anyone who thinks they can handle a couple of hours with this fantastically gorgeous man, we'll start the bidding at five thousand dollars. Eighteen years or older please, unless you've got a legal guardian present. We don't want to get Mr. Stateton into trouble."

"Five thousand!" a blonde girl in the back raised her hand. Jared ignored the woman and scanned the room for the real Jane.

"Do I hear six?"

A redheaded actress smiled coyly and raised her hand. "I'll give you seven."

Jared looked slightly nauseous as he faced Karina and walked back up the runway to the main stage. Karina just smiled and tilted her head to one side, her face a pleasant, perfect blank. Jared mouthed *be nice* before plastering a smile on his face and turning back around to walk down the runway. His stomach rolled at the idea of a stalker being able to purchase him. If she won he and Tyler were going to have a serious discussion about what was a valid seduction technique because this one was failing miserably. He turned again at the end of the runway and nearly groaned aloud at the amused look on the woman's face who was playing stand-in for Jane. She looked like she'd happily feed him to sharks.

"Ten thousand."

Karina shifted her focus from the man onstage who looked like he might vomit at any time to her sister's raised hand in the back of the room. Jane just smiled and shrugged her shoulders, her face turning pink. Karina fought not to laugh. "I have ten. Do I hear eleven?"

"Twelve." The actress smiled. Jared's face took on a greenish hue.

"Thirteen," Jane countered. Jared had turned to watch the bidding war, his eyes lighting up as he recognized Jane, the corners of his mind that usually remained dormant flaring to life and seeking her out.

"Fifteen." The actress began to get angry. Jane reached out mentally and dragged the woman's intentions out of her brain. The woman was mental. The things she was thinking made Jane nauseous.

"Jared, keep walking. Maybe they'll get up to twenty." Karina did laugh and Jared took off his coat to strut down the runway again all the while trying to maintain eye contact with Jane who pointedly refused to look at him. "I have fifteen going once, going twice…"

"Twenty-two." Jane stood and repeated her offer, this time facing the actress's table and feeling like a fool for willingly falling into a trap, though taking some satisfaction in denying her opponent a chance at him. "Twenty-two thousand dollars. Pick your currency." The actress sat down and gestured rudely toward the stage. For some inexplicable reason Jane wanted to knock the woman's veneered teeth in with her fist.

Karina banged her gavel. "Jared Stateton you're sold for twenty-two thousand dollars. Miss, I hope you brought your checkbook."

Jared stepped off stage and tried to not look too eager as he met his purchaser in the back of the room who was giving someone else's name as she signed over the funds. He tried not to appear too curious though he made a mental note of the transaction all the same. "Thank you for saving me from a night of unending torment," he muttered, glancing around to make sure that they were not being overheard.

"That was a very large check, so I'd say you owe me a large thank you." Jane fought to not look up as they stepped away from the crowd. Her suddenly clammy hands gripped her tiny evening clutch tightly. Annoyed she expected that her sudden unease had nothing to do with the astronomical charity donation she had just made. "Besides she looked like a piranha. I couldn't do that to another living thing."

"And here I thought you didn't like me very much or maybe were just planning on avoiding me." Jared shoved his hands into his pockets as they walked more to avoid touching her inadvertently rather than a need to remember what he'd put in there. He felt like bouncing through the ballroom rather than sedately walking, however he highly suspected it might spook his companion if he suddenly burst out into song.

"I outbid her by seven thousand dollars. What on earth would give you that idea? I really think she would have given up at twenty. I could have saved myself two thousand dollars."

"Twenty thousand? I guess that would have made me a real bargain, huh?" Without waiting for her to answer, Jared leaned closer to whisper in her ear. "I was referring to how you ran off last night, Jane. Though this is one helluva way to get a guy's attention. You could've just asked last night or waited until Friday. Of course I couldn't have waited that long."

She did meet his gaze then and smile sweetly. "I'm sorry, but Jane's up there." She pointed to the stage.

"So what's your real name?"

Jane hesitated for a moment, reflecting on her earlier conversation before she chose to answer him. "You're not going to play along at all, are you?" He smiled and shook his head negatively. The boyish grin made her reach out to him and a single erotic thought slipped from his mind to hers almost causing her knees to buckle and leaving her more breathless than her own wanton fantasies. Ignoring the impulse to touch him, she opted for the less frustrating route of playing his game of twenty questions in lieu of a conversation. "Jane Jamison is my name. Though I suspect that you already know the one you're looking for, which I plan to question, by the way. That's my sister, Karina. But let's keep that between you and me. I like having the night off every once in a while."

"You chose to spend your night off at the event you were going to anyway. Isn't that a bit sadistic or is it more of a narcissistic thing to actually see yourself in two places at once?"

"I'm sorry; I could have sworn you just insulted me." Jane picked up her pace, annoyed with herself and with his presumptions, one of which she knew was far too close to correct for her comfort level. For someone who didn't know her he was learning what buttons to push in record time. She did take some satisfaction in forcing him to hurry to keep up with her. Cocky bastard.

"Okay, so what do fallen angels do on a normal night off?"

"Apparently they purchase evenings with the slightly psychotic rock stars they picked up in random sushi bars the night before." She took a deep breath and tried to ignore that her pulse had assumed a rapid staccato beat in his presence. "Don't you want to see how much your brother goes for? He's up next."

"Oh, I have a feeling that a certain redheaded actress will make sure he's well taken care of." Jared moved closer to her, his voice dropping to a deeper, more intimate tone.

"In that case maybe I should stick around." Jane tried to move away but found herself unable to unobtrusively extract herself from the exchange. Though they'd moved to the far back corner of the room more than one auction patron was staring curiously in their direction.

"You can't have us both," Jared joked.

"Just ruin my fantasy." She pretended to pout, keeping her tone intentionally light and conversational to deter him. "Actually one of you is probably more than I can handle."

Jared backed her into the wall behind a potted plant, one hand braced on the wall at her head, the other sliding behind her to touch the tiny black tattoo that he had caught a glimpse of peeking out from under one of the straps of holding her dress in place on her shoulder. He leaned closer and closed his eyes briefly, breathing in her perfume. "You didn't seem to have a problem yesterday."

She pushed him back with a dark warning look, fighting the slightly insane, unwelcome urge to see where he was headed with his comments. "Don't make me hand you over to the redhead." Jane pulled her mental blocks in tightly to shut out the intimate thoughts coming from his mind.

Jared stepped back, immediately dropping the flirtation. He grinned and held out his hand to her. "I'd be honored if you'd spend your night off with me, let me show you my gratitude."

"You know, I think it would sadden me to understand your reasoning patterns." She took his hand hesitantly, remembering the promise that she had made to her sister, the part of her that was curious about the man in front of her overriding the more logical side that was in a full blown panic attack. Jane concentrated on breathing in and out of her nose as she put one foot in front of the other, propelling herself forward and back to the safety of the auction.

"Why is that?" He began to quietly, insistently pull her toward the door.

"You might quit surprising me." Her steps hesitated as she considered the proposition he possibly presented.

"And yet you've only known me for twenty-four hours. I'll try to constantly evolve if you try to do me a favor. Don't ask so many questions. Patience and faith cost you nothing."

"You're sure about that."

"Question or statement?"

"Statement."

"In either case, yes, I'm sure. Now can we go while you still have an alibi?"

"It frightens me that you think I'll need one." Jane gave in and followed him out the back door as Tyler and Karina watched warily from the stage.

"I promise to try to not bite unless I ask permission first."

"Jared, you take me to the most interesting places," I commented as I picked my way carefully down the immense stone staircase to the abandoned beach where Jared waited, laughing. The bastard was laughing at me! Sadly it fueled my sense of adventure and my competitive streak making me want to run down the staircase just to say I did it. My five-inch heels really weren't made for that though. Actually they weren't really made for walking so scaling a cliff was proving to be a slow moving process.

"Chicken shit! Get your ass down here before we miss the sunset!" He laughed, watching me like a hawk circling prey. I really started wishing that not only had I left the shoes in the car but that I'd never gotten out of it in the first place. For a guy that I didn't know I seemed fairly determined to throw myself in his path. Maybe Zane's self-destructive tendencies were bleeding over onto me. I felt my foot slip on the rock and caught myself before the heel broke and I did a face plant down the rest of the stairs. Risking a quick glance down I silently mourned the passing of my shoes. Karina would insist on another shopping trip to replace them.

"I'd prefer to not break my ass, if you don't mind." I finally, gratefully reached the sand and walked over to where he was waiting for me, hand outstretched. Don't get me wrong, I wasn't pissed at him for bringing me to the very romantic, very private beach. I was mad at myself for knowingly falling into this trap. And I wanted to. I wanted to take his hand and follow him anywhere that didn't have the stress and insanity of my life. Honestly, I just wanted to be with him. The short amount of time I'd spent with him had been so nice, so easy. It made wonder what if the rest of it could be that simple. I stared at his hand and I suddenly couldn't see anything else. It was like the world muted around me, shrinking to this one act. What made me hesitate was that I wasn't completely sure if my reaction would be done out of choice or desperation. I took his hand and allowed him to pull me toward the breaking waves, laughing as we tripped across the sand.

"Do you value those shoes?" He kicked his own off, shrugged out of his jacket, and began unfastening his shirt cuffs. I couldn't help it; I wanted to see what was under the shirt. Yeah, this wasn't a slippery slope to go down at all. I was on the express bus straight to Hell.

"I used to. This might be completely worth their demise." I glanced around us at the bright orange glow reflecting off the water and warming the sand. "You are insane, just for the record." I stepped out of the now destroyed dress shoes, not caring about the new scratches adorning the leather and focusing on the much more enticing view presenting itself in front of me.

"Yeah, you're not the first person to tell me that. I won't take it personally. And this gives me the perfect opportunity to get you out of your clothes without you pretending to find it insulting." He stripped down to his boxers and stood waiting for me with his toes in the water. "Take too much more time deciding and we'll miss the sunset. And there'll be pictures."

I unzipped my dress and fought the shiver where the cool evening air met my bare skin. Black lace lingerie is sexy, chill bumps are not. And I wanted to make damn sure that his full attention was on me as I slid my cocktail dress off my shoulders to the sand and stepped out of it. I didn't want to know how much I enjoyed watching the reaction in his eyes. I felt it anyway and pushed it way back behind the purely physical reaction I was having to him. There would be time for me to romanticize the memory later without ruining the present with rose-colored glasses. "There'll be pictures anyway." I couldn't help myself, I lingered just a moment longer than was necessary, just to tempt him, to see if he'd make a move. When he said nothing, just stared, I sauntered into the cold foam and dove into the water, swimming out until my feet could barely touch the sandy bottom and I was numb enough that I could face him smiling rather than shivering. "Now who's waiting?"

Jared waited a moment before he swam out to meet me and I could have sworn I saw his eyes blinking rapidly like he was trying to clear his vision. I took it as a positive sign. "You have to admit, the view is exceptional." He glanced at me and then turned to face the drowning sunlight. He was trying to distract himself. I grinned as I watched him literally will his pulse down to a steadier rate though I found myself slightly disappointed that he could do it with me standing so close.

I slid through the water, stepping between him and the fading sunlight though I didn't face him. "Yes, it is, albeit a bit colder than I imagined." That time I couldn't help shivering, the freezing water feeling like needles against my skin. I wrapped my arms around myself to ward off the chill and ignored the impulse to dive into his mind to see what he was thinking.

"I can fix that." He touched my shoulder with one hand, the other extended in the water between us, his eyes drifted closed and I felt a subtle tug as he channeled my energy through himself and into the ocean. I felt the water warm almost immediately and the panic rise just as fast as I jerked away from him. I hadn't even touched him and it was already coming back to bite me in the ass. His eyes opened and I knew he was watching me, trying to gauge my response. Unfortunately for him the panicked side of my brain was in the midst of staging a coup over the rational area.

"How did you…?"

"I borrowed it from you."

"Is it permanent?"

He shook his head and I felt my breath rush out in relief. I couldn't help a quick survey of my mental faculties just to make sure. "Only works while we're physically touching."

Slightly calmer I reached up, covering the hand that had resumed touching my shoulder with my own and tried very hard to not give in to the impulse to study him for some traces of bionic material that would allow him to use himself as a conduit for energy that shouldn't be transferred. "You're a little freaky, you know that? Wanna teach me how that works?"

He actually looked surprised. "I didn't know it was teachable."

I couldn't help but laugh. I did feel kind of bad that I giggled in his face but not bad enough that I stopped laughing. "You really don't meet other people like you, do you? The trick to teaching someone something simple like that is to make sure that you don't leave a part of you behind when you're done. If the person doesn't already have the latent ability then it takes a connection with that person to give them the ability. You have to build the connection and then share your talents with them for it to work which is why I'm just a little concerned that you managed this without my consent. Some people you may not want carrying around a piece of you forever, you know?" I knew my eyes changed color even though I couldn't see or feel it and I was glad for the plastic lenses that hid the colors from Jared's view. A part of me wanted him to see but a larger part didn't want to play the part of a dead girl for him. And that part allowed me to meet his eyes and keep my distance. Even I know I'm worth more than a forty-year-old faded memory.

I watched him while he stared at me for a long time. I wondered what he saw when he looked at me and then later, why I cared. Jared took a breath, and I imagined the wheels turning in his head, contemplating all possible meanings of his words before he spoke. "What if you wanted to carry someone with you?"

I sighed and opted for the cold comfort of the water rather than the current topic of conversation. Him looking at me like that, like I was still her was turning me off faster than he had managed to turn me on. It was more than a little frustrating to realize that I was never going to be able to outrun my soul's past, even with a complete stranger. So much for nice and simple. I'd had enough of these talks with Zane, with my sister; I didn't need it from Jared too, not when I was trying so desperately to live in the moment, to just forget about it for a minute. "There are ways to do that too, unfortunately, and none that I've found to unbind you once it's done."

"But you know how?"

"How it was done originally, no. That it is done and is therefore possible, yes."

"I have to ask. If you had the opportunity to free yourself, would you take it?"

"Have you been talking to my sister?" I met his searching blue gaze and I felt the defiance radiating off of me. I didn't care if it made him take a step back; I was tired of being expected to be something I wasn't anymore. I did do him the courtesy of tilting my head to one side and thinking for a full minute before answering. I heard my voice coming out angrier than I intended but I didn't stop it. "I don't know if I would break it or not. Sometimes it's a nice fantasy but I know that's all it is, all it can be." I stepped closer to him and I couldn't resist touching the side of his face. "I know what you're searching for but I don't know what you hope to find. I'm not her, Jared. James died. I may have what's left but I'm still my own person despite my connection to Zane. I really like what I know of you but I don't want to be the corpse from your memory and I desperately want to be more than some guy's doormat. And I'm sure as hell not going to be the consolation prize because you can't have the earlier version of me." I slid further away from him in the rapidly cooling water, moving closer to shore in the vain hope that he would take my answer at face value and drop it. The sudden fascination with the proprietary aspects of my soul was beginning to rub my nerves raw. "So what exactly is it that you want, Jared?"

"I want to know you. Trust me, I know better than anyone that you're your own person. But part of that person is James and we both know that I obviously can't ignore that. What good is it doing you to bury it?" He reached for me but left his hand floating on the water between us. I wasn't going to make a move to encourage him. If we were going to play this game I wasn't going to do it while he was pretending I was someone else.

"I'm alive. Yes, it's weird that Zane and I are a little earlier than our normal schedule but right now is all I care about. For this moment I don't want to worry, I don't want to over think things, and I don't want to pretend to be someone else. I have the opportunity to enjoy this sunset right now. Living in the past just ensures that I won't get this opportunity again. I'm not ready to give that up for something I can't change. If there's any of this that you don't agree with, if you brought me out here to play a fantasy role for you then it's best we end this now because I'm trying really hard to be more than a ghost in someone's memory." I used the waves to float a bit further away, silently willing him to shut up and just be the random attractive guy I'd met in the sushi bar for five minutes.

"You're not a ghost." Jared swam toward me, facing away from what was turning out to be a spectacular sunset. "I know that you're different now but the fact is that you've been alive and in my head almost my entire life and I don't know why. I've wanted to know you for so long that yes, it is going to take me a moment to separate out what's real and what is my expectation of you. This may be nothing, what I feel when I look at you might be an old reflex action and I may be completely wrong. But I want the chance to find out. And I want to know that you're happy. That's all I've ever wanted. Just let down the walls a little bit. What's the worst that happens, we waste a few days of each other's time? We're the closest a human can get to immortal and we know it. We've got nothing but time."

He took a step closer to me and I wasn't sure if I wanted to punch him or kiss him. That speech bordered on both the nicest and worst things anyone had ever said to me. I gritted my teeth, clenched my fists, and tried to look at something other than his mouth before I responded. "The worst that happens is that you try to kill me and I end up killing you."

Jared actually smiled and took another step closer. "You think in that fight you would win?"

"I don't go down very often without a fight." All of the tension that had fled that afternoon came rushing back to me. I stalked angrily toward the shore. This is what I get for letting my guard down.

What a perfect way to ruin an otherwise lovely evening. "Unless you intend on starting that fight now I suggest you take me home. Or I'll do it myself."

I knew Jared was frustrated. I could hear him moving through the water trying to keep up. There just wasn't enough fight left in me to argue with him right now. After fighting everyone else in my life, total strangers got the short end of the stick. "How do you plan on getting there alone? There are no cabs out here and you don't have the keys."

I stepped out of the water ahead of him and picked up my clothes. "I'll take your pants." I swiped the dress pants off of the sand and tossed them over my wet shoulder, the keys jangling against my skin. Without looking back I started up the steep staircase hoping that the climb would burn off some of my excess annoyance. Apparently I wasn't entitled to a real night off. Not surprisingly I reached the truck first, tossed our things inside, and was waiting for him, leaning against the driver's side with the keys dangling from my extended index finger when Jared finally topped the cliff.

"I was wondering if you would still be here." He took the keys from me and I stood aside so that he could open the door to put in the rest of his clothing. While I was waiting I took up residence on the fender. I hoped the relaxed poser would help me to not look quite so hostile. I was really trying here and he wasn't making it that easy on me with talk of the generally questionable state of my soul.

"I shouldn't have threatened to leave you here. You didn't deserve that."

He shut the door and turned to face me, shoulder against the window, arms crossed over his chest. I didn't exactly blame him for taking a defensive stance. "You don't apologize much, do you?"

"I'm not apologizing now."

Jared laughed and his stance relaxed. "Go ahead. You've been dying to all afternoon. Look in my head and see what you find. It won't be soul snatchers and axe murderers."

"You don't get a free pass into my brain." I warned him because I wanted him to understand that this would not be a give and take situation. But damn it if he wasn't right. I did want to know what was in his head. He made me nervous enough that I didn't want to lose focus for a moment around him. At least with free reign to see what was really in there I could either stop concerning myself with it or use a rock to bash his skull in before he pushed me off a ledge. I kind of wanted him to turn out to be a threat just so I could be done with it rather than having another person to deal with. Jared nodded his consent and I held his gaze as I took him up on his offer. Just adding another to the tally of points already in his favor, he wasn't trying to kill me but what he proposed just might end that way.

Stepping into his head I felt the cold water close in around me once more and I saw us still standing so close that we were just short of touching in the ocean. He wanted to play a game. His mind was quite adept at recreating me down to my trepidation as I reached for him. He wanted to see if I could touch him without it turning into more. At least in the fantasy he was spinning I failed miserably. When he kissed me the world fell out from under my feet and I fell against the truck, the sun-warmed metal biting into the skin of my back, as a moan that I wasn't sure was real or fabricated tumbled from my lips. In that moment I had never wanted anything as badly as I wanted him inside of me in every possible configuration I could think of even though I knew it was nothing but a daydream that I was experiencing. I didn't realize how strong my actual physical reaction had been until I reluctantly pulled myself out of his fantasy and back into the real world to find him standing directly in front of me, his eyes burning holes into mine and the heat from his body pulling at me like a magnet. Oh, this was not good. And I had played right into it. Damn it. Right now I wasn't even doing a good job of fooling myself. Now the bastard knew it.

"I dare you." He leaned into me, bracing his hands on the car on either side of my waist, close enough that my skin tingled with wont to touch him, far enough away that a deep breath wouldn't end the ache.

It was taking deeper breaths than I was accustomed to without running a marathon to keep my pulse rate down and I couldn't take my eyes off of his mouth. I wanted to taste him just to see if it was as good as the fantasy he'd shown me. This was reality though and he couldn't compel me to give in first. So I decided to do the next best thing. I pushed off of his truck, moving every inch of my lingerie-clad body as close to him as I could without touching him and smiled into his pretty blue eyes. "Is that all you've got? I could do better than that in my sleep."

"You don't sleep." Now I wasn't the only one staring at the other person's mouth.

"Then I guess you'll just have to live with your version." I dropped back against the truck and smiled like a Cheshire cat. Yeah, I called your bluff, motherfucker. Being attractive does not mean that I'm going to fall to my knees for you. He could fall on his knees for me though. I wouldn't mind a little begging for once.

He reached out and just barely brushed his hand against the lace of my bra. My expression didn't change but I knew my brain was screaming for him to do more. "Why don't we just drop the pretense?"

Even my eyes managed to not lose their defiant glare though my body temperature flared higher causing my skin to ache for his, the power of it nearly overwhelming my currently reigning logical thought processes. I sincerely hoped that he couldn't sense the battle for my self-control that I was suddenly very afraid of losing. "I have no idea what you're talking about. Must be rather one-sided." Thank God and Goddess that my voice came out of my mouth more confident than it was resonating in my mind.

"You think so?" Jared closed the distance between us with me trapped between him and the truck. I could feel my heart pounding in my ears and I didn't want to take a breath because if I did there wouldn't be a place below our necks where we weren't touching. His skin made mine feel like heated Jell-O and I wanted to mold myself against him just for the hell of it. Oxygen deprivation did not help my mental capacity and I had to eventually breathe in order to keep from suffocating. It was worse than drowning. All I could smell was his skin and he smelled like spiced chocolate. If I could have formed a coherent thought it probably would have been a prayer to save the soul everyone was so worried about from my sin.

"I will not touch you." Special emphasis was put on the "not" in that sentence. I wasn't sure if it was more for me or for him. I don't think either of us was paying much attention to my protests, hollow as they were.

"I didn't say you had to." His hands and his lips whispered across my skin, close enough for me to feel the air they displaced but not close enough to touch.

I closed my eyes and swallowed past the knot in my throat. "Stop."

I felt his mouth against my ear before I heard his voice and it was all I could do to not turn my head toward him and give in. "Are you sure that's what you want?"

I maintained enough presence of mind to place one hand on his chest and push him away while I slowly opened my eyes. "Yes." There, that came out with a little more confidence.

"All right." His arms dropped to his sides and he stepped back. "Hop in. I'll take you wherever you want to go."

I escaped to the other side of the truck, my face flaming red in the cool night air. I took a moment to jerk my dress back on then groaned when I realized I couldn't zip it all the way up by myself. Sliding back into my irreparably damaged shoes I walked around the front of the truck holding the sides of my dress together in the back to keep it from slipping down my shoulders again. "Will you…help me?" I had to force the words out through clenched teeth.

"Sure, turn around." Jared motioned with his fingers and I turned, releasing the dress and lifting my wet hair out of his way. I couldn't resist a small shiver as his fingertips slid across my bare shoulders and down my spine. "I love this tattoo." His breath blew warm across the spot and a little gasp slid from between my lips. My teeth clamped down on my tongue to keep me from turning and pinning him against his trunk with my tongue down his throat. The snap of my zipper brought me back to reality. "All done." Jared took two steps back with a smug smile on his face. "Ready to go?"

My teeth slowly released my tongue and I nodded, not yet trusting my mouth to say what my mind was telling it to. It took me until I had stepped around to the passenger side of the truck to realize that I hadn't bothered to keep my thoughts to myself. Chances were that Jared had seen or heard everything that had just run through my mind. Go figure that would be what he got out of me. Choosing to ignore it I stepped up into the passenger seat and closed the door with a sharp snap. "Take me back to the hotel."

"I think the auction's probably over by now." Jared climbed into the driver's seat and shut the door, starting up the engine without looking at me.

"The only other option is to my house and I'm not sure that I want you to know where I live." The seatbelt locked into place and I sat waiting as he pulled out of the parking spot and drove down the Pacific Coast Highway.

"What if I take you somewhere else? I could go for some food."

"We're covered in salt water. What do you have in mind?"

He did look at me then and his gaze was purely animalistic. It made my breath catch in my throat and things below my waist liquefy. "Oh, I know somewhere we can go where we're perfectly dressed."

My cell phone vibrated against my thigh, still secure in my evening bag and I nearly sighed aloud with relief. I didn't care who was calling. If it was a telemarketer I might still kiss them in thanks. Retrieving the phone I saw that not only was it Karina calling but that she had called several times in the last few hours. I didn't realize we had been gone that long. "What's up?"

"Are you okay? Am I interrupting? Please tell me you had sex with that man."

"Shut up! I can only answer one question at a time. I'm fine. We're headed back into town. Is everything all right?"

"Everything's fine. Are you all right?"

"We'll talk about it later." I risked a glance in Jared's direction and I saw his face harden with the mask he seemed to wear any time he wasn't directly in my presence. "I'll be back later." I slid the phone closed and turned in the seat to face my companion for the evening. "So you never did tell me, what were you thinking for dinner?"

"Do you want me to take you back to Beverly Hills?" His voice was quiet with trepidation.

"Have you got another date that I don't know about? I'll be happy to reschedule if you need to." I crossed my legs and draped my arm across the back of the seat, amused at the turn of conversation. In the short amount of time I'd spent with Jared he did nothing but exude self-confidence. It was interesting to see that he was the one a bit unsettled, at least visibly. I kept adjusting my position to keep my idle hands to myself.

"So that wasn't a Hail Mary call?"

"A what?"

"You know, you have a friend call with a fake emergency so that you have an excuse for running out on me." Despite his best efforts he did crack a smile, which he tried to cover with his hand.

"No, it was my sister wondering if I'd dragged you into a seedy hotel room for sex." I opted for the truth in lieu of a lie. No point in making something up when the truth was already enough to shock him. "So, food? Still interested?"

"With you, always. Though I want you to promise to do something for me first. I want you to make a list of everything you have ever wanted to do. An honest list, not some bullshit one. And we'll start working on it." Jared divided his focus between glancing over at me and watching the dark road as he drove.

I couldn't help but laugh. "Why? What's in it for you?"

"I want to know you as you. And you clearly need to get out more." He flashed that adorable little boy grin and it was a good thing that I was sitting down. My knees so did not need to betray me right now.

It was an interesting offer, definitely worth contemplation. "When?"

"On our date. You paid enough for it, might as well make it something you won't forget." His eyes betrayed his thoughts and turned the innocent expression positively sinful. Even the devil wears a mask.

"How many items can I put on the list?" I stared stubbornly past his head at the dark evening sky doing my best to ignore both direct contact with his face and the hot, tight feeling I was getting from staring at him until I got my hormones back under control. I did wonder if he would really follow through with this list idea. People in our positions generally had little use for a bucket list seeing as every time we kicked the bucket we just came right back like a bad penny you can't get rid of.

"However many it takes. I'll keep taking you out until we finish it. You can be my self-sacrificing mission for the year." He shrugged noncommittally. Yeah, I believed that if I told him "no" he'd leave like it wasn't a big deal. I had a fleeting thought maybe that I ought to tell him that coffee and a walk through the canyons would work just fine if he wanted to get to know me. It really didn't have to be this complicated to hang out or even date me. I have enough complicated. Then I decided I'd rather see where he was going with this. "I'll use the receipts for a tax write-off or something. Just so you don't feel obligated to think it's a real date." I laughed more at the idea of how hard he was trying to prove his sincerity rather than the intended joke. It wouldn't have surprised me if he knew it.

I thought earnestly for a moment about his proposition. Was there really something that I wanted to do but hadn't done? "I don't think it'll be that long of a list. Other than potentially living longer I can't think of much that I haven't done that I really cared about doing. Got any suggestions?"

"I could think of a few," he murmured, reaching out to tuck a wayward lock of hair behind my ear. When I saw what he was doing I shifted out of his reach. He compensated by making the motion with his hand like he was moving it and the lock moved to the desired spot as if of its own volition.

A heavy sigh slid past my lips. "Don't give up easily do you? Why are you doing this?" My hand unwittingly brushed across the hair that he had moved and I grimaced at the unconscious gesture. "Do you play knight in shining armor for every girl you come across in sushi bars?"

"No, just the intriguing ones who steal my tea." Jared grinned and turned off the PCH to drive through Malibu Canyon. I combed my fingers through my hair and turned up the warm air coming from the vents to dry it.

"When are you going to tell me where we're going?"

"Are you going to make my list?"

"I'll make your list."

"I want it by tomorrow."

"I do have other things to do than amuse you, you know."

He shook his head, his eyes glued to the winding road in front of us. "You don't get a day off yet. Agree to give it to me by tomorrow or I'll drive you in circles all night."

"What happens when we run out of gas?"

"Then you're just stuck with me, in this truck all alone wherever we end up until morning. And it's only eight o'clock. Sunrise isn't for ten more hours. Think of the things we could do in ten hours." To further emphasize his point he turned off the main road and wound up a deserted road higher into the mountains.

"Fine, I'll give you the list." I used the heat from my hands to finish drying my hair and my clothes before turning the heater in the truck down. "So where are we going?" I flipped the visor down to quickly check that all traces of my earlier make-up were gone and that I didn't look like someone who'd just gone for an unexpected swim in the Pacific. The fact that I was about to show up at whatever restaurant with Jared Stateton would send a few tongues wagging. If it looked like we'd been doing precisely what my sister thought we were doing then it would make the papers. I didn't like undue publicity, particularly when it would be right next to a headline featuring my dimwitted fiancé and his latest conquest.

Jared looked over at me, saw what I was doing and stopped the truck in the middle of the desolate road, throwing it into park so that he could turn in his seat and openly stare. "You don't need to worry about that. You're gorgeous."

"I appreciate the compliment but if we're going to be seen in public, yes, I do." I hastily reapplied my lip-gloss and closed the visor mirror. "What's wrong?"

"Nothing, you just don't need to worry about what anyone thinks and I believe you spend far too much time doing just that. I wasn't complimenting you just for your benefit."

"Maybe if you told me where we're going I wouldn't worry about it so much."

"I'm taking you somewhere that I don't take a lot of people. It's very private; no one will bother you. Just trust me for a moment, will you?"

The earnestness in his voice caused me to stop and consider my words carefully before I spoke again. I could see inside his mind and there was nothing in there to alarm me, not even the sexual fantasies that he'd plied me with earlier. "I can't stop being paranoid. I usually have good reason."

"Do you tonight? Do I scare you?" The question was honest and he didn't even attempt to solicit a non-verbal response.

"No, you intrigue me. And that scares me."

"Do you think I would hurt you?"

"Not intentionally. But I think this going much further might lead in that direction."

"How much further do you think this is going to go?" He leaned closer to me across the seat.

"It can't go anywhere. Ever." My voice trembled. I licked my suddenly dry lips and felt my blood pressure spike.

"You know you can touch me. I won't bite." If he moved any closer he'd tumble across the gearshift and I wouldn't exactly be disappointed to have his body on my side of the SUV.

"How disappointing. I do bite. Hard." The lights from the dashboard illuminated just the side of his face and I could almost swear I saw a pained expression as he tried to hold himself back.

"I'll try to not enjoy it too much." His voice was so close I could nearly feel it like a caress on my skin. I didn't remember moving but I was suddenly sitting much closer to the center console than I remembered. "Forget about everything else. What do you want to do right now?"

I don't know what was wrong with me that I had developed this obsession with his mouth. All I could do was fixate on it. I'm not even sure I heard all of the words he spoke and my mind went blank rendering my lip reading skills useless. "I want to know what you taste like."

"I'm not stopping you." His hand was on my bare thigh, his fingertips sliding underneath the hem of my skirt. The part of me that hadn't had sex in a year wanted his hand to be about eight inches higher. I vaguely wondered where the little voice in my head that had been so determined I wouldn't break first had gone.

I should have stopped myself. Without losing his gaze I blinked out my contacts, tossing them out the window into the cold night air. Though I knew I'd only scratched the surface of his attachment to James I needed to see him without any filters right now. Whatever happened I wanted to know that it was real. I pulled my upper body over the center console, using it to hold my body weight as I leaned in to whisper, "You have one time, one place, and you can only use your tongue. Where is it?"

Jared turned his face in to nuzzle my neck and we both sighed at the slight contact. It was more torture than touching. I wanted his mouth on mine, on my skin, and for the moment I didn't care that this was probably the stupidest thing I would do in this lifetime. I wanted to tempt him, touch him, and I wanted to know what it felt like to be truly desired. "If I get to pick a spot then you have to as well."

"So who goes first?" I slid my mouth against the hollow in his throat, just above his collarbone, and breathed deeply. I desperately needed to know if he tasted just as intoxicating as he smelled. "I already picked my spot." I didn't wait for his permission. My tongue licked a path up his neck, ending just behind his ear. I felt him shudder, his breath coming on the heels of a tiny moan and he tilted his head to the side to grant me greater access. One hand left the console to turn his head to the side as my lips took turns alternately sucking and kissing their way back down. I felt him move against me and his muscles tighten as he fought to do nothing more. As I moved I caught a quick glimpse of one white knuckled hand gripping the steering wheel. When I reached the soft spot between his neck and his collarbone again I sucked his flesh into my mouth and bit down hard. I let down the mental wall I had erected between us just a bit so that he could see how I saw him from my perspective. I felt his bright eyes open wide and unseeing, a strangled cry barely escaping his throat as he tried to pull me closer in the tight confines of the car. The sexually charged emotions coming off of both of us nearly made me forget everything else. I dove into his mind wanting to see what it was like for the empath in him and the thoughts that greeted me were enough to make me want to damn the consequences including incarceration for public indecency and straddle him in the car. Common sense took over before I could pull him into the backseat of the SUV like a hormonal teenager and I kissed the spot on his neck gently, grazing it with the tip of my tongue as I sat back. I couldn't resist the urge to touch my still tingling lips as I licked the traces of him off, watching him watch me. The look on his face was almost predatory in the dim light and the thrill of being the prey he sought sunk low in my already overheated body. "Your turn."

"I can't reach what I want from here." His eyes bore holes into me, refusing to blink away even for a second. For a split second I thought he was going to lunge across the remaining space between us and kiss me. A long moment passed before I realized that he was struggling to maintain his control, his rapid breathing slowing to a lower rate. His hands slowly unwound from their clenched perches and he turned in his seat to face forward, the intense look still in his eyes. "I'm saving mine for later." His riveted gaze finally turned from mine to the black unlit road and he put the truck in gear. It was quiet between us for a moment as he turned the car to drive back down the mountain and I straightened in my seat, attempting to mask my anger and embarrassment by fiddling with the previously unused seatbelt. "Please don't take this the wrong way but I don't think dinner's a good idea tonight. I'm not completely certain that I can behave like the gentleman you deserve."

"I didn't ask you to." I retreated further into myself where I knew he couldn't fish around in my mind and tried to not look as uncomfortable as I now felt. Why did I get myself into this?

"I didn't say it was because I didn't want to." Jared finally turned and glanced at me, the smoldering look still in his eyes. "Sure you don't want me to know where you live?"

A harsh laugh escaped my throat and I deliberately stared out the window, watching the steam rise from where my hand touched the cool glass. "That really wouldn't be a good idea."

"Where can I take you?"

This was growing more uncomfortable by the minute. I pulled out my phone and text messaged Karina. She responded in under a minute, which let me know that she really was concerned about my well-being. "Where exactly are we?"

"On Mulholland, roughly in the Palisades on the coast side, north of Van Nuys on the Valley side. If you'll give me a general idea of where to go I can at least drive toward a town."

Great. Karina was in another fight with Craig and I was pettily worried about the guy I was just all over finding out where I live. Screw it; this night was turning out to be half amazing and half disaster anyway. "Just drive back to Malibu. I live on the beach."

"I get an address?" He laughed in surprise. "I'm speechless. I feel honored."

"You should. You may need it later anyway." I tried to shrug noncommittally and ended up laughing in earnest halfway through the gesture.

One relatively short car ride later he was turning into the short drive in front of my complex. "So this is you?"

"This is me. One of them anyway." I smiled and slid out of the truck. "Oh, while I was waiting for you to climb the stairs at the beach I took the liberty of programming my number into your phone. Just to make sure you don't have an excuse for losing it." I shut the door and managed to walk somewhat confidently around the truck to the footpath to the door. Then I heard a car door slam behind me.

"Jane!" I turned and saw Jared leaning against the driver's side of his truck. When he didn't move I shook my head and listened to my heels click sharply on the pavement as I walked back.

"Can I help you?"

"Yes." He grabbed my wrists and turned, pinning me against the car, a hand on either side of my head to keep me from turning away. His mouth collided with mine and I groaned, pulling him tighter against me as his tongue slid into my mouth. His kiss grew more insistent as I welcomed him deeper, his hands moving up my arms to pull me closer, one reaching behind me to massage the area where the tattoo was. After several long moments he pulled back, his blue eyes cloudy with some unnamed emotion as he turned and released me. "Like I said, not because I don't want to." I smiled but didn't say another word as I walked inside. I didn't dare to even look over my shoulder until I was safely ensconced in my third floor condo.

I shut the door and leaned against it for a long moment with my eyes closed before dropping my handbag on the library table in the entrance hall and continuing into the living room where Karina waited impatiently for me. "What happened with you and Craig?"

"He told me to consider a separation." She stood and walked into the kitchen where she'd put hot water on to boil for tea.

"Oh God, Karina…"

"I don't want to talk about it." The words were sharp enough that I let the topic drop.

"Is there anything that I can do?"

"Reprogram my husband's brain?"

"I'm willing to give it a shot."

"I'd rather hear about your evening. What the hell happened to you? Where did you go?" She surveyed the disaster that used to be my outfit critically. "I'm guessing he didn't just take you upstairs in the hotel for a quickie?"

"No, he didn't and I am a moron." I kicked off the ruined shoes and walked back to my bedroom. "Is Zane here?"

"No and if the gaggle of girls he departed with is any clue he won't be back for several hours or possibly several days." Karina followed me, mournfully examining the shoes and tossing them into the trash. "Those were two thousand dollar shoes, just so you know."

That stopped me. "Excuse me? I paid how much for what? They're shoes!"

"No they were shoes, now they're ruined lumps of Italian leather." She sighed, sitting on the bed as I stepped into the walk-in closet. "Hey, Zane moved. You've got more closet space."

"And no need for that rock you were wearing for me tonight."
"Does this mean we can date the hot rock star?"

"We?"

"I get to live vicariously through you in the event that it's good. Otherwise I'll just take your place and tell you how amazing it was later," she teased. "So other than the shoes why are you a moron?"

I sat down and told her the whole story. How he had been so incredibly charming, how he took me to the beach, how I'd nearly attacked him in the car and he'd kissed me like he could fuck me with his tongue in front of the building. "I am a moron. I shouldn't have touched him to begin with and then for him to pull back like that then kiss me like that…" my voice trailed off and I had to lay down to keep from falling over from vertigo. "And now I'm just dizzy."

Karina laughed. "He has really gotten under your skin. Did it occur to you that he honestly is trying to show you that he's the nice guy? Trust me, any other red-blooded straight male would have jumped you in a second with that proposition in the car. I'm so proud of you!"

"You're proud of me? For acting like a horny teenage slut?"

"For acting! For doing something, anything just because you wanted to. The good news is that he wants to see you again."

I sat up shaking my head slowly. "I shouldn't see him again."

Karina's voice became coated with annoyance. "I know that you're not really familiar with this whole dating thing seeing as the only person you've ever been romantically attached to is Zane, but I think this genuinely nice guy might actually like you and not want to just have sex."

"He may like me but he's all enamored with James."

"Correct me if I'm wrong but aren't you still James?"

"Part of me is, a little tiny part that doesn't want to be brought to the surface again anytime soon. Why can't it just be simple? If he wants to be my friend, that's great, if he wants sex that's even better because I could definitely go for that with this man. I just don't know that I'm cut out for any type of relationship other than the completely fucked up one that I've already got." I traded my ruined dress for a pair of flannel pajama shorts and a tank top, returning to curl up under a blanket at the head of the bed. Karina stepped out while I was changing and returned a few moments later carrying two steaming mugs of fragrant green tea. I accepted the one that she extended to me, gratefully curling in around its warmth.

"All right, let's look at this logically." Karina sat next to me, tucking her feet underneath the blanket. "In the past, what, nine hundred years you've had one serious relationship? I know you've had sex with other men, but that's still pretty intense. Now that relationship is ending. Finally."

"I love how it's a good thing to you that my soul mate turned out to be a dud. That's kind of awesome in a weird, twisted way." I leaned back tiredly into the pillows and sipped my tea.

Karina laughed, resting her head briefly on my shoulder. "I still can't believe you bit him."

"I left a mark." I couldn't help but smile at the memory.

"Good girl." Karina toasted the accomplishment with her mug and we both sat back sipping our tea.

6

"So it went well then." Tyler stood from the couch, straightening his baggy black jeans and t-shirt as his brother entered the house grinning despite his disheveled appearance. He eyed Jared's rumpled, salt-covered attire as he walked across the room, taking his used drink glass to the kitchen.

Jared closed the door and followed him through to the kitchen. "You're home and wearing normal clothes so does that mean it went well and you've got a date later or it ended horribly and I should sleep with my eyes open?"

Tyler leaned in closer to Jared, his hands still over the sink washing his glass. "You may not want to do that. I've got two drumsticks. Get what you were looking for?"

Jared smiled and wiggled his eyebrows. "Just wait." He opened the fridge and removed two bottles of water.

"Nice bite mark." Tyler snitched one of the bottles of water and went back out to the living room.

Jared touched his neck and smiled at the memory. "Thank you. I rather like it." He followed Tyler into the other room. "Do you want to go first or should I?"

Tyler dropped down onto the couch cracking open the bottle and taking a large swallow. "If I'm going first this needs to be vodka. I'm surprised you didn't bring a date home."

Jared groaned, his head falling back against the couch. "Oh I wanted to, believe me. It was not the right time."

His brother laughed in surprise. "Seriously? You've been looking for this girl for decades and now that you've found her it's not the right time? This is a sick, twisted game that you're playing with yourself."

"I didn't say it wasn't the right time to be with her, I said tonight did not provide the ideal circumstances that would lead to sex. Just from the glimpses I got I understand that she's adept at having sex without developing an emotional attachment and that's not what I want. From what I was able to interpret she's never had a real emotional connection with anyone but that jackass she lives with. How do I compete with that?" Jared took a swallow of his water and grimaced. "You're right, this should be vodka."

"Because you're the poster child for functional emotional relationships?" Tyler stared at him in disbelief. "You have the perfect set-up. And you're bitching because for once a woman is not in love with you. Have I taught you nothing?"

"I don't want her to walk away. We both know what has to happen this time."

"And you are completely positive that this woman is the right way to go with that?"

Jared slouched further back into the couch, his eyes contemplating the ceiling. "If not, she's close. Probably the closest I've ever gotten."

"You're basing this off of what, two nights and one bite mark? I'm guessing that it didn't go too far if you're still this frustrated."

"I didn't touch her. I nearly broke the steering wheel on the truck when she bit my neck but I did not touch her."

"Oh dear God." Tyler leapt to his feet and walked back into the kitchen, returning a moment later with a bottle of tequila and two shot glasses. "You are insane, just so that you know that." He opened the bottle and poured both of them a shot, placing the bottle in between them on the coffee table before resuming his seat in the chair adjacent to the couch. "Cheers." He downed the shot, grimaced at the burn of the alcohol, and poured another. "So she attacked you and you did nothing?"

Jared downed two shots and poured a third before responding. "Not my brightest moment. In my defense I didn't want to jump her in the backseat like a cheap prom date either."

"You didn't go to prom." Tyler knocked back two shots before Jared could respond.

"Yes, I did. I took Monica Fitzpatrick. I wore a really embarrassing zoot suit because she thought it was hot. We looked like a bad gangster film." Jared frowned at the memory as he drank more tequila.

"You asked her to go, you picked her up, but you most definitely did not go to prom. I was there. You didn't show to save me from the teenage hormones and crepe paper." Tyler saluted him with his shot glass and put it down with a clink on the glass table.

Jared's forehead wrinkled as he concentrated, trying to pull the memories out of the tequila. "We went to the school, I remember it." He paused for a moment then smiled brilliantly as the memory finally resurfaced. "Oh, that's right. We went to prom but we never went inside. I spent all night fucking her under the bleachers at the football

113

field." He drank his remaining shot and put the glass down next to the half empty bottle. "How did I forget that?"

Tyler glared at him. "Is that really what's important right now?"

"No, what's important is that I'm going to see Jane again. She's making a bucket list for me."

"Because nothing says romance like a list of things you want to do before you die."

Jared chose to ignore the sarcasm. "So tell me what happened after we left the auction. Who bought you?"

"Some blonde bimbo that you didn't want to have an emotional connection with a few years ago. She said for me to give you her number if you were still single. Are you still single?"

Jared laughed. "Unless there was a wedding ceremony that I don't know about yes, I'm still single." His brother pulled a crumpled bar napkin from his pocket and tossed it at his head. Jared caught the paper and tossed it back. "I don't want that though. Maybe you should use it."

"I'm not into your leftovers, but thanks for the thought." Tyler took the girl's phone number and tossed it into the wastebasket across the room. "Bimbo Barbie made me suffer through her endless gossip prattling over mediocre food at the Cheesecake Factory for three hours. After you left I did have an interesting conversation with the other Ms. Jamison who started hyperventilating the moment her sister stepped outside and didn't return."

"Twins?"

Tyler nodded, confirming Jared's earlier theory. "They're pretty good. If you hadn't known I wouldn't have because I didn't know what to look for. The other one's real name is Karina."

"What did she say?"

"She found it interesting that her sister who reportedly wanted nothing to do with you this morning spent twenty grand to go out with you. Much like me she assumed that Jane could date you for free. Did she get jealous?"

"She saw inside stalker chick's mind and didn't want to subject me to a night of torture."

"Sure. Keep telling yourself that."

Jared laughed and reached for the bottle of tequila, knocking his shot glass off the table and onto the hardwood floor in the process. "Ah, damnit," he groaned as the glass broke into several pieces at his feet.

"Want to use mine?" Tyler offered, leaning over to look at the mess on the floor.

"Nah, I take it as a sign I'm done with the tequila for now." Jared bent down and carefully gathered the broken shards into his hands, carrying them to the kitchen. "Will you come in here and find something for me to dump this in so that it doesn't cut us when we take out the trash?"

"You mean when I take out the trash?" Tyler walked into the room and pulled a gallon sized plastic storage bag from a drawer, holding it open under Jared's hands. "I thank you for your concern."

"No problem." Jared carefully opened his hands to shake the shards out. Rather than broken pieces, a lump of melded glass fell into the bag. "What the…" his voice trailed off as he bent down to stare at the solid mass that used to be a shot glass.

"That's interesting." Tyler raised the arm holding the bag so that they could examine it better. "Are you sure that nothing out of the ordinary happened tonight? Get struck by any meteors?"

"Not that I remember." Jared poked at the glass through the bag. Testing the strength of the mended pieces he thumped it through the bag. The glass shattered, the melded pieces falling on top of each other causing him to step back in surprise.

"Looks like there might be some interesting consequences to meeting Ms. Jamison." Tyler closed the bag and carefully placed it in the trashcan. "Maybe you should have jumped her in the backseat."

"Maybe so." Jared remained fixated on the cabinet door that hid the trashcan and the broken glass from his view. "I didn't even kiss her until I dropped her off at home."

"Are you kidding me?" Tyler's eyes rolled so far back in his head that he feared they might get stuck. "Who's the patron saint of lost causes? We're not Catholic but I'm considering starting to pray to their God just to see if it keeps me sane."

"St. Jude the Apostle," Jared answered absently. "We've technically been Catholic; you just didn't pay attention in Bible study."

"I forgot about Spain. Dad did not choose well that time. I thought that woman was going to try and burn us out of ourselves thinking she'd given birth to devil spawn." Tyler walked back into the living room. "The guys will be here to record at eleven. Do you want me to tell them to meet us here or at the rehearsal space?"

"Meet here. We can go through it a few times outside before we go to the studio. I don't want to waste time. The rehearsal space in Hollywood is too far from the studio and the studio is too expensive to try things out in. Have them come by at ten just to give us some breathing room time-wise. I'll try to not be so distracted tomorrow."

"Going to get some sleep?" Tyler sat back down with his laptop and another shot of tequila.

"No, I'm going to take a really long, freezing cold shower and hope that I sleep." Jared's voice was suddenly weary as he walked toward the back of the house.

"No drunk texting," Tyler called after him happily. His brother pulled his BlackBerry out of his pants pocket and tossed it at his head as he rounded the corner into the hallway in response. "Good to know that you're practicing protection!"

Jared smiled and flipped him off. "Demonstrating my utter lack of surprise at your lack of sympathy."

Tyler glanced up at him and quickly flicked both middle fingers at his brother. "Demonstrating my lack of surprise at your utter lack of creativity."

"Glad to know we love each other."

"You are not really going to take that to his house. Jane, this is emotional suicide! Why did you even make the damn list in the first place?" Karina slammed a mug of coffee on the table in front of me sloshing the steaming liquid onto the table and my new notebook. I wordlessly blotted the coffee off of the pages and continued to write out the list that Jared had asked for while my sister continued to rant. "I love you. I support you having your own life and I know it was my idea for you to go after this guy for a little fun, but this is not what I had in mind! This requires emotional involvement. You're on the rebound; you should stop at physical involvement."

I calmly put my pen down and glanced up at her. "I am not emotionally involved with Jared Stateton. I haven't spent more than four consecutive hours in his presence. I am intrigued by this list idea and it has made me think of some things that I would like to do with my life given the option. Taking said list to his house affords me the element of surprise and for once I would like to see him unprepared."

I smiled and sipped my coffee. List completed at twelve items, I stood and walked to the kitchen, leaving Karina fuming at the dining table. "What do you want? I'm making breakfast."

Karina's mouth dropped open in surprise. "You are cooking before noon? You never cook before noon. If it wasn't for me and Starbucks you would never survive the mornings."

"You left out Coffee Bean!" I know that my voice was annoyingly happy but it was genuine this morning and I wanted to enjoy it while it lasted. Sadly I am too pessimistic to believe that it would last for more than a brief span of time. I leaned around the door frame to catch Karina's reaction. "Pancakes or waffles?"

"This is insanity. I should have you committed."

"Probably. I might not fight it if you do. Blueberries?"

"I hate blueberries." Karina caught my cellphone as it bounced across the table, the ringer on vibrate. "You've got a text message!"

"Who from?" I frowned at the gas stovetop while I tried to determine which setting would not burn my hastily mixed pancake batter. I do cook. I can cook extremely well and I also bake. I actually bake a lot. I find it to be a good stress reliever. Karina was right though, I don't enter the kitchen before noon other than to pour coffee so I was a little afraid that my first attempt at pancakes would be a disaster. The waffle iron had a timer and well-marked settings. I should have made waffles.

"It's not in your address book. A 310 number..." Karina's voice trailed off. "You gave him your number, didn't you? The man knows where you live and you gave him your number. Have you never participated in a casual relationship with a man before?" I heard Karina sigh and the chair scrape across the floor as she pushed it back to walk into the kitchen. "Do you want to see this yourself or should I read it for you?" When I turned she was standing beside me, holding

118

out my phone. I took the phone and stepped to the side, allowing her to take over the pancake making while I checked my phone. I felt my face heat up before I even opened the message. Not a good sign for any perceived or continued detachment on my part.

Reserved our booth for sushi on Friday. I don't want to wait that long to see you.

I smiled in spite of my best intentions to show no reaction. It was the uncontrollable happiness this morning, my first real day of freedom in my entire existence. Yeah, that had to be what it was. I knew it was a lie but felt it becoming more apparent as the heat spread from my face down to my chest and out through my arms. Well Karina did encourage this; she should see what Frankenstein monster she was having a hand in creating. I slid the keyboard out to reply, jumping when sparks slipped out of my fingertips and caused my phone to smoke. I dropped the phone, stepping back with my hands held stiffly out to the side. "Did you see that?"

"Did I see what?" Karina turned from the stove holding my spatula.

"I shorted out my phone." As the shock began to wear off a jolt of excitement rushed through my veins. Maybe distancing myself a tiny bit from Zane was what I had needed after all. I bent down and picked up the phone, holding it gingerly between my thumb and forefinger. The keyboard was still smoldering. "I shot sparks out of my fingers. Electric sparks." I glanced up at my sister and I knew my eyes had turned a happy shade of jade green. "Do you have any idea what this means?" I continued without waiting for her response. "I'm getting my powers back!"

"It could have just been a fluke, a random fluctuation." Karina's eyes were round with fear as her eyes alternated between me and the phone in my hands. I appreciated her concern but right now I wanted to be excited about the new development. For the last several decades I'd done nothing but slowly lose my abilities. To get one back, one that would give me a real defense against the threats that inevitably appear, that might be a miracle and one that I would gladly accept. Needless to say, the phone had not survived the encounter.

"I guess it's a good thing that I had planned to go pay Jared a little visit. Otherwise he might think I was being rude." I smiled sweetly at my sister as I stood and carefully placed the phone on the granite countertop where it couldn't catch anything else on fire. "Are you still in the mood for the pancakes? I'm hungry."

"Again! There's still something not developing in this section." Jared paced the indoor rehearsal space he'd built on one corner of the property he shared with Tyler, struggling to identify the minute detail that was missing from the music that they were due to record in under an hour. He listened to the section again, his concentration ruined by a persistent beeping noise. He opened his eyes, slowing his steps to focus on the security camera that showed a live feed of the front door to the house. Jane stood there staring up at the camera expectantly. The rapid thump of his heartbeat drowned out his realization of what was missing from the song that his band, Metamorphosis, should be recording in West Hollywood in the next twenty minutes. He chose to ignore the intercom for a moment to finish focusing on the song. "Does anyone else hear that?"

"Hear what," Cam asked from behind his drum kit. "Are you referring to the beeping? It's your doorbell."

"It's the intercom if you want to be really specific. I was referring to the arrangement. Something's off. I can't figure out what's missing." Jared attempted to unobtrusively glance at the screen to see if Jane was still there waiting. She rang the intercom again and extended her middle finger toward the camera impatiently. Jared fought the urge to run to the door and turned instead to face the other three members of the band.

"Are you going to answer that?" Tyler lounged against the wall, a dark pair of sunglasses shading his eyes from the bright artificial light.

"I'll be back in a minute. Fix this?" Jared indicated Jason and Cam, the two band members still clutching their instruments. Tyler nodded affirmatively and pushed off the wall, walking over to the soundboards. Jared reached over and punched a button on the security system panel. "I'll be right there. Come around to the back." He stepped outside amid various cat calls from his band mates. He crossed the lawn to the side gate, puzzled when Jane wasn't there waiting for him. Thinking that she had misunderstood, he opened the gate and stepped through, looking around to catch a glimpse of her. A laugh echoed through his mind, pulling him back through the gate. He turned just as Jane dropped down off the wall, landing beside him, her vintage combat boots barely making a sound on the soft grass.

"You're not very hospitable, you know that?" She straightened, dusting her hands off on her jeans.

"That's a solid stone wall. How did you do that?"

Jane glanced up at the eight foot wall and shrugged. "Not that hard, actually. I'm not a helpless female. And while I appreciate chivalry I don't always have the patience to wait for a man to open the door for me. You're lucky; I could have disarmed your security system."

Jared stared at her, wondering if there was a superpower lurking in her petite frame that he hadn't already found. "You didn't return my text."

"I broke my phone." She took a few more steps into the yard, noting the expansive landscaped area bordered on two sides by a forest of trees.

"How did you get my address?"

"You can find almost anyone in Hollywood with a phone call. You took two. This is where you were bringing me last night?" She glanced back at him and smiled. "You're still weirded out that I jumped your fence, aren't you?"

"A little," he admitted. "I feel awkward knowing that you can jump a wall I couldn't climb."

"Parkour. If I've got to run from something I'd like to know I can get away." Jane reached into her back pocket and withdrew a folded sheet of paper. "Your list. I would've avoided the trip and just texted you but since I'm apparently not good for electronics I brought it by. Do you mind if I walk back out rather than climb?"

"Want to come in and see the house since you essentially stalked me to find it?" Jared took her arm and steered her toward the glass and wood patio area. "I need to read this before you leave and I let you off the hook."

"I did not stalk you, I called your stalker. Well, one of them anyway," Jane laughed, allowing herself to be propelled into the gray stone house. The inside was just as clean and carefully maintained as the exterior. The dark wood beams continued on the interior in the ceiling and the floors. The walls were either an earthy beige or glass. All of the furniture was either leather or some earth-tone, like the entire place was designed to blend into the surroundings. Jane had noticed that this house was somewhat far off the beaten path, close enough to access several neighborhoods quickly and far enough away from anyone else to give seclusion. That it was located in a bend at the top of one of the Hollywood Hills granted a beautiful view in three different directions. For someone who made it his business to remain in the spotlight, Jared Stateton was working very hard to stay hidden. His home portrayed who she was beginning to think he was, relatively modest for Hollywood standards, a meld of ancient culture and modern lines.

"Can I get you anything?" Jared stepped through an open doorway into what Jane could see was a large gourmet kitchen. While he was gone she took a moment to glance around the living room, noting that there was literally nothing out of place in the three rooms that she could see, courtesy of the open floor plan.

"I'm fine, thank you."

He returned with two glasses of water and gestured to the ivory couch. "How long did this take you?" Jared took a swallow of his water as he unfolded the page she had given him and began to read. "Number one on Jane's list of things she's always wanted to do: Do something completely spontaneous for the hell of it. You are not doing me any favors by taking premeditation off the table. Are these listed in any particular order?"

Jane smiled secretively. "I'll leave that up to your superior intellect and interpretation."

"At least you're confident enough to admit that." He winked at her and continued his recitation. "Number two: Not answer my phone for a day. Three: Conquer my fears. Care to be more specific?"

"I will be when we get there. Keep going."

"Number four: Watch a miracle happen. Five: See the Northern Lights. Six: Discover something new. Seven: Travel without an agenda. Do people really do that to such an extent that you need it on a bucket list?"

"Oh, yeah. I have a friend who takes highlighted maps and guidebooks on trips. Schedules every day down to the minute."

"Does this person enjoy their life?"

She shrugged. "I assume so. I've only traveled with him once. It didn't end well."

"Should I be jealous?"

"Should you have a reason to be jealous?" Jane raised one eyebrow in question.

Jared cleared his throat and returned his full attention to the list. "Number eight: Lay on a glacier and listen to it crack. I like that one. Nine: Age gracefully. Ten: Raise children. You want kids?"

"Isn't that something usually discussed on or around the twelfth date?" Jane shifted uncomfortably on the couch.

"This list may take longer to accomplish than previously anticipated," Jared teased.

"I didn't stipulate that you were involved. You asked what I wanted. These are the things that I've never done, even after nine hundred years. I've never had that much time."

"We will change that. I promise. I do not do promises lightly." He reached for her hand. She smiled but pulled out of his reach. Jared chose not to push her, afraid that trying to force her would only send the woman he'd searched for running. He could sense the fear behind her mask of confidence and wished that all it took was a wave of his hand to make it go away. "Eleven: Get lost. Twelve: Wake up one day without fear." Jared folded the list and placed it carefully on the glass and steel coffee table.

"You asked for honesty. So, do I pass inspection?"

"I cannot tell you how sorry I am that you've never experienced some of these very basic things. I will do everything in my power to help you see as many of these items done as possible this time around."

"Don't worry about making that kind of promise to me. It's just a list. What gets done is done. I generally have bigger problems to deal with than completing tourist trips." She smiled and felt when it faltered around the edges and she knew it didn't meet her eyes. "I didn't write that to gain sympathy for things that have nothing to do with you. This was just the first time I've ever really thought about what it is that I want to do. I'm still attached to Zane. I can only block him out for so long but I'm finding that it might be worth taking advantage of the times that I can." Jane stood, staring at him expectantly. "So does the tour end here or are you going to show me the rest of the house?"

"Sure." Jared recovered his composure quickly and stood. He fervently hoped that she wasn't attempting to read his mind because in that moment he was filled with sadness and a profound respect for the creature standing in front of him. "Well you've seen the living room and kitchen. Do you want to continue with the dining room or the bedrooms?"

"Gentleman's choice."

After a brief trip through the remaining areas, Jared stopped Jane in front of the door to his bedroom. "So what do you think?"

"I think my library is more impressive." Jane stepped closer, inhaling the sweet cinnamon spice that came off of his skin. "Do I get to see what's behind door number one?"

"Come with me." Jared took her hand and pulled her inside, closing the door behind them.

Jane's eyes darted around trying to take in some of the room, some identifying marker in the dark. "I'm not this easy," she laughed. Jared threw her back against the door, slamming his hands into the wood on either side of her head to hold her in place. His mouth collided with hers, his teeth pulling on her lips. He felt her hands slide under his shirt and his back arch as she scraped her nails down his spine. "Okay, maybe I am." Her fingertips slid into the waistband of his jeans and she pulled him against her, her body becoming pliant in his hands. Jane wound her hands through his hair, thrusting her tongue into his mouth. His hands fell against her shoulders and pulled her closer into him, relishing the moan his tongue elicited from her throat.

Jared turned her in his arms, pushing her back against the door, his fingers moving both the bra and camisole straps covering her tattoo off of her shoulder. "My turn. I love this tattoo." Jane's head dropped against the wooden door, taking a deep breath as she tried desperately to not overthink the moment. He traced the tiny black skull and crossbones first with his index finger then with the tip of his tongue and Jane couldn't help the tiny noise that escaped her throat, her skin shivering where he touched her. The heat from his body slid across her and she pushed back into him, giving up any pretense at not reacting. When he tried to move away, Jane reached back with one arm almost involuntarily and pulled his mouth back onto her shoulder. Her fingers wound through his hair, forcing his mouth down harder onto her back as she arched into him. Jared was past the point of needing encouragement or caring that he was supposed to be somewhere else. His arms locked around her waist, eliminating any remaining space between them, at the same time his perfect teeth sank into her shoulder blade. The room had grown almost unbearably hot and Jared could feel what felt like literal flames riding under Jane's skin, the heat radiating from every point where they touched. With the walls down between them her mind crashed into his like a tidal wave, the knowledge that she truly wanted him colliding with the high he was already riding from her emotional response. In all the years that he remembered nothing had ever felt this good and he wanted more of it. He wanted her, not the ghost of who she had been. She laughed at the low, possessive growl that escaped his throat and cried out as his caress grew more forceful. Her nails scraped down the wooden plank in front of her and his eyes opened long enough to register the sparks that burned grooves into the door.

Jane's eyes opened and he knew instantly that not only were they bright blue-green but that they saw nothing of the flames that wound around the arm that she used to reach back and pull him in tighter. The hand left on top of his two that were trapping her hips against his contained more heat than the fire that whispered against his skin like a caress. He barely registered her head rocking back into his shoulder when her skin gave way under the flat blades of his teeth and he felt her body spasm in his arms. A wave of his own desire rocked through him, stealing his breath and leaving him desperately wondering how he could slide her under his skin and keep her there. Jared pulled back when he tasted blood and kissed the tiny wounds his teeth had put in her back. He knew he should step away but couldn't bring himself to let go of her. The fear that she would push him away now that she had felt some of what he felt, seen a bit of who he really was, becoming a nearly physical presence between them. "I'm sorry, you're bleeding. You should've stopped me."

"I liked it." Jane thanked God that for once she didn't think. She turned in his arms, grabbing his face and pulling him down until his mouth found hers. Jared could taste her blood on his tongue and moaned when she licked it away. Her hands grappled blindly with his t-shirt until he stepped back long enough for her to pull it off and toss it to the floor. He couldn't register anything but her lips on his and her hands on his chest. Jared fought the urge to pick her up and carry her the ten feet to his bed. He nearly forgot his resolution to not do just that when Jane's mouth slid down his neck and her heated hands moved to caress his lower back.

Jared pulled her against him and lifted her, wrapping her legs around his hips as he devoured her mouth like a starving man, the reality of being here with her like this overwhelming all of his lingering teenage fantasies as he kissed her. "Tell me you don't want me and this ends now."

Jane couldn't stop touching him. She could feel the heat coming off her skin everywhere they touched and she craved his mouth like a drug. "This isn't safe for you."

"Fuck safe. I'm giving you one out. If you want it you'd better take it now."

She laughed, a deep, throaty sound, as her mouth work its way back down his neck. "Don't want an out."

Jared leaned her back against the door and let go of her enough to allow her body to slide down his. "What do you want?"

She reached up and smoothed out his eyebrows, letting her fingers trail down his prominent cheekbones to his mouth. "You. For a lot of reasons that I don't understand and several that I do." Jane watched him curiously as she allowed her hands to drop down to her sides, lacing her fingers together behind her back so that she could observe his unassisted reaction.

Jared's breathing was labored and uneven as he rested his forehead against hers, closing his eyes and reopening them to make sure she was real. He took a small step back to stop her from kissing him again. He stepped away from her a moment later, took a deep breath, and opened the door without a word.

Jane went out into the hall with a smile. "As you wish."

He smiled and pulled her back, closing the door. "Changed my mind."

"Jared, did she murder or kidnap you?" Tyler called, entering the house. "We should've been at the studio recording hours ago and you know how you hate to waste studio time." He reached out with his senses to try and locate his brother without stumbling in on a possibly awkward situation. He heard voices coming from his brother's room and decided that if they were talking they weren't that serious. "If you're alive, I'm coming in!" Tyler called in warning as he opened the door which immediately slammed in his face.

"One minute," Jared muttered from the other side of the door.

Tyler backed down the hall and waited patiently at the entrance to the den, leaning against the doorframe. Jared emerged with Jane a few moments later, their faces flushed. As soon as they entered the hallway Tyler felt an increase in temperature and stared at Jane as heat radiated off her skin in the bright sunlight. "What were the two of you doing?"

"Something spontaneous." Jared grinned. "Turn the eyes in the back of your head around, it's not what you think."

"Sure it's not. Did you know that we're hours late? We amended the arrangement, equipment's all packed. We're just waiting on you." He checked his watch. "Or lunch, whichever you would prefer first."

"We'll go to the studio, take a snack if you're hungry." Jared grinned at Jane, his fingers still brushing hers. Tyler watched the tiny movement and swore he saw a flash of fire jump out from between their hands.

"I apologize for detaining you." Jane faced Tyler and smiled. "Jane Jamison. Nice to meet you."

"Tyler Stateton. And I don't blame you, I blame him."

"You were at the auction. How much did you go for?"

Tyler laughed. "Not as much as him."

Jane shook his hand, giving him a quick full body glance. "Pity. I knew I should've hung around."

"Oh, I think you've exceeded current expectations." His knowing look met his brother's happily cautious face. Despite his outward calm, Tyler could still feel the inner turmoil that Jared was fighting to keep secret. At least from his brother's point of view Jane seemed to have more baggage than a commercial airliner. In that moment he vowed to kill her himself if she caused the downward spiral that Jared had suffered previously because of her. Rather than imparting any of that information he smiled, shook her hand, and stepped back to allow the two of them to pass. "What direction should I give Cam and Jason?"

"We're leaving now." Jared watched Jane walk ahead of him toward the front door. "Hey, can we do dinner later?"

Jane turned at the door and smiled. "No. But I'll let you make me dinner tomorrow night."

"What if I don't want to wait that long?"

"That only works once. I'm told that patience is a virtue." Jane blew him a kiss and swept out the front door.

Tyler heard her car crank and groaned. "Tell me she didn't put a 428cid Shelby engine in that car. I don't give a shit about her but can I fuck her car?"

"Studio. Now. I've wasted enough of our time." Jared put his hands on his brother's shoulders and steered him toward the studio.

The door was unlocked and partially open when I arrived at home. Not a good sign. I pushed the door the rest of the way open cautiously and took a single step inside. "Zane?" Receiving no reply I opted to carefully, quietly set my things on the entryway table and enter the condo on silent feet. I reached out mentally for Zane and slammed into a metaphorical wall. Also not good. This usually either means we're in trouble or he's bombed. I crept around the corner and found him slumped over the dining table strewn with newspapers, unconscious. I guess that means we're working with option two. "Hey!" I walked over and grabbed him by the shoulder, shaking him roughly. He jumped back as soon as I touched him, his dark, blurred eyes struggling to bring the room into focus.

"Where the fuck have you been?" Zane growled drunkenly.

I couldn't help but laugh. All of the times that he disappears for days, I went off for a few hours and he has the nerve to freak out. Standing this close to him I felt all lingering guilt over ending our romantic relationship dissipate on a whiff of his rum flavored breath. I reopened the connection between us for just a moment and felt a part of his drunken haze slip over me. Unless I took a part of his chemical abuse on myself there was nothing that I could do for him other than make some coffee and hope he sobered up. "You finally noticed I was gone."

"The whole world knows where you were and who you were with. We'll try to minimize the damage, of course." A tall, thin blonde in a tight charcoal business suit walked in from the kitchen carrying a steaming mug of coffee. Oh how I hate house pets.

"Good morning, Juliet. Did you forget to leave last night?" I kept my eyes forward as I walked past her into the kitchen and fixed two cups of coffee, ignoring the knee-jerk reaction at finding another woman, particularly that woman in my house once again. If Zane and I were going to live together this would be something that I'd need to get used to without earning attempted murder charges. I took a moment to regain my composure before I walked back into the dining room with the coffee and a tight, fake smile on my face. I sat one of the mugs down in front of Zane, who had fallen back asleep, before taking the seat at the table next to him. I opened the link between us again, absorbing some of the abuse to his body to allow him to recover quicker. Knowing that the woman wasn't just going to go away on her own, I faced Juliet who was still standing by the kitchen doorway, her face a perfect blank as she sipped her hot drink from one of my favorite Jessica Rabbit mugs. "Thanks for making the coffee. So what are you covering today, besides my fiancé's dick?"

"Oh, I think you'll want to look at the morning paper before you start pointing fingers. You created quite a mess last night." Juliet smiled smugly, leaning against the kitchen doorway.

I slid through the woman's mostly vacant brain rather quickly, sighing as I noticed the intense, lingering desire for Zane that was still evident from the night before. Noticing for the first time what was littering my tabletop I idly picked up one of the paparazzi rag papers, flipped it over, glanced at the pictures of me and Jared on the beach, and tossed it aside all while still sipping my coffee. Thanks to my jaunt through Juliet's thoughts I already knew what to expect so I got to feign indifference while noting that the photographer managed to get some quite good shots of us playing in our underwear. I considered calling to see if I could buy the digital files for my own personal use. "Obviously you need to get your stories straight. The photoshopping's not bad, but there are about a thousand or so people who will happily tell you that I was at a charity bachelor auction all afternoon and a good portion of the evening. Jared Stateton was there as well. I believe he was auctioned off for twenty or twenty-two thousand. One of the higher ticket items for the night. Nice guy. Great ass. I'm sure there was a more reputable news source at the event that can furnish names and pictures if you'd like. Now why don't you run along and read something that won't bring down your IQ. I'll clean up the mess you made." Without glancing up from the next gossip magazine on the table, I pointed from her to the door. I looked up long enough to treat her to my bored stare and see if she would take the hint.

"He'll get rid of you," Juliet retorted. Her voice was sadly more hopeful than harsh.

All right, we could play this game. I uttered a long, theatrical sigh, exaggerating my display of annoyance at having to have this conversation again with another woman while loud snores came from Zane's end of the table. "No, he won't. There'll be a thousand of you and still one of me. Now get the fuck out of my house." I stood and pointed to the front door, just in case she'd forgotten where it's located.

Juliet put down her coffee cup and stomped over to the kitchen island, picking up her flashy designer handbag. "It's not just your house."

"Yeah, but I live here, pay half the mortgage, and as Zane's PR rep, well you're just the help. And obviously you've helped him enough for one day."

The woman stormed out on her stilettos, slamming the door behind her. Zane jumped up again as the door slammed, nearly knocking over his cooling cup of coffee. "What did I miss?"

"I threw out the trash." I sat back down and sipped my coffee calmly, continuing my examination of one of the various paparazzi papers. "Nice pictures. Too bad they don't prove a thing and Jared and I both have alibis. But it was a good try all the same."

Zane looked at me across the top of his mug with glazed over eyes. "And you're on a first-name basis with the bastard. Terrific. So it's not you in the pictures?"

"Oh no, it's me," I replied cheerily, perversely enjoying the surprise on his face at my first indiscretion in the several hundred years that we had been together. "Want some more coffee?"

"I may need it." He sat fully upright and blinking as he watched me walk back into the kitchen to refill our mugs. Since his head was clearing I felt fairly confident in pulling back out of his mind, allowing him to bear the rest of his self-destruction alone. Just as I was sliding away, a last thought slipped from his mind to mine, that he felt like he was looking at me through new eyes. "You gonna tell me how this happened or would you just like to know that I can still smell him on you?"

"I'm not surprised that you can smell him on me; I can still smell him. I quite enjoy it, actually." I handed him back his mug and sat down again. "I have a nearly identical twin that no one knows about. Figure it out. And do you think I care? All the years spent linked up to your mind, knowing what you know, feeling what you feel, knowing who you've fucked. Smelling all of them on you night after night, knowing you've even had some of them in our bed. I've pretended that I don't know it, I don't feel it, that I can't see what's inside your head, and I'm sick of it. We're not engaged anymore; we don't have to pretend that we're still in love with each other. We do need to stay together though. I can't leave you defenseless and running around the planet alone."

Zane glared angrily at me from his slumped position in the dining room chair. "You think I'm defenseless? Don't stress yourself trying to save me, Janey."

"Anyone attacking you isn't going to give you time to cast, you have no active powers, and this may come as a shock to you but I'd like to not take this life for granted. I want to live a nice, full, long, healthy, reasonably happy life. It's really not that bad of an idea. It would definitely be a change for the two of us." I wasn't trying to be mean or hurt his feelings. It had suddenly become very important to me that we manage to live for longer than a few years this time. I think I'd kept my head down, just walking through life with no expectation other than to be sucked out of it rather quickly. Now that I'd looked up I didn't want to look away and give up so easily again. If Zane didn't understand that we were going to have a serious problem.

"I didn't say I was ready to kick it yet either."

I motioned to the track marks on his arms. "Really?"

He crossed his arms showing the first sign I had ever seen that he might be just as uncomfortable with his habitual drug use as I was. "That doesn't mean I don't want to live, it just means that I prefer an altered state of existence."

I shook my head sadly. "The only person I can't save you from is yourself, Zane. That's what scares me the most. Not any of the other monsters lurking out there, you."

Zane rubbed his eyes tiredly. "I don't want to have this argument with you again. I'm not walking around with a gun to my head. I don't know why you have been. Is this guy what's making you so concerned with living now?"

I opened my mouth to give him a total denial but felt the words die on my tongue. "No, he just made me realize that I might like it."

"So you're gonna keep seeing him?"

"Why not? It's not like you don't have your fun."

"You can't leave me," he replied stubbornly.

If I couldn't see into it I'd swear the man's head was full of nothing but bricks. I didn't want to argue either but I really would appreciate it if he would pay attention every once in a while. "You think I don't know that? The only active power you have is your sex drive which is what gets you into trouble. No, I take that back. It gets *us* into trouble, which you conveniently leave to me to clean up."

"I didn't want it to be like this." He sipped his coffee, grimacing at the bitter taste. He leaned back in the dining chair tiredly, his blank eyes expecting me to simply give in again. "I really do love you."

"I know you do and that's your answer for everything. It just doesn't work anymore. You know, I kind of always thought that you'd get this out of your system, we'd work it out, or you'd wake up one day and realize that I am enough for you. I don't care anymore. I don't believe in the fairytale, Zane. I believe that we've been put here together for a reason. The reason may not matter anymore, I don't know. You know that I'll love you forever, Zane. And I know we can't be separated, I'm not trying. I just can't do this with you anymore. I'm unbelievably sick of being stuck in the exact same circular pattern over and over again. I want out, or at least as far out as I can get."

"You can't do this anymore but you still want to be with me?"

"I don't really have a choice. No matter what, you're still a part of me. Nothing changes that."

"He makes you very outspoken for very early in the morning."

"It has nothing to do with him. It's also early afternoon, just for reference." I paused, tapping my fingernails against the side of the coffee mug as I studied the contents intently before speaking again. "Thank you for moving into the other bedroom."

"Am I going to wake up tomorrow with him here?"

"No matter how attached we are, I'm still not you." I stood and kissed him on the forehead. "We need to publicly call off the engagement."

He looked up at me with sad eyes. "You care about him, don't you? Don't ever let them get to you, J. You'll end up like me."

"I don't know. Honestly I'm not sure I'd know how to. Friends outside of you and Kari may not be such a bad thing." I caught myself smiling at the thought and immediately shook the thought from my head. I didn't want to get ahead of myself even if the attention was nice. "I can't believe I'm having this conversation with you."

"You've been my best friend forever, J, whatever else has gone down. We don't make it, I still don't want to lose you." Zane smiled wistfully up at me as he pushed his coffee cup aside and laid his head back down on the table.

"You can't lose me. I thought we already established that." I brushed his hair back in one of those rare moments where I saw behind the mask to the man Zane could have been and it made my heart hurt a little just to look at him. "I would do anything for you, you know that. I plan to die for you one day. I just don't want it to be too soon."

"I love you, Janey."

I stopped and pulled my hand back. "I love you too, Zane."

Zane smiled sadly up at me and closed his eyes. "I wish I could remember everything for you, J. I've never known how to be what you want me to be."

"Zane, I never wanted you to be the man I remember because I'm not the woman you'd remember. I had hoped you'd be better; that we'd be better."

"Sorry to disappoint you."

I kissed him on the forehead and walked away. "We're not done yet."

7

"There's a real art to properly preparing tofu." Tyler took over the sauté pan, forcing Jane to move on to salad duty. He was having a hard enough time believing that his brother was asleep on the couch while his new pseudo-girlfriend was invading Tyler's kitchen.

"So what's the secret," she asked as she chopped vegetables to go on top of the lettuce, being careful to not let anything slide off of the cutting board.

He smiled. "If I told you I'd have to kill you, and I would probably get in trouble for that seeing as how my brother's been searching for you my whole life. Probably before that." He left the tofu to check the pasta and moved on to the pesto sauce. Tyler was still a little surprised that she didn't comment over being left alone with him. If Jared had actually spent any of the last three nights sleeping rather than staring at the ceiling muttering to himself Tyler would have dumped the pasta on his idiot head for sleeping through the first part of his date. Jane didn't seem to mind which lead Tyler to believe there would be an inquisition at some point before his signature pesto primavera was done.

"Why?"

Here it was. Tyler turned to peer at her more closely, noting that she wasn't wearing the hazel contacts he'd noticed with her sister. "You really are her, aren't you?"

"That would depend on your definition." Jane avoided his interested stare, her eyes turning bright amber as she concentrated instead on putting more energy into her chopping without taking a finger off.

"The girl with mood ring eyes." Tyler stirred his sauce and waited for the question he knew his brother hadn't answered.

Jane put the knife down and faced him, determined to get an answer to the reoccurring question from at least one brother. "How do you know about that?"

"The song. And I've lived with it my whole life, at least this one. When we first started out as a band he wrote a song about a girl who lived across the street from him and our mom. A girl named James who he told had mood ring eyes. She was murdered along with her boyfriend the winter before I was born. He played it incessantly for years until the rest of us begged him to stop. Jared was just a kid, but he said he could feel it. He prayed, begged, and pulled a lot of things it's better that he tell you about, but he swore she came back, was reborn on his tenth birthday. He's been looking for her ever since. He's been looking for you." He watched her curiously, waiting to see her reaction. Tyler saw shadows of what was running through her mind reflected in her multi-colored eyes and he wondered if the colors worked the same as the jewelry. "Glad we didn't make a bet on this because I swore that either you weren't real or he'd never find you. I probably would've ended up dressed in drag at our next show singing "I Feel Pretty" or something by a boy band."

When the questions in her brain finally slowed enough to form a coherent sentence, she looked up at him with dark gray eyes and he wished he had one of those little slips of paper that decoded what color corresponded to what emotion. "Who are you?"

He smiled and shook his head, unwilling to answer any more of her questions on the subject until his brother was awake. "Two magical little kids, one of whom just happened to fall in love with the girl next door when he was a kid."

"I remember him." Jane smiled at the memory of the dark headed little boy. He'd loved her car. Her smiled turned to a frown as a realization struck her. "Oh, ugh, I used to babysit him. Does that make my being here now really weird or is it just me that's having Mrs. Robinson flashbacks?"

Tyler couldn't help chuckling at what she obviously thought was a horrific turn of events. "You have to remember that he's actually older than you now. I think you're safe."

"It's still a little weird, right?"

Tyler snickered, his brother's bite mark flashing across his memory along with one of Jared's thoughts which told him where to look for hers. Tyler patted her on the tender spot on her shoulder, laughing when she started as he touched the place hidden by her t-shirt. "I wouldn't worry about it if I were you." He went back to preparing the tofu squares.

"How did you...?" Tyler touched his head and pointed to the other room where Jared slept in response. "Of course you'd be telepathic too," Jane laughed at herself for not realizing the obvious sooner. Her expression softened. "Why didn't he give up? Thirty years is a long time."

"I don't know. It wasn't for lack of everyone around him trying to get him to give it up. I guess he always felt like he'd helped to bring you back. And he wants to protect you from some idiot you were dating before. Says the guy's what got you killed."

"Repeatedly, I'm afraid, although Zane doesn't really remember a lot this time around. I'm probably the only person alive who thinks their soul mate is a complete dud." Jane went back to preparing the salad.

Tyler laughed. "How long have you been together?"

"A few times now. Time before this, when your family got dragged in apparently, we were actually supposed to be twins and the Fates screwed us up a bit."

"Understatement. So technically you were screwing your brother?"

"Technically, that's happened a lot. One of us doesn't get made without the other and we're either lovers, brother and sister, or twins, so pick your poison really. What about you and Jared? How long have you been together?"

"Eternity. Always brothers, in case you were wondering."

"Wasn't gonna ask."

"Kind of you. So, what are you gonna do now?"

"Nothing to do. I really like your brother for a lot of reasons that make absolutely no sense to me. I'd like to say I could give a relationship a real shot or, hell, just dating, but I don't know that I can do that and be fair to Jared. I honestly don't even know why I'm thinking about it. I've never had a relationship with anyone other than the non-magical philandering idiot that I'm fated to be with. If I had any real free will I would've left him a long time ago. However, if I leave I can't protect him and we could both end up dead again. The best I can do is to be happy while it lasts and hold back the impulse to scream during the bad stuff."

"You don't think you were ever meant to be happy."

"Not with that idiot. I'm sorry. I'm sure that you don't want to know all of this and I shouldn't complain. I'm sure it's much better than it sounds, really."

"I wouldn't ask if I didn't want to know. What happens to you concerns me now because it affects him." Tyler cleared his throat and waited out a moment of silence before continuing. "What about love? Do you know why you're here?"

"No idea, though this thing with your brother is probably the most reckless thing I've done in centuries. If you have any words of wisdom, please feel free to impart them." She paused. Tyler smiled to himself, shaking his head negatively, completely unwilling to step that far into his brother's mess. He could already sense that she knew the right questions to ask if she'd follow through with it past today. "I was really in love with him once. I remember it, vaguely remember what it felt like, but other than that there's nothing. I care because we've been together so long. I don't know how not to. And whatever happens to one of us happens to the other, so I don't want him to get so much as a cold if I can help it."

"Interesting curse."

"Know a way out of it?"

"Fated souls? Nope, not unless someone higher than the Fates decides to cut you a break."

"I'll hold my breath. So what are your special talents, Tyler?"

"I can cook perfect tofu." He emptied the contents of the sauté pan into the pasta bowl and picked up an oversized wooden fork and spoon to toss the ingredients together. "I can also hear things you don't want heard, sense when you're lying, and know what your powers are given a close enough proximity. I can also spellbind you by manipulating your emotions, but that one doesn't get used very often

143

this century. I am not an alien and tinfoil hats do not help." He hesitated. "Can I ask a question that's truly none of my business?"

"There wouldn't be a point in saying "no" now. I'll answer to the best of my ability and you can feel free to try and pull the rest of it out of my head if you like."

"Would you willingly die for him?"

Jane took a deep breath and stared Tyler straight in his gray-green eyes. "Zane is an extension of me. There's nothing I wouldn't do, nowhere I won't go, nothing I won't forgive. It's not because I want to but because I see no other alternative. And I do willingly die for him whether I'm shot, my heart's ripped out of my chest, or I just wake up in the morning. I die for him because I have to. It's what I'm meant to do. And I'm equally sure that I'll knowingly walk to my death this time just like I did last time, cursing the whole way. For the record, and because you asked, if I got a choice in the matter, I wouldn't do it."

"I really am sorry."

Jane passed him the chopping board with the additional vegetables that she had cut up for the pasta. "Why? You didn't do it. But thanks anyway. It's nice to have someone to talk to other than my sister."

He nearly dropped the chopping board into the pasta. Little bursts of laughter slipped past his lips. "Oh, so I'm a girl now?"

"No! I just meant that you're like me so you get it. Normal human wouldn't. Normal human would run." Jane smiled at him and picked up the salad and bread platter. She slid a stack of plates under the bread platter and carried it into the dining room. "Can you get everything else? I'll pry Jared from the couch." Without waiting for an answer, Jane went back into the living room where Jared was stretched out asleep on the couch. She smiled, watching him as he slept, a small smile on his handsome face. Rolling her eyes, she gave in to the urge to lean over and kiss him sweetly. "Wake up, sleeping beauty."

Jared opened his eyes and smiled. "Mmm, I'm obviously still asleep." He closed his eyes and pulled her down on top of him in a bear hug. Jane giggled, snuggling up beside him, trying to not question her motives or emotions as she briefly rested her head on his shoulder.

"Dinner's ready." She sat up and tried to pull him with her off the couch.

"I've got everything I want right here," he growled in her ear, taking her head in his hands and dragging her mouth across his jaw.

"Don't set off the sprinklers!" Tyler called from the dining room. They could hear the clink of the china as he set the table.

"So everyone knows about my new little heat trick, huh?"

"You should see the scratches you left in my bedroom door yesterday." Jared groaned and sat up, pulling Jane with him. "Tyler, I can feel you staring at me from two rooms away. Stop it, we're coming!" He stood and pulled Jane to her feet. "He was older than me in our last life and he hasn't let me forget it."

"I heard that!"

"Oh, just set the table! We'll be there in a minute!" Jared pulled Jane in the opposite direction, toward the back of the house. "I want to show you something." He pulled her into his bedroom, and shut the door.

Jane laughed as the door closed, cutting off Tyler's protests. "I didn't know you were into repetition."

"I'm not. Unfortunately I'm not looking for another make-out session. I need to ask you something and I need you to answer honestly, no matter how unconventional you may think it sounds." He stepped forward, stopping in front of where she sat on the bed.

Leaning back on her hands, she met his stare, his sudden intensity mingling with the confusion rolling off him in waves. "Okay. What's going on?"

"Have we ever met before?"

"According to your brother I was your babysitter in another life so I think that would qualify." Jane shuddered at the memory, thinking of the way that she'd allowed him to touch her in this very room not that long ago. Even though it was a different life for her, it was still the same one for him. And that made it just a little weird that she'd spent the better part of the prior day fantasizing about him.

"That's not where I was going with this. I keep having these dreams that feel more like memories. I think they're about you, but you would have been a lot younger at the time. Is it possible that we knew each other and didn't know it?"

"Didn't know what?" Jane's voice betrayed her cautiousness. Liking Jared was one thing. Trusting him with things that she'd only told her sister was a completely different situation.

"I don't know how we could have met and I didn't know it was you." He sat down next to her on the bed, trying to display his earnestness by taking her hands in his. She pulled away and moved as far as she could without falling off the edge.

"No, we've never met. Not since 1971 anyway." Jane shifted uncomfortably. "Is that all you needed to know?"

"Yeah, that's it." Jared's face became a total, perfect blank as he watched her stand and leave the room, knowing all the while that she was lying to him. What he couldn't figure out was why she still didn't trust him enough to even tell him this one small detail. "You know that I can get the real answer from you if I want it bad enough, right?" he called after her.

Jane stopped in the hallway and turned back to face him, her expression wary and her eyes a stormy gray. "Please don't threaten me. I like you and I don't want to feel that I have to do something we both might regret later."

"You won't hurt me." He stood and took two steps toward her.

"You don't know me well enough to make that determination. Sticking your tongue in my mouth does not make you an expert." Anger caused her to not care if she was being irrational.

"Go ahead then. Prove me wrong. I'm right here." Jared reached out, took both her hands in his and placed them on either side of his face. "Throw enough firepower into my brain and even I won't be able to recover. Tyler wouldn't survive it either so you've got nothing barring your escape." He felt her hands heat instinctively and then cool as she regained control of her reaction. "What are you waiting for?"

Jane searched his eyes for some explanation that made sense. "You don't belong in my world."

"How do you know that if you won't even let me try? Are you going to fry my brain or stop threatening to every time I say something that hits too close to the truth for you?"

"I never said I'd kill you by electrocution. I can't control it enough to use it as a weapon yet," she confessed, her voice turning soft as he stepped closer, his hands still covering hers on the sides of his face. She suddenly felt thirteen again, talking to her very own version of Casper and wishing he was corporeal enough to kiss her. The man standing in front of her was very real, and from what she could tell, very not human though he looked and halfway acted the part well. "Why did you try to find me?"

Jared watched her eyes lighten from gray to blue and felt himself start drowning. "Because I felt it when you were gone."

"What happens when you wish I'd have stayed dead?"

"Did we know each other?"

Jane sighed and stepped back, pulling her hands away from him. "If the answer was "yes", you wouldn't still be asking the question; you'd know."

"You failed a calculus test in 10th grade because of me." Jared voiced the only solid memory he had of that time just to see if it resonated at all with the woman standing in front of him.

Jane stopped and stared up at him. "Excuse me?"

"You failed a calculus test because I wanted to talk to you. You were supposed to be studying but you spent the night talking to me instead."

She felt the frown creasing her forehead and wondered if she'd been wrong about Jared being the guy she'd seen through her mind's eye. "I never took calculus. I'm terrible at math unless it involves accounting." Jane felt his disappointment. "You don't have to invent reasons to see me. If you want to be with me, then be with me. Just stop trying to make me into someone I'm not. I am so unbelievably tired of not being enough for the men in my life. If you're going to keep chasing a ghost, let me know now so I won't have to threaten to kill you again."

"Do you know what I realized in this room yesterday?" Jared backed her against the doorframe, his hands on her hips.

"What?"

"That you are better than any fantasy."

Jane looped her arms around his neck and smiled. "Wow, you are really good at that. So how many women have you conned into your bed using that line?"

He grinned. "So far, just one."

"You know, we might need to invest in either a larger house or soundproofing for that room," Tyler commented as they all three sat down at the dining room table. "You make him kinda loud." Jane blushed and busied herself with her salad. "Oh, don't take that the wrong way. I'm pretty sure it's a compliment. At least you didn't flambé the house. I didn't check on the cars, but I haven't heard any sirens or explosions." He smiled and helped himself to the pasta.

"Weren't kidding about being able to hear everything, were you?"

"Nope. I have to wear earplugs or monitors in both ears during concerts. Guitarists get to stand next to the speakers." He grinned, taking a bite of his salad.

"Did you ever think it was a strange career choice for someone with bat hearing to play in a rock band?"

"Well we'd wanted to be musicians for a while. Now I can rock out and withstand the noise. Gotta love modern technology."

Jane looked at Jared, wanting to know what made him tick. In under four days she'd already found herself too close to safely extract herself from his life without at least a little collateral damage. Estimating how much damage was a more difficult task than she wanted to admit and after the last hour she was wondering if she even really needed the answer. "Do you both remember?"

He shrugged noncommittally. "Bits, pieces, and most of everything. Oddly enough, we've both "grown up" to look like this every time. Luckily there aren't too many paintings, though now there will be photographs and the internet." Jared grimaced at the thought. Her unease slithered along his skin, bringing a chill into the warm room. Forcing a bite of his food to pass through his suddenly tight throat, he concentrated on chewing, willing his mind to a complete blank before Tyler could start asking questions that Jared didn't want to answer.

"What's your favorite thing this time?" Jane glanced over at him, noting that he was paying more attention to his plate than her question.

"Mass-produced chocolate bars. The good stuff from overseas, not the crap they make here."

"Tyler?" She glanced up and smiled across the table at his brother.

"Earplugs. I can finally sleep."

Jared took a bite of his pasta and turned to look at Jane. "And you?"

"Coffee bars, Red Bull, and Mars Bars. And I agree with you, the best chocolate comes from Europe. I've got a friend in the UK who keeps me supplied. I'm her jellybean contact."

Tyler snorted with laughter, dropping his loaded fork in his plate. "People need jellybean contacts?"

"People need all sorts of things. And jellybeans are terribly expensive in the UK. Shipping kills though."

"Wouldn't that defeat the purpose then?" Tyler wiped his mouth with a napkin before attempting to reclaim his lost fork.

"Not if you're partial to Dr. Pepper flavored jelly beans. This at least saves the import tax. And it keeps me from paying the inflated prices here on real Cadbury products. I'm actually fairly certain that it works out to be pretty much equal, this is just more fun. You never know what you're really going to get."

Jared turned around in his chair, interested. "How often do you ship them?"

"About once a month or so."

"Next time we'll just take them." Jane raised an eyebrow and Tyler nearly missed his mouth with his newly reacquired fork. "Our band tours Europe again next month."

Jane faced straight ahead and continued to eat. "Will you be playing "The Girl with Mood Ring Eyes" in Europe?"

Jared suddenly became very interested in his food, vowing to have a word with his brother later about what was and what was not kitchen conversation. "We haven't played that in a long time."

"Why not?"

He slammed his fork on the table and met her curious eyes with the most horribly haunted face she'd ever seen. "Because I nearly lost my mind looking for you. The band didn't want the reminder. Some of our fans even consider the album it came off of, *Apocalyptic Night Dreams*, a cursed album." He paused for a moment, his expression softening. "I feel like my brain has finally well and truly fried just because I'm sitting here having a conversation with you. I played that song obsessively. I kept thinking that you would hear it and find me."

"I really am sorry, Jared. I had no idea that James caused this to happen to you. You were just a kid when she died. I'm surprised that you even remember."

"Talk much while I was asleep?" He glared across the table at Tyler who shrugged noncommittally, becoming increasingly entertained by his food. "You had to know someone would mourn you."

"Her. Someone mourned James, not me. I am still among the living for the moment. What I don't understand is how you're so attached to me and why I'm suddenly so attracted to you when I haven't really noticed another man for nearly a millennia. Not that you're not attractive, I'd just like to know what's really going on here. Did you do it?"

"No, I didn't," his words were short and clipped. "Are you complaining?"

"No, it's just been my experience that if anyone knows who I was it's not a good thing. I usually end up dead one way or the other." Jane took another bite of her food, trying to chew quietly in the uneasy silence.

Jared broke the awkward moment first, his quiet voice startling both his brother and the woman sitting next to him. "I would never hurt you, James."

"I know that. But I'm also not James anymore. I may be here, but she did die. I need you to understand that if we're going to continue spending time together." Jane touched his arm. "Can I hear that song sometime?"

The dark expression remained clouding his face. "Yeah, one day. We owe James a thank you for the Grammy."

She choked on a bite of tofu. "No shit? I think I just became slightly intimidated."

"Nice to know it's possible." He smiled slightly, watching her as he continued to eat.

Tyler watched his brother watching her as they all ate silently for a few minutes. Finally he put down his fork and had to clear his throat to keep from laughing. "Jer, you can quit looking like the kid from *The Exorcist*. She's not going anywhere. You can eat."

Jared smiled and didn't move his riveted gaze. "You don't know her. She might."

Jane laughed. "You might want me to at some point. The novelty will wear off eventually. You'll need to hunt down a new toy."

"We'll see about that." Jared pointedly stared at her while continuing to eat his dinner.

She chucked him in the jaw playfully, forcing him to face forward. "You watching me eat is weirding me out." On impulse she took his left hand and placed it in her lap, covering it with her own as she continued to eat. "There. Feel better?"

He looked surprised and relaxed almost immediately at the contact. "Actually, yes." Jane swapped hands with her fork and locked the fingers of her right hand with his left.

"Aw. Aren't you two cute?" Tyler smirked. He chewed the last bite of his tofu with a smile and stood to clear the empty plates. "Who wants dessert? Oh wait, you did that first."

"Amusing. Did you come up with that all by yourself?" Jared carried his and Jane's plates into the kitchen.

"I did, actually. You liked that?"

Jared leaned through the doorway to see Jane. "For dessert we have three kinds of ice cream, I might be willing to part with some of my fudge for you, or there are about twenty variations of hot tea." At her questioning look he clarified. "I do a lot of meditation. I like to prepare and relax with tea."

"I vote for the tea, but I'll help you make it." She followed him back into the kitchen. "Do we need to pick something caffeinated so that you don't pass out on me again tonight?" she teased, sweeping past him carrying the remaining dishes from the table to the sink.

"You don't trust me to boil water in my own house?"

"No, I just use less electricity and am a touch more efficient. You're not one of those guys that can't accept assistance or ask for directions, are you?"

"Are you one of those women who has to be in charge of everything?" he countered, leaning back against the counter as he watched her.

"Absolutely. I told you that I'm a distrusting control freak and borderline sociopath when we met at the sushi bar. You just didn't believe me. It takes more than a tinfoil helmet to do my job." Jane managed to keep a straight face as she lifted the tea kettle from the stove and moved to the sink to fill it, continuing before he could respond. "Pick out the tea? I can boil water, but I know nothing about obscure types of tea."

"Who said it was obscure?" Jared smirked as he saw the imprint of his teeth still pink in the skin around her tattoo and found himself thinking of at least three other places on her body where he'd like to put matching impressions.

"What kind of tea do you have?" Jane stepped up beside him and sat the tea kettle on a trivet, laying her fingers against it to heat it. She felt her skin heat up again in his presence and forced it to channel into the tea pot which was boiling in under a minute.

Jared opened an overhead cabinet and examined the contents critically. "Okay, so maybe none of it's that normal. There's a mint, a chamomile, a couple with vanilla, lavender, a roobios, and ooh! Try this one." He dropped a tea bag in a black packet in front of her and went off in search of tea cups. "Dragon ball ginger."

Jane filled the three offered cups with hot water and Jared went behind her adding tea bags. "So tell me more about yourself."

"Tell me about you."

"I'm a carbon-based life form. My favorite author is Oscar Wilde. Your turn." Jane took her tea cup and followed Tyler into the living room.

"I read general fiction and history books, listen to obscure podcasts, and I suck at *Guitar Hero*." Jared followed her and sat next to Tyler on the couch across from where she'd settled in an armchair.

Tyler shrugged. "Don't look at me. I don't play the damn thing. I laugh at him. Some of us have accepted that the *toy* will not play the same way as our real Les Paul."

"It is a game. It will not win." Jared settled back into the couch, crossing his legs and propping an arm across the back of the couch. He smiled and sipped his tea.

His brother raised an eyebrow in challenge. "You want me to tell her?" He leaned forward. "Grab that white Stratocaster over there." He put his tea cup on the coffee table. "Do you play?"

"There are some things that it's better I leave to the professionals, no matter how hot I think it is." Her eyes flipped back and forth between the two of them, annoyed that she wasn't privy to the internal conversation that she could almost see on their faces.

Jared nodded in her direction, saluting her with his tea cup. "Nice to know that you're appreciative."

Jane looked at Jared cautiously as she walked over to the instrument collection in the corner of the room. "*Guitar Hero* I rock at, real guitars I'm shit with." She picked up the Fender guitar and immediately noticed something wrong with the neck. "Why is there electrical tape? Did you break it?"

Tyler crossed the room, took the guitar from her and smiled at his brother who was choking on his tea. "Last chance." Jared shook his head and pounded on his chest. "He marked the chords with the same colors—"

"As the controller!" Jane finished for him, laughing. "Why would you do this, it's a beautiful guitar! At least it's not the vintage one," she nodded to the guitar hanging on the wall behind the couch. "That one's a 1960 Sunburst Strat, right?" Jared choked on his tea for the second time in under a minute, nodding furiously that she was correct.

Tyler whistled his appreciation. "A girl that knows her guitars and cars. Why did my brother have to find you first?" He clasped both hands over his heart and collapsed dramatically back into the couch cushions.

"I told you to go with me to eat the other night. You wouldn't listen." Jared rolled his eyes.

"So, does it help?" Jane ran her fingertips across the tape, watching Jared's face for a reaction.

"No!" Jared laughed. "Sadly my gaming skills have not improved. I am doomed to be the guitarist who can't play the guitar video game. I can't even play my own song on that game and I wrote those riffs."

"That is truly the saddest thing I've ever heard. I still can't believe you taped your guitar up like a toy! How long did it take you to come up with that?" she gasped out between bursts of laughter.

"Not *that* long! I assume if it works one way it has to work the other."

"It's a color-coded game!" Jane collapsed in a laughing heap on the couch.

"I like her." Tyler took her vacated chair along with his tea.

Jared grumped in his corner of the couch, ignoring both of them. "This was completely unnecessary."

"Yeah, but it was fun." Tyler saluted him with his cup.

For the record, I have no idea what I was thinking would happen when I went over to have dinner with Jared Stateton. I don't know what I wanted to happen. I do know that what did happen had me out pacing the largely vacant streets of West Hollywood at two in the morning. After leaving Jared's house in the Hills I took a drive south rather than north, landing on the Sunset Strip near House of Blues somewhere around midnight. I parked with all the intention of wandering into one of the many clubs and listening to someone's mediocre music beat my brain into blissful submission while I nursed a drink at the bar, forgetting all about the man who's scent covered my skin for a couple of hours before I had to go home and face Zane, my sister, and their questions. I was actually hoping that I'd wander into a reasonably good show that would thoroughly distract me until either the place closed or my unlimited credit card ran out. This was turning out to be a very expensive week.

I settled on walking down to the Viper Room and entering during the middle of a fairly good local metal band's set. Moving through the small, crowded room to the bar I retrieved my drink and handed over my credit card for the bartender to run a tab. I worked my way across the room toward the stage as the set ended and another band began to take command of the stage. Leaning back against a post near the stage, I watched the bands exchange equipment, listening to the dance remixes of rock songs that the DJ was spinning. I stayed until last call then walked out into the cool night air, the wind barely registering on my skin as I walked down San Vicente toward Beverly Hills.

Why was I so concerned? People meet other people, feel chemistry, make a connection, have sex, fall in love, get married, and die every day. Given the option of being normal, at least halfway normal, I always thought that I would take it. So why wasn't I jumping at the chance to be with someone who liked me this much? Other than that he wasn't human. Lying in his arms this afternoon that had been my first thought. Nothing about him other than the outer casing was even remotely human. I should be scared, not contemplating my next opportunity to try out one of his creative fantasies. I still have Zane to worry about. Barring all that there's still a book to deal with that is currently only two hundred pages long. I have bigger, more pressing issues than trying to start a relationship with a guy that I wasn't sure I wanted to be in a relationship with anyway. Though granted, he hadn't offered me the relationship; I was getting ahead of myself. I liked to envision all possible outcomes of a situation so that I can plan for all contingencies. That way no matter what happens, I'm prepared. That's the theory, anyway. It seems to lose something in the translation from my head into reality. So I walked downhill through West Hollywood and into Beverly Hills, berating myself with an internal monologue as I tried to make sense out of what I was doing to myself at a rather critical point in my life. I found an all-night donut bakery where I bought a cup of coffee and a bag of beignets to walk around town with me. If I was going to stay up I might as well fuel my unplanned exercise with caffeine and a sugar rush. Groaning, I turned to climb back up the hill into Hollywood to locate my car.

Halfway through my bag of fried dough and powdered sugar I found my car. It had a new accessory. Tyler Stateton was leaning against the hood, arms crossed over his chest as he waited for me. I sighed but didn't slow as I approached the car. The man was slightly infuriating simply because there was no way to hide anything from him. I held the bag out to him as I approached. "Donut?"

"Thanks." He took one of the pastry squares and bit into it, watching as I opened the driver's side door. "You don't seem too surprised to see me."

"I'm more surprised that you managed to find me when I didn't even know where I was going." I dropped the bakery bag into the backseat and sat down in the driver's seat with the door open so that we could talk. "Please don't lean on the fender, your jeans might scratch the paint."

"May I sit with you then?" He walked over to the passenger side, waiting expectantly with his hand on the door.

Sighing, I reached over and unlocked it, settling back into my seat with the rest of my coffee. "Powdered sugar stays out of the car, please."

He held up his fingers to show me that the donut was gone. "Clean hands. May I sit?"

I gestured to the passenger seat and watched the planes fly overhead. "Tell me how you found me and I'll give you another donut."

"Tell me what you want with my brother and I'll tell you how I tracked you down." He turned sideways to watch me while we talked. All of the good humor from earlier in the evening was lost from his face and I wondered if it had been an act for his brother's benefit.

"I don't want anything from your brother. I like Jared, but I've been honest with him. Being honest with myself I'm not even sure how I like him. Does that answer your question?"

"Not exactly but it's better. You realize that he's falling for you?"

I bit my lip and nodded. This is what I'd been afraid of. "I don't know how to stop it other than to walk away and I really don't want to do that at this point."

"You can have sex with anyone."

"You have to know how rare it is to meet someone else even remotely like us, particularly someone who will admit it. To have met Jared who is so comfortable with who he is it gives me hope that I might be okay with it one day too. That's a gift. Having met him, spending time with him, it's all a gift. And I don't understand it, I didn't ask for it, but I can't just push it away before I know why. Very selfishly, I think I need him right now. Obviously there's something in him that needs me too. He spent thirty years looking for me because there's something inside of him that he can't let go of. Are you going to ask me to walk away?"

"No, I'm going to ask you to take into consideration that this is no longer about you. Next time you're with my brother and he's let down his shields I want you to look into his mind, I want you to see the void that looking for your soul caused, and then I want you to make a decision that won't send him back to that place."

"How bad was it when I died?"

Tyler felt her genuine concern and didn't bother hiding that it surprised him. "It wasn't bad when you died. It was bad when you were reborn." He slid out of the car and walked around the back, pausing at the trunk. A moment later his hand appeared in front of her face holding a tiny electronic device. "Fair is fair. This is how I found you. I put a GPS tracker on your car." He dropped the device in the parking lot and crushed it under his boot heel.

"That's actually slightly disappointing." I couldn't help the insane little laugh that escaped my throat.

Tyler's deep laughter echoed mine. "What were you expecting, some magic tracking power?"

"Yeah, I kind of was. All the tricks between you and Jared and you used good old-fashioned technology to find me. It's a little cute and endearing." I felt a tug on my shields and a realization occurred to me. "Jared doesn't know you're here, does he?"

"No, and I'd appreciate it if we kept it that way for as long as possible. I know that at some point you may not be able to hide anything from him and when that happens, it'll be okay but right now he might take my head off. Especially after our dinner conversation tonight. He already thinks that I overstepped my bounds. If he knew I'd tracked you down he'd really become paranoid and I don't want to deal with that tonight."

"I didn't see you."

"Thank you."

I glanced around the mostly vacant parking lot, seeking a vehicle that I thought might match Tyler. The only other vehicle was a boxy black SUV. "Tell me that's not your car."

He pointed to the car and smiled. "Yes, that is my car."

"No wonder you like mine." I resisted the urge to gun the engine of my car as I drove away.

"You had sex with him." Karina met me at the garage elevator and road up to the condo. Yeah, not being able to hide things was sometimes annoying.

"I have six hours before my meeting at Universal. In that time I need to write as many pages of this book as will fly out from my fingertips, drag Zane from wherever he passed out to his bed, and I'd

161

like to sleep. Beignet?" I passed her the bakery bag containing the last few of my dozen donuts.

"You can't bribe me with sugar." Karina pulled one of the pastries from the bag before passing it back to me.

"Funny, it worked for Tyler. Actually, no it didn't. I need to find a better bribe." I unlocked the door and entered my home, immediately searching for Zane. Priorities.

"Tyler? The brother? Wait, you've got something going on with both of them? Are you insane?" Karina stopped in the entryway, staring at me with her mouth hanging open as if it had come unhinged along with her rationale.

"He put a tracking device on my car and followed me so he could find out what my intentions are toward Jared without his brother overhearing." I stopped searching and faced her, assuming that if he wasn't passed out in the hallway that either Zane had made it into the condo on his own steam or he wasn't home. Either way it wasn't my problem at the moment. "Does that answer your question?"

"He wanted to know your intentions? How archaic."

"If you think about it, they're pretty old so I guess it's not really that uncommon of a question." I needed coffee. It was just after five, the sun was starting to rise, and my sister showed no signs of slowing down.

"What are your intentions?" Karina took the carafe from me and poured water into the coffee maker.

"I don't have any intentions. I like him. There, I admitted it. I like Jared Stateton. Does everyone feel relieved, vindicated, happy, something? Other than that I have no intentions toward him as of this moment. I'm pretty sure that he has some toward me though so maybe his brother was asking the wrong person." Frustrated, I sat

162

down at the bar and laid my head on the countertop. "Why can't things be simple and easy for once?"

"Could you trust it if it was?" Karina turned the coffee pot on and sat down next to me, patting my back. "So, tell me about the sex."

"It was an accident that I'd like to repeat a minimum of five times daily. May I please go to bed now?"

"No, you may not. You're up to page two hundred and five. That means that you're reaching the point where one character runs off into the woods with a demon to die and another goes chasing. Your agent says you've got two days before she comes after you with a shovel to turn the entire thing in." Karina watched the coffee drip into the glass carafe. "What did you tell Zane?"

"The truth more or less. I don't know what else to tell him or why he should give a shit other than that if I leave there's no one to save his sorry ass from himself. Have we tried everything to detach me and Zane from each other? I mean everything." I rolled my eyes up to look at Kari without moving. I'd walked around West Hollywood half of the night wondering what I would do if I managed to survive without Zane. I'd spent the rest of my hike thinking about the weird little romantic triangle that I seemed to have dropped myself into. I hadn't come to any conclusions but I had developed a burning need to fully understand all of my available options.

"The only other thing we can do is to try to kill Zane while shielding you as much as possible. And I don't think it would work or that you'd really let me attempt it." She laid her head down next to mine so that our eyes were level. "What's this really about?"

"I just have a really bad feeling that everything's changing and for once I can't see even a microsecond into the future to see what it looks like. I don't want to die and I watch Zane grow more destructive every day. He doesn't care. He just assumes that we'll come back again. I don't want to give up yet. And I don't want to risk losing you as my sister. If Zane and I die now you and I will be separated."

"Maybe you're not meant to see what it looks like." She stood and crossed to the now full carafe, returning with a steaming cup of coffee in the same mug that Juliet had used. "Yes, I cleaned it. You haven't been home and I didn't want your favorite mug exposed to slut germs for longer than necessary."

"Thank you." I kept my head on the counter, staring blankly at the mug two inches in front of my nose.

"Should I find you a bendy straw?"

"Very funny." I straightened and picked up the mug, taking a sip. "Thank you."

"You already said that."

"How's Craig?"

"Halfway apologetic, halfway argumentative. He'll get over it. He usually does." I noticed then that she was staring at me in this weird, distracted way of hers that told me she wasn't concentrating on the current topic of conversation. "Are you doing that?"

"Doing what?"

"Your back's glowing."

"Glowing?" I sat up straighter, reaching an arm around to see if I could feel a difference on my skin. I came back with nothing.

"Yeah, it looks almost like some sort of phantom fire. I can feel it." She moved around behind me, pushing my t-shirt up to examine my skin. "Did you know you have a bite mark?"

"Yes." I felt a hot blush creeping up my neck at the memory and things tighten lower in my body, remembering what had happened after that bite mark was placed there. The room suddenly felt too hot, too enclosed even though it was an open room. I jumped, startled as the coffee in the mug I was holding began to boil, bubbling over the top of the cup and on to my hand. My skin didn't burn and the hot liquid left no mark, not even a red trail on my skin. "Karina, touch this mug." She reached out, gingerly touching the hot ceramic with one finger. When she jumped back I showed her my right index finger and proceeded to dunk it into the coffee, holding it there for at least a minute. It felt like I'd just put it in lukewarm bathwater. The skin was unblemished when I removed it.

"It's not just electricity." Karina touched my hand carefully. "You're an elemental. Can you control it?"

I shook my head, eyes wide as I stared at my hand. From what little I knew of elementals, they were rare. Anything that can control an element, bend it to their will, was dangerous. I might have once wielded fire, but I knew it had never been anything like this before. "It happens whenever I get emotional. This should not be happening."

"This is awesome." Karina genuinely appeared excited about my new ability to set things on fire inadvertently.

"Maybe I should cancel that meeting."

"Just don't touch any electronics and you should be fine."

I rolled my eyes, walking over to the sink to rinse out my cup. "Because upping the temperature and glowing skin won't set off any alarms?" I reached for the coffee carafe, jumping back when the coffeemaker burst into flames. "Seriously!" I grabbed the burning machine, dropping it into the steel sink and dousing it with water.

"At least you saved the coffee." Karina pointed to the now cracked glass carafe that I had dropped on the counter in my haste to put out the fire I'd caused.

I looked back down at the charred, smoldering remains of the plastic coffeemaker and groaned. "Yeah, this is awesome. Remind me to buy more fire extinguishers today."

"So, just out of curiosity, is Mr. Stateton in a burn ward somewhere in the city or did you manage to not set him on fire?"

A few hours, one very cold shower, and several torched targets later I felt in control of myself enough to face my meeting at the film studio without electrocuting anything. Karina had worked with me trying to get my temperature under control. We finally figured out that if I stuff my new-found power into the little box in my mind where I kept my and Zane's mental link that I was better able to control the firestarter impulses. I drove down to Burbank with the windows down still trying to make sure that my skin wasn't glowing with unseen fire and my body heat was around the normal ninety-eight degrees for a human. If stuff like this was going to keep happening that further complicated my life maybe I should rethink my stance on maintaining a relationship with anyone. I'd hate to accidently set someone on fire that I cared about. Hallmark doesn't really make an "I'm sorry I flambé'-ed you" card.

By the time I checked with the guard and moved through the gate security I'd returned most of my mental faculties to their normal functioning levels and had recovered my composure enough to accurately reprise the role of novelist. I had coached myself on the way there, driving through the lot, while taking the elevator up to the correct office. Coming off as a crazy person wouldn't have been in my best interests so I wanted to make sure that I was prepared with intelligent answers to whatever questions they might ask. Much to my disappointment, the meeting went much faster than I'd anticipated with minimal participation on my part. Other than the initial two sentence "discussion" over what the studio's intentions were for my manuscripts I really hadn't needed to be there at all other than to smile and nod at the appropriate times. I was pretty much sold when they gave me the number they were thinking of spending for the option rights to my books. Provided it was mine to dispose of as I wished I might would have considered selling my soul for the offer they gave me. Though, in the event that I was ever placed in total possession of my soul it might take a little more than money to get me to part with it. The damn thing was proving too hard to gain ownership of currently. After promising to review the contracts my agent would send over, I politely shook hands and walked back out to my car, the glare of the bright southern California sun only enhancing my day even though my sunglasses were perched on the coffee table in my condo. I was actually in such a good mood I didn't, for the moment, feel weighed down by Zane, Jared, my life in general, and was considering driving down the street to the mall to buy a new pair of sunglasses. It was a week of trying things new, maybe a voluntary solo shopping trip wouldn't be such a bad thing. Resolved, settled, high on life for the moment, I got in my car and drove off the lot. I wasn't even annoyed that I had to use my GPS device to find the mall conveniently located approximately two miles away. I was annoyed that while trying on moderately expensive sunglasses at a boutique store an increasingly familiar pair of blue eyes appeared in mirror. I turned around and found Jared Stateton watching me try on a five hundred dollar pair of Tiffany glasses. Did the entire family have me bugged with tracking devices?

"Stalking me again?" I returned the glasses to the case and selected another pair to try. Assuming I opted to purchase anything it would probably be another pair of the Ray-Bans I already owned in a different color.

To his credit, Jared wasn't apologetic in the least. If I couldn't have deducted that from his face, his mind was wide open, purposefully allowing me to see that he wasn't playing any games with me. That, if nothing else, was at least a refreshing change of pace. "People usually stalk me, not the other way around. I'm not adept at developing an appropriate response for when the object of your desire coincidentally crosses your path in a shopping mall." He stepped past me and selected a pair of red Versace glasses that he handed to the relatively helpful salesman to ring up. He paid for his purchase and then turned back to me. "I don't believe in coincidence. Do you?"

I discarded the black aviator glasses in my hand, opting for a pair of rectangular Ray-Bans with champagne lenses. "If I believed in coincidence I have the feeling you'd make me lose my religion."

"So, assuming I'm not the draw, what enticed you into the Valley today?" Jared followed me as I walked to the cash register, handed over my credit card and collected my new sunglasses.

"I had a meeting. I don't know how I'm supposed to react when we conveniently run into each other now." I stepped out of the store and started walking through the nearly vacant mall with Jared trailing along beside me. I didn't want to look back because I wouldn't be able to stand it if he was laughing at me after that little revelation.

"I've got an idea." The words came from right next to my ear, causing a shiver to slide down my spine and heat to rise from the blush claiming my face. He wrapped an arm around my shoulders, pulling me in closer. "Is this less awkward for you?"

"It's a little possessive." I tried to unobtrusively put a minute amount of distance between us. Zane and I hadn't publicly called off our engagement yet and I didn't want to give Jared hope for something that might not be even though I really was starting to like him. The bastard.

He held on tighter and just smiled, steering me toward a sporting goods store. "We walked like this the night we met and you didn't seem to have a problem with it. I need new running shoes, do you mind?" Without waiting for an answer he walked back to the shoes, taking me along with him for the ride. While I saw his outward confidence, I could also taste his fear which left me with a no-so-good feeling about being here with him. This had started out so easy.

On the way out the door he pulled me to the side, looking around to make sure we weren't overheard. "While I appreciate the compliment, I just wanted to let you know that you're glowing."

"Seems to happen whenever you're around." I closed my eyes and took deep breaths, concentrating on the smells coming from the coffee bar and food court rather than the intoxicating scent coming from the man beside me, further fueled by my skin's sudden heat flash. "Could you step away please? You're distracting me."

"No." He stepped closer and I felt the skin on the hand he touched flare. I visualized it as a tangible thing that I was reeling in. In under a minute my skin was no longer flaming, seen or unseen. I opened my eyes carefully. "Much better. No one saw anything."

"Sorry. It's still new." I started walking, keeping my eyes straight ahead.

"No apologies necessary. So I've got this list and was wondering which item you'd like to conquer first?"

"The one that lets me go home and finish my work before my agent and publisher put me on their shovel list permanently."

"Shovel list? Should I be concerned for your well-being?"

"Have you ever seen the film *Secret Window*?" He shook his head negatively, shoving his hands into his jean pockets. Until I learned how to fully control myself and figured out what this thing was it was better that he kept his hands to himself. "The killer in the film uses a shovel to kill, bury, and plant corn over his victims. When my sister and I are really angry with someone we say they're on our shovel list."

"Makes sense. Can I tell you something without you freaking out and catching something on fire?"

"Can I catch you on fire?"

"You could but it won't do much good. I seem to be immune, which is a new concept for me." We had reached the parking garage and he was cornering me between the car door and a concrete pillar. "So can I say it or not?"

"Go ahead, speak. Or let your shields down and I'll save you a breath."

"I like you. I know that you're not really single, you're not into that, whatever right now. I just wanted you to know that you will be my girlfriend."

"That's not the way to get someone to like you more. It's a really great way for me to gift you with a shiny new straight pin to pop your overinflated ego though." I opened the car door and he reached around me, slamming it shut.

"I'm not egotistical. I'm confident."

I took a deep breath and ignored the tension headache building behind my eyes. "It's two o'clock now. I have to work for a bit but why don't I come by around nine-thirty? We can have a late dinner, figure out which item on the list to tackle. If you're still interested." The last I admit I said rather suggestively.

"Oh, I'm interested." Jared leaned in for a kiss, causing my eyes to close reflexively and my heartbeat pumped a little faster. A moment later my eyelids fluttered open to see him hovering just a breath away, watching me with no small amount of amusement. "Don't melt the topcoat on your car. I'll see you tonight." With that he turned and walked away. I waited until he exited the parking garage before I sank back against the door. I so did not need this in my life.

Before going home I consoled myself with a trip by the cell phone store to pick up a replacement for the device that I had electrocuted earlier in the week. I did find out that my device's insurance plan covered damage from electricity which meant that I only paid half of the exorbitant price for the smart phone that I left with. Why is it that everyone believes their cell phones should look like part of the controls for a spaceship? I need it to call, text, and maybe check email. Maybe. I ended up with one that would do all three, surf the internet, unlock a car, watch videos, and play music at the same time. I just hoped that Karina could tell me how to work the damn thing.

Karina came in just as I was putting the finishing touches on the three chapters I had written over the last few hours. If I stayed up for half of the night I could probably get the rest of it done well before my new deadline approached. If I ditched Jared I could finish the thing before midnight. I thought about it for a moment then I thought about the time we'd shared the day before and decided that cancelling our impromptu date wasn't going to happen, at least not from my end. My sister didn't share my enthusiasm for the new arrangement of my evening.

"You saw him again. I thought you weren't going to see him again." She stormed over and flopped down on the couch.

"No, you decided that I wasn't going to see him again because I developed a body temperature issue after I met him. I don't remember ever agreeing to that. And I didn't seek him out today, I just ended up at his mall after my meeting at the studio that went exceptionally well, thank you for asking." I saved my manuscript and closed my laptop. "You wanted me to get a life. This is me getting a life."

"I didn't tell you to get this life with this guy."

"You liked him two days ago. What changed your mind?"

"You had sex with him and turned into the female version of the Human Torch. I wonder why I could possibly be concerned, J." She sighed, watching me from under the fringe of her short bangs. "Promise me that you'll be careful, okay?"

"I will be careful. I promise. I know you didn't come down here just to discuss my possible sex life. What's going on?" I set the computer aside and balanced my chin on my hands.

"Are you planning to live with Zane forever?"

"Possibly though I'd prefer to not. Unless we can be separated we need to stay close no matter how uncomfortable it may be. I can't risk anything happening to him and me being too far away to try to fix it. What's this about?"

"Nothing, I just wanted to know." Karina moved to stand.

"How's Craig?" That stopped her in her tracks and had her reclaiming her seat in under ten seconds.

"I'm waiting. He's going to ask me for a divorce, I know it, Jane. And I don't know what I'm going to do when he does." I watched her lip tremble and I wanted to march upstairs with a machine gun.

"He's a moron. I know it, you know it, and he's going to figure it out. He loves you, Kari. Has he said anything about working it out?"

"Yeah, he said that if I wanted to be his wife I couldn't be your sister anymore and he didn't want to hear any more talk about anything occult. Do you think I could live with those terms?" The words were tempered with anger and it took everything in me to keep my fury in check that the man my sister loved would treat her so badly and not even see it in himself.

"I think what he's asking of you is unfair. Take everyone else out of the equation but you and him. What do you want? What conditions can you live with? Barring everything else I want you to be happy." I moved to the couch and hugged my sister while she cried for her troubled marriage. I wanted to be able to take her pain away, to hurt Craig for what he was doing to her with these harsh demands. Above all I wanted her to understand that she needed to make her own decision about what was right for her.

Karina sat back after a few minutes and looked at me with watery eyes. "I don't know that he'll ever love me."

"He already loves you. He's just too stupid to realize it. Do you want to be with him?" She nodded, more tears spilling out of the corners of her eyes. "Then go try to work it out with him. Don't think about any of the rest of this. Forget it. Just talk to him. The two of you love each other, you should at least try. And if he's still being an asshole you can always move in here with me and we'll kick Zane upstairs to live with Craig. They can be grumpy together." That got a tiny smile out of her at least. "I love you, you know that, right?"

"You're my sister, of course I know that."

"If you need me…"

"You're less than a phone call away." Karina touched my forehead. "Thank you."

I walked her to the door. "You know if he still refuses to see reason I can always set him on fire and we can call it an accident."

Karina outright laughed. "I'll keep that in mind. Be careful on your date tonight."

I let my conscious mind mingle with Karina's as she walked upstairs. I knew she wouldn't stand for me walking her to her condo and I honestly didn't know if I could walk in there right now without attempting an experiment on her husband to find out what my new electric heat power did to the human brain. I felt when she stepped inside the condo and her trepidation as Craig greeted her. A warm light filtered through as he hugged her and I slipped out of her thoughts, unnoticed and content at her happiness. I rose from the couch and wandered to the bedroom. It usually took me twenty minutes or less to get dressed. I had a feeling that I was going to spend a lot longer than that tonight and that I'd loathe myself for it later. Might as well get started.

"Are you ready to start on that list?" Jared watched as Jane carefully hopped up into the passenger seat of his truck.

"Is that what we're doing tonight?" She adjusted the short skirt on her wine-colored sundress, draping a leather jacket across her lap. "Which item are we working on and does it involve dinner?"

"Yes, it involves dinner, but we have a long way to go so we'll have to eat on the way. Hope you don't mind." Jared reeled his thoughts back in and pulled away from the curb. "Are you opposed to fast food?"

"I'm not terribly high-maintenance. What are you thinking?"

He grinned, watching her eyes change from hazel to bright green in the dimming light. "Give me twenty minutes and you'll see."

Jared pulled off of the 101 in Woodlands Hills, driving until he found the jammed parking lot that he was looking for. Jane looked around as she slid out of the car and laughed. "Food trucks. I've never eaten at one of these."

"Well you've got a few to choose from and they're all amazing. Take your pick." He followed her as she walked around, looking for all the world like an enchanted child as she weaved through the laughing families and teenagers clustered throughout the high school parking lot. Something caught her attention and she grinned, stopping long enough to turn back to him and take his hand before darting off into the crowd. As she pulled him along with her, he felt his heart literally skip a beat. His steps faltered for a moment as an emotional heaviness settled on his shoulders. Jared saw the concern in her face as she paused to see what was wrong, the emotion that she wouldn't acknowledge behind it, and knew that nothing in his life had moved forward since he'd first encountered her thirty years ago. Fear wrapped around his insides, paralyzing him momentarily at the realization that after centuries of living, the creature clutching his hand on her way to a food truck that served exotic grilled cheese sandwiches could break him. And there would be no escape for him when she did because immortal beings never really died.

Jane stepped up and ordered herself a brie and tomato sandwich before turning to Jared, a smile still playing across her lips. "Will you split the s'mores melt with me for dessert?"

Jared couldn't help but grin. "Yeah. Just order some extra marshmallows." He stepped to the counter and ordered his own sandwich, feeling the happiness that Jane radiated. He laughed to himself, wondering if a grilled sandwich was all it took to make her happy and why he hadn't tried that sooner. Watching her collect their food, he imagined briefly that he was the cause of the fire he'd seen burning in her eyes. He knew from his empathy that the burning light was nothing more than her will to live, regained after longer than he cared to contemplate for fear that he would sink fully into the melancholy that she had lived in for centuries.

They made their way back to the truck, and got in, Jane dividing out their food as they settled in. Impulsively she reached over the gear shift, grabbing him by his over-shirt and kissed him. "Thank you for this. I don't know what it takes off of the list but thank you."

"Well if I cheat then this covers "discovering something new". However, I have something else planned but we need to hurry or we'll miss it. And don't hog the s'mores melt. That's the best one." Jared couldn't help but smile as he drove out of the parking lot and onto the highway.

An hour later he pulled into an empty parking lot and turned off the truck. "Are we here?" Jane looked around suspiciously at the darkened asphalt. "You're not going to toss me off the cliffs, are you?"

Jared laughed, getting out and walking around to the passenger door to extract her from the truck. "Hurry up or we'll miss it!" He turned on the flashlight in his hands, directing it toward the underside of his face. "I brought a light this time. No slipping on the stairs."

"Where are we?" Jane latched on to Jared's arm as he led her toward the edge of the cliffs and down a steep wooden staircase to the beach below. "Crystal Cove. It's a lovely little beach in Orange County that has number four on your list." He turned off the light when they reached the beach and held a finger across his lips to signal that she should keep quiet. Jane slipped across the sand with him to a small group of people congregated near an area illuminated by the moonlight. As they inched closer, Jane saw the nest, settling into the sand to watch as tiny sea turtles hatched and crawled toward the softly breaking waves.

After a few moments Jared sat down beside her, draping her forgotten jacket across her shoulders and pulling her back against his chest. As the last of the turtles worked its way out of the nest, she leaned her head back on Jared's shoulder, turning her face to look up at him. "What was number four?" she whispered.

"Witness a miracle." He smiled as she settled back into his arms, watching the last infant turtle walk into the surf.

After the last of the other observers disappeared into the night, Jane sighed and sat upright, disentangling herself from Jared. "That was really beautiful. Thank you."

Jared sat back in the sand, watching her and knowing that she could sense his confusion at her sudden interest in leaving. "Hope it counts. Where are you going?"

"Back to the car. Or would you rather walk for a minute?" She nodded toward the beach and the breaking waves.

"The beach doesn't go far from here either way. You have to climb over the rocks or wait until low tide to walk down any further." He patted the sand next to him, still warm from where she had been sitting. "Why don't you join me and watch the stars?"

Jane sighed again and he could feel her hesitation though he knew he'd hit on something that was special for her to consider his proposition. "You have to stop doing that." She sat back down and laid back to stare at the stars, taking care to not touch him.

"What am I doing?" He laid down close enough that they weren't touching unless one of them moved.

"You're unnerving me in a good way which just further unsettles me. And that I find extremely annoying."

Jared chuckled. "Put your hands in the sand, firestarter."

"Don't call me that," Jane grumbled, but did what he asked. "Why am I digging my hands into the sand?"

"Patience," he chided. "Concentrate on your pent up energy, the literal heat in your skin, and push it out through your hands into the sand. There's nothing in there that you'll hurt, nothing that will burn. If anything you'll make lightening glass." He didn't need any psychic powers to know that she was skeptical. "Just try it. If it doesn't work you've lost nothing."

Jane closed her eyes, imagining that she felt the fire washing out of her through her hands into the ground around her. After several minutes she sat up, her eyes wide as she shivered on the windswept beach. "I'm cold."

"Is this a new thing for you?"

"It is this week."

He touched her face and felt the minute temperature difference from a few minutes earlier. "Do you feel better?"

"I need to test it." Jane straddled Jared's hips, pushing him back on to the sand. "Should this not work, you're immune, right?" She leaned over him, close enough that he watched her eyes change to bright amber even in the dark. "Mind being my test subject?" Without waiting for an answer she moved forward to kiss him, her eyes keeping his wide-eyed gaze.

Jared reached between them and grabbed her wrists, pushing her hands back into her chest far enough that her mouth couldn't reach his. "What are we doing?"

"I'm attempting to kiss you. What are you doing?" She smiled through her insecurity. Jane felt his hesitation and groaned, pulling back. "We've already talked about this, Jared. I can't give you what you want but I enjoy spending time with you. You need to decide if you can live with that or not." She stood, dusting off her skirt. "I'm going back to the truck."

Jared scrambled up out of the sand and raced after her. He caught up just as she reached the staircase and grabbed her by her arm, wheeling her around to pin her against the cliff wall. He kissed her roughly then threw her away from him, back against the stone. "Is this all you want from me?" Jane could taste his anger on lips still burning from his kiss. "Answer me!"

"What do you want me to say?" Jane shot back angrily. "That I'm madly in love with you, that I want to throw my entire life away to be with you? I don't know you! I like what I know so far but I'm not in love with you. I can't promise you anything. You knew that day one, minute one. So who are you really pissed off at, Jared, me or you?"

"I can try to give you a better life."

"Who are you kidding?" She laughed harshly. "You can't save me. You're not even in love with me. You're in love with a mirage, a memory. And no matter how hard you try, she's still dead. You don't want me. You want the shards left over from a dead girl you barely knew as a child. Don't get all high, mighty, and self-sacrificing with me. You don't know what it means."

"How the fuck would you know? You have no idea the hell that I've gone through because of you, what I've done to make sure you were given a chance." In his anger he pushed her harder against the stone wall, not backing down even when she grimaced at the pressure, wanting her to know, just a little bit, what it felt like to live inside of him.

"Don't think that I don't appreciate the effort but did I ever ask you to do any of it?" Jane spoke softer, regretting the hurt that her words put on his face. "You did this. And I'm not anyone's fairytale." Jane didn't put up the pretense of a struggle even though she knew she might win. She leaned forward as far as she could with her hands imprisoned against the cliff, her eyes closing briefly as she inhaled against his neck. "I do like you like this." Dropping back against the rock, she smiled up at him. "I like you. I like spending time with you more than is possibly healthy for me or you, given the current set of circumstances. I want to get to know you. But this isn't the Stone Age or wherever you're originally from. You can beat me against the wall, I might even get off on it, but I'm still not going to tell you what you want to hear just because you want to hear it. I've been stuck in a literal dead-end relationship for 900 years. I'm not trying on another one just yet. Can you live with that? Or do we need to end this now?"

Jared let her go and took a step back. "Ancient Greece. Around 1634 B. C. I'm not really sure of the exact year. After a while I just stopped counting. Tyler may know. He's better with numbers."

"What?" Jane looked up from rubbing circulation back into her wrists, her mouth open in a little "O" of surprise.

"You asked where I was from originally. Greece."

"That makes you over three thousand years old."

"Roughly 3600, give or take a few years for reincarnation. I don't age the same way that you do and I live to be 179 so I can predict almost down to the day when I will die. Fall of 2150 this time, in case you were wondering." He stared up at the waning moon, wondering why in the hell he had felt that complete disclosure had been warranted in that moment. When Jane ran away like she was being chased by the devil Tyler was going to spend years torturing him.

She shrugged, stepping away from the cliff and back toward the staircase. "So I guess I don't need to be concerned about having been your babysitter anymore."

"Not really, unless you just find it that interesting. I wouldn't use it as a conversation starter with people we don't know. You might get that Mrs. Robinson reputation that you were so worried about." Jared followed her up the stairs, still unsure if his reaction was causing the evening to end or just get started. Emotionally he wasn't sure how he felt about it either way. Physically he wished he'd just shut up and let her fuck him. Rather than watching her walk away from him he could've been watching her moan on top of him. "Jane?"

She turned around at the top of the stairs, glancing down at him. With the moonlight now fully on her face he could see that her eyes had changed back to the sea green they had been earlier when he'd picked her up. "Everything all right?"

Jared closed the distance between them. He rushed at her, pulling her away from the edge of the cliff as he gathered her into his arms, slamming her back against the driver's side door of his truck. A strangled sigh escaped her throat as he crashed into her, lifting her to wrap her legs around his waist, one hand fisting her hair to hold her mouth tightly against his, the other reaching under her skirt. Her hands cradled his face, her tongue drawing circles on the roof of his mouth. Jared groaned, his jeans suddenly growing too tight when he realized she wasn't wearing any underwear. Yeah, he really wished he had known that twenty minutes earlier. Though the epiphany that started this might save him sand in awkward places and a lot of explanations later. The more he touched her, the less he remembered his logic. Her legs tightened around his body, grinding against him, her skirt hiking up enough that it was almost out of his way. "Stop, stop. Just a second."

Jane's hand slid between them, reaching for his zipper. "Jared, I will say anything you want as long as you don't stop and know that I'm just saying it for sex. Unless it's true." She bit his bottom lip, pulling his mouth back to hers. She lowered her body onto his and he had to brace one hand against the car to keep from falling to his knees. Jane's breath caught in her throat and her spine arched. "Oh my god. Jared…" her voice trailed off on a cry as his mouth slid down her neck to her collarbone and he moved inside of her. Her body met his frantic movements, her hands digging into his shoulders.

"I need you to see," he gasped out, his fingers digging into the car door. Jane tightened against him. He placed his hands on either side of her temples and kissed her. All of her mental barriers vanished and everything Jared felt crashed into her, stealing her breath. Jane took the wave of emotion and pushed it back into him, tempered with her own thoughts. She could see everything that he felt for her, every potential outcome played out in his mind. In every scenario she was herself and it endeared him to her in a way that she couldn't fully describe, even to herself. Remembering snippets of her conversation with Tyler, she pushed further into Jared's mind, searching out the place where he kept his memories of her. Moving through the recent memories, she fought her way to the past and the memories that he'd tried to forget. Jared sensed her invasion and started, his eyes flying open, knowing what she was seeing. She snapped back to the present, her gaze meeting the fear in his eyes and she smiled as she kissed him sweetly. Jane pulled him closer, straining to touch him in more places than her two hands could reach.

Jared wrapped his arms around her, holding her as tight as he dared with his face pressed into her neck, feeling her rapid pulse beating against his lips. "I didn't know what I was looking for but I always wanted you."

Jane opened her eyes, her labored breathing growing faster at the intensity in his gaze. "I—"

He shook his head and smiled, his thrusts growing slower, more controlled as he held her gaze. "Don't close your eyes." The intimacy of the act frightened her with its intensity. Staring into his eyes, even though it wasn't possible, she could feel him sliding along every inch of her from the inside out. Jane's mouth fell open as the pressure built inside of her and she struggled to keep her eyes on Jared's as she tightened around him and felt everything inside of her release. He gasped then groaned, dropping his forehead on her shoulder as he started to pull away. "I have to—"

"No." Jane held his face in front of hers. "Do not close your eyes. I want to watch you come inside of me."

He shook his head negatively and she could feel the vibrations from his body as he struggled to maintain his control. The sensation caused her to move with him faster, the movements becoming jerky as she felt the climax building again. "Jane, I can't."

"I want you to."

A primal growl escaped Jared's throat as he lunged into her, claiming her mouth, his body losing its rhythm in his frenzy to take all of her in. He swallowed her scream of pleasure with a kiss and pulled back just enough that she could watch his face while he found his release inside of her body. Jane moaned with him, orgasming again watching his face as he let go of everything but her, falling to his knees in the sand. He slumped against her heavily and she curled into him, supporting both of their weight against the side of the truck.

"You didn't catch me on fire."

Jane laughed against his throat. "It wasn't for lack of trying." She paused to take a deep breath. "Can we repeat that about five times a day?" Her body shuddered against him and she wiggled closer, the movement causing him to groan. "Maybe six."

"Are you trying to kill me?"

"If you die it wouldn't be fun anymore. Though there are worse ways to go."

They both laughed. A flash of light caused Jane's eyelids to flutter open. "Did you see that?" She looked toward the clear sky for lightening. The light flickered again, this time from the road above them. "Shit. Get up very carefully."

"What am I missing?" Jared tried to shake off his lethargic mood, staring past her shoulder to see reflections in the car door.

"I do believe that there's a photographer on the main road taking our pictures."

"Motherfucking hell." Jared's entire body tensed. Jane pushed back, holding on to his shoulders, her knees planted firmly on the ground.

"Do not let them know that you see them. It will just make it worse." Jane stood carefully, smoothing her clothing back into its proper place without drawing more attention to herself. While she stood, Jared straightened his own clothing, pushing his hair back from his face as he joined her.

"Do you care that they probably just recorded that entire thing?" Even in the dark and without her powers she knew that he was truly afraid of her answer.

Jane knew that she should be concerned. This was precisely the thing that she tried so hard to avoid, the undue attention that she did not need. Maybe it was the still surging endorphins but she couldn't bring herself to care that much. Instead she looped her arms loosely around his neck, bringing him back into her embrace. "Maybe we should give them a little more to look at. I'd kind of like the video as a souvenir."

Jared kissed her quickly then reached behind her to open the car door. "Care to continue this somewhere a little more private?"

"There's a continuation?" Jane moved against him suggestively. "Think we'll make it all the way back into town?"

"If we don't there are plenty of hotels between here and there." He grinned and released her.

Once they were in the truck with the doors closed behind them, Jared leaned across the center console and pulled her to him, kissing her roughly. "I'm sorry about the photographer. This is not how I wanted tonight to end."

Jane kissed him again. "Just go. Don't give me time to think and we don't have to end it here tonight."

He started the truck, peeling out of the parking lot and driving back toward the interstate. "What happens if you think about it?"

"I might start to question why I let it happen and I don't want to ruin it. I want to be able to remember that look in your eyes forever." She reached out and pushed his dark hair out of his eyes. "I shouldn't want you the way that I do but I want to be able to remember you like this."

"I'm not going anywhere." His expression belied his confusion.

Jane smiled softly. "You will. But you will have left me with a beautiful memory."

"It doesn't have to be like that." Jared fought to keep his concentration on the dark road in front of him.

"It's who we are. I'm not yours and you're not mine. However if you'd like to enjoy each other while we have the opportunity I'm more than happy to be a willing participant."

He smiled, glancing toward her just for a moment. "I'll let you keep thinking that's all this is if it makes you feel better about it."

"You're never going to just accept what you're given, are you?" She watched his face in the passing streetlights.

"Nope. If I did, you and I would be in a very different place that I'm not sure either of us would like very much." He let the silence stand in between them for a long moment before speaking again. "Should I take you…where do you want to go?"

"You take the same interstate either way," Jane pointed out, the humor falling out of her voice when she realize how seriously he was about to take her answer. Why do men have to make things so complicated? "Where do you want to go?"

"I want to answer that but I don't want your decision to be weighted by my opinion."

"This doesn't decide the course of the rest of our lives." Jane laughed. "Overly dramatic much?"

"Overly dramatic would be me threatening to drown myself if you didn't pledge your undying love to me right here, right now. I just don't want you to make a decision based on what I want. You've made enough decisions based on other people."

"Doing your part to give back the illusion of free will, huh?" When he didn't answer she continued. "I don't want to end the evening just yet but I'm not spending the night with you either. That might mean something that neither of us is really ready for."

"That just told me that you're considering it. I'll take it." The little boy grin that made Jane's knees melt appeared on his face and she sincerely hoped that she wasn't making a huge mistake.

The next morning found me lying in the one place I swore I wouldn't end up. Dawn was just breaking across the gray-blue sky and I lay on one side of Jared's bed, watching the sunlight spread across his skin. He was sleeping on his stomach and it took everything halfway brilliant in me to not reach over and push the hair out of his eyes, curling up beside him. He was...all right so I don't have a word for it. The more I tried to tell myself this was a bad idea, the deeper I seemed to fall into it. And I wanted to. There was no denying that, not after last night. Lord help me, but I wanted to wrap around him and forget the ugliness of everything else. It wasn't assisting my one track mind that he was incredibly beautiful lying on the white sheets with the sunlight crisscrossing over his skin. Before I did something else stupid, I slid out of bed and found my bag with my new phone. I needed to get out of here. Fast. Jared stretched and rolled over on his back, smiling in sleep. I felt something in me melt and I wanted to reach out and touch him, to lay with my head on his chest to listen to his heartbeat. Another thing I didn't have words for was how impossibly bad this could be if I continued to let him get to me this way. I crept around the room, feeling like an intruder while I got dressed and collected my belongings. I knew I should stay, that he would be upset to wake and me not be there. Yet another in a long list of brand, shiny new emotions and reactions for me to deal with. Zane had never cared if I was there when he woke up or not, even when things were good between us.

Introducing me to Jared Stateton was a cruel trick on behalf of the Fates with no way for us to be together. He'd accused me of thinking about it the night before. I wouldn't tell him that he was right but I knew that he knew it anyway. I don't want to hurt him. I don't want to be a manipulative bitch who twists the situation to my advantage without regard for his feelings. But I had warned him. And I didn't want to stop seeing him. But I couldn't let myself get involved either. Tyler had been right. I'd had a glimpse of that dark place in Jared's mind and I couldn't send him back there. I wouldn't do that to someone else, certainly not someone that I was starting to care about. And like it or not, I did care what happened to him. I did not want to be the thing that hurt him. So I called for a car and left.

I returned home to find Zane passed out on the living room rug. Glad to know that he was concerned for my wellbeing. After a quick survey of the condo to make sure that he was alone, I left Zane to his sleep and went to take a very long, very hot shower and see if I could scrub Jared's smell off of me. Halfway to the bathroom I heard the familiar *ping* of my phone receiving a text message. I glanced at the clock on my way back into the living room and groaned. Who the hell thinks it's a good idea to call before eight in the morning? This had better be an emergency. Zane was still sleeping when I grabbed my phone from my jacket pocket. I read the message as I walked back to the bathroom and I couldn't help the smile that blossomed on my face. Damnit.

In a habit of running out on me? - J

I dropped the rest of my belongings on the bed and flipped the keypad open to message back.

Tried to avoid most of the scandal. Want to get into more trouble?

187

I took the phone with me into the bathroom to await the response that I knew wasn't far behind. I didn't have to wait long and I honestly think that I would have been disappointed if I did. I had just turned on the shower when the phone beeped.

I want to get into you. Got a present for you. Might help for the next time you need to make a getaway.

I bit my lower lip, blushing as I remembered the night we'd spent mostly not sleeping. Shaking off the memory, I hit the reply button and messaged back, opting for honesty.

I didn't want to leave, I had to. You're too beautiful when you sleep for me to wake. Getting in the shower and would love to have you here.

Tease. Half an hour?

Bring caffeine.

8

Jared handed Jane her Starbucks cup as she slid into the passenger seat of his SUV. "Caffeine as requested."

"Thank you. I'd kiss you but we're being watched." She hid her grin behind the coffee cup, using her eyes to indicate the not-so-discreet photographer that was parked across the street, a long-range camera lens pointed in their direction.

"I thought you didn't care." He propped one arm casually on the steering wheel as he turned and reached for her, the position designed to allow the paparazzi photographer a clear shot.

Jane ducked shyly out of his reach. "I wasn't going to ruin your spotless reputation."

"I'm a rock star. We get off on bad reputations." Jane smiled impishly at him and grabbed him by his t-shirt dragging him close enough to kiss. His lips met hers for one hard, brief moment before he pulled back, straightening his clothes and grinning. "Don't know about novelists though." He put the truck into gear and pulled away from the curb. "Let's find out later. I feel like boring them to death today. We paid for some kid's Ivy League education last night."

"Just think, that kid might be the future governor of California."

Jared grinned impishly. "Is that a legitimate aspiration for someone?"

"Depends on whether or not they want a bid for Senate. Or a political tabloid career." Jane took a large, grateful swallow of her coffee and relaxed back into the seat. "You're going to ruin me, you know."

"Why do you think that?"

"Coffee, amazing sex, you're fire resistant, and you surprise me with gifts first thing in the morning. What more could a girl ask for in a fling?"

"Who said this was a fling?"

"I did. Nice try though."

"Hey, I should at least get bonus points for the attempt." Jared laughed while Jane did a quick cursory scan of his brain to see if he was really as unaffected by her rejection as he was pretending to be. She was slightly disappointed to find that the reaction was honest. "I do have something new to show you." He braked for a stoplight and pulled his shirt collar to the side, exposing his unblemished neck.

Jane touched the spot where she knew she'd left a bite mark that had been healing when she'd left him alone a few hours earlier. "How did you do that?"

"Funny story. If you hadn't been so quick to get up this morning you would've seen it. There seem to have been some entertaining side effects to having met you." He glanced over at her out of the corners of his eyes as he drove.

"Like what?" Jane asked cautiously.

Jared stopped for another red light and turned in his seat to face her. "Got anything broken?" She shook her head. "Anything you can break?"

She thought for a minute, reached in her bag and pulled out a pencil. "Will this work?" At his nod she snapped it in half and handed over the two pieces.

When he stopped for the next red light, he laid the two wooden pieces on his thigh, fitted them back together and held them tightly in his hand. Jane heard a few soft snapping and cracking sounds. The light turned green and Jared drove through it, passing back the whole pencil without a word.

"Frick." Jane took the pencil and examined it. "It's perfect. This just happened? You weren't thinking about it, trying anything, nothing?"

"Yeah. I was examining it in the mirror with my hands and it just, I don't know, healed itself. I tried it out on some other stuff. It doesn't seem to be limited to anything, which is useful." Jared shrugged his shirt back into place and kept driving, staring straight ahead. "It seems to weaken the longer I'm away from you."

Jane quickly dropped the pencil back into her handbag and drank her coffee, pretending to ignore the underlying intimate turn of the conversation. "So when are you going to tell me where we're going?"

Jared's face lit up like a little boy at Christmas. "Okay, I know that we need to always live this life and there's enough shit that reminds us of the past. You, as it has been clearly pointed out to me numerous times, especially do not want anything that draws undue attention or brings back bad memories. But while I understand that, I think there should be exceptions to every rule, don't you?"

She watched him deliver the monologue with some amusement at the quick redirect of the conversation. "Is there a point to this speech?"

"Yes, I'm getting there. Even though we need to move forward sometimes there are things that we miss that it should be okay to hold on to."

"You practiced this, didn't you? Please tell me it was in the mirror with a hairbrush for a microphone." Jane clutched her coffee cup in her hands and batted her eyelashes.

Jared stubbornly ignored the question and pulled into a car storage facility. "I kept something for you." He stopped in front of a garage and turned off the truck, handing Jane a set of car keys, complete with a mood ring keychain. "Those are yours." He got out, opened the garage door, and flipped on a light, waiting anxiously for her to follow.

Jane slid from the SUV, her eyes wide and unswerving from the dark silver gray car in the small garage space. "Where did you get it?"

Jared stood back and watched her examine the Corvette. "It's, um, how you, James was identified. James didn't have any living relatives and no will, so my mother took over everything; the preparations, the estate or what there was of one. There really wasn't much besides the house, which was a rental, and the cars. Eighteen and twenty-one are pretty young to pass away. Regardless, she couldn't part with the car because she knew how much it meant to James, to you. It's had a few minor cosmetic modifications over the years."

"Like what?" She looked at him with the clearest green eyes he'd ever seen across the hood of the car and he knew they weren't contacts. He watched her fingers drift up to the roof of the car, like she was getting reacquainted with something beloved.

"Well, for starters, the interior had to be redone. You kinda ruined it. I replaced it again a couple of years ago with more modern leather and carpeting. And I liked the gray racing stripes for the seats. Upgraded the sound system. New paint job, original color, new tires and hoses. Otherwise it's just as you left it." Jared watched her examine the car, hesitating before broaching the subject that he knew she didn't want a reminder of. "What happened to you must have been horrible to cause that kind of damage."

She looked up at him from across the car, her bright eyes a dark gray blue. "My chest was ripped open while I was driving."

He mentally kicked himself for asking and causing that haunted look in her eyes. "I'm sorry."

She smiled, her eyes lightening to a bright blue-green. "I was too. It wasn't very comfortable." Jane slid into the driver's seat and ran her hands lovingly across the steering wheel. "Why did you keep it?"

"Ask my mom. I was a kid." He sat in the passenger seat. "This was my first car." He smiled at the memory.

"You should keep it." She pulled her hands away reluctantly, dropping them in her lap as she continued to stare at the instrument panel.

He shrugged. "I always knew it was on loan. Don't insult me by not keeping it."

"I'm still not her, Jared. James unfortunately didn't make it far past the driver's door of that car." She tapped her chest in illustration, still refusing to look at him for fear that he'd read her emotional response in her eyes.

"I know and I'm sorry for what she lost." He moved closer in the tight confines of the car, cradling her face in his hands to force her to meet his gaze. "Oddly, other than the eyes, you really don't look like her at all. I'm not sure what I was expecting when I found you. Jane, you're not some old dream and I'm not looking for a fairytale. The car's just a piece of the past that I thought you might not mind coming back to you. I don't want you to read anything into it other than that. There's no ulterior motive on my part."

Jane felt hot tears of gratitude well up in her eyes and she blinked them back, refusing to show the emotion or the perceived weakness. "Thank you."

"I'm just returning it." Jared smiled and brushed her tears away with his thumbs.

"You don't get enough credit for being one of the good guys, you know that?" She reached across the gearshift and hugged him, overwhelmed by his gift.

"You know, I've been trying to tell people that for years." He nuzzled her neck then slid further down into his seat, a little unsettled by her response and the need he felt to protect her. "So are you ready to tackle today's list goal?"

Jane swallowed her uncharacteristic emotional response and smiled brightly. "What number is on the agenda for today?"

Jared grinned and held out his hand. "Give it."

"Give what?"

"Your phone. Right now. One of the list items was to not answer your phone for a day. You can have it back in the morning."

Jane looked at him warily as she handed him her cell phone. "Why in the morning?"

His smile turned more intimate. "Because I'm waking up beside you in the morning." He frowned at her slider phone. "What the hell is this?"

"It's my phone."

"Did the eighties give this to you?"

"Very funny. I just bought it."

"It's huge! And there's no keyboard."

"I'm told they're getting bigger to enhance the viewing options on the screen. Not that I understand yet why anyone needs to watch television on their cell phone. I'm just happy if the damn thing dials correctly. Open it, genius. The keyboard slides out from under the giant screen."

He played with it for a moment then set it aside. "Got a pen? I'm adding something to this list. We're buying you a new phone."

"Buying a new phone goes on a shopping list, not on a list of things you've always wanted to do unless your life is far more sheltered than ours ever will be," she commented drily. "So, what are you packing?" Jared pulled out his palm-sized PDA from his front jeans pocket and handed it to her. "Oh my god, you're a crackberry freak. I should've known."

"Yeah, I'm gonna turn you into one of them too. Make you join our cult." He snatched it from her hand and returned it securely to his pocket taking a moment to check its safety.

"Oh, so it's like that, is it? You love that thing more than a child?" Jane stifled a giggle at his concern over the phone's wellbeing.

"I don't have any children. Never have." He readjusted the phone in his pocket nervously.

"Quit fidgeting with it. Your jeans are tight enough it's not getting out, believe me." She laughed and held out her hand. "Your turn. Hand it over."

The shock was evident on his face. "I am not giving you my phone. This is not my list."

"Give it to me or I'll take it from you."

Jared leaned back in the seat, gesturing for her to come over with his fingers. "Come get it." Jane reached over and he caught her hand. "I'm not giving it to you without a fight."

Her eyes twinkled various shades of violet. "What if what I had in mind was a little more creative than that?" With Jared still holding one arm, Jane leaned over and undid the button on his jeans with her teeth. "Interested?"

"Mmm, but I think I'm hanging on to your hands." He shifted lower in the seat, enjoying the direction the morning was taking.

"Well, you'll need to hold on to something and I don't need my hands." She leaned back over him. Jared's head fell back, his blue eyes wide, his breath coming in quick gasps as he gripped her wrist tightly. Jane slid against him, her mouth moving over his jean-clad body seductively. He moaned when she pulled back and blinked in surprise when she sat up holding his phone in her teeth. She dropped it in her free hand, glancing at him briefly with mild interest. "What did you think I was going for?" She punched a key sequence on the device and began speaking into it. "Jared will be available to return calls tomorrow. Please leave a detailed message."

"What was that?"

"Changed your voicemail. Your password really should be more original. Our birth date? Come on." She turned the phone off and slid it into her back pocket. "We'll trade them back tomorrow."

"Oh, I'm answering yours. Especially after that little performance you just gave." He swallowed hard, sat up straight and re-buttoned his jeans.

"Hey, you're the one who didn't want any P.D.A. issues today. I'm just following the rules," Jane teased, reaching over to brush a wayward lock of hair out of his eyes. He smiled at the contact, his eyes dipping down to keep her from seeing how much he enjoyed the almost automatic gesture that to him seemed more intimate than anything else they'd done together in the last few days.

"Fuck the rules." He pulled her over to the passenger seat. "Think we can have sex in this car?"

Jane laughed, falling over the gear shift into his lap. She gazed up at the suddenly serious expression in his face and felt the most absurd overwhelming need to kiss it away. Opting to embrace the physical response rather than the emotional one, she licked his neck and kissed her way up to his open mouth. His fingers wrapped in her hair, framing her face as he held her, kissed her. A surge of heat shot through her and into him. She reached for him, frantically trying to touch every available part of him, causing his caresses to become more hurried, more insistent as his hands slid up her back under her t-shirt. Jane felt her body temperature rise quickly and opened the car door, climbing off of him. "Too bad I didn't wear a skirt today," she whispered in his ear as she stood. "We're flambé-ing anything it's not going to be my mint-condition, newly reacquired Stingray. Get your adorable ass out of my car."

"If I get out, can we continue this now?"

She shook her head negatively. "My body temperature's too high. We'll set something on fire. Not good in a place full of flammable objects."

"Where's the beach when you need it?" Jared obliged her, closing the car door and leaning against it. "So do you want to take this with us now or come back for it later?"

Jane looked at the car longingly, her fingertips dragging lovingly across the rear fender. She sighed. "Later. We'll come back. Otherwise I'll be distracted by either it or you all day. Or both."

"Okay." Jared pushed off of the car and walked back toward his SUV. "Stay here for just a minute?" He backed the SUV into a parking space across from the Corvette's garage. A moment later he returned with her handbag. "What are you looking at?" He tossed the purse to her and slid back into the passenger seat. "Uh, you driving?"

The driver's side door opened and Jane jumped in, a wicked smile on her face as the engine roared to life. "Hang on." She backed out of the garage and waited while Jared hopped out to close and lock the garage door. At the entrance to the parking deck she brought the car to a halt and looked at him expectantly. "Where am I going?"

"Why are you looking at me?"

"You seem to be the guy with the plan. So am I going right or left? I don't recommend straight. There's a building there."

Both hands dropped to his lap and he sat back, staring straight ahead. "You're driving. I'd say it depended on what you want to do."

Her look was challenging. "Anything?"

He opened his hands in a submissive gesture. "This is about your free will."

The light turned green and Jane turned left. The little gray car roared down the road, Jane speeding up to glide through the lanes of traffic. "Uh, this is going to take a minute. Got any music in this thing?"

Jared flicked on the radio and began flipping through the dials. "I didn't leave any discs in here, but maybe we can find something on the radio."

Jane reached under her feet and pulled out her small black leather handbag. She tossed it onto Jared's lap. "My IPod's in the front pocket."

His face screwed up and he curled back from the purse like it was a poisonous thing. "You want me to look in your bag? From my experience I understand that would be a bad idea."

"What woman screwed you over? It's not gonna bite you. Just reach into the pocket and pull it out."

"Seriously?"

An impatient groan escaped Jane's throat. She reached into the purse still resting on his lap, pulled out the tiny device, dropped it on his lap, and returned the dreaded purse to its resting place beneath her feet. "There, you didn't have to touch the terrifying object. Can you touch the IPod or do I need to plug it in for you?" she teased.

"I just wanted your hand in my lap."

"Uh-huh, sure." Jane rolled her eyes.

While Jared looked at the IPod like it was still a snake sitting far too close to his favorite body parts, he obligingly picked it up and plugged it into the stereo system. "Anything particular that you want to listen to?"

She looked over at him and smiled impishly while changing lanes and sliding around two cars. He forgot about the IPod and looked slightly nauseous as she drove through an intersection without looking to see what color the traffic light was. "I think you're in there somewhere now. Karina was screwing with the playlists the other day so I really can't tell you what all she put on there and what she took off. Surprise me." She slid the car seamlessly through another busy intersection without looking once at the road or the cars around her. The car picked up speed and Jared felt his nerves start shaking.

"Do you know where you're going?" He randomly pressed a button, unconcerned with what song came out of the stereo.

"Yes." She glanced quickly back at the road. "Does this bother you?"

"I don't die easily but I do still die." He fiddled nervously with the IPod. "How have you not hit anything?"

"Supreme concentration." She obliged him by turning her attention back to the road. "Better? Do you know how those things work? You need some help?" Jane reached for the IPod.

Jared snatched it away. "Fuck that, I can operate a damn IPod." He pressed the click wheel and rock music poured from the speakers. "How are you doing that?"

"Watch this." She accelerated coming up on a red light. The light turned green right before they would've caused a traffic accident by not hitting the brakes in time. "Kind of a cheesy mental issue to have, but very handy when you're in a hurry. The other I was doing by watching the road through you."

"Through?"

"Through your eyes, actually. Form a mental link tight enough and whatever you see I'll be able to see. Though we might need to be careful using it too much. Sometimes what the other person sees will override your own vision when you let your guard down if you're not careful and they have a strong enough emotion while they're looking at whatever. You have your new abilities and I have mine, though I suspect if you tried you could do both of those fairly easily." Jane parked the car next to a café on the side of a park and got out. "We're here. Are you coming?"

Jared alighted from the car and followed her into the café, relieved that for once she wasn't overanalyzing their connection or asking too many questions that he wasn't yet prepared to answer. She purchased an energy drink and looked expectantly at him. "You want anything?"

He shook his head and stepped away from the counter. "I'm good."

They left the café and wandered over to the park. It reminded Jared of an oasis. A little spot of green amid the concrete and glass of the city. He watched parents playing with their children on the playground as they walked by. He smiled as unbidden, wistful thoughts about how life could be came and went, as fleeting as he feared the relationship with the woman beside him would be. Fear borne from the seed of doubt planted deep in his psyche by his own determination to chart the course of his own destiny. He'd known what he wanted for over thirty years. Reality tended to twist fantasies into something different and as he watched Jane walk through the park, oblivious to the people around them, he wondered exactly how much his vision of the future would change. If he would even have one without her. Jared knew what was expected of him, what he would never escape because of her. And his time was quickly running out, a near impossibility when time seemed to be all you had. He looked sideways at her profile glowing in the bright sunlight as they walked and felt his stomach churn. He knew she'd leave, that she wasn't really his. Though he desperately hoped he was wrong. The one thing he'd never understood was why he cared so much about this particular woman. "Can we sit down over here for a minute?" He indicated a nearby bench underneath a tree, a little isolated from the nannies and parents with kids, the joggers running along cement paths, and the kids on random types of wheels that seemed to be on virtually every American sidewalk. Jared took her and pulled her across the grass to the bench. As they sat down, he pulled her IPod out of his back pocket with her headphones plugged in. Staring straight ahead at the late morning sun, he handed it to her. "I already selected the track. Listen to it if you want." He slouched over and watched the other park inhabitants pass by. "You know, it's completely ironic. I wrote that song for you. I hoped you'd hear it, that it would bring you to me, if nothing else asking questions, so that I could at least see you. It never occurred to me that you wouldn't hear it. And now, when I guess it doesn't matter, the freaking thing's on your IPod."

Confusion marred Jane's delicate china-doll features as she took the player. She reached over and brushed his shaggy hair back from his eyes. Even at the now-familiar gesture he wouldn't change his focus. "Jer, what's wrong? I feel like you just went to this whole other place."

Jared gripped his hands together so tightly that his knuckles began to turn white just so he wouldn't start shaking. He stared determined into the horizon, ignoring the sunlight glaring in his eyes and the fact that he felt like he was breaking apart. "Please don't touch me. Just listen to the damn song."

A quick touch turned the player on and a haunting melody filtered through the headphones into Jane's ears. The song was more of a ballad than the other Metamorphosis songs that she had listened to over the past several days. It felt like a dark ribbon swirling through her head, the lyrics breaking her heart with their intensity. It took her a moment to realize that what she was hearing was nothing but an electric guitar and the man sitting beside her's voice. And it took everything in her to not reach out to him, grieving the pain that she had caused him, no matter how inadvertent it was. Watching his face in profile she listened as his voice begged her to find what was missing, pleading to rip out all of the things that made him remember what should be forgotten. As the last mournful note faded away, she pressed the stop button but continued to sit there, listening to nothing and staring at the man seated next to her with unblinking eyes. Knowing that the song had been written long before they'd met at the sushi bar didn't make it any less difficult for Jane to determine exactly how she felt about it. It didn't lend any clarity to whether or not he really wanted to be with her or who she had been either.

As she continued to watch him, his grim expression became more tense, and she felt her brows knit together, her confusion growing with the intensity of her reaction to the song which she tried to keep to herself as much as possible sitting next to an empath. Several moments passed before Jane removed the headphones and sat with him in silence, contemplating the horizon. Finally he turned to her, his eyes as shielded as the rest of him from her. He felt something in him start to break.

"You'll never be in this the same way that I am. I get that. But now you know."

"Know what?" She touched his forearm, breaking the barrier that seemed to have popped into existence between them during the three minutes length of the song.

He finally met her eyes, and his eyes were the most startling blue she'd ever seen. "That I'm in love with you. I've always been in love with you, all of you, not just what died or what's living. It's killing me to be your fuck buddy and give you back. I realize this is a lot to dump on you, but you have to know and probably had already figured out half of it. You deserve honesty, Jane, and I've waited half a human lifetime to tell you that." A horse laugh escaped his lips that sounded almost like a cry. "All your talk about being fair to me and I'm fucking this up royally." He looked away from her, almost as if he couldn't stand to see her face anymore or the eyes that reminded him of what had been lost.

"May I say something?" Jane continued without waiting for his answer as if the question was just a mere formality to warn him of what was coming next. "I want you. I can't seem to stop touching you and I swear that you feel like an addiction, which creeps me out a bit since I babysat you and remember you when you were about two feet tall. You've gotten better looking as you've gotten older, by the way." They both laughed but it was nervous, hesitant. "Jared, I like being with you, but you know what I am. There are no options for me." She touched his face, bringing his gaze back up to meet hers. "You have no future here, just the present. If that's enough for you then I want to be with you, despite all of my best efforts to convince myself otherwise. But there is no real choice; no alternative. Essentially, I'm already dead; it's just a matter of time."

"You don't look dead to me." His hand covered hers and his bright eyes grew serious. "What if there was an option, a way out? Would you take it?"

She shrugged and smiled sadly, gripping his hands tightly in her own to stop them from shaking. "Doesn't matter. It doesn't exist. Sometimes free will is just a myth. I come with no promises and no guarantees. I'm sorry."

He blinked then squinted in the bright sunlight. "Think you ever will be ready to let go?"

She watched his profile as he watched the children play in the light. He was so beautiful that she almost cried. The urge to tell him what he wanted to hear to just not hurt him was nearly overwhelming. She gave him the only thing she felt she could, as much of the truth as she dared without raising his hopes over what might never be. "I hope so. But it's really not up to me."

He smiled softly, the smile more genuine as he wrapped an arm around her shoulders and pulled her to him. "So when are you going to tell me what we're doing here?"

"Should I be suspicious at the sudden turn in conversation or just take it at face value?" Jared shrugged and continued to smile. Sighing, Jane turned, propping her feet on the bench and laying her head in his lap. She slid her arm around his back, her fingers caressing the bare skin just under the hem of his shirt. She felt calmer just touching him and was glad that he had dropped the serious mood he'd been developing. "To answer your question, we're here just to be here. Taking a moment that's not filled with something else." She looked up at him curiously. "Don't you ever do something to not do something? Be still, enjoy the moment." She turned her head to gaze back out at the park.

Jared laughed and relaxed some, his fingers playing on her free arm. "The last couple of days are the most time I've taken off in years. And I highly suspect that either Tyler's covering for me or the world as I know it is falling apart and I just don't know it yet." Jane covered her mouth to cover the giggles trying to escape. "Don't laugh at me! I'm serious! I usually only sleep four hours a night."

Her body shifted against him so that she could meet his eyes. "What do you do with all that time? Don't you miss the sleep?"

"Being a rock star is hard work!"

A laugh bubbled past the hand she tried to clasp quickly over her mouth. She gave up the fight then struggled to compose a very serious face for Jared's benefit. "I'm sure it is." The face cracked and she began laughing again.

"It is!" he protested. When Jane didn't comment, he unceremoniously dumped her off his lap.

"Hey!" She sat up and flipped around on the bench to face forward, punching him playfully in the arm. "What the hell was that for?"

"You're not taking me seriously." He stuck his lower lip out, pretending to pout.

Jane nuzzled his neck. "Oh, don't be so pitiful!" She kissed him behind the ear, making him smile. "It's not my fault that you're missing the entire point of being nearly immortal."

He turned sideways on the bench to face her. "Enlighten me. What am I missing?" Jared draped an arm across the back of the bench, resting his hand on her shoulder.

She turned in toward him, propping a knee on the bench. "The joy of living! Of breathing, of just enjoying being because you are. Our lives are a gift. What's the point if you just work all the time? Are you capable of just having fun? Relaxing?"

He looked truly injured. "Of course I am. And I'm a little hurt by that statement. I thought we were having fun."

Jane straddled his lap, her arms looped loosely around his neck. "What do you do for fun other than this?"

A deep sigh escaped his lips. His hands slid possessively up and down her back. "I lose really badly at video games. I read books. Don't watch a lot of TV. Go out with my friends. I go to friends' gigs. You know we're going to get our pictures taken again for this."

Jane turned his head to one side and placed soft kisses down the side of his neck. "Mmmm...I love your skin. The way you feel, the way you taste. I think my favorite spot today is either right here," she demonstrated, "between your neck and collarbone or here," her

mouth moved again, causing an involuntary shiver, "behind your ear."
She pulled back a tiny bit and smiled. "I read everything from
children's books to Dante. I like going to the movies, I tolerate
shopping with my sister because she loves it, and I collect weapons.
Pictures being made yet? I'd kind of like the souvenir."

"Is that the only reason you're touching me?" His fingers
locked in her dark hair, holding her face less than an inch from his.

"I already told you. You're my new addiction. So what's your
favorite book?"

"*The Metamorphosis* by Ovid, hence the name of the band. What
was your old addiction?"

"Refrigerated Mars bars," she whispered in his ear. "This is
much healthier. You know *Metamorphosis* is an epic poem, right?"

Jared slid his face into the curve of her neck and breathed her
scent in. Vanilla, jasmine, and something else he couldn't quite
identify but enjoyed the curiosity of not knowing exactly. "Ovid
wrote a poem that's three hundred and eleven pages long. That's a
damn fucking book." Temptation won out and he closed the inch
between them, sliding his tongue into her mouth. A tiny, helpless
moan came from deep in her throat. At the sound, Jared's fingers dug
into her back pulling her further down on his lap. Jane tightened
around him, her mouth feeding eagerly at his. His crotch began to
vibrate against her thigh. She jumped, her mouth reluctantly sliding
away from his.

"That's a new function."

He slouched down and reached for his front jeans pocket. "I'd
like to take the credit, but I think that's my first call of the day." He
extracted her phone, slid it open and held it to his ear. "Hello, Jane's
phone...No, she's not answering her phone today...How did you?..."

He made a face and handed the phone to Jane. "I think you need to take this. It's Zane."

Jane took the phone wordlessly. Jared suddenly looked terribly uncomfortable. She reaffirmed her seat on his lap to insure that he wasn't going to try to leave, laying her head against his chest to hear his heartbeat while she dealt with the main source of stress in her life. "What's going on, Zane? Must be important for you to use a phone."

"That's why I'm using the phone. Have you tried using the normal way to contact me today?"

Her eyes met Jared's and she smiled, ignoring the blatant anxiety in Zane's voice. "I haven't exactly been thinking about you today which was the point of our conversation about separate bedrooms, if you remember."

"Yeah, your cabana boy's even answering your phone now." He rushed on before she could respond. "I can't reach you through the link anymore, J."

"What are you talking about?" Jane cuddled in closer to Jared, closing her eyes to calm her frustration at the unwelcome interruption.

"I mean I feel you but otherwise it's like you're not even there. Try it. What've you done?"

"Nothing. You interrupted me. Hang on a minute." She put the phone down on the bench and pulled back from Jared. She took a deep breath and reached deep into herself, searching for the silver strands that linked her to Zane. She found the strongest of them, the ones that attached them at the heart, and followed it, running into a metaphorical wall where Zane should have been. She pulled back into herself and as she did she noticed newer, stronger strands, gold ones that went from her in a different direction. Apprehensively, she began sliding slowly down one of the gold threads. She started, curling back into herself when she saw two bright blue eyes watching her from the

208

other side. She sat very still for a long moment before slowly reaching for her phone as she opened her eyes. She spoke into the phone but her attention was focused on the man in front of her. "Zane! Are you still there? Any idea what happened?"

"I don't know. I thought you did it."

"I can barely feel you; I just know you're alive. This is not good."

"No, shit. Why do you think I called?"

"I could come up with several reasons," Jane sighed, glancing up at Jared. "The only thing I know to do is a normal binding spell until we can figure out how to fix this permanently." Jane ignored Jared's warning look. She slid off of his lap reluctantly and stood. "I'm sure our connection's not nearly as fractured as I'd like it to be."

"Well I hate to interrupt your date." The words dripped with so much disdain that Jane felt a sudden urge to take a shower.

"Don't, Zane. Just start the prep. We'll be there as soon as we can."

"You're bringing him here?"

She gritted her teeth, giving up on hiding her irritation. "You fuck fangirls in my bed and don't change the sheets. Spare me. I'm coming because we need to fix this, no other reason." She ended the call and walked back over to Jared. "We have to go. I'm so sorry."

"It's all right. I'll catch a cab back to the garage." Jared stood, dusting his hands off on his jeans.

"You don't want to come with me?"

"You want me to?"

"Of course. This shouldn't take that long and I'd really like you there with me. I could use some magical back up in case Zane loses it on me again."

He hesitated for another moment before rising and taking her outstretched hand as they walked back to the car. "This is probably a really bad idea."

Jane stopped and faced him, all humor lost from her expression. "I could really use you there. Just in case something goes wrong." She licked her lips, pausing as she considered her next words before just coming out with it.

He sighed and put his arm around her shoulders, guiding her through the park. "Come on then. Let's get the uncomfortableness over with."

"I also don't want you to read more into this than there is. Zane publicly called off our engagement today which means he's probably already a little more pissed off than usual which generally leads to a destructive warpath." She held up both hands to display her naked fingers. "I've known you for all of a week, so I shouldn't give a shit what you think, but I do for some frighteningly idiotic reason, so just don't say anything, don't take it for more than it is, and if he goes off on you, please just ignore it and know that he says it out of self-destruction and spite just to get a reaction from you."

Jared grabbed her by the shoulders and bent down until they were eye to eye. Jane's face turned bright red with embarrassment when she saw that his blue eyes were sparkling with barely contained laughter. "I got it." He noted her mortification and hugged her quickly. "I think it's cute when you ramble." He felt her shut down mentally and kissed her sweetly to reassure her that he meant what he said. "Don't ever feel like you can't say anything to me."

Jane mock glared up at him, irritated that he was so close to perfect when her life was such a mess. "It irritates me that I can't even be annoyed with you. How's that for a start?"

Jared laughed, sliding his arm around her waist as they walked to the car. "Now why do I feel that there's another question lurking back there?"

"Do you feel any different today?"

"Yeah. I'm happy. Though I don't think that's the answer you're looking for. What gives, Jane?"

"It's probably nothing." She unlocked the car doors and slid into the driver's seat. "If it turns into something, I'll let you know. Is that all right?"

Jared smiled at her, slouching in the passenger seat. "I'll live with it for now."

Jane raised an eyebrow in question, but didn't comment as she put the car into gear and drove away.

9

Zane greeted them at the door to the condo. "You're screwing with me, right?" He eyed the other man defensively. "I let her out of my sight for one damn day and she comes home with a stray. I should've eaten the damn sushi." With a deep, not so heartfelt sigh he stood aside and allowed Jared to enter with Jane. He led the way through to the living room where he had laid out a large glass bowl already full of salt water, various glass containers of herbs, four white candles representing the four corners, as well as red and green indicator candles and two athames. A thick circle of salt surrounded the majority of the room with the spelling equipment securely in the middle. Zane stood at the edge of the circle and flicked his lighter. "Ready to begin?"

Jane stepped into the circle and knelt between the red candle and silver athame. Zane joined her, kneeling facing her with his oak-handled dagger at his right and his green indicator candle on his left, a mirror image of her actions. "I need another red candle."

Zane looked back and forth between her and Jared. "Oh, no. He cannot be in the circle. For all we know he's the one who did this."

Jared looked disgusted, maintaining his stance just on the periphery of the circle watching them both carefully. "And what is it that you would like for me to have done, Zane?"

"Ah, he speaks! Is my girl treating you so good that you need to come between us like this?" he sneered, looking Jared up and down. "Is that the problem, Janey? This one's your hot little chew toy?" Zane turned his attention back to Jared. "Or are you not special like we are?"

"Fuck you, Zane. It has nothing to do with you." Jane stood, moving to leave the circle. If all Zane wanted was to taunt her, she saw no point in staying despite the possible consequences to her and Zane's connection. Right now being rid of him was sounding more and more like a brilliant idea and this temporary separation might be as close as she ever got to the real thing. It might be a good idea to enjoy it while it lasted.

"You haven't done that well in a while, baby," Zane remarked snidely from his position on the floor, directly in between Jane and her exit.

Jane leaned down to look him directly in the eyes, her face inches from his. "I wasn't particularly motivated and you don't give a girl a lot to work with."

Zane smiled. "Funny how you didn't say that before he showed up."

"You never lit me on fire," she quipped lightly.

Zane reached up and yanked out several of her hairs, pushing her away. "I will."

Jared reached across and caught her, his foot brushing some of the salt in the circle out of place. "What the fuck are you doing, man?" He tried to pull Jane to him and out of the circle, but she pushed away angrily, her focus on Zane.

Jane dropped to her knees beside him, reaching out to take the hairs back from him. Zane slapped her away, knocking her to the floor. He dropped the hairs in the salt water along with several different herbs as he muttered a prayer to ask for the blessing of his work. Jared pulled her into a sitting position, his hands on her shoulders. Zane pulled out his athame and cut his right hand before Jane could recover and stop him. "I'm getting you out of her life." He lit the candles with a wave of his hand.

The force of the energy threw Jane back against the opening in the circle, tossing Jared halfway across the room and into the coffee table. He stood up quickly rushing back to the perimeter of the circle, being careful not to touch the pulsating energy composing the circle. He noticed the tiny hole in the circle and knelt in front of it as he watched Jane pull herself up from the floor. Jared shoved a hand through the small opening that his foot had made in the circle, vainly attempting to reach her. "Jane, get out of there!"

Jane watched, suddenly afraid as Zane's blood dripped into the potion he had made. "I can't. I didn't make the circle. He did." Her connection to Zane flared back to life with a vengeance, pouring his conscious mind into hers. Jane could see the spell that he'd cast to temporarily disconnect them, the hands of the witch that he'd siphoned his temporary power off of while they'd been in bed. A scream tore from her throat, the pain of his spell searing her brain.

Zane knelt down in front of her, his face filling her line of sight. "Yeah, I did all of that. Surprised that I could do something without you, baby?" An ugly grin twisted his face as he turned back to the potion he was creating.

Jane waited until he was occupied with his casting before she reached back through the small hole in the circle for Jared's hand.

"Touch me," her voice whispered through his mind. Watching Zane, Jared very carefully crouched behind her and slid his fingers under hers. She gripped his fingers tightly as she concentrated on the potion. Within a few seconds it began to bubble and boil like it was sitting on a hot stove rather than a hardwood floor.

Zane jumped back as some of the liquid popped up and stung him. "Nice try, baby. Doesn't matter if the water's hot or not." He slid back a bit, moving the bowl out of her reach. "You gonna let go of cabana boy to get to me? Didn't think so," he remarked snidely. Zane closed his eyes, put his bleeding palm into the flame of his indicator candle and started the incantation. *"Bring a piece of her soul to me, exchanged for mine. A piece of my heart for hers…"*

Jane looked back at Jared. "Don't let go." She watched Zane, absorbed in his work as she squeezed Jared's hands and closed her eyes, concentrating all of her energy on the emotions that he caused to rage in her. She brought them to the surface and felt the flames licking just below the layers of her skin. Jane shoved the heat outward, engulfing everything in the circle in fire. Zane cried out in pain, turning away from the bright glow erupting around him. Seeing an opportunity arise, Jane dropped down on her back and kicked the potion bowl over, extinguishing both of the indicator candles. The hot water surged across the wooden floor, scalding Zane's legs. It continued to wash around him in waves, held in place by the magic of the circle. "Damn it to hell!" His hands hit the perimeter of the circle, breaking the magic. The water sloshed over the salt barrier and Jane fell backwards, unconscious, her hand still gripping Jared's as if her life depended on it.

Jared dragged her limp body fully out of the circle and away from Zane. "What did you do to her?"

Zane stood calmly, brushing off his burned hands. "She's mine. Don't stress yourself, cabana boy, it never would've worked. Jane's always been mine. Though if you'd like to keep trying, feel free to hang around. *Our* bedroom's down the hall on the left. I'd stick around to chat but I've got a date." He looked down and grimaced at his charred, wet jeans. "Guess I need to change. You think?"

Jared glared up at him, disbelieving as he cradled the other man's fiancé in his arms. "She means nothing to you, does she?"

Zane knelt down so that he was right at eye level with the other man, but just out of his reach. "That's where you're wrong. She's everything. She keeps me alive. That's why she's important to me. She's fated to love me, that's why I'm important to her. She knows that she only breathes as long as I do. So you see, cabana boy, no matter what she thinks she feels for you, she doesn't, not really. Not because she doesn't want to but because she can't. There will always be a part of me living and breathing inside of her. No matter how far in you get, you'll never eradicate me. Janey just needed a little reminder." He smirked and stood. "See you around, cabana boy." He left toward the indicated bedrooms.

Jared sat silently for several long minutes, holding Jane, waiting for a sound signaling Zane's departure, not wanting the man to try to stop him though he seriously doubted that Zane gave a damn what Jared did for Jane. Finally he was rewarded by the outer door slamming shut. He slid Jane's phone out of his pocket and flipped through its internal phone book until he found the name he was looking for. His call was answered on the second ring. "Hey, this is Jared Stateton. I'm with Jane at her condo. Can you meet me here? I think Zane's hurt her…" He ended the call a moment later and dialed his brother's cell phone from memory. "Ty? Jane's in deep shit. I need your help."

Tyler gave an audible sigh. A mental flash of Tyler rubbing the back of his neck in irritation flashed across Jared's mind. "I knew this would end badly. What do you need?"

"Zane did something to her."

"I thought he wasn't supposed to be special anymore. That is what we're talking about? Magic?"

"Apparently that's not the case anymore because I just watched him pull some shit that you wouldn't believe. Ty, I need you to find out what he did to her."

"How bad is it?"

"She fought back and she's been unconscious since."

"Blood magic that went wrong I take it? You know who that means I've gotta ask for a favor." Tyler silently groaned, more irritated than he wanted to admit at his brother's insistent involvement in an unknown woman's life.

"I wouldn't ask if it wasn't important," Jared pleaded, hugging Jane's limp body closer.

"This better be damn important. This is like ten Christmases and birthdays rolled into one," Tyler warned, still hoping in vain that Jared would drop the matter and step away from the precipice of his own madness.

"I owe you."

"Yeah, you already owe me. Gimme a couple of hours. I'll call and see where you are when I've got your answer."

"Thank you."

"You're my blood. Even if you are a crazy bastard." Tyler sighed again before ending the call.

Jared set the phone aside and pulled Jane closer while he waited for reinforcements to arrive. He wanted to go and tear Zane apart. He held his hands over Jane's forehead and concentrated, praying that his healing powers could sense whatever was wrong inside of her.

Several minutes passed with no result and he slumped back in defeat. In all his memory Jared didn't remember ever feeling so helpless.

10

Karina arrived within a few minutes, confirming Jared's belief that Jane kept her little-known twin close by. He heard the outer door open and close, followed by rapid footsteps and a sudden screech of sneakers on the wood when she found them on the living room floor. "Jane?"

"Down here," Jared answered peering back at her over his shoulder. "I'd get up and introduce myself properly, but I don't want to move her." He watched Karina enter, surprised by how different the twins looked when they weren't trying to be perfect replicas of each other.

"We've already met." Karina came closer and to the side of him so that she could see the rest of the room more clearly. She took in her sister's unconscious form, the various magical paraphernalia, and knelt down beside the person left standing in the wreckage of her twin's living room, unfazed by his presence or the intimate way that he held her sister. "Maybe you should start at the beginning."

"I don't cast, not like this anyway, so I'm not completely sure what he did. I haven't moved anything but the cell phone since he left and that was in my pocket." Jared felt just as defensive in Karina's presence as he would have if he were being interrogated by the police.

"If you can tell me what's wrong with her, I might be able to heal her. I don't want to try without knowing what it will do to her."

A look of mild interest crossed her face. "You're a healer? I see that there are some things my sister left out." She smiled when his ears turned pink from embarrassment.

He shrugged, clearly uncomfortable. "It's a newly acquired skill." He turned his gaze back to Jane's pained sleeping face.

Karina crossed the salt circle and examined the remains of Zane's work. "What did he use?"

"The two colored candles, the white candles, and a bunch of herbs that he must've already mixed that he tossed into the saltwater. They went in too fast for me to be able to identify any of them. He cut his hand and dropped blood in along with some of her hair."

"Blood and candle magic, which you're not supposed to mix, and holy water. Fantastic. Even Zane's smarter than this. Whatever he wanted done he was trying to make stick and it backfired all over my sister."

"How can you tell?"

She gestured to the still-unconscious Jane. "Blood and candle magic are both high magic. When they backfire it hurts you, kills you, or at the very least knocks you out for a while, though I suspect you already know that." She grabbed a throw pillow off the couch and handed it to him. "Here. You might as well get up. You'll be more useful and she's not waking up for a while."

Jared took the offered pillow, slid it under Jane's head and gingerly stood, being careful to disturb her sleeping form as little as possible. "Why would it backfire on her and not him?" He watched Jane's brow furrow in pain then ease in her sleep.

"Do you remember anything he said, any part of the spell at all?"

"Yeah," he watched her as she examined the spilled holy water and herbs. "I don't think he finished, but he apparently thought it was enough. He broke the circle after Jane set it on fire and kicked over the bowl. He said something along the lines of trading a piece of his heart for hers and a piece of their souls."

"Ah, shit." Karina knelt beside her sister, one hand over her chest and the other on her forehead. "But you said he didn't finish it, right?"

"Yeah, well at least I'm assuming he didn't. Those two lines were all he got out before she stopped him. Why "ah, shit"? I thought he was supposed to be magically neutered or something anyway."

"He is. I don't know what he's done to get his powers back, but it can't be good. Did you say that Jane set the circle on fire?"

"Yes, Jane lit the circle on fire. I've been trying to help her control it. Guess it's working."

"Since when is my sister taking magical advice from you?"

Jared sighed. "Since I seem to be the only thing that she can't set on fire." Karina opened her mouth to respond but managed nothing but a surprised "O" before they were interrupted by a knock at the door followed by Jane's phone bouncing across the floor as the vibrate ringtone started. "That would be my brother, Tyler. I called him after I called you. Figured we could use all the magical reinforcements we could get." He went to answer the door, grateful for the interruption.

Tyler hung up the phone as the door opened. "You didn't answer your phone or hers. You always answer your phone. Freaking

223

crackberry laid babies in your head." He pushed past his brother and entered the condo.

Jared closed the door and followed the younger man back through to the living room. "Jane's got my phone and I strongly suspect it's heavily doused in salt water."

"What?" Tyler looked back at his brother as they entered the living room. In response, Jared gestured behind him. Tyler turned and stopped, gawking at Jane and Karina, who was attempting to straighten up some of the mess. "Holy hell! You weren't kidding. I mean I knew you weren't kidding but this is…this is interesting, to say the least."

Jared stepped past him and sat back down on the floor next to Jane. "How did you find me?"

"Not the hardest address to find in Los Angeles. I didn't hear back from you so I assumed you would still be here." Tyler carefully stepped around the debris in the living room to get to his brother's side.

"Were you able to find anything out?"

"Yeah." He glanced at Karina and rubbed the back of his neck like it was a nervous twitch. "You want to do this somewhere else?"

Jared wouldn't even look up from his vigil at Jane's side. "No, she's cool."

Tyler smiled tightly at Karina. "No offense."

She glanced up at him and went back to her work. "None taken."

He peered at her a little more closely. "You really don't look that much like her when you're not dressed up. You were doing a damn good imitation the other night."

224

"We're not truly identical." She didn't look up from the mess on the floor. Tyler knelt down and caught a glimpse of her dark green eyes. She glanced up at him curiously, slightly annoyed at the unwanted attention before returning to her inspection.

"You had a point?" Jared prompted.

"Oh, right." Tyler looked back and forth between the two of them and stepped further into the room. He pointed at Jane. "She's carrying a piece of his soul. Her whole one plus a small part of his. It's why she's still unconscious and why when she does wake up she'll probably be very sick until the spell's undone. If it's not undone, she'll eventually die because her body can't hold it."

Jared just stared up at him. "Thanks for the good news."

"No, the good news is that you saved her life. If you hadn't been here, were you touching her?, she'd already be dead."

"Why isn't this happening to Zane?"

"She's carrying it for him. She has a part of his soul now. Think of Jane as kind of like Dorian Gray's painting. She's taking whatever he does. Involuntarily, in case you were wondering," he looked pointedly at his brother. Tyler knelt by her head and stared at her face, in pain even in sleep. "I didn't believe them when they told me," he said softly as if his voice would wake her.

"When who told you?" Karina asked suspiciously, really looking at him for the first time.

Tyler looked at Jared. He shook his head negatively. Tyler turned to Karina who was still clearly expecting an answer then back to his brother. "Time to take this outside now?"

Jared nodded, reluctantly got up and led Tyler down the hall. They ducked into the first room they found, Zane's home recording studio, and shut the door behind them. "I didn't want to give her the opportunity to lock us out after you wouldn't answer her." The other man nodded his agreement. "What did you find out?"

"The good, bad, or straight up you're fucked part?"

"You choose." Jared leaned against the back wall, crossing his arms over his chest, feeling a headache forming behind his eyes.

Tyler paced the middle of the small, cramped room. "Zane's soul's on probation. He fucks up this time, he either goes to an eternity of hellfire and brimstone or cherubs and harps, depending."

"Jane?"

"She's free, Jer, as soon as the decision's made. You know dad's gonna make you choose eventually, right?" Jared nodded, his normally large eyes even wider. "He's agreed to give her the choice. You have to know that she has the option to stay with him to either try and save him or go with him. Or she can choose you. You know what happens if she chooses you. She has to know, Jer."

"I know that but I'm not going to unnecessarily scare her away."

"If you're serious about this woman you'll have to tell her eventually. Just promise me that you'll give it some thought and her some time. Please. Eternity with a woman who's pissed at you could be a very long time."

"What happens to you?"

Tyler smiled sadly and shrugged. "I don't know. You may not get to keep both of us, Jer. Most people don't get two soul mates."

"Four thousand years we've been together and now they decide I get to fall in love." His stubborn gaze met his brother's. "I will not lose you, Ty."

"Jer, you fall in love every couple of decades. Really in love? I remember a few times. Like this? Not once in all that time. And she's important to them too if they're willing to allow it. But you've still got bigger issues. There's a bounty hunter after that guy's soul. They killed a succubus last time and they don't just let their people die quietly. Now part of him is in her which makes her a target and she's gonna be too weak to defend herself. That idiot's also dating a black witch, in case you forgot."

"Terrific. He's hit the trifecta of bad shit for one lifetime. How do we reverse the spell?"

"Here's the kicker: you can't; he has to. Or she has to give him up. And until she's bound to you, she's a target for the black witch who's after Zane and the bounty hunter who wants his soul."

"What is it with this guy? He doesn't even have good hygiene!" Jared pushed off the wall and joined his brother in the pacing. "Why can't her body support the extra piece of soul? Aren't women made to be able to carry two souls?"

"You're thinking of a pregnancy. In that case there's an extra body in there to provide some insulation. In Jane's current dilemma there are two souls in there that are fighting for dominance."

"They're pieces of the same soul. It should be fairly compatible."

"No, they're not. She doesn't know that and you don't want to know what it cost me to find that bit of information, but she's not his soul mate. She's his protector. That's why they're reincarnated together, why they're tied to each other. It is literally her reason for living to make sure he keeps breathing. Believe it or not that moron was supposed to be a prophet."

"You're kidding me. A prophet for what? Drug use or the end of the world?"

"Neither, as it turns out. He's lost his powers because he used them for personal gain without adhering to his purpose. He drowns what's left over in drugs because he doesn't want to deal with it."

"That's great. How the fuck am I supposed to get her away from him now? If she's a protector she won't willingly leave him. It's not in her programming, not that I didn't already know that."

"Are you sure about that? It's taken you less than a week to seduce her away from him. She's choosing you."

"Sexually doesn't count. Not really, anyway."

Tyler fidgeted with impatience. "Zane has a very vulnerable soul so it's very desirable by people on the black magic side of things. Jane is a programmed protector, so it's in her to try to save him, not to mention that she's been attached to him for 976 years which is a helluva long time for a human. Most of them have been recycled in that time. She's the reason he hasn't been. Without her, he's gone. Our side will essentially do the proverbial washing of the hands of his soul. Left to his own devices he's not powerful enough to run amuck or anything anymore. He's fairly effectively destroyed what's left of his power which leaves him relatively useless to anyone who would intervene on his behalf. Other than Jane, of course."

"Really? What happened today?" Jared stopped and stared at his brother expectantly, his anger evident.

"Inadvertently courtesy of his new girlfriend. I have a feeling she'll shut that down real quick once she figures out what he did. However, Jane's now vulnerable to her magic til either she's dead or she's rebound." Tyler did his best to ignore his brother's bad mood and the sinking feeling that was taking hold in his own stomach the further the situation progressed.

"Shit." Jared began pacing again.

"You stand a good chance. We already know that she's attracted to you physically."

Jared grinned involuntarily at the flash of memory. "We need to know what repercussions this will have on us before I do anything."

Tyler ignored the statement, continuing with his train of thought. "The two of you obviously share some kind of connection. You've been healing things left and right. And you know she's unhappy attached to him. You can give her a lot he can't. Including life. The wild card is that we don't know who she's really supposed to be attached to, if anyone."

"How much time do we have?"

Tyler looked out the window and sighed. "Not much. She'll wake up soon and they'll approach her with the choice tonight. If she chooses you, you'll know when you wake up day after tomorrow."

Jared flexed his left hand, rubbing his thumb absently across the palm and the thin scar that decorated it. "Shit."

"Are you afraid?"

He smiled brilliantly. "No. And I really thought I would be."

Tyler shook his head, returning the smile. "You really are crazy as fuck. This girl Karina, how pissed is she gonna be?"

Jared hesitated, reaching for the doorknob. "What was your three-part scale again? This'll probably land us somewhere around totally fucked." They were laughing when they re-entered the hallway.

Karina met them in the hallway, blocking the door to the living room. "I would beat the shit out of both of you for keeping something from me that could possibly save my sister's life, but since I'm aware that would take a very long time which we don't have, I'll try to contain myself for the time being." She turned back toward the living room. "Oh, she's awake, by the way. And asking for you."

The two men stopped and looked at each other. Tyler stared at him, his hands flailing. "I don't think she meant me! Go!"

Jared took a quick, deep breath and went swiftly into the adjoining room, still rubbing his left palm like it was burning. He broke into a run when he saw Jane trying to sit up with Karina's help and Tyler watched any doubts fly out of his mind, the burning palm forgotten. Karina left her sister's side and held Tyler back with an angry whisper for an abbreviated explanation.

Jared knelt down on the floor beside Jane and pulled her into his lap, ignoring her struggling attempts to sit up straight. "You're okay! Are you okay? When I find that son of a bitch I'll..." he paused and backed down for a moment. "Shit. I forgot."

Jane righted herself and stared at him, her curiosity evident. "Screw him. Forgot what? What the hell happened?"

Jared reached out for her. "You're carrying a piece of Zane's soul, Jane. Until it's removed you'll bear the consequences for his actions."

"Then let's get it out of me."

"It's not that easy, honey." Karina knelt down beside them. "Zane has to remove it himself. If he doesn't, it'll kill you. Your body's strong, but it's not meant to hold two people's souls, not even one and a part."

Jane's whole body fell still as she sat back and absorbed the shock, feeling panic rise in her throat. "No. It's not possible. Zane doesn't have active powers. He couldn't have done this." She glanced around the room, her eyes searching. "Where is he?"

"We don't know where he is. We were hoping you could tell us." Karina exchanged a look with Tyler and answered the lingering question. "We think he borrowed them from a black witch."

"Which would bring me back to how do we fix it?" Jane demanded angrily, panic starting to creep into her voice. She closed her eyes briefly to seek out Zane and received a blinding amount of bright, shattered impressions from more places than she could readily identify. "I can't see him." Her eyes popped back open, her voice breathless with the pain in her head.

Jared cupped her face in his hands, staring straight into her multi-colored eyes. "We'll find a way. I will not let him take you again."

Jane's hands covered his and she attempted a weak smile. "I know." She reached into her back pocket and withdrew something which she held up for him to see. "I saved your phone."

Jared kissed her again, a little harder this time and she felt her knees begin to melt. "I love you. Give it back to me in the morning."

Karina interrupted. "She can stay with me."

Tyler glared at her. "She'll be safer with us. You're welcome to join."

Jane spoke up. "Not that I get a vote in my own well-being or anything, but they are right. Two people protecting me is better than one and a half. I feel like shit."

"Will one of them count if he's distracted by having you in his bed?"

Jared helped her to stand. "Whose bed I'm in or what I'm doing there is none of your business."

Karina's eyes narrowed as she regarded the protective way he touched her sister. "Glad I could help. Is there anything else you need from me or can I go?"

"Why are you being like this? They're just trying to help." Jane turned pale, swaying as the blood rushed from her head to her feet.

"No, they know more than they're saying and I don't trust it. I'm not leaving you with them."

"That part's true." Tyler rubbed the back of his neck again.

Jane stepped toward her sister, away from Jared. "Do you trust me?" Karina nodded and Jane continued. "This man will not hurt me. He saved me. And that one," she pointed to Tyler, "would rather die than hurt his brother. I'll be safe with them. If you don't think so then come with us, but I can't stay here. If Zane gets the opportunity to finish what he started I will be dead. They know something I don't need to know, I don't care." She turned to Jared. "If it's important that I know—"

"I'll tell you," he finished for her.

She turned back to face Karina. "There. Problem solved. Please don't worry. Do either help me pack and get out of here or leave. Please, Kari." Jane struggled to stay upright as she felt her strength waning. The piece of Zane's soul felt like a cancerous weight in her chest. Her eyelids fluttered shut for the briefest of seconds as she fought to pull it under control and stay conscious.

"You're completely impossible and a pain in the ass." Karina stepped over and wrapped an arm around her sister's waist to help support her as they walked. "I hope you know what you're doing," she whispered in Jane's ear as they made their way carefully down the hall.

"I haven't the slightest idea. I think I might be more insane than normal lately." Jane smiled wanly at the attempted joke, allowing Karina to help her into the bedroom to pack.

11

"Are you sure you have everything?" Jared queried for the umpteenth time as he loaded Jane's messenger bag full of notebooks, a laptop, and various electronic paraphernalia behind the passenger seat of the Corvette, the bag joining her duffel bag on the driver's side.

"Laptop, notebooks, clothes, toothbrush. Yep, I'm good. I'm only staying for a couple of days. Not like I'm moving in or anything." She laughed weakly at the attempted joke, leaning heavily against the car for support.

Jared pushed the seat back and straightened. "I've never seen a woman that packed this light before." He pulled her into a quick embrace, his kiss little more than a tease. "And don't give me ideas." He stood back and held the door for her. "Get in the car."

"When you have to run you learn to pack light." Jane stepped past him with a smile and slid carefully into the passenger seat. "And was that a proposition, Mr. Stateton?"

"Are you considering it?" With that he closed the door and crossed the short expanse of circular drive to where Karina was loading her overnight bag into the back of Tyler's Dodge. Tyler closed the door and awaited instructions. "You guys are going to follow us to the garage, right?"

"Don't you think it would be safer if we changed cars with her then," Karina asked. "You can move her to your car and I can drive the 'vette."

Tyler nodded his approval. "She's right, Jer. The 'vette's more conspicuous than a black SUV in Los Angeles. Maybe you should just put it back in storage til this is over. They might already have it marked with something."

"No, you'd know, wouldn't you?"

The nervous tick reappeared. "I don't sense anything, no. But, Jer, I've never seen this," he gestured to Jane watching them impatiently from the car. "This should not have happened."

"We'll take the car with us. If it is marked we don't need to leave it in a facility full of unaware people." He turned to Karina. "Anything happens to that car and she'll kill you."

"Noted," she remarked drily.

"Can we get this moving?" Jane called from the car.

Jared rejoined her, sliding into the driver's seat and putting the car in gear. "You still considering?"

She didn't look at him. "After all this is over, you may not want to know the answer."

"Give me three months and I'll change your life," he joked then sobered quickly at her expression. "I'm going to have to convince you, aren't I?" Jared remarked softly.

"It's not that I don't believe you, it's that I don't know how to trust it."

"I am who I say I am."

"I know. I just don't know a lot about who that is," she answered staring sightlessly out the window. Storefronts, billboards, miles of concrete slid past her gaze without notice. Instead of the streets of Los Angeles, she saw the world as Zane saw it. A hard, shiny place full of possibilities of ways to use his newfound power. And she could see her. The woman who would take her place. She reached a dark, manicured hand out and pulled a taste from Zane's aura, Jane's aura. Suddenly Jane was back within herself, the streets of the city flying by. Her pained cry caught Jared's attention.

"Jane!" Jared slammed on brakes, trying to watch her and the traffic as he frantically searched for somewhere to pull over. She seized, her hands frantically clawing at the air as the hole worked its way into her aura. Almost as quickly as it started, it stopped. Jane collapsed in the seat, breathing heavily as the pain slowly subsided.

"Don't stop. Keep driving. I'm okay," she croaked out in a low voice.

"What the hell was that?" Jared signaled to move back into the other lane, his attention divided between watching traffic and keeping an eye on Jane.

"My first turn taking something for Zane. It shouldn't have hurt like that. She didn't pull that much energy from his aura." Her breathing started to slow back to normal. She laid her head back against the seat and looked over at him. "I'm really fine. I promise." She reached a hand across the gearshift and squeezed his thigh reassuringly.

"Somehow I think you'd still say you were fine if you were shot and bleeding from the head," he grumped, covering her hand with his. "I'm worried about you, Jane."

"Keep holding my hand. I'll be fine." She turned her head to gaze out the window again.

Karina held her hands out for the key to the Corvette, watching as Jane moved from the car to Jared's truck under Tyler's careful scrutiny. "Before you start, yes, I know it's an antique, I'm aware it's important to her, and I will do my very best to let nothing happen to it. However, you need to realize that this is a car. You have my sister. I'm not sure what the two of you have going on, but if you do anything to hurt her, I will hunt you down."

"And kill me, right?"

She looked him up and down and smiled, snatching the dangling car keys from his fingers. "No, I'll turn you into a six year old girl." Karina turned and flounced off to the Corvette.

Tyler stepped up behind Jared; they both watched Karina walk to the car. "And that was about…" he muttered under his breath.

Jared grimaced and slapped his keys against his hand. "Let's just say if things don't go my way tomorrow night, you might want to start praying for me." Tyler made a sour face and returned to his own automobile without another word. Karina roared out of the garage in the Corvette. Jared winced at the sound as he climbed into his own vehicle. "Should I call and up the insurance on the car?"

"Possibly," Jane smirked. "Or just don't worry so much. She's only wrecked four cars, though two were at one time."

"Two at what? How?" he stuttered.

Jane laughed. "She flew into the driveway in mom's car and smashed into dad's truck. Totaled both of them. Took out part of the back porch too, if I remember correctly."

He held out his hand, fingers gesturing urgently. "Give me my phone. Right now."

"Not until morning," she teased, dangling it just out of his reach.

"Does it still work?"

"Of course. You think I wouldn't save your most prized possession?" Jane answered playfully, returning the phone to her back pocket.

"It's not," he replied honestly, stealing a glance at her. "How are you feeling?"

"Tired." She sighed, silently contemplating her next move. "I'm sick because of whatever Zane's done, but I don't need to be saved, Jared. I don't want you to be here out of obligation because of who I used to be or some white knight complex because my life sucks more than usual all of a sudden."

"So is it that you think I have nothing better to do than chase you around Los Angeles or that I'm this hard up for a date? Or maybe I get off on playing the hero?" Jared felt his anger getting the best of him but didn't bother to tamp it back down, wanting her to at least begin to understand how her words hurt him. "I've been in love with you my whole life! There are women out there who hate you because they could never measure up!"

Jane just stared at him, becoming more defensive because of his anger and her fear at how quickly their relationship seemed to be progressing. "Did it ever occur to you that I might not measure up? That I might not even want to?"

Jared cut across three lanes of traffic, jerking the car to a stop barely on the side of the interstate out of the way of oncoming cars. He unbuckled her seatbelt and dragged her halfway across the gearshift, until she was close enough that their breath mingled and she could see the torrent of emotions behind his eyes. "Tell me again that you don't want this."

She pushed his hands off of her angrily but stayed where she was. "I shouldn't and that's what makes me think there's something wrong with it."

His face shut down completely and the air rushed out of his lungs on a pained breath. "You think I bespelled you?"

"No. I'm afraid that someone did. Maybe bespelled both of us," Jane admitted quietly, her eyes downcast to avoid the pain she felt radiating off of him.

"No," he shook his head in denial. "Tyler would be able to tell if there was some sort of spell on us. He'd tell me."

"Are you sure?"

"Yes! My god, does it matter if there is?"

"I don't want you to wake up one day and wish you were beside someone else."

"You said *me*, not *you*. You wouldn't regret it?"

"I don't know what I want, Jared! Do I have to decide the rest of my life this minute?"

"We may not have a lot of time so you might want to start thinking about it." Jared smacked the steering wheel in frustration.

"I am not going to die today. Not like this," she touched his sleeve, realizing the déjà vu that he must be feeling. Jared glanced at her but didn't reply as he continued driving.

Karina drove her sister's car carefully through the early afternoon traffic. She became annoyed with the IPod and looked over to change the stereo back to the radio setting. Satisfied with her selection, she looked back up just in time to see a man in a Navigator barreling down on her in the wrong lane. "Oh, shit!" She slammed on the brakes with both feet, praying that the person behind her saw the oncoming truck and her brake lights. She squeezed her eyes shut as the truck came closer and she realized she had nowhere to go. When the loud crashing noises never came, the impact from the truck wasn't felt she opened her eyes cautiously and found the 'vette nose to nose with the Navigator. Its young driver looked as stunned as she felt. He stared at her for a moment then drove off, moving back into his correct lane of traffic.

Karina took a deep breath and kept driving, ignoring the encroaching sense of dread stealing over her being.

12

"All right," Jared remarked as Jane waited for him to unload the truck in the driveway, "where do you want these?"

"You're giving me options?" She rose up on her tiptoes, sliding her arms around him from behind and placed a soft kiss behind his ear, attempting to make some sort of amends for their earlier argument in the car. "I appreciate the gesture, but I am perfectly capable of carrying my own bags."

"And I'm perfectly capable of being a gentleman in my own house, so get over it." He touched the hand she had placed over his heart and leaned into the hug for a long moment before pulling away. He slung both bags over his shoulder and led the way to the front door. "We have a very nice guest room. I'll boot Tyler out of his room, but you really don't want to stay in there."

"Where do you want me to stay?" Jane followed him into the house knowing the answer to her question but wanting to hear what he had to say before giving in to her desire to be near him.

"Wherever you're the most comfortable," he answered diplomatically. Jane yanked her duffel bag out of his hand and walked off toward his bedroom. Jared smiled and followed her. "I hoped you'd say that."

Tyler jumped out of his truck as soon as Karina pulled in behind him. "Where the hell did you go? You were supposed to be following me. I just spent the last twenty minutes driving around parts of Los Angeles County I'd rather not think about."

Karina got out and slammed the car door. "Will you let me explain? Some spell-bound moron just tried to kill me."

Tyler's temper cooled in mid-rant. "What?"

"A guy driving a Navigator drove into oncoming traffic and stopped just short of creaming me."

He crossed quickly over to her. "Are you okay? Did you hurt the car?"

"Nice to know you care," she commented sarcastically as he knelt to inspect the front end of the car. "It's fine."

He stood, dusting off his hands. "Whatever drew the spell to you is gone now. Nothing on you or the car."

"How do you know there's nothing on me?" She crossed her arms defensively over her chest. "Are you going to tell me what's going on now?"

"I just do. Trust me." He hesitated then motioned her toward the house. "Jared and Jane are inside." He entered the house ahead of her, yelling for his brother. "Jared! Family conference! Tell Jane little Jared can come out and play again later." Jane came into the living room from the kitchen carrying a glass of ice water while Jared entered from his home office.

244

"Oh, you're just full of them this week, aren't you?" Jared dropped down onto the couch.

Tyler sat in the chair across from him. "The two of you can be separated. I'm in shock."

Jane flipped him off with her free hand and curled up next to Jared on the couch out of spite. Karina opted for the remaining leather armchair across the room, facing everyone else. "The two of you are awfully cozy for a few stress-laden days," Karina remarked. Her sister smiled at her and wrapped tighter around Jared, nuzzling her face in his neck. "I'm just saying." Jared smiled, his ears turning red from Karina's comments as he settled Jane closer against him, reading enough of her thoughts to know that this was only partially a show for her sister's benefit.

"You should've watched him obsess. This was expected," Tyler countered.

Jared blinked at him innocently. "As usual, I'm assuming you had a point?"

"I apologize in advance if anyone is offended by me being direct." Tyler turned to stare at Jane intently. "Time to hear the part we were hoping to avoid telling you. There's a bounty hunter after Zane's soul because of the succubus you killed. Since you have a part of his soul, you're pinging on their radar. They just tried to go after you. They got Karina instead and stopped. This could be a good thing. Maybe they just want that piece of his soul which we need to get out of you anyway. If you could just figure out a way to give it to them—"

"No!" Jane interrupted. "I'm not condemning his soul, even in part, to save me."

"This could save your life and by extension ours as well. I think you know it's not just about you and Zane anymore," Jared said quietly.

"One life against someone's soul. I won't do it."

"He's already fractured his soul. Willingly. You don't come back from that."

Jane pulled away from him, curling defensively into her own side of the couch. "He didn't know what he was doing!"

"We were both there. You heard the spell as well as I did. He knew. He knew and he did it anyway. To rip you apart. You wanted to be free of him, this is your chance. Give up the piece of his soul before it kills us both." Jared got up angrily and left the room.

"Zane has to take it back," Jane said quietly to the room at large, curled defiantly into a corner of the couch alone. "I won't leave him to die alone."

"He'd have to take it back willingly," Karina said gently. "Do you really think he's going to do that?"

Jane slumped back in defeat. "No."

"Are you willing to make that decision when he won't?" Jane thought for a minute and nodded affirmatively. Karina held out a hand to her. "Then let's find out what he's planning to do. Come on. I brought my herb kit. Let's get started." She glanced at Tyler who stood with them.

Jane nodded again and stood, still taking comfort in holding her sister's hand. She turned to Tyler who was watching them with more than just mild interest. "Where's the nearest holy ground?"

"Burying a body?"

"Casting off old demons."

"Ah." He stood. "In that case, you're standing on it. The house, the grounds are all built on consecrated earth. This used to be a church."

"You're sure?" He smiled and nodded. "How do you know?"

"We built it in the 1920's, when the church was beyond disrepair. We knew we were at the end of our life cycle, so we entrusted it to a family we knew would take care of things until we got back and were old enough to take it back again."

The sisters gaped at him. Jane recovered first. "That took a lot of planning. How did you even know that you'd be back to reclaim it?"

"Thirty-six hundred fifty-seven years and an average lifespan of one hundred and seventy nine years gives you a lot of time to practice. If you want to get your stuff, there's a nice, secluded spot in the garden where you won't be disturbed."

"Huh. Jared was only off by a few years." Jane followed Tyler to the patio doors while Karina went to fetch her herbs. "That's why you brought me here. You knew I'd be safe on holy ground."

"Black magic can't enter this place. You wouldn't be safer at the altar of a church. Just don't step off sanctified ground. Most recently the house and immediate vicinity have been resanctified. We haven't really gotten around to doing the rest of it yet."

"So why build over a church?"

"It's a nice spot and it's safer for us too." He held one side of the French doors open for her as they stepped out onto the back lawn. "The hardest part was trying to guess at the future of the area. Didn't want to make it conspicuous if at all possible." He shoved his hands into his pockets and regarded the position of the sun as he led her further away from the house. "We liked it here, before the Depression. Got tired of moving around so we just decided we'd come back from wherever we ended up."

Jane looked around appreciatively, enjoying the tree-filled yard which barely looked landscaped beyond the pool. "You couldn't have picked a more beautiful place."

"Thank you." He paused and faced her, squinting in the light. "I'd ask you not to hurt my brother, but I'm not sure you can help it. I do believe that you can try and be considerate of him though while you're going through whatever you're going through. He deserves better than this, but in all the time we've been together I've never seen him this bent over anyone or anything. So if you can't, don't, okay?"

"I want to."

"Yeah, but wanting and doing are two totally separate things, don'tcha think?" He motioned for her to keep going and led her to an open space between two trees. "You should be safe here for your spell. I'll go make sure Karina finds you. You okay?" She nodded and he turned to walk back toward the house, leaving her in the small clearing.

After waiting for what seemed like several minutes, Jane began to get restless. She wandered around the clearing and inspected her surroundings, finding little to interest her. She finally stepped into the shade, still within sight of where Tyler had left her and sat down wearily, leaning back against what at first appeared to be a piece of moss-covered tree trunk. Just as she was beginning to think that her sister had to be the slowest person on earth, Jane felt a sharp pang as something warm and wet seeped through her shirt. She bolted upright, wiping frantically at her back. The hand she pulled back was covered with bright, sticky new red blood. Rotting arms came up from the ground, seeking her. Before she could react to move, they snaked around her upper body, clamping her to the damp ground.

Jane did the only thing she could think of with her hands trapped beneath her: she screamed.

Tyler had just stepped on to the glassed-in patio when Karina rushed over to him, followed closely by a very concerned-looking Jared. "Where's Jane?"

Tyler looked confused. "I told you where she was five minutes ago." He looked annoyed by their oblivious expressions. "The clearing?"

"I haven't seen you since I left you with my sister to get my bag." She held the small backpack up to illustrate her point.

"I just saw you at the edge of the garden," Tyler insisted, pointing behind him.

Jane's scream echoed across the yard. Jared took off running toward the wooded area that enclosed part of the property. "Graveyard."

"That really won't do you any good. I can keep any living thing out of this clearing until I'm done with you. Now the dead ones…" The arms around me tightened. "…that's another matter entirely."

I looked up and saw a nightmare, a relatively young woman with darkly tanned skin and long flowing black hair approaching me. The same woman I had seen earlier through Zane's eyes while she ate a piece of his aura, my aura, with or without his knowledge. I wasn't sure on that last part. The woman would've been beautiful except…there was something *wrong* with her skin. It appeared to be crawling with something. As she came closer I realized the things moving across the surface of her skin were symbolic tattoos, each one black and written in an ancient text that should've made no sense at all to me. Surprisingly, I found that as their movement slowed, I could read them. Every one was a dark rune. This was just getting better and better. I tried to concentrate on using my new fire ability to burn my way out of my rotting prison. The flames sparked and died along my arms, refusing to burn even a leaf attached to the reanimated corpse that held me down. So much for a usable power. "You must be the wicked witch. You broke holy ground."

"Do these give me away?" She watched one of the tattoos float across her hand. With a flick of her wrist and a hastily uttered word they all vanished, leaving behind, as I had suspected, a quite beautiful young woman. I guess she would have to be at least reasonably attractive to attract Zane's attentions to this extent. From her appearance, I would've guessed mid to late twenties. From the power she exhibited, I knew that estimate needed to be much older. The woman leaned over me, studying me curiously like I was a science experiment. I didn't find it very flattering. "It wasn't that hard. You stepped past the barrier. This place hasn't been consecrated in a while and your soul's like a homing beacon now that I've tasted Zane's. Since I'd like to keep this as pleasant as possible while I kill you, you can call me Glenda. I have a great sense of irony." She straightened, flicking invisible grit off her fingernails. "So do we need to go through the whole "oh, why me?" thing or can we just get on with it?"

I pulled once more against the macabre bindings holding me to the ground before slumping back in defeat and settling for propping on my hands so that I could better address my adversary. "Yeah, I think we are. Personally, I like to know what I'm dying for. I assume this has something to do with Zane and his idiocy?"

"He's mine." A few of the tattoos reappeared and flitted across her angry face before disappearing again.

"Do I look like I'm arguing with you? I don't want him, I just don't want you to kill him." I sighed as I looked to the heavens for an answer. "So yeah, I'm afraid that warrants a "why me" as in why do I always have to die for that idiot? Things were finally just getting good." In vain, I pushed against the rotting arms again before my strength began failing me, causing my eyes to close. I took a deep breath before continuing trying to get the woman to see logic. "He can be your little bitch for all of eternity for all I care. I just don't want to die for his sins since I finally decided I'd like to live, at least for a few more years until I get a gray hair or a wrinkle. Does that work for you? Now will you please let me go?"

"And there's where we reach an impasse, you and I. Because he'll never want me completely until he's unbound from you." The long fingernails on one hand flexed out and back in, forming miniature daggers then returning to their normal form. That looked uncomfortable.

"You know if you kill me while I'm still bound to him, you'll kill Zane too?" I watched understanding dawn on the other woman's pretty features. "Forgot to tell you that part, huh? Did he also forget to mention that he shoved a sizeable chunk of his soul in me this morning?" I resumed my pointless, angry struggles against the corpse out of sheer frustration. "Go ahead, check me. Wanna kill me now? I dare you." I glared up at the witch and I knew my eyes blazed black.

Glenda the bad witch leaned down and sniffed me. I stifled the urge to recoil and held still while I was inspected. "You tell the truth."

"You sound surprised." I fell back to the ground, suddenly drained from trying to hold myself up. "The bastard's killing me. Again."

"Yet you would still keep him."

"No, I have no option in the matter." My eyes fluttered shut for an instant, snapping back open as I realized just how badly Zane's soul was draining me. Maybe it would be the best way to end everything if it just ended now. As usual I couldn't stop it, help wasn't arriving, and damnit if Zane hadn't gotten me into this mess again.

"What if I could give you one? Would you take it, white witch?" Glenda watched me interestedly. It took me a long moment to register what she was saying and even then it didn't make much sense.

I felt my strength waning and forced myself to stay alert, focused. "What do you want?" I tried to carefully reach out to Karina and I felt her panic as she looked for me.

Glenda stared me straight in the eye and I shut off the connection to Karina for fear that the witch would be able to see her through me. "Your freedom for the segment of his soul that you hold. You'll go off, do whatever you wish, and leave Zane to me. Unbound for eternity," she said simply.

"All right," I relented, "I'll play devil's advocate. No strings? You can get this piece of his soul out of me?" Glenda nodded affirmatively, rising from her crouched position on the ground. "He wouldn't be condemned?"

"That's his choice, not yours. I guarantee nothing concerning his free will."

"Where's the catch?"

"He belongs to me, not you. He will not be returned to you and you cannot interfere. You will no longer be his protector."

I thought for a moment then nodded slowly. The proposition definitely had merit. If she could do what she said she could it would solve a lot of my problems with one wave of her metaphorical wand. I felt Karina searching for me and could hear Jared's rapid heartbeat as he ran for the woods. I didn't have much time left to consider my options and I needed to save who I could. As much as I wanted to care for him I really couldn't say that Zane was worth my death as his savior anymore. And she would kill us. I knew that without a doubt. If I said no, this woman wouldn't hesitate to kill both of us and anyone else that happened to run into the clearing in the interim. The question became what was I willing to risk? "That's fair. I do this and you'll leave me and mine alone?"

"You wouldn't come back after him?" she asked curiously.

"Jane!" Jared came crashing through the trees and we were out of time. Glenda caught him in a wave of energy and sent him flying through the trees.

"No!" I watched in horror as he disappeared from my line of sight and threw myself against the corpse's arms, struggling to break at least my hands free, silently vowing to set the woman on fire. "Let him go!"

The witch's attention turned back to me, her captive, her arm still extended in the direction she had tossed Jared. "This one you would save, but not the man who would give you his soul. How interesting." She pulled her arm back and Jared came back through the trees into the clearing like a puppet on invisible strings. My heart leapt into my throat and I struggled to control my reaction. She'd kill him if she thought it would force me to make a decision. He glared at her defiantly even though her power held him suspended motionless several feet above the ground.

Tyler and Karina came breathlessly to the edge of the clearing, stopping when they saw the chaos in front of them. "Stay there! Don't interfere!"

Glenda barely spared a glance in their direction, her attention absorbed by her new toy. "Pay attention to your friend. I'll crush the life out of him before you can blink," she called to them before returning her full attention to Jared, beginning to strangle him slowly. "Though I realize you'd just come back, Anyasis, I do believe that she'd be dead before you got old enough to do anything about it."

"Let him go! He has nothing to do with this!" I slumped back to the ground, my body exhausted from struggling and carrying the extra weight of Zane's soul.

"Calm down before you kill yourself," Glenda remarked drily. "You're no good to anyone that way, least of all your little demi-god. Though if you're here, Anyasis, that means that Traegar's somewhere nearby."

Tyler pushed Karina behind him and stepped into the clearing. "Right here, Sabina."

The witch smiled. "So that was you who so kindly gave me directions earlier." Her form seemed to shimmer in the sunlight and suddenly she appeared to be a mirror image of Karina. "Though I believe you prefer this version, do you not?"

"Stop it." Tyler felt his face warm as his anger rose. He dared not look back at Karina for fear of her reaction. I could feel his concern through Jared and it frightened me momentarily that I could read him that easily. "That particular party trick never was that amusing."

She blurred again, reforming as herself. "The Golden Princes. I'm touched you remember me."

"I remember you trying to mate with my brother and being pissed when he rejected you. What do you want?"

"I found a new candidate."

"The musician? Isn't he a bit beneath you?"

"Not beneath your brother's precious mate, or is she even aware of that clause yet?" Sabina spared a glance for me, the person who was still pinned securely to the crumbling gravestone. I had a feeling I should really put more effort into paying attention to the conversation than trying to break or burn my way out of my prison.

The thing holding me down was already dead and impervious to anything I could do to it short of sawing my way out. Where were the hand tools when you needed them? And maybe an extra hand that wasn't trapped under my ass so that I could use them.

I looked up and caught the look of fear in Jared's eyes as the witch continued to strangle him. Pressure started building up around my throat. I glanced over at Karina and gestured to Jared with my eyes. Karina gave an almost imperceptible nod and melted back into the trees. The witch continued, unaware. "Are you already keeping secrets from your mate, Anyasis? *Tsk, tsk*. I always knew you were a bad boy."

Tyler's ears perked, listening intently to Karina creeping just this side of silently through the trees. When she got almost too close to Jared and Sabina, he held up a finger behind his back to caution her, praying that she could see him. I watched them, willing her to see Tyler's gesture without using our telepathic connection for fear that the witch would find her and use it against us. Thankfully the noise stopped almost immediately. Tyler closed his eyes for the briefest of moments in silent relief. He heard her bag unzip and drew the witch's attention back to him. "Is this payback or something else far too dramatic, Sabina?" He used her ancient name since she used theirs.

"Traegar. Ever the diligent guardian and protector. Don't you ever get bored with your role in his life? Truly it's only by happy accident that you're here as well. I just want her mate." She tightened her hold on Jared's throat and I felt the pressure increase around my own. This was not good. I could sacrifice myself but how far the ripple effect of that would go remained to be seen. If she killed me I no longer knew who I'd take with me. Watching Jared's face turn blue, feeling my own heart seize, I suddenly knew what I wasn't willing to risk. I would not die today.

"Take it!" I screamed, unwilling, even for Zane, to watch Jared die for having simply been unlucky enough to meet me. "Just let Jared go."

"You would permanently severe yourself from your soul mate for the whore Anyasis? I don't understand humans."

"I'm giving you what you want! Besides, you're getting the real whore here. Wait, does Zane count as a whore if he doesn't charge?" It wasn't sarcasm; I really wanted to know.

The witch laughed. "You know nothing about this one, do you?"

"People trying to kill me's kind of cut into our quality time. You make two attempts in one day."

"Better brush up on your mythology, girl. Anyasis and Traegar, the Golden Princes, beloved sons of the great god Apollo. Soul-bound to each other because no mortal or immortal woman was ever good enough for the perfect children of the gods. But you like to play with the humans, don't you? Reinvent yourselves every hundred or so years so that you never get bored and the women stop chasing you. By the time you come back around, they're so old they just think they've seen a ghost and go along to die in their lonely beds." She stepped back to me and knelt to speak in a stage whisper. "You know I've even been there once upon a time. Not a bad choice, but I must say I think you might be reaching a bit high."

I tore my eyes away from Jared's tortured blue gaze. The witch's monologue made a lot of sense if it was true. If we all survived this there would be plenty of time to talk about this later. "Are you doing this or not, Glenda?" I mocked, ready to get this over with one way or the other.

"Fine." The witch stood. "Would you like me to hold on to this or let go?" I glared at her in answer. In hindsight, probably not the smartest idea but the woman was seriously beginning to piss me off. "As you wish." She released Jared and he began hurtling toward the ground. Karina tossed a hastily mixed potion onto him and he stopped falling inches from the ground. She immediately released him and he caught himself on his hands and knees, coughing from the lack of oxygen. I saw the rise and fall of his chest and could breathe a little easier knowing that the witch's targets had dropped from three to two. Now I just had to keep myself, and by extension Zane alive. "Ah, look, the other white witch. Are we all just one big, happy family now?" Karina stepped out from behind the trees, keeping eye contact with Sabina despite her fear. "You people are just no fun." She turned to me. "Let them know that you do this of your own free will."

"I agreed. Please don't interfere." I stared straight up at Sabina. "Unless she kills me in which case murder the bitch."

A translucent bubble popped up around me and Sabina, separating us from the others. If she killed me now maybe everyone else could get away before she went after them too. I wasn't ready to go yet but it would serve Zane right for walking around with his head up his own ass. "Oh, I'm going to make sure this hurts." Sabina raised her hands to the sky in a chant, the tattoos flowing back into view along her skin. I felt a tug deep in my chest and a note of fear bubbled up inside of me. Suddenly, through my other sense, I saw Zane and the silver threads that bound us together. They quickly began to unwind and separate and suddenly I was back in my own body, staring sightlessly at the bright blue sky as I screamed, the burning in my chest growing until it felt as if I was being ripped apart by something with large claws from the inside out. Then, as suddenly as it had begun, the spell ended, leaving me feeling drained, empty inside and not at all a part of my body. My eyes were still staring unblinking, the irises gone completely translucent, when Sabina leaned over me, wiping my blood off her hands with a rag that had materialized from nowhere. I didn't have the energy to blink. I wasn't sure I was breathing. There was nothing but the white-hot pain still searing through my chest. It occurred to me then that I hadn't negotiated for my survival in all of this. "Nice doing business with you, Janey." The woman smiled and then vanished.

The circle fell and Karina ran to my side. "Holy shit, what did you do?"

Oxygen began to slowly return to my lungs and I blinked the film from my eyes. I struggled to sit and found myself still bound by now limp corpse arms. At least the grotesque thing wasn't still moving. "He's gone now. There's nothing in my head where he's always been."

Karina struggled with the dead arms, trying to free me while touching them as little as possible. "Just be still, tell me about it later. Where's this blood coming from?"

"My back and probably that giant hole in my chest. There's some sort of broken headstone back here." I tried vainly to help Karina pull apart the rotting limbs. "Who is this?" I blew at a piece of green decayed skin trying to get it off of my arm.

Tyler groaned as he recognized what was left of one of his brother's headstones. "You do not want to know. Trust me." He knelt down beside me and pushed Karina out of the way. Tyler ripped the arms off of the corpse and very gently eased me into a sitting position. "You feel okay?"

"I feel great. I just had someone else's soul ripped out of me. I feel like shit and smell worse. Where's Jared?" I put a hand over the sore place on my chest, bringing it back with a disgusted grimace when I realized it had landed directly on bone and muscle, Sabina's spell leaving a large, self-healing hole in my chest. As a bonus it didn't hurt anymore. The flip side of that was I looked like something from a bad zombie movie.

"Over here!" he called, his voice still horse from abuse to his throat. "I'm okay! Or I will be." I saw him rise up on all fours and roll over on to his back, still struggling to breathe correctly, as Tyler and Karina helped me to stand.

Karina saw the bright red soaking my back and I could practically feel the worried glance she shot over my shoulder to Tyler. "Can you hold her?" He nodded. She spared a sympathetic look for my benefit. "Sorry about this, but wounds come before modesty." With that she grabbed my shirt by the holes in the back and ripped it open, causing me to wince in pain, gripping Tyler's forearms for balance. Karina *tsked* at the deep gouges on my back, formed from scraping against various pieces of gravestone in my struggles. "If you're going to keep this up, we need to invest in a leather wardrobe to protect your skin, hon."

"I liked that shirt." I gritted my teeth against the pain of my sister's prodding. "How bad is it?"

"Flesh wounds. Cleaning it out's going to be a bitch. You got a lot of dirt in there. Now turn and let me check the front." I let go of Tyler and did as I was told. As Karina was peeling my shirt off, I looked back over to where Jared was still breathing unevenly on the ground. Involuntarily I touched my neck, the memory of the choking sensation returning.

"Please go check on him. We're fine here."

Tyler looked unsure. "I know he's okay. I leave you and something happens again..."

"You're two steps away. Please." I knew my eyes begged him to do what, at the moment, I could not.

He conceded and walked the few steps over to where his brother lay panting on the ground. "So, was she as good as you remember?"

Jared laughed. "Better. I think I passed out for a minute there." He doubled over in a coughing fit. "Of all the black witches that dumb fuck would have to pick the one I had an affair with a millennia ago." His voice lost its good humor and his face grew serious. "It's done?"

"It's done."

"She's all right?"

"She will be." Tyler nodded and held a hand out to help Jared up. "And the good news is she fought for you, bro."

Jared too the offered hand and groaned as Tyler helped him to his feet. "Don't call me that, it sounds weird."

"Would you like for me to drop you on your ass?"

"No, thank you." He watched me arguing as Karina fussed over my wounds and I pretended that I wasn't paying attention to their conversation. Karina's ministrations were breaking my concentration. "She still has a choice."

Tyler followed Jared's gaze back to the two women. "So make her choose you."

I watched Tyler help Jared stand and breathed a sigh of relief when I saw the brothers laugh. While they were distracted I turned my attention to my sister who was examining the rapidly healing crater in the center of my chest. "I still want to do what we came out here to do."

"The vision quest?" Karina answered distractedly, still watching the wound close itself. "What's the point now? You just said he's gone. This is creepy that you're healing yourself without trying. I'd like a chance to clean it before it closes up."

"Just trust me, Kari." I pushed my sister's hands away, annoyed. "I need to make sure I'm doing the right thing here. Don't look at it. I'm trying not to think about it. It feels gross. And Zane's not the only voice that's been in my head."

The last statement earned Karina's undivided attention. "Are you kidding me? Since when?"

"This morning. Maybe earlier if he's really who I think he is which I still don't understand, for the record. And the strands are gold, Kari, not silver. What does gold mean?" My voice was a tense whisper even though I knew Tyler could hear if he chose. The man could hear a needle drop within a three mile radius if he so chose. I was beginning to see the disadvantages of his situation.

Karina looked over her shoulder at the brothers with a newfound respect borne of a healthy fear of powers far greater than herself. "Gold shows the blessing of the goddess. If you're bound by god or his goddess, that's a whole different ballgame, Jane. It'll change any fate, destiny, or anything else you had going."

"Meaning?" I prompted.

"I hope you like each other." She turned her attention back to me. "I'm assuming you'd like to do that spell now?"

"I think now would be good. Let's go back to the house though. They're not going to leave us out here alone and that bitch already broke holy ground once today. I'd rather be somewhere that's been resanctified recently." I began walking slowly over to where Jared and Tyler were waiting with Karina close at my side, still holding my bloodied shirt.

"Glad you wore a good bra today," Karina commented remembering my half-dressed state. She watched Jared's eyes on me as we approached and leaned in close to whisper, "Do you love him?"

I absently rubbed my hand over the newly healed, unblemished skin on my chest, unconscious of the large amount of drying blood that still lingered there. "I don't know. I'd kinda like a little more time here. It's been one helluva day."

"You may not have more time."

"That's what he said earlier. I thought it was because he thought I was dying." I watched the brothers from new eyes, going over everything I knew about them in my head. "He's really sweet, hot as hell, and fantastic in bed. Does that help?" I turned my distracted gaze back to my sister.

"You offered a black witch your soul to save him. What's that?" Karina crossed her arms over her chest, unwilling to back down.

I looked up and caught Jared watching me, the brothers being unusually quiet. I had the sneaking suspicion that Tyler was eavesdropping. "I have no idea," I answered honestly.

"Figure it out."

Karina and I sat in the middle of a hastily made circle of holy water and candles on the dark stone tile floor of Jared's bathroom. Karina was focused on the small pewter bowl in between us that she had already added holy water and several herbs to. She was in the middle of sprinkling in jasmine when she looked up at me. It didn't take any special talents to see the concern in her eyes though at this point there wasn't a lot I could do to get rid of it other than to walk away and bury my head in the sand. Standing this close to the truth I wasn't willing to do that. "You're sure you want to do this?" I nodded affirmatively. "Do you have something from each of them?"

I passed her one of Zane's favorite silver rings that I had taken from our condo when we left which Karina slid around the base of his indicator candle. "How appropriate. Jared?" I couldn't help but snicker as I reached into my jeans pocket and handed over the blackberry that was still residing with me, thankfully no worse for the day that it had endured in my pocket.

"Don't hurt it."

Karina bit her lower lip to hide her amusement and said nothing as she placed the phone next to his red candle. She handed me a round rose quartz star crystal and a small piece of paper. "All right. Hang on to this, say the spell with me, close your eyes and clear your mind. We'll do this as long as we have to. The important thing is for you to not fight it and let it take you where it needs to take you, show you what it needs to show you, not what you want to see. Any questions?"

"What if it doesn't work?"

"Then you're not meant to see. And it may show you something you don't like. Just keep an open mind. I'll be here the whole time. If you're out too long or something bad starts happening I'll pull you out. I promise."

I nodded, suddenly nervous. "Thank you."

"Don't thank me yet." We each looked down at our pages and began reciting the spell. My eyes drifted closed and my breathing slowed as I relaxed. Bits and pieces of pictures flashed by like a film in fast forward playing on the backs of my eyelids. When it slowed to real time, I saw myself as an old woman in a turn of the century house with high plaster ceilings and oak floors, standing in front of a large wooden staircase. I was hugging two small children, a boy and a girl, and greeting their parents, my own children. Children I'd never dared to dream I'd have. They were followed by a man with silver hair and bright eyes that glowed when he looked at me. I felt my heart both surge and break a little at the sight of him, knowing that what I was seeing would be both the beginning and the end of two very different dreams. I watched the day happen with what could be my family. Watched myself curl in a very familiar position with my head on the man's chest and my hand over his heart as he drifted off to sleep with me in his arms and exhaled his last breath. When I knew he was gone, I felt myself going too, and I woke up, lying on the bathroom floor with silent tears streaming down my face and Karina leaning over me, a worried frown creasing her brow.

"Did you see what you needed to see?"

I sat up, nodding, not sure how to fully express what I had just experienced and a little afraid that if I voiced it, it wouldn't happen. I reached around blindly grasping at my athame, my vision still blurred by tears. I found the small dagger, picked it up and sliced open a small section of my left palm, holding it over the goddess's candle. "I ask that you bind me to my soul mate." My determined stare didn't flinch as the flames rose up to lick the blood that dripped from the self-inflicted wound. I don't know why I was so certain in my decision but I was. I actually don't think I'd been that certain of anything in a long time. And I wasn't frightened. "In the name of the god and goddess, I ask that you bind me to my true soul mate."

Karina sat back stunned as the flames rose up around my hand, accepting the gift, then slowly receded, leaving my hand healed and unharmed except for a small raised scar. She swallowed hard, still staring at my hand and the slowly extinguishing candles. "Blessed be."

"Blessed be," I echoed, staring at the new shiny scar on my left hand. "Please don't tell Jared or Tyler. Let me."

The shocked expression remained stagnant on Karina's face. "Jane, even if I would tell them anything, I wouldn't know what to tell them right now. What did you just do?"

264

"I chose." I rubbed my palm absently, staring at nothing while Karina drew back from me. I think for the first time she was afraid of me.

13

A while later I stood blissfully in the shower, allowing the hot water to slide calmingly over my abused body. I opened my eyes and looked around at the large walk-in natural rock shower with its waterfall showerhead and copper-plated hardware. Steam rose from the floor and I sighed as my muscles began to relax, reaching for Jared's organic ginger shampoo. I soaped up my hair, being careful to rinse it forward to avoid soap dripping in the marks on my back that still burned. I looked down and watched the blood drip off my fully healed chest, the red a vacant reminder of what wasn't there anymore. Honestly I don't know if I was really that calm about it or if I was still in shock. Most of my days, even my worst ones, don't end with me still alive. I'd put off so much waiting for the end to come. Now that the future stretched out before me I didn't know what to do with it. And I didn't know what to do with the man who had at least been partially responsible for giving it to me.

My fingers massaged conditioner into my long wet hair and I closed my eyes, instinctively reaching out with my mind and finding absolutely nothing where Zane used to be. I felt a momentary sadness at the loss followed by a surge of relief as the realization of my sudden freedom set in, tempered with the knowledge of what I had done just after being given my life back. I had tied myself to someone else.

Someone who I really didn't know, if Sabina was to be believed. I had faith in a higher power, I believed in God. I wasn't sure that I believed in the same gods as the ancient Greeks or that the man I'd been sleeping with for the last several days was one of them. That was kind of a big thing to leave out of conversation when we were supposed to be getting to know each other. It did make a certain amount of sense though. Explained why I couldn't get a good read on him. Demi-god wasn't something I normally looked for in a person, magical or not. Regardless, I couldn't just dismiss that he had been in my head. I wouldn't tell him he was right the other night but I was almost certain he knew that he was. I also knew that whether I liked it or not someone upstairs had decided to bind us together, for better or for worse. I didn't know if that meant I couldn't get out of it if I pitched a bitch fit but the twisted part was that I wasn't sure I wanted to. What if I could have the life I saw in my vision quest? Did I really want a husband, kids, the white picket fence? Or would someone else just come after me? Would I burn the fence down?

What if I just didn't tell him, ran away to London or Rome, somewhere I'd never been before? I could go lie on my glacier and listen to it move forever or until it cracked and swallowed me into oblivion. Even there I had the sneaking suspicion that Jared Stateton would somehow find me. And the thought wasn't nearly as unwelcome as a part of me wished it was. I washed the conditioner out of my hair and began to smile at the thought of being able to go anywhere without the cloud of worry hanging over my head that I would soon die for someone else's mistakes. It was a very liberating fantasy. I could move, start over. I smiled in earnest as the increasingly familiar scent of Jared's soap grew stronger in the hot steam rising from the water as I bathed and I knew that despite my lingering fantasies my decision had already been made.

Memories flooded my senses, images of his smile, flashes of his hands gliding along my skin and I shivered even in the hot water. A tiny moan escaped my throat and I felt my body quiver in places that

268

hadn't felt really alive in years. I felt a tug on the gold strands that would bind me and I started to panic, feeling my freedom being ripped away, replaced by the lead that had resided on my shoulders for my entire existence. Panicking, I took a washcloth and began to vigorously clean my skin, more of an attempt to wash away the unseen brand that seemed to be forming there than anything else. The washcloth scraped against the still tender spot on my left palm and I looked down at the barely visible thin, shiny scar. I rubbed at the spot thoughtfully with my thumb, going over the vision and my decision from earlier, remembering Jared rubbing the same spot on his own hand when I had woken up that afternoon. There had been a choice. I knew it. I pictured the bright blue eyes waiting for me at the end of all of those golden strands and the panic drifted away with the water rushing down the drain. For the first time I felt at peace with the future and the certainty that I knew existed for it. A future that for once did not center around my imminent demise. A life alone suddenly didn't seem so entertaining anymore. I closed my eyes and stepped back under the running water. I had begun to gently clean my back when a knock sounded at the door. "Yes?"

The door opened a bit, just enough to let sound in to the bathroom. "You all right in there?" Jared's voice was still a little muffled by both the door and the running water. He leaned against the doorframe, his head against the small opening. I could hear Karina and Tyler arguing in the background.

"Yeah, just enjoying your shower. And trying to clean out these cuts on my back." I struggled with the impulse to mentally reach out and see what his reaction would be.

He paused at the opening I had given him, and I could almost feel him wondering if it was too obvious. Curiosity won out and he quickly decided he didn't care. "Want some help?"

There was a long, silent moment before I responded. I didn't want to seem too eager. I knew he wanted a relationship but I wasn't entirely sure he knew precisely what he'd signed up for. I sure as hell hadn't. Really, I was waiting for the buyer's remorse to set in. "Sure."

"I'll go get Karina." He held his place at the door, listening to see if I took his out. Why would I need an out when I was the one who'd given him the opening in the first place?

"I meant you, if you don't mind."

Jared stepped inside. I could hear him closing and locking the door. He walked across the tile floor to the shower door silently on bare feet. "Are you coming out or should I come in there?" He leaned against the wall beside the door to await my answer. I watched his silhouette through the opaque glass of the shower.

I opened the door and leaned out, a sarcastic glare to compliment his smile. "You're really going to make me work for this, aren't you?" I grabbed him by the shirt and pulled him into the shower with me. I'd already thrown caution to the wind and under a bus. Might as well jump in with both feet. No point in doing anything halfway at this point. "Get in here."

Jared laughed, pulling the shower door closed behind him. "Yes, ma'am."

I drug him under the showerhead with me. His smile lit up the space as I brought his mouth down to mine. That little boy grin of his hadn't failed yet to make my knees weak or keep me from falling willingly into his arms. His hands slid down my back and I felt no pain, just a warm prickling sensation where the wounds were. His lips kissed their way down to my shoulder, then he turned me in his arms, moving me far enough away to trail his fingers across the newly smooth, unblemished skin of my back, checking his work. One hand stopped at the tattoo on my shoulder which I knew still held tiny, flat shiny scarring imprints of his teeth surrounding it. He kissed the mark reverently, causing me to shiver even in the hot water. When he pulled back, he held his hands over the mark to heal it. I turned and stopped him, grabbing his wrists, realizing that I'd made myself truly vulnerable to this man and not caring. I was suddenly more aware of him than anything else. "Don't. I like that it's scarring. I had hoped it would," I finished almost in a whisper as he stepped closer.

"Wounds are clean." He took another small step toward me in the close confines of the shower. I could feel him fighting with himself to not reach out and grab me.

I didn't move. "If you're asking if I want you to stay or go, I most definitely want you to stay. Hence the invitation."

His smile grew impish and his eyes darkened as he gazed at me. "Do I have an incentive for this?"

My head tilted to one side as I regarded him curiously. "You must be really uncomfortable." I allowed my hands to drift lazily up under the wet t-shirt plastered to his skin. He held his arms up over his head, making it easier for me to pull it off while continuing to passively watch me touch him. I tossed the wet shirt over the top of the shower to the tile floor.

"So where's your one place today?" Jared growled in a low voice, his hands sliding along my skin and I felt it heat instantly at the relatively small amount of contact.

"Oh I think I should get more than one now. Don't you?" I batted my eyelashes playfully at him. "I think I'll start here, right over your heart." In light of the rest of my week, slowing down now didn't seem like a plausible option. It didn't help me at all that I didn't want to, that the thought of leaving this place and never looking back didn't cross my mind. I wanted this, didn't I? One glance at the man standing half-dressed under the water in front of me let me know that at least part of me really wanted this new arrangement to work. I decided to let that part of me run my body for a while. I first kissed then licked the spot over his heart, bracing myself with my hands on his stomach. "I can't decide if my favorite spot today is here," I ran the tip of my tongue up the center of his chest in illustration, "or here," I started at his collarbone and worked my way up to just behind his left ear.

"Do you go lower after that?" his voice was a tiny bit shakier than he had intended and it made me smile with satisfaction knowing that I unnerved him just as much as he did me.

"Of course not. My hands go lower," I demonstrated, fingertips gliding down his stomach with the trails of running water to the waistband of his low slung jeans, watching him watch me the entire time. "My mouth stays up here." I bit the spot between his neck and collarbone that had already once held impressions of my teeth as my fingers worked to unfasten his belt and jeans. I pushed his remaining clothing to the floor, my face back just far enough that I could meet his eyes. "It's no fun for me to be the only one with an addiction."

Jared's eyes searched mine for some hint of uncertainty as he pulled me to him. I knew what he saw and he found no hesitation in my gaze, in my touch, nothing but a burning need for him in my kiss. I felt my body give in to him as all of my other fears and concerns floated away on the steam. Jared's mouth latched onto mine and suddenly his hands were everywhere, fingertips memorizing every nuance of my arms, chest, back. Like he was trying to remember everything for when I was gone. If he knew what I knew he wouldn't bother. Or maybe he would. It hadn't occurred to me until that moment that even though he wanted a relationship on the surface that at his core he might not want what we'd both been signed up for. He had just as much of a reason to run from this as I did. Maybe more considering I'd almost died twice in one day. A little voice in the back of my head screamed at the insanity of the situation. I pushed it away, wanting to enjoy my life for just this moment, whether it lasted or not. Nothing that we were doing was wrong. Even if I wanted to try to convince myself that it was it wouldn't have worked. Touching him felt too much like home and it gave me the only true peace I'd known in my entire existence. In that moment, all I wanted was to feel Jared's body light my skin on fire. Little incoherent, helpless noises came from deep within my throat and I could physically feel his reaction. He picked me up, wrapping my legs around his waist. He leaned us both back against the wall and I felt his desire build as he relished the feel of me sliding against his body. A tiny moan of protest escaped my throat as he broke away from my mouth to trail hard kisses down the front of my body. I sagged against the wall, my fingers locked in his dark hair, the flames building and setting my skin on fire. When my fingertips began to tingle sense returned long enough for me to pull one hand away and put it under the running water, the fire bolt sparking out of my fingertips, flames extinguishing under the hot water, absorbed as easily as it was in the sand. Jared jumped up and back as one of the tiny embers touched his shoulder on its way to the drain, his movements nearly sluggish and his eyes passion-glazed. "What was that?"

I smiled lazily and reached out for him, pulling him back into my embrace. "I learned a new trick. You may be fire resistant but I didn't want to set your house on fire."

His smile returned, his arms wrapping around me. "Mmm. Would hate to call the insurance company for that." He met my eyes and his expression softened even further for a moment. "Jane, I…"

I placed a finger over his mouth to quiet him. "Not right now. Right now, just be with me."

Jane lay on her side, watching the rise and fall of Jared's chest as he slumbered. Tiny slivers of moonlight filtered through the windows to break up the shadows obscuring his face. The light brought back flashes of the night they'd had sex on the beach, the deep honesty, intimacy that she'd felt watching him like that. Like there was nothing left to hide. She gazed at him, relaxed and peaceful in sleep, while thoughts and memories ran a riotous pattern through her head. The very thing she'd wanted for so long, dreamed about, had been just within her grasp. And the only thing she could think about was the one thing she shouldn't want. Jane couldn't reason going from one completely bound relationship to another. And with someone she knew basically nothing about. It was irrational, illogical. And as she watched him sleep, she wasn't completely sure if it mattered anymore. She was actually pretty sure that nothing else mattered anymore. She reached out and tentatively touched his chest, wondering what she would feel, or if she would feel anything if she walked away now. It had only been a few days. That was nothing compared to the lifetimes they had lived through. Jared's sleeping form didn't flinch at the touch of her hand. Her eyes closed briefly, her mind considering the possibilities, the consequences of her actions, the longing that she'd felt during the vision quest when she'd seen herself as a much older woman laying her head on his chest and her hand over his heart. Jane had a moment of self-loathing for feeling so vulnerable in this man's presence. But as she opened her eyes and saw the look on his angel face as he slept, she truly didn't believe she could sleep next to him another night without touching him.

Jared watched Jane watch him from under the fringe of his long black lashes. He couldn't quite fathom how she found just being with him more intimate than sex. It amazed him at how comfortable he was with the whole situation, how easily he'd adapted to having her in his life. And how much he didn't want her to fear being with him. He kept his breathing under control and fought to not smile at her hesitation as she touched his chest. He wanted badly to see what she would do and he knew she'd recoil to her own side of the bed the instant she knew he was awake. After all the years of living alone, just him and his brother, Jared enjoyed the idea of continuing his existence

274

the three of them. He'd never be unbound from his brother, he knew that as well as he breathed. He didn't want to lose Tyler, not even for Jane. But the idea that they could all three co-exist… There had to be a way for him to keep both of them. He watched Jane slide across the narrow expanse of the bed separating them, being careful not to disturb him, to settle curled against his side, her head on his chest and her hand over his heart. He instinctively relaxed against her, his arms wrapping protectively around her before he could stop it. Jared felt her start, then relax when his breathing didn't change. Her breathing slowed to deep, even breaths and he held her a little tighter as he drifted off to sleep.

14

Consciousness slowly returned to Jane's being. She rebelled, keeping her eyes firmly shut against the bright intrusion of sunlight. She snuggled in closer and sighed contentedly just before she felt what she was curled up against shift and stretch. Jane jerked into awareness, jumping up and falling onto the opposite side of the bed, her eyes wide with fear. Jared laughed and pushed up on his elbows, his blue eyes shining.

"Wow, you wake up fast."

Jane scooted back to the edge of the bed, pulling the sheet with her, covering herself to her shoulders, her fuzzy brain still trying to piece together the last several hours. "I'm sorry, I shouldn't have…" she stammered nervously.

"Sorry for what?" he laughed. "Sorry you went to sleep in my arms or sorry you enjoyed it?"

"No, it's just, I didn't mean…"

"To touch me?" He pushed the sheet aside and crawled closer to her. "Yeah, because you've never done that before."

"It's not the same. Shit! What is wrong with me?" Jane held up a hand to stop him from coming any closer. "Oh, no. You stay there. You make everything all weird and fuzzy and I don't need that right now so stay there."

Jared laughed again and sat back on his heels, respecting her request for distance. For the moment. "Are you always this grouchy before coffee in the mornings? This might be something I have to get used to."

Jane stared at him, his eyes bright and his black hair tousled and stuck out in odd places from falling asleep with it wet, and felt the frustration melt out of her, against her will. "How do you do that to me?"

"Do what? I haven't done anything." He offered her his best, most disarming smile. She didn't buy the innocent act for a minute.

Jane just cocked an eyebrow and shook her head. "That work for you often?" The smile morphed into a grin as he nodded enthusiastically. "Damn it, Jared." She lunged for him, catching him off guard, their lips colliding as they fell back onto the bed. Jane straddled his hips, her hands caressing his chest and upper thighs while her tongue thrust in his mouth. Jared groaned and pulled her down tighter onto him, his body arching up to meet hers in all the places he couldn't reach with only two hands.

Jared shoved both hands in her hair and forced her mouth from his, releasing her and allowing her to work on his neck. "Jesus, Jane, you can't do this to me and I want you to."

Jane pulled back and smiled. "What exactly am I doing to you that you're not a willing participant in? Make that sound for me again."

He caught her face, stopping her from resuming her progress down the front of his body. "What are you doing?"

"What do you mean?" She paused, staring down at him, suddenly uncertain. Fear of his ultimate rejection rose high in her and she attempted to squash it down before he felt it too.

"What do you want?"

"Honestly? To not fall in love with you," she laughed.

"I want you to tell me it's too late." Jared brought her mouth to meet his in a hard, crushing kiss. He rolled over, pinning her beneath him. "I want you to more than want me." He shoved his hand between her legs, she arched into him and gasped, her fingernails digging into his back.

"Jared," she breathed.

"What do you really want?" he demanded.

"Don't do this to me. Please," Jane begged, her voice barely more than a whisper, her body's responses completely out of her control.

His head dropped down beside hers, his labored breathing hot on her neck. "I'm sorry, Jane, but I can't wait. You have to let me know. What do you really want?"

"I want you, inside of me, now." She moved up against him. Jared pushed her back down on the bed.

"More than that. What do you want more?"

"You." She gasped and reached up, framing his face between her hands, forcing his gaze to meet hers. "I need to know if you really want me. Because I chose you."

Jared braced himself on his hands, staring down at her. "You did what? Are you sure?"

Jane bit her bottom lip nervously and held up her open left palm, sliding the new scar across his lips and down his jaw. "I chose."

"Oh god, Jane." Jared kissed her hand, her wrist, and buried his face in her neck. "You shouldn't have done this. There's a lot that I should have told you before you did this."

"It doesn't matter; none of it matters." She held him close, running her fingers through his hair. "You really are his son aren't you? The witch wasn't lying?"

"Not exactly, no. Are you afraid?" His fingers slid down her arm and he twined his with hers.

"Of what?" She watched him curiously.

"Of what you'll become. With me." He looked up from their joined hands to gaze into her eyes.

"What are you talking about?" Nervousness mingled with her uncertainty at his sudden seriousness. "We're already of the same kind. What do you think you're going to do to me?"

"You still have a choice. If you stay, you'll become as I am."

"Is that so bad? You don't have anyone trying to kill you, do you?"

"Not that I know of, no."

"Then shut up and kiss me."

He laughed and pulled her into him. "Tease."

"I'm not telling you to stop."

Karina awoke to the sound of her cell phone pinging under her bed pillow. She groaned and rolled out of bed, simultaneously dragging her robe off the foot of the bed and her phone out from under the pillow. "Hello?" she answered sluggishly, more of an attempt to stop the annoying noise than to find out who was on the other end of the phone line.

"Good morning. Where did my wife sleep last night or should I pick up the *Times* and find out for myself?" Karina groaned inwardly at how angry her husband sounded. "Before you say anything, I already know that you weren't at Jane's. Zane was up here already looking for her so I'm assuming that wherever you are you're together."

"Then you know I'm not having an affair as I'm not narcissistic enough to fuck my twin." Karina shrugged into her robe and sat on the edge of the bed, looking out the window into the backyard where Tyler was already up, doing yoga stretches. "Otherwise you wouldn't believe me if I told you."

"You might want to try me. Zane's about to lose his mind and I'm not sure how much more of this I can take, Kari. We don't have a life together. There's you and Jane, and then there's me. If you don't let me in, how are we supposed to be together?"

"I can't tell you where we are. If Zane's so worried, maybe he should ask his girlfriend why Jane left. You're just gonna have to trust me a little while longer, Craig."

He sighed deeply. "When will you be home?"

"I don't know. Soon, I hope, but what does it matter? Will you be there when I get there?" she shot back, her pent up frustration with his continual mistrust and ignorance of who she really was coming to the surface.

"I don't think so this time. I really didn't want to do this over the phone, Karina, but I can't do this anymore. I want a divorce."

"Who are you divorcing, me or that image you have of me in your head, Craig?" She felt the rage building up inside her and it made it worse that she felt like crying, not out of sadness, but just because she was so mad. "You didn't ask if I was okay, if Jane was all right, or what could have possibly caused us to go off the radar and leave you and Zane behind. You don't want to deal with the messy parts, do you?"

"It's all a fake! It's a ruse that the two of you cooked up to hide behind when something goes wrong that you can't deal with."

"No, it's not. You've seen it and you know it's real."

"I'm sorry."

"I'm not. We'll talk about this when I get home, all right? You still want the divorce then, you can have it."

"Will you please at least tell me where you are?"

"Go read the *Times*, Craig." Karina ended the call. She yanked jogging pants and a t-shirt out of her suitcase and changed quickly, glancing up every few minutes to make sure Tyler couldn't see her from his spot in the backyard. She tossed her cell phone onto the bed and left the room, slamming the door behind her.

Karina made her way quickly down the hall, stopping briefly in front of the closed door to Jared's bedroom. She raised her hand to knock, considered it for a long moment before deciding against it and continuing on to the kitchen. Once in the kitchen, she helped herself to a cup of coffee from the full carafe on the counter and looked out the window to where Tyler was still practicing his yoga. He looked up, caught her watching him and nodded his acknowledgement before continuing with his exercises. Her fingernails tapped absently on the side of her coffee mug as she replayed the conversation with Craig in her head. He was right; she didn't belong with anyone who couldn't accept who she was. At the same time, she didn't want to acknowledge the end of her five year marriage either. Five years, seven months, and sixteen days, she mused silently, sipping her coffee and staring out the window absently. And absolutely nothing to show for all that time but a lot of empty promises and fake words. She refilled her mug and opened the backdoor, walking out into the sunlight.

"Should I pretend that I didn't hear that little exchange, or do you want to talk about it?" Tyler didn't face her, but continued to look into the steadily rising sun as he finished his workout.

"You don't even like me. Why would you want to talk about my personal life?" Karina took a few steps closer and sat facing him on the grass, squinting up at him in the early morning light.

"I never said that, so don't assume. And I don't have anything else to do, so if you need to talk, I'm willing to listen." He glanced over at her before turning his face back into the sun.

"Can we talk about something else? Just don't say anything about what you heard, okay?" she requested, her face softening just for a moment before returning to the smiling mask she wore every day.

Tyler dropped down onto the lawn, turning so that he could see her face. "I didn't hear anything. What do you want to talk about?"

"How have you been doing that looking straight into the sun without sunglasses?"

"I'm good that way. And I had my eyes closed," he confessed shyly. "I like the sunlight. You miss it when you're dead."

"You remember being dead?" Karina asked incredulously.

"No," Tyler laughed. "We're immortal so we're never really dead, there's just a little lag time switching bodies. One minute you're a senior citizen, the next an infant. Oddly they're both very similar forms once you reach a certain age."

"Interesting. Will you teach me how to do that?"

"Stare into the sun or grow old and feeble?"

"No, those stretches you were doing. How do you do that?"

"It's called yoga. I'll show you if you give me some of that coffee." Karina passed him the coffee mug and he took a deep, grateful swallow as they both stood. "All right. Let's get started." He placed the mug on the ground off to the side and stood next to her facing forward. "Put your arms over your head like this and breathe deeply." Tyler stood behind her, coaxing her body into the correct position before stepping to the side and taking the pose himself.

Karina giggled. "You've got to be kidding me!" She mimicked his actions.

Tyler watched her out of the corner of his eye and fought to not laugh out loud. "You'll get the hang of it." Karina lost her balance and fell to the ground, laughing. "Okay, maybe not like that." He reached down and pulled her to her feet. "Want to try again?"

She smiled a genuine smile and dusted herself off. "Yeah. Show me again?"

Jane wandered through the darkness, quietly discarding the things that weighed her down. She reached the dark, empty beach and stepped out onto the sand. Her quiet footsteps took her closer to the dark water. She stood at the edge of the breaking waves, watching the moonlight dance across the surface of the sea before turning and continuing down the otherwise vacant beach in silence. Somewhere out of the darkness she saw someone walking toward her, his stride more purposeful than hers as he approached. Jane smiled in happy recognition and reached out for his hand. Jared took her hand and kissed it.

"Are you ready?" He smiled at her, pulling her further down the beach.

"Yes." She placed both of her hands in his and they stepped away from the water, walking further into the darkness. The night faded into the day and Jane sensed the presence of another being, a higher being, on the beach with them. The presence was a peaceful, calming one and she was unafraid when Jared stopped walking and turned to face her. The landscape surrounding them seemed to melt away into an infinite open sky full of all colors and none of them at the same time. The being materialized as an old man floating in the air above and beside them. Jane faced Jared, holding his hands tightly. "Are you sure about this?"

His expression darkened and she looked down to see the palms of both of their hands slit open, the cuts crossing all the lines on their open palms. Without even thinking it, her right hand was bound to his, palm to palm, by a long white cord wound with gold. Their left hands were tied together in the same manner with a red silk cord. The being placed his hands over their joined hands and bowed his head in blessing as he stepped back, nodding for them to begin.

"What do the colors mean?"

"Red blesses our union and white with gold blesses us with children from the Goddess."

"Personal friend of yours?"

Jared gazed at her with a thoughtful smile on his lips as he gave her one last chance. "What do you believe?"

Jane stared at their joined hands, feeling the warm, sticky blood dripping down her wrists. "We've been joined for two days." She raised her eyes to meet his searching gaze. "You bleed for me. I bleed for you."

"You bleed for me." Jared tugged the red binding tighter around their left hands. "I bleed for you." He pushed their joined hands over their heads moving his face so close that his eyes filled her vision. "Blood of my blood."

"Blood of my blood," Jane repeated her eyes wide and her voice a little breathless.

"Flesh of my flesh."

"Flesh of my flesh."

"Soul of my soul." Jared gritted his teeth, tightening his hold on her hands, refusing to allow her to back out.

"Soul of my soul." Jane flexed her fingers and reaffirmed her grip on his hands through the blood. She felt the being's expectant gaze on them and Jared's glowing bright blue eyes were all she could see.

"Heart of my heart."

"Heart of my heart."

"Never shall we part." Jane hesitated. Jared came as close to her as he dared, the expression on his face almost violent. "Say it, Jane. Never shall we part."

"Jared..." Jane's voice was a whisper as the magnitude of the decision they were making came at her full force.

"Say it. Please." The words were a command and they reached straight down to the core of Jane's being, obliterating her lingering doubts.

She took a deep breath. "Never shall we part."

The sky around them darkened from dawn to dusk, and as the darkness filled with stars Jane suddenly realized that they had somehow ended up floating horizontally, the only space between them marked by their joined hands. She vaguely heard the being bless the union before he disappeared, leaving the two of them alone, lying on the darkening beach with the waves crashing and the sun just past setting. Jared gently slid against her, being careful of their still bound hands. Jane moved against him, cuddling closer as he kissed her reverently. "Now you're mine."

"And you're mine." She wrapped one leg around him and pulled him tighter to her, her body arching up to meet him, her fingers wrapped in his. "Love me."

"I already do."

15

Karina paced the kitchen impatiently, finally stopping in front of the sink, banging her coffee cup down on the kitchen counter. "It's been over two days. What is going on in there?"

Tyler walked in from the living room and calmly washed her coffee cup out, placing it in the dishwasher. "She chose him. Apparently it takes a while. Not that this is any of my business, but don't you want to talk to your husband? At least let him know that you're okay or something?"

Karina brushed the questions away with a dismissive wave of her hand. "He prefers to believe that all of this doesn't exist. He doesn't want to believe in what he can see, only in what he can't."

Tyler turned around and looked at her in surprise. "He meant what he said? He would really go through with it?"

She shrugged her shoulders. "My sister accuses me of having a charmed life. My husband and I don't even see each other to sleep most nights. My magic and my sister are my life and she's stronger than I could ever be."

Tyler opened the freezer and pulled out a chilled bottle of vodka. "Seems to be a lot they take for granted, doesn't there? Get a couple of glasses. For this commiseration we'll need something stronger than coffee." Karina retrieved the glasses from a cabinet and followed him into the living room.

"I thought you were both the perfect children or something?"

Tyler took a seat on the couch and poured vodka into the glasses Karina set down on the coffee table. "Technically we're the same person. Part god, part mortal, one true soul split exactly in half. Originally we were created at the same instant, so neither of us is truly older or younger than the other. Our destiny was to sit at the feet of the gods at Olympus and play. Eventually choose some mortal or immortal and make little gods or goddesses."

"But it never happened?" Karina took a sip of her drink and grimaced.

He downed his entire glass in one large gulp and went to refill it as he continued his story. "We didn't come out as adults, we came out as children. Our father gave us to a mortal woman to raise. We knew we were different. Our magic was never a secret. But we didn't want what our father wanted for us once we were old enough to choose for ourselves. Eventually he agreed to let us remain here on earth as long as we agreed to die and be reborn every couple hundred years."

"What happens to you when you die?" Karina leaned forward, enthralled with the story.

"We just die, just like everyone else. You don't cease to exist, you just become something different for a while. Like returning to your original state or something." He laughed. "What do you want me to say?"

She giggled and carefully downed more of her drink. "I don't know! There's some light at the end of the tunnel, a reason to believe in God?"

Tyler laughed and poured himself another drink. "You need to keep up." He gestured to her half-empty glass. Karina downed the remaining liquid quickly and thrust the glass out for more. "That's my girl." He refilled her glass then sat back with his own, smiling at her. "To answer the question, you've got a lot of reason to believe."

"That my sister's fucking a god is not a good reason," Karina laughed, drinking the vodka like a shot.

Tyler raised his eyebrows and refilled her glass again. "That's not what they're doing now and he's not the only one in the house."

"Yeah, but you don't act like it. He kind of does." They both laughed. Karina quieted after a moment. "How do you know what they're doing?" Tyler touched his ear in answer. "Oh, right, I forgot. What's going to happen to her now?"

Tyler's smile disappeared. "She's one of us now. Or she will be anyway. Neither of us has ever done it, so I'm not 100% on how it works. From what I get, they do both rituals, their blood is mixed, and by taking his blood, the more powerful of the two, she will become as we are."

Karina set her glass down on the table, not trusting her shaking hand, all good humor lost from her expression. "What rituals?"

"The marriage and fertility rituals. Justice of the Peace kind of doesn't hold up with our family. It takes a little more," he searched for the right word, "commitment."

"Explain, please."

"You know, blood-letting, ritualistic binding, you get the idea."

"How is it undone?" Karina paled.

"You can't." Tyler laughed and finished off his drink. "The only person, and I use the description loosely, who could break it would be our father or the goddess herself. And do you really think dad's going to let them out of it now that he's finally got one of us bound to a woman for eternity?"

"That's a long time." Karina picked her drink back up.

"Why do you think I'm still single?" Tyler poured another shot into his glass and saluted her with it. "Cheers!"

Jared awoke tangled in Jane's hair and a ripped bed sheet, his body covered in sweat, blood, and random other bodily fluids, all little souvenirs from the carnal activities of the past two days. He groaned as he rolled over, his abused body protesting the movement. Very carefully, he unwound the long, dark hair that trapped his arm and smoothed the remainder of it back from his wife's face. He looked down at his hands, stained with drying blood, the ends of the ropes still securely fastened around both wrists. He wanted to untie them so that he wouldn't disturb the beautiful angel sleeping at his side, but something stopped him, an unnecessary, unwarranted fear that if he untied them that the magic that bound them would be undone. He knew it was an irrational fear, that what was done couldn't be undone. But even though the wounds on his hands were physical markers that she had freely given herself to him, he still wasn't confident in the knowledge that the woman at his side was fully his.

Jane stirred, cuddling in closer to his warmth. She smiled, sighing contentedly. Jared felt what was rapidly becoming a familiar ache steal over his chest as he leaned over and kissed her on the cheek, more desperate than he wanted to admit to know her unconscious reaction. Jane's smile brightened and she turned, reaching blindly for him in her sleep. "Jared." He went to her, his uncertainties set aside as she welcomed him into her embrace. Her arms wrapped around him, arching into his warmth as their lips met.

It was with no small amount of regret that he broke away from her a moment later.

"We have to get dressed." Jared kissed her again softly, his teeth pulling on her lower lip, dragging the contact out just a moment longer.

"What a fabulous way to wake up." She finally opened her eyes to smile up into his face. "Did we do what I think we did?"

He held up one of his bound hands, the cord pulling hers up with his. "What do you think?"

Jane glanced at her palms and thoughtfully rubbed at the quickly healing wounds in her hands. "Guess that means it wasn't a dream. At least not totally," she commented, lying down and wrapping her arms back around him.

"No regrets?"

"Is that a real question?" She kissed him quickly, passionately and pulled her mouth away while pulling his body down against hers. "I could never regret you." She placed his hands on either side of her face. "Pay attention. I want you to see something. Look at my face." He obliged her, fighting not to smile into her sea green eyes. "This is what me happy looks like. I know you might not recognize it as I've never managed to hold this expression for very long but you did this. Thank you."

Jared kissed her again long and deep, his tongue sliding just along the edges of her lips. He finally pulled away, sliding off the bed and taking her with him despite her protests. "We have to make an appearance. Nice new tattoo," he commented, indicating their intertwined left hands as he guided her toward the bathroom.

Jane looked down and saw the words in Latin inscribed in bright metallic gold where a ring would be on her left hand. "What does it say?"

"To know light in darkness." He looked down at his own matching mark and squeezed her hand reassuringly. "It means that the goddess, my true mother, gives her blessing."

She stared up at him in surprise as he dragged her under the lukewarm fall of water. "Anything else I need to know?"

He pretended to think for a moment. "I love you. And you smell a little funny. Shampoo?" He held the bottle out to her, wrinkling his nose in illustration.

"So romantic." She took the bottle and squirted a massive amount of shampoo on his head. "Thought you might want some too, baby."

Jared raked his fingers across his face, clearing the soap from his eyes. "Oh, you're gonna play it like that? See if I share the conditioner!"

Jane pushed him out of the way so that she could rinse her hair. "Try it. What's yours is mine, sweetheart."

"Now you bring that up," he groaned good-naturedly.

"Any regrets?" She smiled, switching places with him.

"Not one." He grinned, ducking under the running water.

"So if you're basically two halves of the same person, how did you end up becoming the sidekick?" Karina's words slurred and she flopped back on the couch, vodka sloshing over the top of her glass.

Tyler mock-glared at her from over the rim of the nearly empty bottle. "I am not a sidekick, I will have you know. Though it was my idea to become musicians." He cracked a grin and raised the bottle to her. "Jer may get more attention, but I'm still better looking."

"All in your head, Ty. All of it," Jared laughed as he entered the room, snatching the nearly empty bottle from his brother's hand. "You've had enough."

"Says the man who's been in bed for two days. Well rested?" he called after his brother who went into the kitchen with his bottle.

"Very well, thank you," Jared yelled back, washing the remaining vodka down the drain.

Jane entered the room still adjusting her earrings and stopped, taking in the sight of the two people slumped over various pieces of furniture in front of her. "Are they smashed?"

"We're celebrating," Tyler answered happily, slumping over in his leather armchair.

"I see that," Jane replied cautiously. "What are we celebrating?"

"You're a goddess!" Karina burst into laughter which rapidly turned into hiccups.

"And you're trashed." She sat down next to the other woman who fell over into her lap. "Oh, no. Head down and you're done for. I know you." She pushed Karina back up into a sitting position. "You two think you can pull yourselves together long enough to go out and have dinner with us?"

"Where are we going?" Karina slanted her eyes to her sister at the mention of food.

"Sushi place." Jane glanced at Jared and blushed. "Apparently we have reservations."

Tyler perked up. "Will there be sake?"

"You haven't had enough?"

"I'll be alone for the next millennia, thanks to you. I deserve a little drink." He squinted at her, holding the fingers of one hand as far apart as possible in front of his eyes in illustration.

"You've had a very large drink and you're not alone. You've got more company now." Jane walked over and pulled him out of the chair. "Think you can stand living with both of us forever?"

"I will not be a sidekick."

"Wouldn't allow you to be. Now both of you go change. We have to leave soon and you smell like a distillery."

Tyler pulled Karina up and they leaned on each other as they stumbled from the room. "Distillery's not so bad." He sniffed her.

"You're definitely hotter."

"We are not smashed." They giggled as they stumbled down the hall.

Karina sniffed Tyler's arm and turned her head away in disgust. "You need a shower."

"So do you." Tyler flicked Karina's nose playfully.

Karina rubbed her nose and pushed Tyler toward his bedroom. "Go clean up."

Tyler smiled impishly as he grabbed both of her hands in his. He wasn't sure if it was the vodka, but suddenly all he could see was his reflection in her green eyes and he liked the way that she saw him.

"Come help me." He pulled her with him toward his room half-heartedly.

Karina laughed, showing him her wedding rings. "Bathe yourself." She shoved him through the doorway, laughing as he crashed into the foot of his bed. Karina stumbled into her own room, slamming the door behind her.

"So how long should I tell the restaurant to hold the reservation?" Jared came up behind Jane, handing her a glass of wine over her shoulder.

She accepted the glass with a smile. "We might need to make dinner and get dessert at the restaurant."

"They'll sober up on the way."

16

"Enough sake?" Jane teased, raising her cup to her new brother-in-law.

"Yeah. I'm good." He laughed and the smile was genuine. "I really am happy for you guys."

"Thank you, Ty." Jared drank his sake and settled back into his corner of the restaurant booth, one arm around his wife's shoulders. He allowed some of the fear that had settled in his abdomen to subside a bit at his brother's acceptance of Jane. Jane relaxed as Jared did, immediately sensing his relief at the positive answer to the unspoken question.

"I just can't believe that after all that searching you met her in this dump." Tyler raised his hand to indicate their questionable surroundings with his empty sake cup.

"This place is not a dump. It has character," Karina said defensively on her sister's behalf, turning sideways in her seat to punch Tyler playfully in the arm.

"Thank you!" Jane laughed as Tyler, pretending to be injured, shied away from Karina before sliding back across the bench seat and settling close to her. Jared raised an eyebrow at his brother who shrugged helplessly in response. Jared bit back a laugh, returning his attentions to his wife.

Jared held up a cucumber roll to Jane with his chopsticks. "Will you lick my chopsticks?"

"Hmm." Jane obliged, then sat back in her seat to chew, blushing. "You're never going to forget that are you?"

"Nope." Jared smiled at her unwarranted embarrassment, reassuring her with a soft kiss. "I quite enjoy it."

"Everyone having fun? Nice party?" Zane strode to the table angrily, followed closely by Sabina who seemed reluctant to be dragged further into the emotionally messy situation.

"We are actually." Jared's hand tightened reflexively on Jane's shoulder as he watched them approach, suddenly fearful of his wife's reaction in the company of her former soul mate and his new conquest.

Jane smiled, gave Jared's hand a quick, reassuring squeeze and slid out of the booth. She went right past Zane, ignoring her ex completely. Zane turned red at the intentional insult while Jared and Karina fought not to laugh. Tyler watched the whole scene with obvious amusement, settling back to eat as he watched the mini-drama unfold. Jane continued past Zane to Sabina, exuberantly hugging the startled woman. "It's so good to see you again!"

Zane's jaw dropped open in surprise. "You two know each other?"

Jared readjusted his seat so that he had a better view. "Just wait; it gets better."

"You're a strange human, Jane Jamison." Sabina took a step back, her arms still held tightly at her sides, uncomfortable with the public emotional display.

"Um, that would be Jane Stateton now," Jared interrupted.

Sabina looked at him in surprise. "The prince surrendered?"

He showed her the wounds on his palms. "Happily."

She looked back at Jane. "Our agreement?"

"Stands." Jane nodded affirmatively. She looked back at her husband with a soft expression on her face before glancing back at the black witch who had tried to kill her. "Thank you. For everything."

"You are welcome." Sabina smiled stiffly, her movements still tense. "Congratulations on your wedding."

"Wedding!?" Zane's eyes nearly bulged out of his head. "You married *him*? Jared fucking Stateton?" The words exploded viciously from his mouth causing the other diners to turn and stare.

"Please don't yell and yes, I did." Jane looked around nervously in the sudden silence, fully expecting to see a reporter on the phone or the flash of a paparazzi camera.

"Jared fucking Stateton?" Zane continued to yell.

Jared watched someone snap a picture with a camera phone and inwardly groaned. "That's not my middle name. Please lower your voice and sit down. We all have an interest in discussing this in a less public forum."

"Bite me, pretty boy," Zane sniped, his expression dark. "I cannot believe you dumped me for Jared fucking Stateton."

"Perhaps we should go to our own dinner, Zane." Sabina said quietly, trying to pull him away.

"We should go shopping, do lunch next week, Sabina." Jane smiled, ignoring Zane's childish outbursts.

"Of course." Sabina tugged vainly on Zane's arm, more than a little irritated at the attention Zane still showed Jane.

"I'll call you at the condo."

"I'm in hell," Zane commented, rubbing his eyes in frustration.

Jane finally acknowledged him. She stepped up to him, her eyes turning black. "Not yet, but you will be. There's a bounty hunter after you and Sabina's got the part of your soul you stupidly shoved in me."

"How?"

"We traded. She wanted you, you wanted her, and I wanted to be rid of you. It's a win-win. Now that she's not trying to kill me I might rather like her." Jane smiled at him sweetly. "I warned you that one day you would push too hard, we would break. Thanks to your stupidity you no longer have any hold over me. Not since yesterday. Thanks for giving me the out."

"I can't believe you did this to me."

"Go fuck yourself, Zane." Jane leaned in closer to Zane, her eyes sparking red and black with her anger and whispered intimately in his ear, "Though you might want to run. You've pissed off a lot of people."

"What's that mean?" His own eyes flickered black for a moment, a relic from their once-shared bond.

Jane sighed and stepped back, her eyes fading to a stormy gray-blue. "It means go live your own life, Zane. I'll have my lawyers draw up papers in the morning to separate our assets."

"The condo?" Zane's anxiousness slipped into his voice.

She looked over her shoulder to Jared. "Honey, will you hand me your napkin?" He looked at her curiously and slid the indicated cocktail napkin across the table to her. She pulled a pen out of her jeans pocket and glanced back up at Zane as she wrote. "Got a dollar?"

"What are you doing?" He tried unsuccessfully to peer over her shoulder.

She finished writing and straightened. Jared leaned over to read the napkin and had to fight to keep from laughing. Jane finally turned to stare at Zane. "Have you got the money or not?"

"If you don't, I'll loan it to you," Jared offered.

"Kiss my ass, cabana boy." Zane made a rude hand gesture in Jared's general direction.

"Answer the question, motherfucker," Jane ordered sternly, crossing her arms over her chest as she firmly planted herself between Zane and Jared.

Zane's eyes widened a bit at Jane's tone. "Yes."

She held out a hand. "Hand it over and sign here." She pointed to a hastily written "x" on the napkin.

He pulled out his wallet and gave her the dollar bill, stepping up to the table to see the scrap of paper. "What the hell happened to your hand?" he asked, noticing the scars on her palms.

"I got married. Sign under my name and date it. I'll have more formal papers drawn up in the morning." Jane stepped out of his way and held out her pen.

Zane took the pen from her and promptly scribbled his name on the napkin, barely glancing at the handwritten words. Jared took it from him, signed it, and passed it to Tyler who repeated the process. "What am I signing?"

Jane smiled. "You really should read more." She held out her hand to shake his. "Congratulations, you're the proud owner of one condo for one dollar. I didn't want to pay the gift tax and this keeps arguments regarding our assets to a minimum. According to that I'll have my stuff out by the end of the week. You can keep all the furniture except my desk. I rather like it."

"Are you shitting me?" Zane grabbed the napkin, holding it nearly against his nose as he read.

"Nope. I officially want nothing to do with you." Jane snatched the scrap of paper out of Zane's hands and snuggled back into her side of the booth with Jared. "Enjoy your dinner."

Sabina hauled Zane away as he continued to mutter, "Jared fucking Stateton," in an endless loop under his breath.

The whole table erupted into laughter as soon as they were out of earshot. "I cannot believe you did that!" Tyler choked out.

"Let me see that!" Karina took the scrap of paper from her sister's hand. "That was insane, J. Do you know how much that place is worth?"

"Do I care, is the question, Kari." Jane leveled a bright green gaze at her sister. "Money's just money. You make more of it every day." She wrapped an arm around her husband's chest and rested her head on his shoulder. "This is more important than all of that crap. You guys are more important."

"I still can't believe you did this." Karina shook her head and dropped the napkin back on the table.

"What's the problem? I wanted it to be done. Now it is. I found it very effective." Jane grinned. "Stopped his hissy fit."

"I found it very entertaining." Jared curled into his corner with his tea.

"Thank you, dear." Jane patted him on the leg as she straightened, then polished off the last of her sushi roll.

Jared leaned over to kiss her, ducking to the left as a dark shadow passed by. "Shit."

"Okay, that was weird." Jane blushed, turning away.

"It's not you." He kept staring off into the distance, moving like he'd crawl over her to get out of the booth.

Tyler reached out, grabbing him by the arm before he pushed Jane out into the floor. "What is it?"

Jared looked back at him. "Did you see that?"

Tyler glanced over his shoulder. "See what? There's nothing there."

"In the shadows, over by Sabina and Zane." Jared tried to discreetly point, all too aware that they were still being watched.

Tyler turned to look. He saw the dense shadow curled behind the table. "What the hell?" He paused for a moment, leaning closer to squint at the image. "Is that... Why would?"

"I don't know. You don't think?"

Tyler looked back and forth between his brother and the shadow curiously. "Which one?"

"Alecto," Jared answered grimly.

Karina spit her tea across the table, narrowly missing her sister. "A Fury?"

Tyler shot her a warning look. "Shut up. We do not want to draw any more attention." A meaningful glance was directed at Jared who obediently sunk back into his seat, slouching down further in the corner.

Jane looked back and forth between the two of them. "We'll talk about this later?" Tyler nodded. Jane slid out of the booth. "I'll be right back."

Alarm crossed Jared's handsome face. "Where are you going?"

She smiled. "Where you can't follow." She turned and walked toward the back of the restaurant, melting into the jumble of servers and patrons.

Jared watched her until she disappeared from view. "Before you say it, I know, I'm paranoid."

"I think it's cute." Karina laughed as she drank more sake.

"I'm glad someone's impressed," he commented drily.

"Don't start that shit," Tyler warned.

"She loves you," Karina protested on behalf of her sister.

Jared's tortured blue gaze rose to meet hers. "She can't say it."

Karina reached across the table and grabbed his left hand, holding it up in front of his face. "Doesn't mean she doesn't feel it. If she didn't love you, that tattoo wouldn't be there."

He pulled his hand back, gazing at the gold tattoo. His eyes drifted back toward where Jane had disappeared. When he turned back around, he noticed that the shadows had receded a bit and he panicked. "Where did she go?"

Tyler barely looked up from his food. "The bathroom. Chill, she'll be back in a minute."

Jared looked at him like he was mentally challenged. "Not Jane, you idiot. Alecto." He got up and looked toward the back of the restaurant. "Jane should've been back by now."

"Jared, don't do it." Tyler got up, pushing Karina out of the booth. He followed his brother to the back of the restaurant, Karina close behind. He pushed her ahead, toward the ladies room. "Go check on your sister." She nodded and entered the room. "Jer, stop worrying."

Karina came back out shaking her head a moment later. "She's not in there."

"Okay, now start worrying."

Jared turned and stomped through the restaurant. "I'm gonna kill that bastard son of a bitch."

Tyler stopped him. "Not yet. Someone's trying to get our attention."

"Yeah? Well it worked." Jared jerked away from Tyler's hold on his arm but stayed where he was, his jaw clenched and arms folded angrily over his chest.

Tyler's gaze never left his brother for fear of what the other man might do. He handed Karina his wallet and she went to pay the bill, collect their things, while he escorted Jared to the door. "Come on. Let's take this outside."

Jared grudgingly obliged, waiting until they were a block clear of the restaurant but it was still within his line of sight, before blowing up. "Why did you do that? Why the fuck wouldn't you let me take that little shit out? My wife is gone for Christ's sake!"

"And we will get her back. But killing someone in a restaurant won't do anyone any good. Do you hear me, Jared? Do not go after him. Whatever's happened, they'll come to us."

Karina joined them. "I couldn't find her. What the fuck happened to my sister?"

Jared hesitantly dragged his eyes away from the restaurant to look at her face, so like Jane's. "She's been taken." He looked to the left and saw the dark shadows waiting for him. "Now apparently it's my turn." He turned and began walking toward the darkness.

"Jer, don't."

"You coming with me or not?" Jared didn't look back and stepped into the shadows.

"I'm going on record as saying this is not one of your better ideas." Tyler stepped up to the edge of the shadows and looked back to Karina, holding out his hand to her. "You coming?"

She stood right beside him, close enough to touch and took his hand. "Where are we going?"

Tyler took a deep breath and pulled them both forward into the abyss. "To hell."

"That was literal, wasn't it?" She gripped his arm nervously and closed her eyes.

"Don't let go of my hand." His fingers tightened around hers as they stepped forward.

17

Hands reached out and pulled on Karina's clothes and hair as she was dragged through a dark tunnel, her face hidden in Tyler's shoulder. When the world stopped spinning, she opened her eyes to a world of dark red rocks with clear rivers and occasional outcroppings of palm trees. The water and trees were the only sign of life other than the two men she had arrived with. Karina noticed the dark shadow clouds flitting around. She couldn't explain it but she felt like they were watching them. She let go of Tyler and stepped away curiously. "This place looks nothing like what I'd pictured."

One of the shadows approached her. "Are you disappointed?"

Karina jumped. "Holy shit!"

A lilting laugh slid across the nearly barren landscape. "There's very little "holy" about it."

She turned to look at the brothers. "Am I the only one who hears this?"

Jared sighed impatiently. "Quit fucking with her, Alecto. Why did you bring us here? And better yet, where's Jane?"

The cloud of shadows in front of Karina quickly materialized into an ethereally beautiful young woman. She shook the remaining gloom out of her gleaming bronze hair and met Karina's gaze with bright blue eyes that rivaled her cousin's. Her dark skin, high cheekbones, and tall thin frame made her a striking contrast to the deep landscape. She smoothed her black free-flowing gown, more out of a carefully cultivated habit than any true necessity. "Thank you for accepting my invitation."

Jared got right in her face. "Where's my wife?"

Alecto smiled sweetly. "Do you truly find it prudent to anger a Fury?"

"You won't kill me." A tight, nasty smile crossed his face as he called her on her empty challenge.

"Ah, but we both know that there are so many things far worse than death." She slid a hand down his chest and stepped away. "Your mortal has taken your place, Anyasis. I thought that she should get to know her in-laws."

"You can't do that to her! She won't survive there yet." His brother held him back to keep him from physically attacking their cousin. Tyler turned his gaze to Karina to keep all of the violent thoughts screaming in his brother's mind from running riot in his own.

"So feisty, cousin. Were you this passionate with some of your former lovers we could have avoided this mess." Alecto laughed callously at his anger, disregarding him completely.

"Who I choose to spend the remainder of my existence with is no concern of the Furies. Give me back my wife!" Jared broke free of Tyler and leapt at Alecto who stood perfectly still, amused at his dramatics.

Tyler stepped in between them and pushed Jared back. "We're listening."

"Are you certain?" She paused a moment to make it clear that she required their full attention before continuing. "I have been charged with "retrieving" Zane's soul. But he is protected by the black witch. Who has a special place for our Anyasis. You will get his soul for me. His whole soul. Or I will take the other half in trade."

"Take Sabina." Jared shrugged.

"Not Sabina. Your mate, Anyasis. Your blood, your scent covers her well, but she remains somewhat attached to him. One perfect half of the same imperfect soul. Not naturally, of course, but really, what's the difference? Hers still reeks of him."

Some of the fight slid out of him as he shook his head in denial. "You're wrong. We're bound. You don't have the power to undo that."

"You're right; I don't. But I'm willing to take hers anyway in trade. Perhaps you should ask yourself: what is your own soul worth and that of your brother? To not do as I ask would condemn you all."

"My father would never allow this."

"Your father has no choice," she spat back. "I am being kind in giving you one. You either live or you die. You don't like the pond scum anyway." She handed him a shining, wicked looking gold spear-like contraption from within the folds of her robe. "Extract his complete soul. Bring it to me and I'll give her back. While you are busy making sure her former mate is not a problem, I'll make sure she's well entertained."

Jared snatched the sharp gold instrument from her hand. "No one touches her."

311

Alecto smiled and shrugged her seemingly delicate shoulders noncommittally. "You know how gods can be with mortal women. I would hurry if I were you."

Alecto vanished and suddenly they were standing on the dark sidewalk in the Valley, one block away from the sushi restaurant. The only way that Karina knew it had been real was that Jared was still holding the golden instrument. "Oh, shit, what just happened?"

Jared smiled grimly. "You just went to hell and back. How did you like it?"

No one said anything else until they were securely hidden behind the wood and stone walls of Jared and Tyler's home. As soon as the door closed behind them, Jared dropped to the floor in a miserable heap and screamed. The sound was the most wretched, heartbreaking thing that Karina had ever heard. She went to him, wrapping her arms around him from behind and held him while he cried. Tyler knelt before him and gingerly pried the golden weapon from his hands. He laid it on the coffee table and returned quickly to his brother's side.

"We will get her back," he said quietly.

"We get her back and she'll never forgive what I've done to free her."

"Jer, you have no choice. If he lives, we die, and you condemn her soul to hell in his place. Explain it to her. She'll understand. You have to do this."

Karina let go and moved a little away from Jared. "Give it to me. I'll do it. Never liked the bastard anyway."

"It's not that simple. First, you can't. You're mortal and that thing will kill you the second you touch it. Second, Zane's soul is

312

split. He fractured it of his own free will and part of it resides in Sabina who, for all her faults, does not in any way deserve what that thing would do to her."

"What does it do?"

Jared finally looked up. "You shove it into their chests, open it up, and extract their still-beating hearts. And I have to do it. There is no other choice. Alecto is a punisher of evil-doers. And no one ever accused my family of not being creative."

Karina paled. "Where's Jane?"

"Olympus," Tyler answered for him.

"Isn't that like the home of your people or something?"

The misery returned full force to Jared's face. "Have you ever read anything about the ancient gods? Do you know what they did, especially to mortal women? They force them to have sex, bear children, tortured them. And they have no choice because they're being faced with a god. What do you think they'll do to a mortal woman, a prisoner, in their territory? Being my wife won't help her."

Karina struggled to maintain her resolve. "How can I help you get her back?"

"Can you put Zane's soul back together?" he asked quietly.

"I can try."

"I don't want to kill anyone. But I won't let her die for him again. I'd like to keep Sabina out of this if possible."

"She won't be happy."

"She won't want to die like this either."

Karina rose and went for her supplies. "I'll need something of hers."

Tyler looked up at her. "I'll get it. Whatever you need."

She nodded. "The more personal the better. And from this incarnation."

He looked at her strangely. "She's only had one. She can be killed, it's just extremely difficult."

Karina glanced across the room at the weapon. "I bet that would about get anybody."

"That's kind of the idea." Jared laughed bitterly.

"Will he ever come back from this?"

"No. And neither will we if I let him live."

"We," Tyler corrected. "We either live together or we die together. This is not just your cross to bear."

"We make the decision together." Karina stared at the wicked looking gilded device resting almost innocently on the coffee table. "I vote to kill him. If Sabina dies, I'm sorry, but she's not my sister."

Tyler looked from her to his brother and took a deep breath. "All those reincarnations without bloodshed. I don't want this; I think it sucks. But they'll take him anyway, with or without us."

"You would both take his life?"

"We're of the same blood. I can take his life."

"No, it has to be me."

"Not if you can't do it. If you can't, I will, Jer."

"I still think you should let me do it," Karina insisted. "I've wanted to kill him for years and I can get closer than either of you."

"You're not one of us," Tyler said quietly. "That thing kills you and we've accomplished nothing."

"No, but you're a god and now so is my sister." Karina held out her left hand, palm up, to Tyler. "Make me one of you."

Tyler's eyes darkened and Karina wasn't sure if it was from lust, anger, or fear. "I can't do that to you. Not when we have other options."

Karina glanced back at Jared. "Are you sure about that?"

"Positive. Don't ask me again. You may not like the answer next time." Tyler met her eyes and the intensity in his gaze caused her breath to catch in her throat. After a long moment passed in silence, he returned to rationalizing the situation with his brother. "This isn't a discussion, Jer. One of us has to do this. There's no way out for him, there is for us. We should take it. It will save Jane."

"Don't you think I know that!" Jared roared. "I love my wife and my family and this life. Alecto chose me to do this because I finally have something to live for."

"So let's figure out how to do this. We sure as hell don't want to get caught."

"Before anything else, at least let me try to separate them," Karina offered, her voice still a bit breathless.

Tyler stood. "You get set up, I'll go get what you need." He brushed past her without daring to meet the questions in her eyes.

Jared put his head in his hands and sighed wearily. "Just be careful. Let's get this part done by morning. I don't want to leave Jane there longer than I have to."

"Will they really hurt her?" The fear in Karina's voice matched the answer in Jared's eyes. "I'll hurry."

"No mistakes."

Karina saw a familiar black staring at her from out of Jared's eyes. "None."

Jane coughed as she walked through the dark cloud of smoke on her way back from the ladies room. She looked back curiously, thinking the smoke was random since it was illegal to smoke in the restaurant. She sat back down and curled up next to Jared. Jane looked across the empty table to the vacant seat curiously. "Where did they go?"

Jared pulled her closer to whisper intimately in her ear. "They thought they'd leave us alone for the night. Took off a few minutes ago."

"Together?"

"Maybe they have the same idea I have for how to spend a productive evening alone," he whispered.

Jane touched him, but felt like something was *wrong*. She looked up into his happy gaze and shook the feeling off. "Ready to go home?"

Jared smiled down at her and kissed her sweetly, almost predatorily. "Absolutely."

18

"How's it going out there?" Jared called to Karina who had parked herself on the glassed-in patio where she said the karmic energy was better.

"I can't work with you hovering," she ground out through gritted teeth.

"Jared, shut up and sit down. Your pacing is driving me crazy!" Tyler watched his brother stalk from one end of the room to the other while watching Karina through the French doors, and he pulled on his own short dark blonde hair in frustration.

"I cannot accept that there is nothing I can do." He stopped at the window to watch the sunrise, thinking how different things could be in such a short time.

"There is something you can do," Tyler said seriously. "Help me figure out a way to get to Zane after she finishes. We don't have much time left."

"He still cares for Jane. If we summon him somewhere, he'll come. It won't leave a trail of people or paper to come back to us. We'll have to make sure that's he's not followed, that Sabina's distracted. This comes back to us, we're fucked, might as well be dead anyway."

Tyler looked out the open porch door at Karina still meditating over her spell of crystals, candles, and her herbal potions. "She'll do it. She might not hold her off for long, but dressed up she looked enough like Jane to convince you. It ought to be enough to fool Sabina long enough for us to get Zane away from her."

"Think she'll go for it?"

"She was gonna turn you into a six year old girl. I think she'll be willing to fool the wicked witch for a few hours. I'll ask her."

Jared raised an eyebrow. "Oh, really?"

"She's married."

"Where's the husband?"

"MIA 90% of the time, apparently."

"And that doesn't leave an opening for you?"

"Isn't it kind of sick for you to fantasize me with your wife's married twin sister?"

"What can I say? You're a sick fuck," Jared laughed. "And I'm not so sure it's a fantasy. Just stick with that one and leave mine alone."

"Are you kidding me? Jane's too high maintenance. I couldn't deal with the constant stress."

"I'm just hoping I don't get divorced over getting her kidnapped on our honeymoon."

"Have you noticed that seems to happen a lot? I mean, twice in one week? High maintenance."

"Yeah, but it seems to be the men in her life that keep losing her," Jared stated bitterly.

"We'll get her back."

"I worry that she won't want to come back. At least not to me." Jared returned his gaze to the brightening sunlight through the windowpane.

"Finished!" The voice cut through Jared's dreams, waking him from an unsettling sleep. He sat up, swinging his legs to the floor. He lobbed the throw pillow that had been used to sleep on at his brother who was still sprawled across the couch, snoring. "Get up. We've got work to do."

Tyler groaned in protest, tossing the pillow back in the general direction of his brother, missing him by a wide margin. He cuddled his own pillow and rolled over, sliding off the couch. He jumped up as soon as he hit the floor, his head banging on the underside of the coffee table. "Shit!"

"Now that you're up," Jared reached over and picked up the golden spear, "let's go kill somebody."

Tyler looked up at him with sleep blurred eyes. "You sure you're up for this?"

"As ready as I'll ever be. I want to get this over with and get Jane home."

Tyler groaned and sank back down on to the couch. "Don't look so happy about it. I'd hate for you to have to face your inevitable disappointment when things turn out to be anticlimactic compared to the insanity running rampant through your mind. Breathe. We'll take care of it and we'll get her back. I don't promise you much, but I will promise you that. We will bring your wife home to you. I don't care what it takes or who we have to kill." He lifted his face from his hands and looked across the coffee table at his brother. "Now can I please have some caffeine before we begin the mayhem?"

Jared laughed a little and stood. He walked toward the kitchen, pausing to squeeze his brother's shoulder. "Thanks, Ty. Hey, I'll even go make the coffee for you."

Tyler stood and followed his brother into the other room. "Only because you want some as badly as I do."

"Only you could get away with jokes today."

"I'm special that way."

I rolled over in bed, sliding further away from Jared. "Are you feeling all right, Jer?"

He gave me that weird, sly, predatory smile and folded his hands behind his head. "I'm fine. I enjoyed last night."

I shifted uncomfortably, feeling the strange energy rolling off of him, tasting like an oil slick. "Yeah, me too. You were different last night."

"I hope you meant that in a good way. Hey, we're playing tonight. You wanna come?"

"Of course. I wouldn't miss it. Where are you playing?" I wanted to ask why he hadn't told me about this earlier. Wouldn't he have told me in advance if they were playing? Had I heard anything about a Metamorphosis concert in L.A.?

He shrugged noncommittally. "Just some club downtown."

"You're not playing something bigger, like House of Blues?"

"Nah, it's too big. We were going for something more...intimate."

"If you'll let me know where, I'll get Karina to come too. I'm sure she'd like to be there. She and Tyler seem to have really gotten to be good friends in the last few days." I watched him warily. I didn't want him to read my reactions too readily but I didn't want to be overly comfortable with him either right now. Watching him watch me, I'd never felt this uncomfortable with Jared but I couldn't place why I felt this strangely either.

The hesitation showed on his face. "I'd rather it just be you tonight, if that's all right."

The feeling of unease that had started the night before tightened into a cold, hard knot in the pit of my stomach. I slid out of bed, pulling on one of his oversized t-shirts. "I'm going to take a shower."

"Would you like some company?"

Knowing now where the sense of dread had come from, I looked down at the thing that so resembled my husband and tried very hard to hide my disgust. "I like to shower alone. You know that, babe."

"Right, sorry. I guess I forgot. Bubble bath later maybe."

Tears welled up in my eyes and I turned away so that he wouldn't see. "Yeah. Maybe later." I crossed the room quickly, closing the door to the bathroom behind me and turned on the hot water, the entire scene a cruel mimic to my new life. I sat down under the spray, forcing my body back under control and my mind to not panic as I reached out mentally for Jared. He would find me, I could figure this out. Whatever was going on, we weren't dead yet so that meant there was still a chance to come out of this unscathed. I bit my knuckles to keep from crying aloud as the tears I'd fought to hold

321

back ran down my face when I found nothing but an endless loop at the end of all those golden strands. I was alone. And I had no idea where I was or who was holding me prisoner this time.

"Wow. You look amazing." Tyler blinked as Karina came out from the guest room.

Jared's voice caught and he had to clear his throat before speaking. "You look just like her. Almost."

He walked over to her and ran his fingers across her open eyes, muttering an intelligible phrase in Latin. "What did you do?" she asked fearfully.

Jared stepped back and turned away from her without looking. "I gave you her eyes. It's just a trick of light, but it may buy us some time."

"I'm meeting her at the Starbucks down the street in an hour. You guys had better get going. Do you know what you're going to do?"

He nodded. "We already psychically "called" him using some of Jane's DNA from her hairbrush. We're going to get him to follow us out into the desert. No cameras, no paparazzi, no witnesses. We're leading him off-road and going from there to Vegas. Some of our friends will already be there making a big deal along the way about being there for a bachelor party giving us an alibi. You show up as you and hopefully one of us will have Jane. Everyone's story checks out and Sabina is Jane's alibi along with whoever else sees you in Starbucks."

"What about you guys?"

"We're not exactly going to Vegas as ourselves. Don't worry about it; we've got it covered."

"You sure about that?"

"Positive. I wouldn't risk this if I wasn't."

Karina picked up her sister's purse and the keys to the Corvette. She handed Jared Jane's overnight bag and a messenger bag. "Just in case she winds up with you after this is over. See you guys on the other side."

Tyler hugged her awkwardly. "I hope so."

Jared smiled wanly at her as he slid the spear in the back of his waistband, hidden underneath his shirt. "Good luck."

"Just get my sister back."

19

Zane sat in his recording studio listening to the familiar voice spinning inside his head. He knew the only reasons for her to want to see him now had nothing to do with the way either of them had hoped their lives would be. He knew hers was better without him in it. Yet he was still compelled to follow it, still felt that irresistible urge to go to her. Despite everything he knew, everything he felt for Sabina, he would still go to her. Without, of course, sharing that with Sabina. Regardless of how well the two women seemed to be getting along.

Zane sat back, shook his head, and turned up the volume on his headphones. Whatever Jane wanted, he didn't want to know. She could send him the mortgage papers by messenger. Or mail. This was not happening. She asked him to stay out of her life and he was staying his happy ass at home. With his headphones turned way the hell up to drown out the quiet noise of her voice in his head.

"All right, you guys got everything you need?" Jason, Jared's best friend since grade school, handed him the keys to a cheap junker car.

His friend nodded, trading key rings with the man. "You paid cash for it?"

"And gave them a fake name for the registration just like you asked. Can you tell me what's going?"

Jared smiled. "Just need to redirect the paparazzi for a while. Think Jane and I announced the wedding a little too early if you know what I mean."

"So where are you going?"

"Just taking a little other world detour on our way to Vegas. I made your and Cam's reservations at the Palms, my treat. Charge anything you want to the room, pay for anything else with cash."

"How does us going to Vegas help you?"

"That's the truly genius part. You're not going. We're going."

Tyler handed him what looked like two murky bottles of water. "Drink this half an hour before you leave, which would be about now. Sorry about the taste. I don't expect it to be good. It's just glamour, but it'll make you two look like us, at least for a day or so. There are wallets with IDs, cash in the car, and a couple of credit cards that we'll need back. Oh, there's also luggage for us and for the girls. You'll be checking all four of us into a suite. We should meet you in Vegas tonight or tomorrow. We'll check you in when we get there so that there'll be two rooms and everyone's covered."

Cam eyed his potion bottle suspiciously. "I'm not asking questions because you're my friends, but this makes no sense, not even to me, and I've known you my whole life. This'll really work?"

"Yeah."

"Which one of you will I be?"

Jared and Tyler looked at each other and shrugged. "We don't know."

"We mixed them up."

"Thought you'd enjoy the element of surprise."

"You're both twisted." Cam screwed the top off and downed the contents of the bottle in a few giant swallows.

"You're not really concerned about the press around the wedding, are you?" Jared shook his head in answer. Jason tilted his head to one side nodding his acceptance. He mimicked Cam's actions, drinking the mixture a little more slowly. "So if we're you, who are you going to be?"

The two brothers checked their watches and smiled. "We'll know in a few seconds," Jared answered, his tone a bit unsettled.

Before their eyes, Jared's black hair bled into blonde and shortened into a living copy of a Ken doll's haircut. His pale skin darkened, his angular face filled out, and his bright blue eyes turned brown. Tyler's height improved by a few inches, his green eyes turning black to match the long straight hair that had grown. His body seemed to lose mass before their eyes, making his clothing literally hang on his gaunt frame.

"Did that hurt?"

"Did we scream?"

"So, who are you?"

"No one." Tyler followed his brother out the door. He waited until they had gotten into the old four door sedan before voicing his one concern. "Zane's not leaving the condo even for Jane, is he?"

"We're going to make him," Jared said grimly, throwing the car into drive and pulling out onto the busy West Hollywood street.

Zane lay on the couch with the television volume on high, not particularly caring which of his illustrious neighbors he was disturbing. Jane's voice in his head continuously grew louder. The more he ignored it, the more insistent it became until the presence was so overwhelming it was like she was still in the room with him... He looked around and suddenly all the things that were hers, the things that reminded him of her seemed to jump out at him. That was it. Too many memories of Jane in this place, that's why he couldn't concentrate, couldn't breathe. He just needed to take a walk, clear his head. Maybe then the voices would stop.

Zane leapt up from the couch, barely remembering to turn the TV off in his haste to spare the neighbors anymore sonic torture. He spared a thought for his keys and wallet, forgetting his cell phone, as he rushed out the door.

Jared drove the old, beaten LeSabre out of Los Angeles toward the open desert and Las Vegas.

"Where are you going?" Tyler panicked, looking over his shoulder at the shrinking skyline.

"He's out and headed this way. We're back to plan A." Jared stared determinedly at the road.

"What was plan B?"

"I was going to make it up as we went along. That it's working out this way is probably better for everyone concerned."

"So what's going to be our random place in the desert?"

"There's an exit about thirty miles up. Small place, plenty of back roads."

"No more mob movies for you after this."

His brother glanced over at him. "Don't worry. After this I'll probably never drive through this desert again."

"I wonder how Karina's doing."

"You can't call her until we get to Vegas. Turn your phone off. You can't call anyone. The last thing we need is to get caught because our phones were roaming."

Tyler turned his phone off and slid it back into his back pocket. They rode the rest of the way in an uncomfortable silence, heavily laden with all the things they dared not say.

20

Zane pulled off the highway at a small exit in the middle of nowhere. His little silver car screeched to a halt in the otherwise vacant parking lot of one of two truck stops off the exit. He went into the liquor store and bought a fifth of Jack Daniels and two packs of cigarettes.

"One-man party?" the young man behind the cash register joked.

"Yeah, something like that." Zane paid him in cash and reached for his purchases. "If I wanted to get lost, which way would I go?"

The kid laughed. "You must be running from a chick. Go to the left. Once you get past town there's nothing that way for a hundred miles at least. Make sure you've got gas though."

"I'm good." Zane saluted him with the bottle. "Thanks." The kid watched him get in his car and drive off in the indicated direction like demons were chasing him. He shook his head, feeling sorry for the man and what he was sure were women troubles. He didn't notice when another car came off the highway, also going to the left.

Karina ordered her sister's customary caffeine-laden non-fat latte and sat at a table in the back corner of the restaurant. While she herself would have preferred the café table near the window, she knew her sister would want to sit where she could see everyone yet wouldn't easily be overheard. She gingerly took a sip of the hot drink and grimaced, setting it aside for when Sabina got there. She didn't have to wait long. The other woman slid into the chair across from her, drink in hand, a few moments later. "Hello."

"How long did you think this would fool me?" Sabina watched her curiously as she sipped her jasmine tea.

"What are you—"

"I am not stupid. You are Traegar's white witch, not Anyasis's. Yet you disguise yourself and meet with me. I could kill you for the insult."

Karina tamped down her fear and opted instead for the truth. "You would've done that already."

"The human twin? The resemblance is good, but not exact. You have no tattoos, and you grimace when you drink the coffee. It's one of Jane's few pleasures. She never grimaces."

"I'll remember that for next time. And I do not belong to Ty-Traegar."

"Are you certain?"

"Of course. I'm married. To another man."

Sabina smiled. "And that means what, precisely? You came to meet me for a reason. What could it be, little white witch? Do you want me to do for you what I did for your sister?"

"I have nothing to trade you."

"Everyone has something to trade; it just depends on how far they're willing to go to get what they want."

"What if I don't know what I want," Karina admitted quietly.

Sabina held out her hand. "Give me your hand and let us find out, shall we?"

Zane pulled his car to a stop off the side of a deserted dirt road and stumbled out, clutching his half-empty bottle of Jack Daniels. He fell back against the car and took a long pull on the amber liquid. "Find me out here, you bitch!"

The sound of another car pulling up behind him and two car doors slamming shut barely registered in his wasted mind. A shadow fell over him and he caught something glinting in the sunlight as he looked up. "Fuck, man. What are you doing here?"

After what seemed like an eternity of trying to scrub my skin clean, I finally shut off the still scalding hot water and stepped out of the shower. That it was now red and raw didn't bother me. I used the lack of comfort to keep myself focused. I couldn't concentrate on what had happened, on what might happen, and as a result I was hyperaware of the present. I took my time dressing and drying my hair, all in an attempt to prolong the moment when I would have to face the nightmare waiting for me in the bedroom. When I knew I couldn't put it off any longer, I pulled my hair back into a severe ponytail, matching both my mood and the black jeans and t-shirt I was wearing that covered my body from toes to neck, and opened the door, a fake, sunny smile plastered on my face. If I wanted out of here I had to play along until I found a way to escape and I didn't dare display my fear. In light of my non-existent options I thought it best to play along as long as possible. The thing that looked like Jared was waiting for me with breakfast in bed. Even if it got me killed that thing would not touch me again. I didn't care what form it had taken.

"Will you join me?"

I forced the smile to be brighter and continued on to the bedroom door. "I appreciate it, but I promised Karina I'd meet her for brunch today. You remember, don't you?"

"Cancel." He stood and I noticed for the first time that he was fully clothed. Thank God for small favors.

"I can't. She'll already be on her way to the restaurant and I think she needs to talk girl talk." I backed over to the door.

The man advanced on me. "Tell her it's still our honeymoon. She'll understand."

"I've really gotta go." I opened the door and started moving out into the hallway. I was about ready to throw caution out the window and make a run for it.

The thing turned my husband's normally handsome face into an ugly snarl and slammed the door, catching me in the middle of the doorway. I sucked in a breath in a quick *whoosh* and bit the inside of my lip to keep from screaming at the sudden harsh rush of pain shooting up from my trapped shoulder. "You will stay here. Do you understand?"

I nodded, letting the pain show in my face to prove my sincerity. He released the door and backed up several steps to allow me to re-enter the room. I kept my face sincere as I rapidly tried to consider my options. Obviously the jig was up. The second he moved out of reach I ducked out of the room, yanking the door closed behind me. I ran through the replica of Jared and Tyler's house, ignoring the pain in my side and the odd sense of déjà vu.

"Jane!" I heard him coming after me and ran for the French doors. My goal almost reached, fingers outstretched for the handle, I tripped and fell into the dark oblivion. With the monster right behind me.

The two men stood alone in the desert, their hands, arms, and clothes sprayed with fresh blood, none of it their own. The gold spear lay on the ground, innocently clean and appearing to have never been used for its dark purpose though its trophy was already taken and claimed. They watched as the rapidly disintegrating body flaked apart, the pieces blowing away like fire ashes on the desert wind. When it was all but gone, a dark storm cloud formed overhead, finally tearing their attention from the gruesome scene before them.

Tyler looked up and pulled on his brother's sleeve. "We should get out of here." Jared neither moved nor responded, his blue eyes still riveted on what they had done. "Jer, we've gotta go." Jared backed up, allowing himself to be pulled away. He looked back once just before they made it to the car. The dark, clouded sky opened up. And his wife fell out of it, hurtling toward the bloody ground.

Jane fell for what seemed like a short time for as far as it felt. As suddenly as she was staring at nothing but black, she was staring at wide open sky, and the thing wearing her husband's skin like a gruesome costume was tumbling out after her. She landed on her back, on something hard and sharp. Before she could process the thought clearly, she reached behind her for the sharp object and thrust it into her nightmare's chest as he fell on her. Jane watched the light die from the bright blue eyes that she loved so much and felt something inside her scream and pass away. As his blood gushed over her hands, she realized that the scream she was hearing wasn't just internal, that the hoarse sound was coming from her own throat.

Jared grabbed Tyler, turned and ran back towards his wife. As if being shown the scene in slow motion, he watched her fall on the spear, take it, and stab a man in the chest who could've been his twin. "Jane!" He ran up to her and dropped to his knees. Tyler skidded to a halt next to him.

Jane's glazed over eyes caught Tyler's as shock began to set in. "Help me," she whispered.

Tyler knelt on her other side and touched her face, the blood on his hands mingling with the blood still pouring from the man on top of her. "It's all right. You're safe now."

Jared pulled on the man's body still pinning her to the ground. "Ty, help me with this." They pulled the body off of her. Tyler removed the spear and set it aside for Alecto to collect later. He knelt beside the fallen man, silently comparing his face to that of his brother.

"Who the hell is he?" Jared kept his voice low so as to not disturb Jane.

Tyler looked up at him and shook his head. "No idea."

Jared sank back down next to his wife. "Jane? Are you okay?"

She screamed, her hands flying at his face. "Get away from me! I killed you! I killed you."

He caught both wrists and held her down, trying to calm her as best he could despite his stunned reaction. "Ssshhh! Jane, it's me, Jared. It's okay. You're okay."

A sob escaped her throat and she quit fighting him. She reached up to touch his face, her hands shaking. "You're real?"

Relief washed over him as he pulled her into his arms, her body still stiff and unwilling. "We got you back." He moved to kiss her and she turned away.

"I'm sorry, but I can't look at you right now, Jared." The dark gray remains of Zane's body caught her eye and she looked to Tyler for an answer. "What is that?"

Tyler shook his head to try to warn her. "Not now…"

Jared sat back from her, his head bowed. She finally did look at him, her fear outweighing the horror of the last several hours. "What did you do?" There was a quiet terror in her voice that cut through Jared's heart like a knife.

He looked up at her, his eyes clouded with his pain and guilt, but it was Tyler who answered. "We did what we had to do to get you back."

Jane clamped her hand over her mouth and fell back, moving away from the entire mess. "You didn't. Not Zane. I didn't want this! You should've let me die."

"That wasn't an option! If you had died we all would've died. Don't you see? He was dead anyway and he knew it. Three for one who was already going to die was not a choice. We didn't want this either."

"How?" Jared gestured to the golden spear still lying on the ground. "Did you give him a choice?"

Tyler nodded. "He knew and was accepting. He tried to do it himself but couldn't. A human can't touch that thing."

"I did."

"You're not human anymore. You wouldn't have survived where they put you if you were, Jane."

"You're like us now," Tyler offered in explanation at her terrified expression.

"Which one of you did this?"

Tyler cut Jared off. "It doesn't matter."

"It matters to me."

The brothers exchanged a look. Jared opened his mouth but it was Tyler who answered. "I did. Jared was afraid you'd never forgive him so I did it."

She looked back and forth between the two of them, as if she could sense the lie. "He might've been right. Why do you two look so funny?"

Jared helped her to stand. "It's a glamour. So that we wouldn't be recognized. You, Kari, and Zane are the only ones who can see. Could see." He grimaced at his red hands and looked away. "Come on. We've got to get to Vegas."

"Why? What's happened? What's in Vegas?"

"Our alibis."

"What about?" She turned back to see what was left of her former lover and the man who had tortured her.

"Alecto will clean it up. It's what she does."

Jane looked up into her husband's eyes and met his haunted gaze with one of her own. "I killed that man. I thought he was you at first."

"I don't know who he is, but I can assure you he's not dead." He helped her into the backseat of their car. "You didn't remove the heart."

A hard glint entered Jane's eyes as she looked out the open car door up at Jared. "Remove it with that thing?" She pushed past him out of the car and rushed back over to the bodies, her stride determined as she approached them. She knelt in the mess of dirt and blood, picking up the golden weapon and shoving at the man who had taken on the appearance of her husband. "Help me move him!"

Jared ran to her side. "Jane, no!" He knelt down beside her. "Sweetheart, no, you don't have to do this. Please."

Her face was entirely devoid of emotion as she looked down at the man who had held her captive. She looked up at her husband and he saw the agony wrapped inside the rage she was feeling. "Turn him over."

Jared saw the resolution in her eyes then did as she asked, looking away from the man in front of them. "I can't watch you do this."

Tears began to fall from her eyes. "Please sit across from me. I need to see your face, Jared. I can't do this if he still looks like you."

Jared finally looked down and saw his own blue eyes staring almost lifelessly up at him. "Oh, god." He reached across and touched her hand. "I'm so sorry. I did this to you, Jane."

"No. But you're going to tell me how to fix it." Jane pulled her hand back and used both hands to shove the spear into the man's chest, causing the body to convulse and spray both her and Jared with blood. "How do I remove the heart?"

Jared placed his hands on top of hers and helped her to twist the device. "You open it like this, then close it," he gripped the spear tightly in both hands and turned away, "and pull. You won't want to look for this."

Jane turned away as she ripped his heart out. As her eyes slowly opened, she saw Alecto materialize and approach them. "You did this."

"Another soul. I don't believe I required this one."

Jane tossed the spear still holding the heart at her feet. "You should've thought of that before you had him rape me disguised as my husband."

Alecto made a disgusted face at the bloodied mess at her feet and with a wave of her hand sent it and the two dead men to the underworld. "Your little goddess has backbone, Anyasis. I might be impressed after all."

"We're finished, Alecto. Stay away from my wife." Jared stepped in front of Jane protectively.

"Such bold words from the prince." Alecto stepped forward and smiled, enjoying his obvious discomfort in his show of bravado. "Do not worry. Your pretty little toy won't be on my list for quite some time. And when she is, you'll both be on the other end of my spear." She evaporated in a cloud of fog before either of them could say anything more.

Jared looked back at Jane and saw her face crumble as her courage finally completely failed her. He pulled her to her feet and into his arms. "You're okay, sweetheart. Everything's okay."

Jane clung to him, burying her face in his neck where she could breathe nothing but his scent and wound her fingers deep in his hair, desperate to just be near him. "Please get me out of here."

He nodded and helped her to the car. Tyler helped them both settle into the backseat. As they drove away, the brothers looked in the rearview mirror and watched while a dark storm cloud enveloped the area and swallowed it down. Tyler pressed down a little harder on the gas pedal, just to reassure himself that they weren't being taken down with it.

342

21

"Jane? Wake up, sweetheart." Jared reached across the backseat and gingerly touched her knee. "We're almost to the Palms and if we're going to keep our cover we've got to pretend that we're happily married and nothing's wrong."

"We're at the airport. And how could you say that?"

"We're ditching the car in the parking lot. And you're renting another one to drive us to the hotel." Tyler parked the car in one of the economy outer lots and Jared got out without looking back at her. "And it's easy. You can barely stand to look at me."

Jane slammed the car door shut and stomped past him. "Forgive me for being traumatized by being held captive by a man with your face and still being covered by his blood even though no one can see it. I thought he was you, Jared!" She turned to face him and her rage stopped him in his tracks. "I slept with him. I thought he was you until he touched me and it felt wrong." She stepped closer to him. "I willingly touched another man because I thought he was you and then I shoved a spear in his chest all so you could kill my ex for a Fury who was too diabolical to do her dirty work herself. Oh, and then we killed him together. Do you know why I wanted him dead? Because I couldn't take the risk of waking up next to someone

343

else who has your face again. I think I deserve a minute to be in shock. Now if someone's got my purse, I'll call for a driver for me, my bodyguard, and my cousin."

"Just for you. We can't arrive together because Tyler and I are already supposed to be there. Jason will meet you. His glamour makes him look like me, at least for the next couple of hours, so you'll have to act like he's me until you get up to the room." He shoved his hands into his pockets, his head ducked low as he walked past her.

Jane reached out for him, tilted his blue gaze up to meet hers. "Jared, I do love you."

"That's the first time you've ever said that to me."

"Doesn't mean that it hasn't been true the whole time."

Tyler, who had been observing up until now, clapped his hands together, catching their attention. "This is all very touching, but we're kind of on a timeline here."

Jared jerked like he'd been stung and pulled away from her. "There's a reservation at the Palms for us. I'll meet you in the suite later. I'll look like me, just so you know. Karina will be in some time later tonight."

"Where is she?"

"She's in L.A. trying to salvage what's left of her marriage after being your alibi," Tyler answered. Both Jared and Jane started at the obvious anger in his voice.

"I had no idea," Jane said softly.

"Maybe if you paid a little more attention you would."

Jared got in his brother's face, allowing Jane time to slip away. "What are you angrier about, that she's having marital problems or that she chose to stay and fix it?"

Tyler took two steps back, his jaw clenched in anger. "Just because you got a fucking fairytale doesn't give you the right to be an asshole."

"Not now," Jared ground out under his breath, glancing back to see how far away Jane was.

His brother followed his gaze and felt his anger explode. "What? You don't want her to know how scared you are, how miserable you've been? How you torture yourself when she's not looking because you're terrified she only wants you for your dick?"

"Shut the hell up!"

Jane marched back and shoved the two men apart. "Go get in the damn cab! Take this up behind closed doors at a lower volume." She turned and walked toward the shuttle to the terminal without another word. The brothers glared at each other, but obediently waited for the next shuttle and followed her to the terminal to catch their cab.

Jason left the gaming tables and walked outside to meet Jane. She exited the hired Town Car surrounded by flashing photogs and paparazzi. He watched a fake smile bloom on her face when she saw him. She crossed to him with open arms and planted a very realistic kiss on his lips. "Hey, sweetheart. I missed you."

"I missed you too." Jason placed his arm around her waist, watching as his friends alighted from the cab. He turned a blind eye and escorted Jane inside. "Let's go upstairs, shall we?" he whispered in her ear. She nodded coyly and cuddled up beside him as they walked to the elevator. Cameron as Tyler met them on the twelfth floor just in front of the bank of elevators. Jane hugged him, greeting him with the same familiarity she showed the real Tyler. Both men escorted her to the suite adjoining theirs. Jason followed her inside, playing every bit the part of her lover while Cam went to his own room next door. Once the outer doors clicked shut all three of them dropped the pretense, Jane collapsing in exhaustion on the beige couch while Jason went to the interior door to let Cam in from Tyler's room.

"They're checking in," he announced upon arrival. "They'll be up in a minute."

"Can't wait," Jane commented, her head falling back wearily on the couch. She groaned and stood awkwardly. "Do I have a change of clothes here?"

"Yeah. You've got the stuff that Jared asked us to bring in the bedroom."

"Thanks, guys. I'm going to take a shower."

Jason looked confused. "But they're in the elevator. Don't you want to wait for Jared?"

She sighed heavily and turned her back to him. "No offense, but I can't deal with seeing two of him again right now." Jane went into the suite's bedroom, closing the door firmly behind her.

Cam looked at Jason. "Did we miss something?"

"Whatever it is, I don't want to know about it. This is already too weird for me."

Jane took a short, very hot shower and walked back out into the dark bedroom wrapped tightly in the hotel robe. She pulled open the closet doors, flipping through the contents in the light coming in from the bathroom. "So are you going to say anything or just sit there and watch me?" She didn't look up or turn around.

Jared pushed off his perch on the windowsill and walked halfway across the room before stopping, still partially concealed in shadows. "I was wondering when you'd notice me."

"I knew you were there and I knew it was you. Now that I'm back from wherever, out bonds are visible to me again." She selected a dark Jersey cotton dress and laid it on the bed, walking past Jared to the dresser to select accompanying lingerie.

He hesitated as he considered his next words, though he desperately needed to know her answer. "Do you hate me?"

"No, of course not. I could never hate you, Jared." She appeared to be surprised by his question.

"Then why won't you look at me?"

"You know why. Just give me a minute." She took her selections to join the dress on the bed.

He grabbed her by the arm, his fingers digging in as he forced her to look at his face. "I'm not him."

"I know that," she answered softly.

"Jane, you're my wife! Do you know how terrified I was that I would lose you? That you'd never come back from that place?"

"Jared—"

"No," he interrupted her, "let me finish. You came back, we did unspeakable, horrible things to get you back and in less than twenty-four hours you're treating me like I'm a stranger. I feel like I sold my soul for a taste of what could've been and now I don't get

347

that either." He took a deep breath, his fingers steepled beneath his chin. "I know that what you went through is horrible. I can only imagine. But you don't know the hell we went through to get you back either. And I won't spend the rest of my life with you pretending to be in love with me. I need to know if you're going to be able to move past this."

"You think you get to ask that now?" Jane shoved him out of the way and went to the bed, grabbing at the clothing she had laid there. "I've been back five seconds and you're wondering when you're going to get laid? That's great, Jared. Really."

"Damn it to hell that is not what I said!" Jared grabbed her by the arm and spun her around to face him, trapping her between him and the bed. "Do you love me or are you repulsed by me? Which is it?"

"I love you and I hate what you've done!" Her eyes flashed an angry black. "I hate what we've done. I believe you when you say that there was no other choice, that Zane would've been taken anyway. It just doesn't make it any easier to reconcile that he's gone, I'm still here, and I'll never see him again."

"What did you think would happen when you married me?" He jerked her like he could shake some sense into her.

"There's a big difference between him being with someone else and being dead for eternity." She yanked her arm away from him and stumbled, nearly falling back on the bed. "Give me a minute to mourn the man I spent the last several lifetimes with. I don't think sleeping with his murderer shows a proper amount of respect, do you?"

Jared felt a burning pain in his stomach and he fell back like he'd been shot. He held up his hands in defeat. "Fine. Have a nice night." He backed out of the bedroom and slammed the door behind him.

Karina and Tyler watched him leave the bedroom, headed directly for the suite's minibar. Karina grabbed Tyler by the hand, pulling him out of his chair as she stood from her position on the couch. "Let's go to the casino."

Tyler glanced over at his brother's hunched back and slid his hotel room key into his pocket as he was pulled out the door. "Maybe we should get a room that doesn't adjoin theirs."

Karina happily skipped down the hall, her fingertips still lightly wound in his. "I love Vegas." She pushed the button to call the elevator and stood back to wait. "So, was that your way of telling me you're afraid to be in the same room with them tonight or that you're interested?" she teased.

A low *ding* signaled the arrival of the elevator. Tyler walked through the open doors, bringing her with him. As soon as the doors closed, he pulled her into a crushing, seductive embrace. "I'd tell you what you want to hear, but," he twirled her and dropped her into a waltz dip, "you're married." They both laughed. He pulled her back up and released her, kissing the top of her hand as they stepped apart. "I'm sorry for whatever happened today."

The elevator doors opened on the first floor and they walked out to the casino. "You were right. I can't be with someone who doesn't really love me, just the idea of me. And he couldn't accept me. Really it's been over for a while. Don't feel bad for me." She pushed the corners of his mouth back up into a smile. He obliged her with a cheesy grin. "There. That's much better."

"So, does Jane know yet?"

"Nope. And you're not going to tell her. Not right now. She's got enough to deal with."

He held up his hands. "It's none of my business. Just thought you might need a friend."

Karina laid her head on his shoulder and steered him toward the blackjack tables. "Thanks. Now let's go play!"

Jared sat in the living room of the suite and drank the mini-bar dry. After he ran out of tiny bottles of alcohol he called room service and ordered a large bottle of scotch. While he normally found the stuff to be completely vile, tonight he felt like making an exception. And the already substantial various kinds of alcohol he had in his bloodstream probably was not aiding his logical thought processes.

He sat on the floor, in front of the couch, drinking straight from his bottle of scotch, staring at the closed bedroom door, wishing that his will was all it took to open it to him. At some point his vision split in two and he saw two versions of the same door. Another swig of scotch cemented the idea that it was just his luck that not only had his wife ditched him after less than a week but that there would also be two possible doors for her to be hidden behind. *Let's see, behind door number one we have Jared's sweet, wonderful, loving wife Jane. Behind door number two we have sexually anorexic Jane who can't stand the sight of Jared because he's a bad, bad man. Heaven forbid anyone kill the dead guy to save three living people. Oh no, we should all just sacrifice ourselves and die. For nothing. For a dead guy.*

Another burning gulp and he decided to try his luck and go in there. Just in case the Jane from door number one happened to be in there. He took another gulp and decided it was a really good idea. Maybe. Possibly. By the next swallow he'd decided he might need to stop talking about himself in the third person and just do it if he was damn well going to do something. He drained the rest of the bottle and stood, wavering as he walked toward the bedroom door. It occurred to him then that he possibly shouldn't have drunk the entire bottle by himself. He reached for the doorknob just as the carpet came up to greet him.

"Jared, sweetheart, wake up. Come on, baby. I can't get you out of the floor by myself." Jane grabbed Jared under the arms and pulled, trying to drag him into the bedroom. He moaned, his eyelids fluttering open and his eyes rolling back in his head, trying to escape the bright light overhead. He pushed up into a kneeling position and stood slowly with Jane's help. "What have you done? Why were you in the floor?"

"I think I was trying to get to the bedroom." He welcomed the darkness of the bedroom and tumbled gratefully onto the cool sheets. Jane pulled off his shoes and socks before attempting to pull his t-shirt off as well. "You don't hate me." He blinked and reached up to touch her face.

Jane rolled her eyes and tucked the sheets in around him. "Just because I don't agree with you does not mean that I hate you. I'm sorry for what I said earlier. I didn't mean it, Jer."

"You still won't touch me." He curled up on his side, his lips pursing in a sullen pout.

Jane closed the door and got into bed beside him, closing her eyes to fight off the bad memories. She curled up against his back, resting her head on his shoulder and wrapped her arms around him, embracing his warmth and familiar smell. "We still haven't finished my list."

"You didn't answer your cell phone for at least one whole day and we got married impulsively. That's two. And you only regret one of them."

"Yeah, but that still leaves travelling without an agenda and conquering my fears. And I don't regret anything," she murmured against his ear.

"You really want to conquer your fears?" He felt her nod and he turned in her arms to lie on his back. "Start with me. Kiss me."

She knew he needed this, but Jane wasn't sure what her reaction would be and she didn't want to freak out on him. In her heart, she knew she still wanted him, she wanted him badly, but her brain still held images of the man they'd killed. She took a deep breath and nuzzled his neck, relishing the scent of the man she loved. "Where would you like for me to start?"

"Anywhere." His eyes darkened as she slid over him, his fingers raking through her long, dark hair.

Jane turned his head to the side and kissed the spot behind and just under his left ear, smiling when he shivered and pulled her tighter. Taking his response as encouragement, she sucked harder on his neck, making him bow off the bed, his fingers digging into her scalp. A deep, gasping moan escaped his throat and Jane pulled away to look into his wide eyes. "I love that noise." She kissed his open mouth, nipping lightly at his bottom lip with her teeth. "I love you. Please don't ever doubt that. Nothing changes that."

She moved to kiss him again and he caught her face between his hands before she touched him. "I didn't kill him. I set it up, I would've done it, but I didn't take his life." His eyes searched hers for her true reaction in the shadowed darkness of the room.

"I believe you. But Tyler was right, it doesn't matter. You're mine." Jane slid on top of him, lowering her lips back to his.

Jared deepened the kiss, sighing contentedly as his wife moved against him, pulling him as close as she could with their clothes on. Her fingernails bit into his shoulder blades while her tongue slid into his mouth as she tried to exorcise the ghosts in her memory. Jared felt his control slipping and he arched into her, feeling her desire override her fear. He started as another emotion slipped in and took hold over Jane, a sigh escaping from deep within her and he felt all of her shields drop. Every barrier that she had held against him collapsed and left, finally leaving nothing separating them. Without even meaning to, Jared saw inside of her, saw all of the woman he loved for the first time and realized that the emotion he couldn't identify was love. For him. Jared broke the kiss and pushed her just far enough back that he could see her eyes. He finally understood what the blue-green color they had been turning over the last few days meant and he smiled at the knowledge, deciding that the color would definitely be his favorite in the future. Jane's kiss-swollen lips frowned at his suddenly serious expression.

"What's wrong?" Her thumbs smoothed out his eyebrows and she combed the hair back from him eyes with her fingers.

Jared smiled as the blue-green of her eyes intensified with her concern for him. He kissed away her frown and brought her back into his embrace, settling her head under his chin and moving her hair to one side to kiss his favorite spot on the back of her neck. "Thank you."

"For what?" Jane nestled against his side. "I should be thanking you. You saved my life twice this week." She smiled against the side of his neck. "I take it back. Three times."

He shifted so that he could see her face. "Three? I only counted two. Did I sleep through one?"

"Yes, actually." Jane held her left hand up, drawing his attention to the permanent scar there. "Once when you came to rescue me from Sabina, the second time was when you pulled me back from hell…"

"Um, that wasn't hell," Jared interrupted.

"Well it definitely wasn't Valhalla. The third time was when you married me. While you were asleep, technically."

He smiled, his fingers intertwining with hers. "Ty did say that you are high maintenance."

She shrugged and laid her head down on his chest to listen to his heart beat. "No one's perfect, not even you. But you come damn close." She pulled their joined hands closer and kissed his fingertips. "I do love you, Jared. I have no explanation for it, but I do. Does that make any sense?" Jane licked a spot on his chest directly over his heart and slid further up his body to kiss his neck.

Jared redirected her progress from his neck to his lips. "Does it have to make any sense? Fuck sense and logic and all that other bullshit. Mmmm..." he groaned hiking her thigh higher across his stomach. "Fuck me." As he kissed her again, he caught just the tiniest shimmer of fear inside of her and held her for a moment longer before pulling back, cuddling her back against his chest. "At the risk of sounding like a total dork, can we just do this tonight?" He rubbed the spot on the back of her neck then trailed his fingers absently up and down her spine while trying to read her emotions, realizing that he could read her mind almost as well as his brother's and that despite her feelings, the forty-eight hours before still left her afraid. Jared was determined that he would not be another thing for her to fear, not when she finally loved him. Jane nodded and cuddled in closer, desperately clinging to him as she fought off her own inner monsters.

"So when are you going to tell me what happened with Sabina? How long were you able to hold her off for?" Tyler picked up his chips and followed Karina to the roulette table.

She smiled, taking her place next to him at the table as he placed his bet. "She knew immediately that I wasn't Jane. It ended all right though."

"Obviously. You're not dead. You gonna tell me what happened?"

Karina looked over at him and put an arm around his shoulders. "We'll talk about it later."

He looked at her strangely as the wheel on the roulette table spun. "What did she offer you?"

She smiled softly and turned away. "You. I told her no."

"Why?"

"We're friends," she said as if the answer should be obvious. "I wouldn't do that to you."

"You could've asked." He placed his third bet at the table and watched the wheel turn. "What if I had said yes?"

"Your phone was off. And I wouldn't have asked that from you. We came to a different understanding." The little ball came to a stop and she looked back at him one more time before walking away. "You won."

Tyler watched her walk away, not really understanding, but somehow feeling like he'd lost. And without even knowing he'd been playing. He had the sneaking suspicion that he should've been paying more attention. He took all his chips and placed one last bet. He won, he went after her. He lost, he went back upstairs to bed alone. He kept his eyes on his bet, not sure if he was willing the ball to stop on thirteen or not. The dealer called it at seventeen and Tyler looked one last time in the direction she had gone. Deciding that the Fates were not on his side and noticing that his glamour spell was starting to fade, he turned in the opposite direction, toward the elevators.

Karina watched him walk away, hidden behind a bank of slot machines. She turned around on her barstool to face the bar and sighed into her amaretto sour. It was probably for the best. Really. She was almost sure of it. She ordered another drink and continued to stubbornly face away as he walked in the opposite direction.

22

Six months later:

"Is Jane doing any better?" Karina flipped her newly dyed, longer black hair over her shoulder as she crossed Wilshire with her brother-in-law in the twilight.

"She's still holed up writing. The new book's almost done and she finally went to the condo this week and cleaned out all of Zane's stuff. Sabina didn't want anything to do with it, not really surprisingly. Anyway, it's done, the condo's sold, and we're all headed for Europe next week. I'm glad you decided to come with us."

"Me, too." She ducked her head closer to his as a photographer snapped their picture, a usual occurrence when she was with him, mistaking her for Jane. "Thanks for coming by the office and picking me up."

"Not a problem. Nice to have company to walk with. I can't believe you got a real job."

"I don't live in Malibu and Jane doesn't need me to hide behind anymore. Though the new hair helps when she does."

"Thanks for covering for her so much lately. I know the last few months have sucked for everyone."

Karina laughed, bumping her shoulder into him playfully. "Not a problem. You're not so bad to hang around with."

"Thanks." He laughed. "Tyler told me to tell you 'hi'. He'll be at dinner tonight. He's riding into town with Jane. I think he misses you."

"Jared, don't make me tell my sister that you're being a bad boy," she teased as they stopped for another picture.

"You think one day they'll figure this out?"

"I'm sure they will."

"And nice try, don't change the subject. I'm just saying you're divorced; your life's ironed out, or at least as much as it's going to get. Maybe you could cut him a break. Unless I'm imagining things."

Karina sighed, shoving her hands into her pants pockets. "Another time in another place and I would've fallen in love with your brother, Jared."

"But not this time?"

She ignored his questioning stare and checked her watch, quickening her pace. "Can we hurry up?"

"Where's the emergency?" He lengthened his stride to keep up with her.

"Nowhere. I just—" her voice trailed off as she saw Jane and Tyler waiting for them in front of the restaurant, Jane still furiously scribbling in her notebook and Sabina standing across the street. "— just want to get there."

Jared saw her lock gazes with Sabina and grabbed Karina by the shoulder, effectively halting her in her tracks. "You knew?"

She looked up at him and smiled sadly as her eyes filled with unshed tears. "I couldn't let you or Tyler do it. I couldn't take the chance that Jane wouldn't forgive you. Tyler told me what Sabina is when we were drunk. This was the only way. She gets the life she needs and the three of you live."

"Kari, I can't let you do this." Jared's grip on her shoulder tightened.

Karina looked down the block to where Tyler and her sister were watching. She pulled away from Jared, backing toward the busy street. "It's done. Please help them understand." She watched Tyler's expression change when he realized something was wrong. He and Jane began to hurry down the sidewalk toward her and Jared. She looked across the street to where Sabina was waiting and then back to Jared. She reached in her pocket and tossed him something small and flat, which he caught and held tight in a closed fist. "Tell him I'll look for him next time. I love my sister."

Jared lunged for her and was too late. Karina stepped out into the oncoming traffic and closed her eyes. He heard the screams as his brother and wife realized what was happening. He saw Jane toss the pages of her novel aside as she ran. And he couldn't reach her sister before the Hummer hit her. He grabbed Jane before she followed her out into the ensuing car crash and pulled her down to the sidewalk, shielding her from the flying glass.

Tyler stopped at the edge of the street, watching three cars collide over the spot where Karina fell before everything became still. Sabina made her way carefully through the mayhem to the center of the wreckage. He saw a bloody hand reach up for her out of the carnage and ran, ignoring his brother's warning to stay. He climbed over two cars that were twisted together, their owners stumbling out, dazed and confused, just in time to see Sabina drain the last of Karina's life away. He knelt beside her limp body, cradling her head in his lap. "Why did you do it?"

"It was her choice. I offered her eternity with you. She chose to take the burden of extinguishing Zane's life on herself rather than make you live with it. But I had to have a life and Alecto needed his. So I took his life and Karina gave me hers in exchange."

"I never should've told her."

"You should know that the white witch's life was worth more. She made another deal. For you."

"Get away from her!"

Sabina nodded and turned away, vanishing into the crowd of onlookers. Jane clambered over the crushed cars followed closely by Jared who had retrieved her forgotten notebook. "Karina?" Her mouth opened to scream when she saw her sister's body but no noise came out as she ran over and knelt down in the glass and metal shards next to Tyler. "Oh, god, what happened? Kari, why did you do this?"

"For us. So we wouldn't have to live with anything we weren't willing to do." Tyler knelt over her, tears running down his face. "I didn't know. I wouldn't have let her do this."

"This isn't your fault."

"She gave her life away so that we wouldn't have to take one. She wouldn't have even known how if I hadn't told her. How is this not my fault?"

"You didn't make the choice." Jane reached back for Jared as the sirens grew louder.

Jared hesitated for a moment, knowing what they were seeing, listening to the approaching sirens. He finally went over and pulled

Jane away. "Come on. We've gotta get out of here. There's nothing you can do for her."

"Please let me stay with her," Jane whispered, her tears trailing down to his hands that held her back.

"These cars could catch fire. We need to get out of here." He pushed Jane behind him and forced Tyler to his feet. "Come on. There's nothing you can do here."

They climbed back out and sat on the sidewalk, watching as the rescue teams arrived. The police came over and took their statements. Jared watched Jane the whole time as he lied, making up reasons why Karina would've stepped into the road. They were released right as the paramedics moved Karina's body to the waiting ambulance. Jared reached into his coat pocket and handed Tyler the thing that Karina had tossed to him just before she stepped into the intersection. A chip from the casino at the Palms. "She wanted me to give you this. She said she'd look for you next time. That in another time and another place she would've loved you."

Tyler pressed the chip between his palms still wet with Karina's blood and knelt over them as if in prayer. "You're gonna tell me how to get her back. I know you know how. You did it when you were nine."

Jared shook his head. "Ty, this isn't the same thing."

Jane looked up. "How is it not the same thing?"

"If you bring her back, she won't be who you remember. You know that. And she won't come back as an adult. She can't."

Tyler's hands were wound together so tightly that his knuckles turned white. "Damn it, I will get her back."

Sabina knelt in front of him, staring up at him with Karina's green eyes. "What are you willing to give?"

362

ABOUT THE AUTHOR

Author, music lover, avid film watcher, and devourer of literature Arianna Swain lives under her own personal rock in the Hollywood Hills. When not writing, rock climbing, gallivanting across the planet, or doing all three at once, she can most likely be found baking under the careful supervision of Angeles, the vampire kitty.

www.ingramcontent.com/pod-product-compliance
Lightning Source LLC
Chambersburg PA
CBHW070733180626
46818CB00007B/2827

pulled him into the apartment with him. Alek and Luka followed them in, wandering further into the space.

"It's not huge, because, you know, we're not rich. Yet. But see?" Alek gestured around. "This is the living room. The dining table would go over there, next to the kitchen. There's enough space on that wall for Luka's exercise equipment and the bedrooms are through there." He gestured to a short hallway to their right.

Evan took a long look around. To the left were some tall windows overlooking the street and the majority of the living area. To the right was the kitchen, with counters that wrapped around in a U shape, along with new-looking appliances, the hallway and a door.

"That door leads to a walk-in closet," Alek said, going over to open it and let them look inside. "The closets are all huge. Great storage. It makes up for the limited space out here. At least all our stuff will be hidden away."

"And two bathrooms!" Brennan exclaimed, smiling hugely, more happy than Evan had ever seen him before. Evan wanted to tackle him to the floor and kiss his breath away. They could christen the space, mark it as theirs — and no threat of anyone unwanted walking in, unannounced. "One off of each bedroom. Isn't it great? We won't have to share anymore."

Luka cleared his throat, loudly, on purpose.

"What?" When both of Luka's eyebrows shot up, Brennan — oblivious — demanded, "What'd I say?"

Then, Luka gave Alek a look, which Evan understood perfectly. Brennan was still playing catch-up, though.

"For now," Alek said, seeming to speak for both of the Popovićs, "we'll be split up into two bedrooms. It doesn't mean anything though, if we don't want it to. We can ease into the living arrangements before deciding how things are going to work between the four of us."

Evan wondered when they'd discussed things between them, suspecting it was while he and Brennan had been allowed to sleep in Alek's bed as long as they wanted to, the night before.

"Ev," Luka said, "you and Alek wake up early for work, so it makes sense anyway that you're together. Bren and I have weirder schedules with his classes and my flex hours at the gym. We're more likely to all get our sleep with the wall between the bedrooms in place. Other than sleeping though...."

The Popović twins again shared a look of agreement which Evan wasn't privy to.

Alek picked up where Luka left off. "We share everything. Food, sex—"

"Sex *with* food," Luka added.

Brennan elbowed him in the side, saying, "And clothes. You would look really hot in my yoga pants, Ev."

"You would, actually," Alek agreed with a dreamy expression as he seemed to mentally play dress-up with Evan's body. After a moment he blinked his eyes clear and said, "Where was I? Oh. Yeah, and most importantly, we share whatever is on our minds. That's a rule."

"He threatened to make a sign for the wall and everything," Luka told Evan behind a hand.

"I heard that," Alek warned. "This is only going to work if we talk about anything that's bothering us before it becomes a problem. Agreed?"

He looked at each of them in turn. Luka nodded, humming, "Mm-hmm."

Evan muttered, "Yeah, okay."

"No problem," Brennan echoed.

"I mean it."

"Okay," Evan insisted. "So, wait, can I sleep with Luka or Brennan once in a while if I want to?"

"You have to ask Alek for permission first," Luka answered, quite seriously, without a hint of a smile.

"You're kidding, right?" Evan asked, laughing a little.

"No, I'm not kidding."

Evan looked over at Alek, who had trouble holding his gaze without glancing away. He was embarrassed, Evan realized.

"What if I fall asleep on the couch next to them?"

"I'll carry you to bed," Alek said. "Sleeping is mine. It's my time with you. We've agreed."

"You and Luka agreed?"

"We all did," Brennan said softly, biting at the edge of his lip.